EDEN'S BONFIRE

LIAM JACK

PART ONE

CHAPTER ONE

Kartik MacNair lay on the grass and tried to ignore the world around him. It was his favourite pastime.

However it was becoming increasingly difficult, as there were two things that were bothering him. Previously there had only been one problem, but now there were two. In the space of a year, the number of problems in his life had doubled. Things were becoming unmanageable. As he felt the grass beneath him, he realised that ignoring the world in its entirety was going to take some effort.

Before, when there had only been one problem, it hadn't been so bad. Well, it was bad, but it wasn't a problem that he had much control over, so he didn't have to do anything about it. Many people assume that having a problem that you have no control over is a bad thing. But not for Kartik. Having a problem that you have no control over meant you didn't have to do anything. Fate has played its hand, the dice have been rolled, the gods had their say, and you're just stuck with what you get dealt. No need for further worry or energy expenditure.

The second problem—now that was a real issue, and something over which, hypothetically, he had some sort of control. Addressing things, however, wasn't one of Kartik's strong points. In fact, it was pretty much the thing he was worst at. If there was a league table for avoiding complications, Kartik would be in the title chase every single year.

Wispy clouds floated overhead in the clear blue sky. He shut his eyes and tried to drift off, but just when he was about to reach a state of stillness, someone asked him about his more pressing problem.

'So what exactly are you going to do with your life?'

Kartik sat up and looked over at his friend, Cameron Fitzgerald, who was sat cross-legged next to him.

'I don't know. What are you going to do with your life?' Kartik asked quietly, congratulating himself for turning the tables and using his own question against his friend. The interviewer would now become the interviewee. His mind was as quick as a flash sometimes.

'Not drop out of university,' Cameron replied. She hadn't looked up from her book, *A Companion to the Iliad* by Malcolm M. Willcock, when she had spoken.

Well, damn! She had just turned the tables on him. He was meant to be the table-turner, but the tables had been turned around again. He didn't know which way they were pointing now. He tried to work this out, but his brain got tired so he lit the joint he had rolled earlier.

'And not smoke enough weed to wake the dead,' Cameron continued contemptuously.

'You smoke as well,' Kartik protested, taking a drag and offering it to Cameron. She shook her head.

'On occasion. Not constantly.'

'Meh,' Kartik shrugged and withdrew the offer.

'Anyway, you didn't answer my question. What are you going to do with yourself?' *That bloody question again. Why did people keep asking it?*

'Well, first, I'm going to finish this joint. Then I'm going to lie on the grass for a while. And if I'm feeling particularly proactive, I may go and get a coffee. But that's only if I'm feeling really ambitious.'

'You've always got a glib quip, haven't you?' Cameron said, looking up from her book.

'It's one of my many talents.'

'Many talents? And what are the others?' Cameron sceptically asked.

'I can make a very good cappuccino,' he replied looking Cameron deep in the eye to ensure she understood the complexity of his skills. 'Best in town.'

'I'm being serious, Kartik. I worry about you sometimes.'

'I appreciate the sentiment,' he said.

'So are you going to do something about it?'

'About what?'

'About what? About life.'

'Probably not.'

'You're hopeless.'

'And you're my dearest friend.'

'Sometimes I question if I even like you.'

'You sure spend a lot of time with someone you don't like.'

'Having you around makes me feel better about myself.'

'See? And there we have another one of my talents. I make others look good via proxy.'

'That's not what proxy means.'

'Hey, I'm showing you my talents and you're criticising my syntax.'

'That's not what syntax means either.'

'Really? No wonder I didn't make it through that English degree.'

Cameron looked at him and smiled, despite her best efforts.

But he was being honest; he did appreciate the sentiment. Or at least he thought he did. He wasn't always very good at judging the emotions he felt towards other people. But what he was more focused on now were Cameron's eyes.

He often thought about Cameron's eyes. They were a deep brown, but just around the pupil of the left eye, there were a few uneven streaks of blue, like lightning shooting out of the centre towards the milky white. A long time ago Cameron had explained that this was a minor form of heterochromia before going into lengthy detail of the science behind it. Kartik hadn't remembered much of what she had said. What he did remember was how it made her face one of the most distinctive, unusual, and memorable faces he'd ever seen.

She had mid-length, brown hair that she was currently wearing up. This framed a pale, round, serious face, with a slightly upturned celestial nose, and large eyes. When her eyes watered, the lightning bolts of blue danced in the brown background.

Kartik was the one to break eye contact first, and he shifted himself on the grass. They were sitting on Jesus Green, which Kartik considered the best park in Cambridge. They were towards the southern end of the green, a couple of metres from a small stream that separated the public space from the private grounds of Jesus College. The college was partly obscured by a thick ring of trees and shrubs on the other side of the stream, teasing of its existence, but never fully revealing itself.

A few ducks floated on the stream, lethargic, relaxed, taking things one day at a time. Kartik felt a stab of envy for the simple, trouble-free way of life. What an easy way to pass the day, floating on the water, eating bread, quacking your way through any inconveniences the world may throw at you.

Sadly, his occupation was not so carefree. He had just finished his morning shift at Café Ristretto, the faux Italian coffee shop where he had been employed for the past nine months. Cameron was currently on her summer holiday from university, which Kartik thought was rather misleadingly named as it would encroach all the way into early October.

'Something will turn up eventually,' Kartik said. 'I'm still young. I'm just not going to rush into a career that may not be good for me.'

Cameron wasn't entirely convinced by this answer, but went back to her book.

Even though it was still only the first week of September, his friend, as always, was being insanely productive. The reading list from her tutors was close to being completed, so she even had time to read things that weren't even part of her course. For example, seeing a twenty-one-year-old girl in Cambridge sitting on the grass reading a book on the Iliad would make one assume she was studying classics, or at a push, history. But Cameron was a mathematician. She studied *A Companion to the Iliad* by Malcolm M. Willcock for fun. No one studied *A Companion to the Iliad* by Malcolm M. Willcock for fun! It took a strange kind of demented lunacy to study degree-level Ancient Greek for recreational purposes.

This was especially confusing for Kartik who had always considered reading lists to be silently prefixed with the word 'suggested'. When he had been at university he'd rarely read the books he was assigned, let alone something voluntarily. He'd written essays on books he'd never even picked up. Cameron read books on topics that she'd never even use.

However, this did perhaps go some way to explain why she was about to start her third year at Churchill Collage Cambridge, and Kartik hadn't even managed to get through two years at Oxford Brookes, before quitting and returning home.

Kartik looked over at a group of Spanish teenagers kicking a football nearby. They were arranged in a circle, using their feet, knees, chests, and heads to make sure the football didn't touch the ground. They moved the ball with a deft skill that was synonymous with the current generation of Spanish footballers. On their shirts, they proudly displayed the names of their heroes: Torres, Xavi, Iniesta. A group of girls watched with mild interest. The girls all wore matching orange backpacks—a clue that they were part of a student tour group. Kartik thought back to his own brief football career. His record for keepy-uppy was two-hundred and thirteen touches before the ball touched the ground. But that had been eight years ago, when he had been fourteen (around the same time he had become friends with Cameron), and since then the amount of football he played had dramatically decreased. He had barely touched a ball in the past couple of years, and he was sure he'd be a lumbering embarrassment if he attempted to join in with the Spanish teenagers.

'Don't you think serving coffee and getting high is a waste of your youth?' Cameron asked, not feeling she had interrogated him quite enough for the day.

Kartik took a drag of his joint. 'It's not the worst thing in the world.'

'What about going back to university? I'm sure once you catch up with some modules you'd be fine. We may even end up graduating at the same time.'

There had been a consideration on his part to remediate his scholarly failure, but he had decided against it. 'I don't particularly want to go back. It wasn't for me. I mean, what the hell was I meant to do with a degree in English literature anyway? Being able to write an essay on the themes of *Middlemarch* hardly prepares you for the world of real work.'

'Did you ever even read *Middlemarch*?'

'Umm... yeah.'

'What's it about?'

'The perils of living in Coventry?'

Cameron sighed. They'd had this conversation many times before, not about *Middlemarch*, but about his future. They'd likely have it again.

'Well, why not at least try for something a little more challenging than what you're doing now?'

'Serving coffee is challenging. Do you know how particular people are about their decaf, half shot, soya, and dry cappuccinos? Pleasing pedants isn't easy.'

Cameron looked at him again with a stern look to let him know she was getting tired of the snarky responses.

'Look, it's just not a good climate at the moment to look for jobs,' he continued.

'You could at least try.'

'We're in a recession, Cameron. Companies are tightening their belts. They're reluctant to spend too much time looking over the curriculum vitae of someone whose greatest achievement is when he beat his friend Andrew 11-1 on a game of Fifa two years ago.'

'Please, tell me you don't still have that on there,' Cameron said, horror in her eyes.

'Not since you decided it was "inappropriate" to include on a professional resume.'

'You really would be doomed without me, wouldn't you?'

'You're the wind beneath my wings,' he replied with biting sarcasm.

'Well, as the wind beneath your wings, I want to guide you into getting a better job.'

'No one is hiring, Cameron. People are getting made redundant, and these people are all clambering for the same jobs I'm going for. Meaning I'm competing with people with skills. With actual experience! How can I get experience when no one will hire you to give you experience? It's a catch-22. I read in the paper the other day that one entry secretarial job had had over two hundred applications. Two hundred! To be a secretary?'

'Well, don't just give up,' Cameron said.

'I like giving up. I'm good at giving up.'

'I know. That's what worries me. You're like Benjamin Braddock but without the charm.'

'Or the degree,' Kartik conceded.

'The *Not-Even-a-Graduate*. Doesn't quite have the same ring, does it?'

'Look, I'll just ride out this recession for a while. When things start getting better, then I can start looking for a more "challenging" job.'

'Why wait for things to get better? Why not be proactive about it? You're relying on things getting better. What if they don't?'

'Well, history suggests otherwise. It's the natural economic cycle. Remember the public expenditure after the Wall Street crash to help mediate boom and bust capitalism? That's happened after every crash of the twentieth century, and that's what's happening now. We'll be out of this in a year's time.'

'Ah, Keynesian economics? So, you do read some of the books I lend you?' Cameron smiled. She was always trying to educate Kartik, to 'make him a more rounded person', and there was no easier way to get in her good books and, more importantly, to get her off his back, than to placate her ego and demonstrate that her teaching was paying off. Naturally, Kartik had never got past the first ten pages of the mammoth tome *The General Theory of Employment, Interest and Money* by John Maynard Keynes, but he had done a diligent sweep of the economist's Wikipedia page, and could now say some vaguely pseudointellectual things about the theory of economics. He wasn't always entirely sure if the things he said were entirely true, but most people would believe him if he showed enough confidence.

And he'd managed to bluff Cameron this time, which was impressive as she knew everything. She was a person who was in a permanent state of study. Kartik had never met someone who thought, calculated, and generally pondered as much as she did. She was constantly having ideas, or working on some project, or expressing some esoteric opinion that Kartik could barely fathom. For every moment that Kartik spent vacantly thinking about nothing, which was most of his spare time, Cameron spent processing information and ideas like a supercomputer. No one was sure how or why their juxtaposed friendship worked, but for some reason it did.

He stubbed out his joint and looked over at the Spanish teenagers. One of them had dropped the ball one too many times, and was now required to stand by a tree, bending over, while the other three took it in turns to try and kick the ball at his arse. The third spot kick got him square on the left cheek and the guy let out a squeal of pain and hopped around holding his backside. The others howled with laugher, but the girls looked on indifferently. It was nice to see footballing punishments transcended national and cultural boundaries.

'As I said, things will get better,' Kartik said. 'But it just seems like a lot of work right now.'

Cameron looked at Kartik, gave a quick snort of derision and then returned to her book. Kartik returned to lying on the grass. They were, for that moment of time, in their respective elements.

CHAPTER TWO

Ryan Stanfield looked across at the nervous wreck opposite him. The young man, no more than twenty, maybe twenty-one, was palpably shaking. There was sweat running down from his temple. Despite his youth, his thin hair was already prematurely receding, meaning the beads of sweat, which started high on his forehead, had a long journey to go before they would reach an eyebrow. The shaking hand was too petrified to wipe it off. It was too busy rattling around on the end of the young man's forearm. In contrast to the person he was about to fire, Ryan was imperturbable. This was a situation that he excelled at. It was a situation he had been in many times in his career, and the efficacy that he brought to his work gave him an undeniable thrill. Ryan pitied someone that couldn't find the joy of firing an underachiever.

'I'm sorry, but I have to do this,' Ryan said, affecting a tone of sympathy that he had seen other people use before telling someone the bad news. It was the sort of tone doctors used in TV shows before giving the patient their terminal diagnosis. . Ryan hoped it came across as genuine, but didn't mind too much if it was an obvious act. 'Looking over the numbers over the past few months, it's just not working out.'

'But I'm about to place a new candidate,' the shaking man said. His name was James Sorensen. It was a name that Ryan would forget within a couple of days.

'Is it confirmed?'

'Not yet. But I'm close. I just need another week.'

'I've heard this before. You told me that last month. So far, you're six months in and you've placed, what? Three low-level candidates? The best people in this company can place a person a week. They have strong pipelines. Looking at your pipeline...' Ryan looked over the spreadsheet report on his laptop. 'You've got very little in the way of opportunities that look like they will progress.'

James was trying to speak, desperate to think of a counterargument. His mouth kept opening to say something before closing due to the absence of words that would actually give credence to any form of defence. The stats spoke for themselves, and the stats were poor. James shuffled in his cheap, ill-fitting suit. The shirt was too baggy and the sleeves of the jacket too long. How were you meant to succeed in business if you couldn't succeed in taking your suit to a tailor? Dressing well projected confidence. Dressing like shit resulted in you being a nervous wreck. It resulted in you failing to cling onto your job after a disastrous probation period.

Ryan adjusted his tie that probably cost more than James' entire suit. 'Look, I appreciate the work you have put in over the last six months, but it's time to face the fact that this isn't working out for you. Being a recruitment consultant is a tough job. Some people can do it. Some people can't.' Ryan opened his palms face up towards James to imply, in case there was any doubt, that his shaking frame was most definitely in the latter category.

'Is there any way I can stay on just for one more week? Try

to finalise this placement. Work on my pipeline.' A bead of sweat had just missed James' right eyebrow and was travelling down his cheek now. Ryan was getting slightly annoyed with his persistence. Why hadn't he showed this sort of stubborn attitude with his clients? Why was he fighting so hard with Ryan, even though it was clear he was out? Ryan had a million other things that needed to be done, and this probation review was meant to be a quick job on Monday morning. Ryan's ability to mimic patience and sympathy was wearing thin.

'No, it hasn't been good enough. I need you to clear your desk and leave by lunchtime.' James' face fell. He finally wiped the sweat from his cheek. Ryan sighed. 'I'll make sure I'll do my best with a positive reference.' He kept his voice flat as he told this lie. It is important to keep your voice measured when lying. It makes everything more convincing.

James got up from his seat and mumbled thanks, before shuffling out the door, shoulders hunched, an aura of defeat surrounding him. Ryan shuffled some papers as he watched him leave. He didn't need to shuffle the papers. It just gave him something to do as people left the office. It was what presenters did at the end of the news, as the lights dimmed and the camera moved away. It gave the perception of importance.

When James was outside his office, Ryan stopped shuffling the papers and put them neatly back on his desk, just slightly to the left of his laptop. He reflected on successfully completing his first task of the day. It was good to get the first task out of the way, and to do it correctly. It put you on the path of success for the rest of the day.

To add to this sense of early-day satisfaction, Ryan was also pleased that he was safe in the knowledge that it wasn't a problem that he had created in the first place. It had been his idiotic predecessor who had hired the gibbering wreck, and it had been up to him to clean up the mess.

His predecessor, Harry Underwood, had been naively patient, had been conned too easily, had hired people on their affable personalities rather than their ability to get a job done. Underwood, who had previously occupied Ryan's now uncluttered office, was the sort of person to look at his team's underperforming results and take the blame himself, to apologise to the underlings, and to promise them he would work harder for them next time.

What sort of self-destructing maniac operated like that? If someone is shit, tell them. If they don't stop being shit, get rid of them. It was a simple, mathematical formula. Success equalled good, failure equalled bad. And all failures should be reflected on the most culpable person for that mistake. He didn't have time for any of this managerial psychoanalysis nonsense, where responsibilities should be deflected under a mountain of technical jargon to take the pressure off, letting people thrive in a relaxed work environment. People shouldn't be relaxed at work. Pressure was good. It spurned you on and got results. The only time you could relax was when targets had been met and exceeded. Then you could wipe your brow. But even then you should still have one eye on the prize, looking to always be one step ahead of your competitors.

He rubbed his hands over his sleek, glass desk. One of the requests he'd made when transferring to the Cambridge office was that the old wooden desk, decorated with rings of coffee stains, ink marks, and a surprising number of carved notches, be removed, and a new one ordered. He couldn't work on a desk that had more in common with the one he had sat behind in secondary school back in the Midlands than with a high-level professional's. The new desk was minimalist and L-shaped, with three black drawers underneath. On top lay his brand new white iMac (work) and his silver MacBook (work and personal). Next to the laptop were the recently shuffled papers (work), and a picture of his wife and daughter (useful to humanise him in the work environment, but he supposed also somewhat personal). The desk was cleaned every evening by a Spanish cleaner whose name Ryan refused to remember so as to keep a sense of appropriate status. In the morning it caught the light coming through the window wonderfully, shining in all its affluent glory. It felt good to sit at a desk that cost more than many of his colleagues' monthly wages.

Ryan had been transferred to Fusion Vision Recruitment's Cambridge branch three months before to help rescue the failing operation. It wasn't a move he had welcomed, as it had meant moving from the main London office to a branch that was small enough to be considered provincial. However, it had ultimately been the board's decision, and they knew that he was the only one good enough to turn this ship around. They respected him for his management abilities.

And now he was in, there were going to be changes. For example, he wouldn't have hired someone as incompetent as James in the first place. Part of being a good recruitment consultant was being able to tell who is good for your firm, and people likes James certainly weren't.

The problem was, it was hard to find good, entry-level people these days. It was how the new generation had been raised. They had been pampered, made to believe they were special and deserving without having to do anything themselves. They expected their employer to work for them, not the other way around. Reward without effort. That's what happens when you have an entire generation raised under a Labour government.

The defining moment of Ryan's youth had been watching Maggie send the fleet off to kick out the Argies when they'd invaded Commonwealth soil. That was how you inspired a generation. What inspired James' generation? Probably nothing. They expected to waltz into the world with an insipid humanities degree and to have everything handed to them on a platter.

There was a knock on the door.

'Come in,' Ryan said, picking up his papers and resuming the shuffling. Philip Lawson walked through the door.

'So, Mr. Sorenson is no longer with us then.' Philip had an annoying habit of referring to everyone by their second name no matter how junior and insignificant. If Ryan wasn't such a consummate professional, this way of addressing junior members of staff would annoy him. But he didn't let little things like that get to him. Philip was good at his job and was therefore allowed a couple of irritating quirks.

'Yes, sadly it wasn't working out,' Ryan said, focusing on the shuffling of papers to indicate his preoccupation.

'He didn't have much time.' Philip sat down in the chair that moments before had been occupied by James. Ryan hadn't asked him to sit down, and again, this would have annoyed him if it wasn't for his professionalism.

'Three months is our standard probation period. He had six. We expect at least six placements in that time, if not more. I placed four people in my first month when I first started my career.' Ryan was fairly confident this was a correct stat. It had been twenty years ago, so he was allowed a slight margin of error.

'It was a different climate back then,' Philip said. It was clear from the way he tilted his head as he spoke that he didn't believe that Ryan had actually made four placements in his first month. 'We're in the middle of a recession,' Philip continued. 'People aren't recruiting like they used to.'

'Exactly. That's why we can't afford to keep members of staff that cost us money.'

Philip didn't say anything for a while, but rubbed his palms together. He was a short, black man. At forty-three, he was three years older than Ryan, but he annoyingly looked younger. He had a youthful frame that was maintained with regular exercise and he had few wrinkles on his face. He had no hair on the top of his head, but there was a thin ring of hair that started at his ears and circumnavigated his skull to his neck. He shaved this off completely, and the only times he truly showed his age was when this hair was left to grow and a grey band curled around the back and sides of his head. Currently, this wasn't the case, so if someone were to guess their respective ages, Ryan would almost certainly come off worse.

'Shall we start the search for a new candidate?' Philip asked. He was the office's accountant, but been around for so many years it seemed like he got involved in everything, hiring included. It was odd that one of the chief influences on the hiring process was an accountant. It was a practice that seemed to be commonplace in the provincial offices, and one that Ryan was keen to remove.

'Get Aaron to start collecting CVs and I'll have a look through them.'

'I can start going over them if you like,' Philip said.

'No, it's all right. It's something I'd like to do myself.'

'Right. Okay then.' There was a slight tension around Philip's face. Ryan kept looking him in the eye. Eventually the accountant looked away. 'I'll get Aaron to send in the best now.'

'Good stuff,' Ryan replied, leaning back in his office chair. It was a large, comfortable chair that had his initials sewn into the arm rests. He'd insisted that it came with him from London when he'd transferred. It was even in his contract. 'Is there anything else?' He'd picked up his papers again to suggest there shouldn't be.

'Well, there is something.' There was a glint of excitement in Philip's eye.

'What?'

'There's a rumour someone's solved Eden's Bonfire.'

'Really?' Ryan asked sceptically.

'Still only a rumour. Some lecturer at MIT. He thinks it's to do with the US government's infiltration of the deep web.'

Ryan snorted. 'You believe that?'

'Could be true.'

'It's a viral marketing thing. I wouldn't get too excited.'

'Maybe.' Philip got out of his seat. 'I'll keep you posted.'

'Thanks,' Ryan said smiling. He considered it a genuine smile, but he wasn't entirely certain if he was conveying it correctly.

Philip left and Ryan was alone again. He reclined in his office chair and gently rubbed the initials on the arm rest with his fingertips. He was looking forward to hiring a new employee. It would be his first at this branch. He could start the process of moulding this new place in his own image. Sure, the place lacked the glamour of his old office, right in the heart of the Square Mile, where the focus had been executive search. In the Cambridge office, the goals, the quality of candidates, the job titles and placements all seemed smaller. He still considered himself to be an executive search specialist, but outside London it was going to be hard to make the sort of placements that made his heart race: directors at the big banks, C-suite at hedge funds, the crème de la crème of the financial world.

Still, this Cambridge gig had a certain, quaint charm. And he knew when he had delivered the required results the board would be so impressed they'd have to welcome him back to London with a debt of gratitude and, more significantly, a large pay rise.

An email from Philip popped up on his computer. It was the details of the MIT professor and his supposed explanation of Eden's Bonfire. He read through it while he shuffled his papers. Then he realised there was no one around to impress, so he put down the papers and got on with some real work.

CHAPTER THREE

The bed was large. Much too large. Larger than his own by far. And it was much too soft. And the sheets. He sniffed them. They smelt fresh. They'd been recently washed with some expensive detergent-fabric softener combo. They were also impossibly white, unlike the slightly greying covers on his mattress at home. As he breathed in the scent, Kartik realised that there was a significant difference between the cheap own-brand detergent that he used and the premium stuff that was used to clean these sheets. This was bloody luxury. If only he had some spare money, he knew where he'd be spending it.

He stretched out but there was no one next to him. There had been at some stage during the night, but now there was only a well folded sheet and a pillow with a tiny dent—the sole hint that someone had previously occupied that space. He rolled again on the opulent mattress, and his eyes settled on the bedside table. A copy of Ayn Rand's *Atlas Shrugged* sat next to a glass of water. The bookmark suggested the reader had not made much progress. Behind the book and the water was a downturned photo frame. The first few times he had been in this bed he had wanted to turn it over, but now he was glad it was always tactically facing downwards before he entered the room.

The glass of water was a lifesaver. He usually woke up with the dry taste of weed in his mouth, but whenever he woke up in this bed, he would have the instantly recognisable taste of a red wine hangover. He downed the water in three large gulps and considered sitting up straight. If he did that, he would have to face the reality of the day, to properly acknowledge what he was doing. So he continued to lay there. The bed was just too comfortable to consider anything else for the moment.

As he was lying down, ready to forget the world and its problems, he heard the sound of the shower from the en-suite. And then, if that wasn't enough stark confirmation that he had indeed been in there with someone else, the person started singing *Moon River*. But this voice was certainly not Audrey Hepburn's. The voice was that of a woman who had taken up the considerable challenge of singing every single note off-key, making the tune instantly recognisable but the listening experience utterly unbearable. Luckily the large pillows, when tactically employed as giant ear muffs, were able to provide temporary shelter from the sound.

'What are you doing under there?'

Kartik woke suddenly. He had drifted off with the pillow wrapped around his ears. He pulled his head out from the pillow and was about to respond but something stopped him. The woman standing at the edge of the bed was naked.

'How are you feeling today?' The naked woman asked.

'I'm good. Fine. Yes. Good,' he stuttered. 'How are you?'

Well this was a new development. Nudity was an obvious prerequisite for when they were having sex, but that always involved a strange tangle of expensive bedsheets and dim lighting. This was the first time she had let him see her in the cold morning light. He tried not to stare, but it was hard not to. She was tall, blonde, and her body showed none of the signs that she was almost twice his age. Maybe, just maybe, she had had some work done on her breasts. He had noticed it the first time they had sex a few months ago. They were perhaps a little too firm, a little too upright. Despite this, they still looked great. As did the rest of her body. And Kartik, frankly, was very pleased to be able to say he had seen it in all its uncovered beauty now.

'Great, thank you.' The voice sounded better when it wasn't singing. Money had certainly been spent on elocution lessons a long time ago. However, as the years had gone by, the refinement of her accent had slowly but surely dwindled. When she was with certain people, Kartik was sure it would sharpen again, but for moments like this, a more relaxed approach was deployed.

'Kartik...'

'Yes?'

'That's an unusual name.'

'Yeah.'

'How did you end up with a name like that?'

'My parents.'

'Was that humour?'

'An attempt at it.'

'What I was asking, is why do you have a name like… what is it? Pakistani?'

'Indian.'

'Why do you have an Indian name?'

And this was the first of Kartik's two problems, the one he had no control over. It was to do with the fact that he had an Indian name, but he himself was very unmistakably white. The result of this was that every time he met someone he had to explain exactly why he had an Indian name. This was annoying and time-consuming but, ultimately, it was something he was powerless to change. Next, she'd be asking about his future.

. . .

'My parents went travelling around India when they were young. That's where they met. Somewhere in Delhi. They did the whole gap year experience in the early eighties.'

'Sounds exciting.'

'Yeah. Bear in mind this was long before gap years became a mandatory rite of passage for kids who head off to Thailand and take cheap drugs at a beach rave and have a "transcendental" experience.'

'Don't judge. Some of my fondest memories have involved taking drugs at parties. Mind you, it's never cheap. I don't really go in for that sort of thing, darling.' Some people Kartik knew were embarrassed about their wealth, as if they must have screwed someone over to live a life of middle-class comforts. The woman standing in front of him certainly didn't have those concerns.

'Yeah, I never really got into anything heavier than weed.'

'Weed? That's a waste of time, darling,' she said. 'What did your parents do while they were in India?'

'They say they "found themselves."'

'So, they probably spent their time taking cheap drugs at beach raves.'

'Probably. Whatever they did, they loved the culture so much that they decided to curse their only son with a completely inappropriate name. Back then they thought it was a good idea. Nowadays I think it'd be referred to as cultural appropriation.'

'Well, I like it. It makes you sound mysterious. Exotic.'

'I'm sorry if I don't live up to my name so well.'

'I think you do a fairly good job.' She brushed back her blonde hair and rubbed her neck.

'What time is it?' Kartik asked, rolling onto his front to avoid the risk of turning the bedsheets as a tent.

'Around eight,' the woman said in a sing-song voice. Bad memories of the shower came back.

'Right.'

'You should probably be making a move.' It wasn't a command exactly, but it would be unwise to argue the point. There wasn't any hint of regret in her voice. In fact, she was being decisively natural. She moved to her drawer, took out a pair of underwear, and put them on. Well, that was one distraction out of the way. 'Do you want a shower first?'

'Yeah, probably a good idea.'

'Towels in the usual place.'

Kartik was about to reach for his boxer shorts, but decided that new ground rules had been established now. He got out of bed and walked over to the en-suite naked. His companion, who had now added a bra to her ever-escalating items of clothing, looked at his erection as he walked past and smiled. 'If only we had more time.' She gave him a quick kiss and then turned back to picking out an outfit for the day.

The bathroom was just as expensive and clean as the bedroom: porcelain white tiles, gold taps, and a full-length mirror next to the bath. Kartik had never seen a full-length mirror in a bathroom before, but he supposed it would be valued by someone with a sense of narcissistic vanity over for their own naked body. Some people would have found the place vulgar and tacky. Kartik had no such opinions. If he had more money than sense he'd probably buy gold taps as well.

He turned on the shower, and attempted to relax. This task was sadly rendered impossible by the renewed sound of the horrendous singing that permeated through the walls. It's hard to relax when *The Sound of Music* is being sung by someone who, ironically, isn't aware what music should sound like. He gave up in frustration.

Once showered and dried he walked back into the bedroom to find the woman fully clothed and applying the day's make-up in front of the bedroom mirror. She barely paid him any attention as he got dressed, brushed his short brown hair, and attempted to look presentable for the day.

When she was done, she turned to him. Any warmth that

she had shown to him previously had evaporated. 'Right, we don't have time for breakfast unfortunately. And I've got to be out of the house very soon. So, I'm afraid you'll have to be on your bike.' She laughed mechanically. 'That's funny, because you actually came here on a bike.' Kartik didn't really get it.

They went down two flights of stairs to the large hallway on the ground floor. Kartik did his best to avoid looking at the pair of children's scooters that were left near the door. It was lucky there were no pictures hanging on the wall around there. Or had they been removed in advance as well? He tried his best not to feel guilty, but this was difficult, especially when he accidentally stood on a child's trainer. The woman didn't react. The door was opened for him. He hesitated before he stepped outside into the sunny morning air. 'Look, Camilla… Do you really think this is, well…'

Camilla looked at him vacantly. 'What?'

'Well, is this a good idea?'

'Look, we both know what it is. And it's fine. As long as it stays like that.' There was something robotic in the way she spoke.

'Well, okay then. But I was thinking if, maybe you wanted to do something more than this.'

She tilted her head to the side quizzically, like a child hearing a new word for the first time. 'What do you mean?'

'Well, you know, we seem to get on well. And the only time we ever see each other is when we, you know…'

'Fuck?'

'Exactly. And maybe if we get on well together, maybe there's something there.' Kartik was now being gently pushed out of the doorway by Camilla who still wore her mask of incomprehension.

'Kartik, are you still drunk?' She looked like she was trying not to laugh.

'I was just thinking that there must be something. It can't just be the sex you enjoy.'

This time she wasn't able to suppress her mechanical laugh. 'Oh, darling.' She placed a long, wet, passionless kiss on his lips. 'I barely even enjoy the sex.'

And then she slammed the door shut on him.

He was left staring vacantly at the number twelve on the door, a butchered version of *Fly Me to the Moon* emanating from inside. Kartik blinked a few times, realised that the door wasn't a particularly interesting thing to spend his day looking at, and went around the side of the house to unlock his bike. He pulled a pre-rolled joint from a cigarette packet, and lit it as he cycled to work.

He rode down a couple of quiet streets and then joined the steady flow of rush hour traffic. The cycle took him past Newnham Common and across Fen Causeway, a little wetland park that was protected by the university to conserve the local flora and fauna. This was tourist Cambridge at its finest—green, old, photogenic. Pictures to show the folks back home in Paris, or Madrid, or Tokyo or wherever. Had these visitors had a transcendental experience when visiting Cambridge like his parents did in India? Have any of them returned home to give their first-born son a typically 'English' sounding name? Were there little Charleses now running around the streets of Shanghai? Or frustrated Henrys having to explain their unusual name to their lovers in Bogotá? Kartik hoped so. The frustration that this would cause would hopefully offset some of his own misery, like some kind of universal, cultural karma.

The bike ride helped clear his head, and the joint clouded it again, giving him a perfectly balanced equilibrium of clarity and carelessness. He cycled past the punts moored at the Mill Pond—a few early bird tourists already getting the tour, eagerly snapping away with their cameras as if their lives depended on it—and then onto King's Parade. King's College loomed large on his left. In the summer months, the entire college would lie mostly empty, as the students enjoyed their unfairly prolonged holidays. When he had dropped out of university himself, he had the vague idea of becoming a radical MP who would run on the promise that the college grounds would house the homeless in the summer and winter breaks. He hadn't given much credence to the practicality of this, but was certain if this plan hadn't seemed like such hard work, he would have been able to pull it off. He flicked the end of his joint onto the grass outside the building.

He locked his bike near Market Square, and headed into work. It was your regular, high-street coffee chain that looked identical in every city, except he was certain that no other café in the country had to deal with quite as many pedants as he did.

'Morning, Kartik,' Gabor said as he walked in. 'How was your day?'

'Only just started, mate,' Kartik responded. Gabor had a tendency to ask someone to review the events of their day, even when it had just begun.

'Americano.' Gabor handed Kartik an already made coffee. He took a sip. Shot and a half of fifteen-second dripped espresso (added to the water after, not before), a half centimetre of cream, one sachet of brown sugar, and served in a double takeaway cup. Gabor had a couple of interesting linguistic ticks, but he had excellent timing and made great coffee.

'Thanks. How's it been?'

Gabor indicated the sleepy interior. 'Slow.'

'Excellent.'

'No, not excellent. We are behind target.' Gabor was the manager of the Market Street branch of Café Ristretto and took his work a little bit too seriously for Kartik's liking. Kartik had already risen to the esteemed rank of Gabor's assistant manager, but their willingness to hit their weekly targets represented a large gulf in their respective managerial styles. A slow day for Gabor meant constant stress, phone calls from their regional manager asking about sales, like-for-like performance, cutting hours on the rota, and panicking about low footfall. Slow for Kartik meant he could probably catch a twenty-minute nap in the staff room twice a day.

'Look, you need to have faith,' Kartik said as reassuringly as he could.

'Faith? What should I be having faith in?'

Kartik hadn't expected this question. He was just supplying unspecific optimism to his stressed manager. 'Err... Capitalism?'

'You are not helping me.'

'Gabor, I would walk through flames for you.' Kartik put a comforting hand on his colleague's shoulder. Gabor looked unimpressed. Gabor always looked unimpressed. Maybe it was because he was Hungarian. Kartik had never met any Hungarians prior to working with Gabor, so maybe it was something to do with their national character: stressed, hardworking, and unimpressed.

Kartik continued with his motivational morning speech, whilst thinking the exact opposite of whatever he said.

'Look, it'll pick up.' *I hope it doesn't.* 'We'll be having a cracking day, be really busy, and get management off our backs.' *None of that will happen.* 'Then we'll go celebrate with a pint.' *Or commiserate, which was more likely, but no less enjoyable.*'

'We better,' Gabor said. 'If we are inspected and things go well, we win Regional Store of Month,' Gabor said with aspiration in his eyes. 'We could even get Gold Star Store of Excellence Award,' he said this in a reverential hushed whisper, like an actor speculating about being nominated for an Oscar.

'I think it's going to happen, Gabor, I really do. For today is a new day, and we are going to aim for dizzying heights. Coffee will be made, customers will be served, toilets will be scrubbed, and we will run this place better than any franchised, high-street coffee shop has ever been run in the history of the United Kingdom. Trust me, I too want the Gold Award for Store of Regional Excellence Prize.'

'Gold Star Store of Excellence Award,' Gabor corrected him.

'Yep, that one too,' Kartik agreed. Did Gabor suspect that he wasn't taking things quite as seriously he was? Surely not, he was nothing if not convincing.

Safe in the knowledge that his manager was now unrealistically reassured, Kartik headed upstairs to the staff room to get changed. The coffee shop was two stories, with large wooden steps at the back. It was all cheap wooden chairs and tables, with the occasional smattering of soft, worn, brown sofas that attempted to give it a lived-in feel, but only served to highlight the lack of money spent on the place in the past decade or so. On the walls, pictures of 'authentic' Italians drinking espresso at roadside cafés laboured the facsimile of continental living for customers that had seen *Roman Holiday* too many times. The place was deserted apart from the few regular early risers: an overweight espresso-sipping workaholic who was permanently glued to his laptop and an elderly couple who sat in silence all morning reading the free papers.

Kartik went into the tiny staffroom that made a coffin look like a spacious flat, and sat in front of the CCTV monitor. On the blurry black and white screen Gabor was busying himself, wiping down all the tables at the front of the café to make it more attractive to passing traffic. He got changed while thinking of Camilla standing naked at the end of the bed. What had that meant? She had deliberately changed the dynamic of their relationship. She had specifically allowed him to take a long look at her. She had wanted him to look over her in the clear morning light. She had wanted him to examine all the brilliant details he had previously only got a passing glance at in the dim light and drunken haze of their ever-shifting positions that they made love in. But then she had completely rebuked him when he had checked if there was more to them than what they were.

Did he want anything else to happen? Could he image sitting in a coffee shop like this, talking, getting to know her, experiencing life away from the bedroom? Probably not. Mostly because of the constant fear that her kids, or even worse, her husband may turn up. But also because, as seductive and beautiful as she was, he really didn't know how much they would get along. As far as he could tell, they had nothing in common, other than a taste for cocktails—a taste that Kartik had mostly faked the first time they had met, as a way to keep her interested.

With a concerted effort, he pushed the thought of Camilla out of his mind and went downstairs to spend most of his waking day serving coffees to people he hated. Around halfway through the day, just past lunchtime, he started to daydream about Camilla again.

CHAPTER FOUR

Ryan was trying to assuage his anger. He was trying to deflect it into something productive. This was his technique. This was what got him through. Using the frustration that he had—with the world, with the general population, with everything and everyone—and turning it into fuel to power his own ambitions. It'd been so successful for him in the past, so why wasn't this working now?

Looking out from his private office into the open-plan office before him, he surveyed his flock. The assessment was bleak. They weren't the workforce he was used to. Sitting around, avoiding work, chatting to each other, surfing the internet, doing anything but getting on the phones and making their calls. What was networking to this generation? They were meant to be the most connected generation ever, with their phones, and their computers, and their social media. But what did they do with this power? Did they turn it into worthwhile work relationships? No, all they seemed to do was send stupid pictures of cats to their friends.

He was eyeing further cuts. He wanted to get rid of all the deadwood. But it was becoming increasingly obvious that if he did, he would be left with an incredibly slim workforce.

He caught Philip out the corner of his eye coming out the office kitchen. Coffee in hand, a serious look on his face. At least this was one person he could count on. A bit disrespectful maybe, but dependable. Could he be trusted? He was on good terms with the office, and Ryan knew that he was the sort of person whose support he would have to gain before completely stamping his authority on a bunch of kids who had the collective backbone of a bucketful of snails.

He fumed for a bit, sat back at his desk, picked up the phone, but didn't have anyone to call. He had passed most of his decent leads to his team, and the few contacts he had in Cambridge that he wanted to keep to himself he had already spoken to. Some had turned into productive meetings, both with candidates and employers.

But now things seemed like they were stalling. Everything he could have done, had already been done. He was beginning to see the limits of this small town. In London there was always someone to call, someone to have lunch with, some financial big shot to schmooze, action that he could be part of. But here? You reached a certain point and everything suddenly came to a halt. He felt like he had been demoted to the role of the orangutan from *The Jungle Book*.

He flipped through his online book one more time and found a half-decent looking lead. A quick phone call later and he had arranged a meeting with a logistics manager looking to switch roles. Mid-level. On £90k. Young family. Named Michael Fitzgerald. Needed something to fit around the two kids a little bit better. It wasn't glamorous, but at least it was a meeting. It'd get him out of the office. He let Philip know he was going out for a few hours, and to make sure he kept an eye on the team. He then went over to the sales desk, shouted at a couple of the younger staff for playing with their phones instead of working (the instant fear that crystallised on their faces gave him a little jolt of pleasure) and then jumped in his car. The meeting wasn't for another hour or so, so he drove around aimlessly for a while, hoping this would relieve some of the tension.

Unfortunately, his frustrations only increased when he once again became aware that the majority of traffic in Cambridge was pedal-powered. In front of him was an ocean of cyclists. What was wrong with these people? It was as if they had been born with two wheels in place of their lower limbs. They moved erratically on the road, treating proper traffic with haughty disdain, somehow not realising how easy it would be for him to mow them down on their rickety little frames and have them under his wheels in less than a second. There was a self-righteous smugness about their behaviour, a holier-than-thou attitude that came with some delusions of grandeur that they were saving the planet. But in reality all they were doing was slowing him down. And he was a busy man.

He honked at one of them as they swerved down a right turn without signalling. The cyclist shot him a disapproving look, so Ryan gave him the finger.

There were a couple of cyclists at his own work. You could tell them from a mile off. Too polite on sales calls, but arrogant in every other aspect of their lives. They would arrive in the office, backs sweaty and suits crumpled from their morning commute. Some would arrive in full cycling gear—preposterous, tight-fitting, garishly coloured lycra—and change into their suits in the bathroom. How long did that ritual take? How long did they waste, peeling off their lycra and changing into clothes that they should have put on first thing in the morning? How many sales calls could they have made whilst they messed around with their bloody outfits? Cycling, in all forms, was a waste of everybody's time.

The drive did nothing but heighten his tension, so he put a stop to it. He turned back towards his office, pulled into the parking space he had left fifteen minutes earlier, and made the short walk to the city centre to the café where he was meeting Michael. He was still half an hour early, so he knocked back a couple of double espressos to calm himself after the small-town traffic nightmare. He was served by a contemptable barista, with rude manners and a laissez-faire approach to service speeds. When Ryan returned to the counter on his second espresso to complain that the coffee was clearly burnt, the barista shrugged laconically, made him a new one and barely even mumbled an apology. He had a mop of brown hair that should have been too short to be messy, but somehow achieved it. His slovenly stubble was what Ryan understood to pass as fashion these days, as if trendy fashionistas were lifting style trends straight from Big Issue sellers. His red eyes suggested he was stoned and his manner reflected it.

Coffee remade, he returned to his table. Weed was no drug to go to work on. It just gave rise to a useless apathy. Cocaine, now that got the job done. Ryan had been a big fan a few years ago and it had assisted him during the most productive point in his career. It was a sad day when he went to his doctor with some serious sinus problems and was told he had to cut it out all together to avoid his septum collapsing. He had quickly done the maths: cocaine may have been productive, but it would have been a disaster to turn up to client meeting with a crater where his nose had once been.

Since then, he'd had to rely on coffee to see him through the day.

He'd just finished his second double espresso when Michael Fitzgerald appeared at the door and Ryan greeted him warmly, slapping him on the shoulder like an extended family member he hadn't seen for years. He bought two more double espressos (his insistence that it had to be made correctly was met with a vacant nod from the stoned barista) and then he started with the meeting. Ryan noticed that Michael barely touched his coffee throughout their talk and considered the notion that it may have been wise to ask first if he drank coffee.

It was tedious conversation, but productive. Michael liked to talk. He liked to speak about his kids, about how his wife had made him rethink his work-life priorities, and how he wanted to work in an environment that was receptive to this, but he could also work hard and progress. Michael was a gaunt man, with a long face, and prematurely greying hair. He had thin limbs and Ryan was suspicious that he may be a cyclist. However, ever the professional, he put aside his own prejudices, and cracked on. He made it look like he was making notes on his new iPad as a professional courtesy. In reality he just typed in some nonsense to make it look like he was paying attention. People felt reassured when they had a visual indicator that what they were saying was being listened to and recorded. It was like they assumed he was too stupid to remember all the mundane detail that he was being forced to endure.

Ryan didn't need any notes to do that. He was capable of remembering even the smallest detail of someone's life. It was what made him a good head-hunter. If a client had kids, he'd remember their names, ages, schools, and even birthdays. If the client played tennis in their spare time, he'd always ask how their backhand was coming along. If they'd taken a year off work to go travelling he'd find out where they'd been, and usually be quick enough to invent a story of how he had visited the same place and was 'just blown away by the scenery.' Remembering the details of other people's lives was a sure-fire way of gaining someone's trust. Appearing to give a shit about people's lives was crucial to his success. Ultimately, it meant that the interviews he sent them on appeared especially selected for that particular candidate, and not just an arbitrary company that Ryan knew needed a corresponding position filled (which they were).

The meeting concluded with both parties satisfied:

Michael because he had a new trusted advisor and Ryan because he had a new candidate and had also drunk six shots of espresso in just over an hour.

'Well, it's been great learning what you're after,' Ryan said. 'The job market is tight right now, but smart, experienced people like you are still highly sought after.' Flattery got you everywhere in this game.

'Thanks, I try to do my best. But if you want smart, you should see my niece.'

'Really?'

'Oh, yeah. She's the real brains of the family. Going into her third year at Cambridge, studying maths. Beats us all at University Challenge every week.'

Ryan laughed, but in his head he was making some calculations. 'Has she got plans for after university yet?'

'Some vague ideas. They change all the time though. At the moment I think she wants to go on to get her PhD and then stay in academia as a lecturer or researcher.'

'Hmm... Great thing to do,' Ryan said philosophically. 'Pity there's no money to be made as a lecturer.'

'I don't think that's her driving force. She's into expanding her mind and helping others. All very noble,' Michael said. 'I'd like to think I would be like that if it weren't for the kids. She'll change when she's got mouths to feed of her own.'

'That's the nail on the head right there. Arabella's the most important thing for me as well.' Ryan had dropped in his daughter's name when Michael had started talking about his own kids. Instant rapport.

'Yeah, I know. I love them. But it doesn't give you any time for anything else. It's just work and family, work and family. Don't get me wrong, I wouldn't change it for the world. But I missed having, you know, a bit of a life. Having hobbies. My niece, she seems to have all the time in the world even though she's doing one of the most advanced degrees she could choose. She's even doing some extracurricular puzzle for her tutor because he couldn't solve it. Some mad science and maths thing that no one can work out. Apparently, Stephen Hawking is working on it. It's called Adam's Bonfire or something.'

Ryan tried to disguise his sudden alertness at those words. 'Eden's Bonfire?'

'Yeah, that's the one. Do you know it?'

'A little bit. I didn't realise Hawking was working on it.'

'Do you know what it's for?'

'Just some kind of puzzle for the academics, I suppose' Ryan said. He may have been sceptical about the whole thing, but he liked the sound of the girl. 'I'd be interested to meet her. There are a lot of companies that would be interested in having a chat with her. I've got a lot of contacts in financial firms in the City. Hedge funds and the sort. They're always looking for top talents. And for someone like your niece, even at entry-level, the pay is light years ahead of what she'd get in academia.'

Michael was apprehensive about giving out too many details, but after some gentle persuasion he gave Ryan her name, college and email address.

'Cameron?'

'Yeah.'

'Interesting name.'

'Bit different for a girl. I think my sister regrets it a bit though. She turned out to be a...' Michael looked around conspiratorially and then whispered, 'A lesbian.' Ryan smiled. His wife would often lower her voice in the same way when she swore. 'Not that I've got a problem with it understand. Just funny. Maybe they were hoping for a boy.'

'Well, it's a distinctive name,' Ryan nodded diplomatically.

The meeting concluded and the two men shook hands before parting ways.

On returning to the office, Ryan headed straight to his

office and did some more research on Eden's Bonfire. He found out a string of theories but nothing concrete: viral marketing, MI5 recruitment, the key to contacting extra-terrestrial life, and everything in between. He then sent an initial approach email to Cameron before setting up an interview for Michael with a suitable company. He put more than the usual amount of effort into finding good roles. Next, he went to have a chat with Philip and filled him in on his day.

'I thought you didn't believe in all this Eden's Bonfire stuff?' Philip said when he had finished.

'I believe it exists. It definitely does. I'm sceptical about its purpose, or if it indeed does have a purpose. But if it is a recruitment tool, it could be interesting in meeting someone who knows about it.'

'It would be. I've looked over it myself a couple of times.'

'And?'

'I couldn't get anywhere on it,' Philip admitted.

'I don't mean to interrupt.' It was a desk jockey called Aaron, who annoyingly, had been eavesdropping on their conversation. 'But what exactly is Eden's Bonfire?'

CHAPTER FIVE

'Eden's Bonfire is a multi-level, multi-discipline puzzle of unknown origin that was distributed over the internet to a select group of academics around the world six months ago. No one knows who made it or what's it for. Few people know about it. Many of the people it was sent to didn't realise what it was and therefore failed at the very first stage. So far no one has come up with a reasonable solution for what it could be. A lot of people don't think there even is a solution. I think there is.'

Andrew was looking at Cameron slightly slack-jawed. 'I don't get it.'

'No one gets it,' Kartik said. 'That's the point. It's a waste of time.'

'It's not a waste of time. It's actually very interesting.'

'So, what do you do? Are there, like, tests and things? Do you get a grade at the end?' Andrew asked.

'No, it's not an exam. There are several dozen stages, with clues hidden all over the place. Once you complete a stage, you'll be sent a new clue, and then you have to work through that stage. However, there are multiple ways to solve each stage. I often speak to people online who have gone about each stage in a completely different way. It momentarily leads them down a different route, but it seems that you always come back to a central path.'

Andrew was struggling to get his head around the concept, let alone attempt the mental gymnastics required to tackle such a thing. His mouth was ajar and his face was vacant, like someone had removed his brain with an ice-cream scoop. It was impressive that he hadn't gone cross-eyed.

Cameron continued, 'Look, think of it like a car journey. You're trying to get from one city to another. You don't have a concrete idea where the second city is, but you've got a vague inkling of the general direction you should be heading. And there is a motorway, which is the quickest route, but you're forced to leave this from time to time and take some winding backroads. People will take detours, get lost, but ultimately they will end up back on the main road, hopefully travelling in the right direction.'

'But the problem is that it's just a bunch of people driving aimlessly with no destination,' Kartik said.

'What do you mean?' Andrew asked.

'Well, no one knows what lies ahead. Or if there's even a reward at the end. Or if there is an end at all, right?'

'That's true,' Cameron agreed. 'But it's not aimless. There's a great sense of collective purpose. And a sense of self-fulfilment for taking part. But you wouldn't really know much about self-fulfilment, would you Kartik?'

'Look, I'm not the one driving on some "intellectual motorway of discovery."' He said the last words in a silly voice that was meant to mimic Cameron's but ended up sounding more like Alan Partridge.

'Life's more about the journey, not the destination. What's wrong with enjoying the ride?'

'What's wrong with not speaking in clichés? Think you could try that?'

'Well, I think it sounds very interesting,' Andrew said playing peacemaker.

They were sitting in the beer garden of The Maypole, a pub that was a stone's throw away from Jesus Green. Although the term 'beer garden' was perhaps a little bit generous for the short strip of concrete that separated the pub building and the multistore car park next door. With the early September nights still warm, the outside area was fairly crowded. There were several groups of people sitting around, drinking, and killing time, before having to drag themselves out of bed the next morning to face another grim day at work. It was a Wednesday evening and Kartik had convinced Andrew to join him down the pub, which was an unexpected treat considering that his girlfriend, Louise, rarely let him off the leash on a weeknight. Kartik had been working the afternoon shift, and hadn't quite got the smell of coffee and steamed milk out of his clothes, no matter how much deodorant he sprayed himself with.

'So what sort of things do you have to do? Where do you get the clues from?' Andrew asked.

'Well, it was initially sent to my tutor,' Cameron answered. 'He gave up on it, claiming he didn't have enough free time to work on it, but I suspect it was because he couldn't do it. So he sent it to me, with some notes. At the moment I am working through a logic-based coding system that is directly related to the work of M.C Escher.'

'The guy that did those steps to nowhere?' Andrew said. He seemed pleased that he finally understood some of the conversation.

'*The Penrose Stairs*, yes.'

'I think those steps are a metaphor for this entire endeavour,' Kartik sighed. 'Maybe the creator is giving you a hint?'

She ignored him this time, much to Kartik's consternation. 'And before that there were a series of sentences hidden in archived newspaper articles from the tabloid press from the week Diana died. You had to work out a formula, to find out which word in which article in which newspaper to use, then put them in the right order, then go to another website and type in the sentence, which operated as a password.'

Kartik considered making another pithy remark, but stopped himself. As much as he enjoyed making glib comments about Cameron's interests, he sensed it was only because of a lingering jealousy of her talents.

When they had first become friends in secondary school, Kartik had fancied her immediately. So much so that he had somehow convinced himself that he was in love with her and her hypnotic, multi-coloured left eye. Even the fact that she had a boy's name didn't prevent him from believing that she was perfect for him. However, as the years went by, his teenage infatuation had given way to platonic familiarity, and now she was the closest thing he had to a best friend. There had also been the small fact that when she was sixteen she had told him she was a lesbian, which had put a dampener on any lingering romantic intentions he may have had. But still, it didn't stop him from occasionally glancing at her and thinking, 'What if...?'

'Does it make a bit more sense now?' Cameron asked Andrew.

'I think so,' Andrew said uncertainly.

'Look, as fascinating as all this is, we're going to get the next round in.' Kartik said, rising from his seat and pointing at Andrew.

'We are?' Andrew asked.

'Yes. We are,' Kartik said, keen to get Andrew alone for a couple of minutes. He had important things to talk about that didn't revolve around a silly puzzle.

'Both of us?'

'I can't carry all the drinks by myself.'

'You can't carry three drinks by yourself?'

Andrew was not getting the hint. 'No.'

'I'm pretty sure you can.'

'I hurt my hand at work.'

'Oh, no problem then. Give me the money and I'll get them.'

'That's the spirit,' Kartik said. 'I'll help you.'

And with that, he swept Andrew inside the pub, leaving a dangerously suspicious Cameron behind them.

When they were at the bar, Kartik owned up to the Camilla situation, which he was feeling moderately guilty but also quite excited about.

'You're sleeping with her again?'

'Yeah.'

'I thought you'd stopped.'

'I did.'

'What happened?'

'I started sleeping with her again.'

'Brilliant.'

'Yeah, I know. That's why I started sleeping with her.'

'I was being sarcastic. Is she still married?'

'Yeah.'

'So why are you sleeping with her again?'

'Because it's fun.'

'But she's married!'

'Yeah. I'm starting to think that's what makes it so fun.'

'You're a terrible human being.'

'I know.' Kartik smiled at his friend. Andrew didn't reciprocate. He had a moral rectitude that didn't quite gel with Kartik's outlook on life. 'But you can't tell Cameron.'

'Didn't Cameron help orchestrate this in the first place?'

'Yeah, but that was before she knew Camilla had kids.'

It had been three months ago, back on a warm early spring evening in May, in a cocktail bar just around the corner from his work. He had been drinking with Cameron and had noticed Camilla drinking alone. She had asked to join them at their table as there was no other space. She had been drinking a Manhattan, Cameron and Kartik bottled beers. Kartik had introduced himself and his sister (Cameron caught on quickly) and then switched from beer to a cocktail on the menu that he thought sounded the most sophisticated and grown-up.

They talked about nothing in particular for a while; Cameron made a tactical manoeuvre and left. Camilla had then bundled them into a taxi and back to her house. 'Remember, there will be no questions,' she had said as they arrived at the door. Upon entering, Kartik understood what she meant as it was clearly not a house that was inhabited by one person. From then on, Kartik had never asked and Camilla had never spoken about it. The pictures on the bedside table were always turned down and the children's shoes—with the exception of the incident in the morning—were tucked away out of view.

It had been a semi-regular thing for the first two months, but then it had seemed to stop, and Kartik had put it down to a bored housewife having a quick, no-strings-attached affair. Then, two nights ago, he had got the call. He had considered saying no, drawing a line in the sand, and standing up for what was—probably—morally right. Unfortunately, he was only human, and a fairly sub-standard, weak-willed human at that, so he had resumed the affair.

'So now Cameron's not keen on the idea anymore because she's not just married, but also a mother?' Andrew asked.

'No, she's like you. She's got, I don't know, principles or something.'

'She'll find out.'

'No, she won't.'

'Yes, she will.'

'The only way she'll find out is if you tell her.'

'Or because you're a bad liar. And she's much smarter than you.'

'I'm a great liar.'

'No, you're not. She'll see right through you.'

'Andrew, please have some faith.' Kartik put his hand on his friend's shoulder reassuringly. 'I've got this under control.'

'Yeah, just like you said you had your housing situation under control.'

'It is under control.'

'Sleeping in Louise's—sleeping in *our*—spare room isn't a housing situation under control.'

'See? You called it Louise's spare room. You're totally under the thumb.'

'Don't change the subject. You're living in our spare room and you're sleeping with a married woman.'

The barman placed three pints on the bar and frowned at Kartik. Kartik smiled. 'Don't worry. It's not your wife. I don't think.'

The barman muttered 'cheeky shit' before going to serve someone down the other end of the bar.

'You know he's going to spit in our next drinks?' Andrew said.

'You worry too much. Anyway, we can always go somewhere else.'

Andrew tutted like a pensioner seeing teenagers littering outside his house. Andrew worked in media sales, a job that screamed of disappointing lack of fulfilment. From what he'd told Kartik, he spent most of his time leaving voicemails and sending unopened emails to potential clients that didn't really need to buy online advertising space on whatever platform he was focusing on that week.

He was two years older than Kartik, and they had become friends at secondary school when Kartik's precocious footballing talents had allowed him to play for the school's Year Nines when he'd just been in Year Seven. Andrew had always been the more sensible of the two and used to carry a sense of controlled calm that, for some reason, had made him fairly popular with women (his first girlfriend at school had been Cameron before she'd come out). But since meeting his current girlfriend Louise at the University of Bristol, that dependable placidity had given way to a desperate need to please and obey. Louise didn't just wear the trousers in the relationship but also bought them, measured them, and got them tailored to the specifications she thought looked best.

Kartik picked up his pint and, not for the first time, thought that his friend could do better than his current girlfriend. He was a handsome guy, with short, curly brown hair and a hint of something Mediterranean about his features, even though his mother was English and his father Danish. They were about the same height, a respectable, if not impressive 5'10', although Andrew seemed to be putting on a little bit of weight around the middle, probably due to his sedentary office lifestyle. Still, nothing a couple of months down the gym couldn't fix, and once that was done, he could start attracting girls that were less constricting than Louise was.

They took their pints and headed to the beer garden.

Kartik gave Cameron her drink as they sat down and lit a cigarette. Andrew made a point of doing a fake cough and brushing away the smoke. Kartik told him to grow a pair.

Next to them sat a group of middle-aged men. They were moaning loudly about people at their respective offices. It was the same boring conversation that you heard at any midweek post-work session. They still had their suits on, with the top buttons of their shirts undone and their ties hanging loose: the unofficial white-collar signal that someone was off duty. They had a ringleader; a large man with thinning hair and a voice that could fill a canyon. His chubby fingers were wrapped around his pint in a tight grip, like an overprotective parent desperately holding onto his child in a crowded area. Every now and again one of his friends would venture an opinion or contribution but these were few and far between, because the ringleader's monologues were longer than Shakespeare's. He looked familiar, and Kartik was pretty sure he had served him in Café Ristretto recently.

It was times like this that Kartik pitied the nine-to-five drones, almost as much as he pitied himself. At least he wasn't restrained by the monotonous, Monday-to-Friday grind that served as an unflinching template to their whole lives. Sure, he had to work long, irregular shifts, but shift work had its benefits. For example, tomorrow was Thursday and he didn't have to go to work at all. And who doesn't want Thursday off? Tomorrow the world would be his oyster. He could do anything he wanted while everyone was at work. For a glorious twenty-four, midweek hours, he was only responsible for himself and had no other commitments. He'd most likely spend this time watching a *Twin Peaks* marathon on DVD. Some people would consider this a waste. But Kartik felt that it was the little things that made life worth living.

'Are you ready for your final year?' Andrew said to Cameron.

'Still got a few weeks before things start up again. Term doesn't start until October.'

'What a joke,' Kartik said.

'Yeah, because I don't do any work in the meantime,' Cameron responded sarcastically.

'Look, all I know is if I had eight week terms, I probably would have finished university. Nice easy ride. I could have fit it all in that first year and still had time to beat Andrew at Fifa.'

`'Yeah, I'm sure you would have.' Cameron turned away from Kartik, indicating she wasn't going to be lured into an argument for the sake of it.

'Louise isn't coming out then?' Cameron asked Andrew.

'She's working late again,' Andrew said.

'And she hates fun,' Kartik added.

'Kartik,' Cameron snapped.

'It's true,' Kartik said defending himself.

'How's her job going?' Cameron asked, again not stooping to Kartik's perpetual goading.

'Yeah, she likes it. It's just the commute that she doesn't like. An hour on the train down to London every morning, and then back again at night.'

Louise worked for a media agency that designed marketing campaigns for travel companies. Her title was something nonsensical like Senior Digital Marketing Team Coordinator, which meant as much to Kartik as Ancient Greek. From what he could gather, her job mostly consisted of client meetings, client lunches, client dinners, client drinks, associate drinks, forward planning drinks, after-work drinks, and team bonding drinks. He was certain there was probably a lot of work involved somewhere, but it always seemed to gravitate around this blanket term, 'networking'. But that was the central hypocrisy of Louise's mentality that didn't sit well with Kartik: whilst it was fine for her to spend her evenings at some fancy bar in central London it was rarely fine for Andrew to spend time at the pub. Just because she was with clients and wearing a suit, it didn't make it much different from sinking a few pints down the local.

'I think she's thinking about making the move to London,' Andrew continued. Kartik's ears perked up and he was suddenly paying full attention.

'Wait, what?'

'We're thinking about moving to London sometime soon,' Andrew said.

'Whoa, whoa, slow down. Why?'

'So she can be close to work.'

'Well, what about you? You'll be further away from work.'

'I can get a new job.'

'Well, why do you have to change jobs? Why doesn't she get a job around here?'

'Because her job is actually a good position at a company she wants to progress in. There are a million media sales roles in London. Shouldn't be too hard for me to make the move.'

'She's convinced you to think like that, hasn't she?' Kartik said. 'She's smart and manipulative. Making you think you want to move when it's actually all just her self-interest.'

'You want to talk about self-interest? I know why you're protesting so much. Because it will mean you'll have to move out from Louise's—from *our*—house.' Andrew said this with an authority that was rare for him these days. He then went back to talking to Cameron about the different areas of London. Kartik sulked until it was time to go back to the bar.

On his way back, as he struggled both with the fact that he may soon become homeless and the three pints and two packets of crisps he was carrying, he bumped into one of the middle-aged office drones' chairs. It was the ringleader, the fat man with thinning hair. Half a pint descended on to the man's shoulder.

'Oi, what the fuck are you doing?' the man shouted as he got to his feet. His jacket was darkened with sticky larger.

'Sorry, mate. Didn't see you there.'

'You didn't see me? You've got beer all over me. Do you know how much this jacket cost?'

Kartik didn't. 'No. How much did it cost?'

The man paused and for a second it looked like he didn't know the price of anything. Clearly he hadn't anticipated his question to be answered with another question. 'A lot of fucking money, you idiot.'

His face started to redden as he snarled at Kartik. Although Kartik had youth and, hypothetically, speed on his side, the man who now stood in front of him was definitely superior in height and bulk. He was overweight, a bulging belly sagging over his belt, but still retained a muscular presence that suggested someone who was previously quite athletic—a rugby player or boxer perhaps. His broad shoulders rotated in their sockets, like a bull flexing before it charges. The knuckles in his right hand tightened into a fist. The left hand hung loose by his side, but twitched rhythmically. It looked as if the man may be ambidextrous, but this was perhaps not the most convenient time to find out.

Two full pints, one slightly spilt pint, and two packages of salt and vinegar formed an obstacle between the two of them, not allowing the aggressor to get too close, but it also meant that Kartik's hands were already occupied if it did come to a fight. The only limb he had available was his leg, and although a swift kick to the kneecap would likely be effective, it would also result in him getting beer all down himself as well. He didn't particularly want that to happen, although it would be preferable to getting punched in the face.

'Who are you calling a fucking idiot?' Kartik said, voice raised.

'You, you fucking idiot,' the reply came instantaneously. Kartik had no response to this. It was an entirely logical answer. The man held up his Fosters-soaked jacket. 'You're going to pay to get this cleaned.'

Kartik hadn't been in too many fights before, but he was pretty sure that the threat of dry-cleaning bills wasn't common.

The man's two friends were standing up next to him. Both looked a little apologetic, as if this wasn't the first time this had happened. Andrew was still sat down looking confused and concerned. Cameron was smirking, as if there was a sense of poetic justice taking place. The shorter of the two friends, a black man around the ringleader's age, put his hand on the man's shoulder. 'Come on, Ryan, it was an accident.'

'Fuck off, was it an accident? He did that deliberately,' the man replied.

'Why would I do that, Ryan?' Kartik asked, not entirely rhetorically.

Again Ryan paused. His face became even redder. The use of his name got right under his skin, but he couldn't come up with a decent response.

'You don't know me,' he said eventually. 'Don't think you fucking know me.' He pushed Kartik's shoulder, causing more lager to spill. This time it landed on Ryan's shoes.

'Now you're getting beer on my shoes?' Ryan shouted.

'To be fair, that was your own fault,' Andrew piped up from behind them.

'Shut up.'

Andrew shut up.

'How much did the shoes cost?' Kartik asked.

'What?' Ryan shouted.

'Come on, just forget it, Ryan,' his pacifying friend said.

'You seem to want to tell me the price of everything that you get covered in beer. How much were the shoes?'

'You're a cheeky prick, aren't you? Think you're funny, do you?'

'Sometimes.'

Ryan pushed Kartik again. More beer spilt. Ryan's shoes managed to dodge another soaking but Kartik's jeans weren't so lucky. The three glasses now contained about half the amount of lager that they had when Kartik had purchased them. At this rate, there would be nothing left to drink.

Luckily, for the sake of the preservation of the beer, the owner of The Maypole appeared and made his way in between the two combatants. He seemed to know Ryan and told him to calm down. It obviously wasn't the first time he had to deal with a situation like this.

The owner dealt with things swiftly, professionally, and calmly. He managed to soak up Ryan's aggression and to toss it away like he was pouring a bucket of mop water down a drain. Kartik stood there awkwardly and nervously as things were sorted out, without anyone really addressing him at all. The group of suits were told they could stay as long as they moved inside. It was a compromise that Ryan accepted grudgingly, the threat of being expelled mollifying him.

Kartik sat down at his table and was told that he would need to stay out of trouble or he wouldn't be allowed to drink there anymore. He was about to explain that he had done nothing wrong, but Cameron gave him a look that suggested that he shut his mouth. He shut his mouth.

'What a dickhead,' Cameron said.

'You looked like you were enjoying it, from where I was standing.'

'Well, it was quite funny.'

'Really? Funny? He could have beaten the shit out of me.'

'Please. He was all talk. I've seen people like that before. Mr Big Shot when they're shouting at you, but nothing comes from it.'

'Oh, really? Where did you learn these lessons of the street?'

'I've been in more fights that you,' Cameron said. Kartik was about to argue, but then did the maths internally and realised it was probably true. 'He was the sort of person who wanted to look tough in front of his friends. But he's not stupid enough to actually hit anyone.'

'He pushed me. Twice.'

'I think you'll live.'

'I've got beer on my jeans. It looks like I've pissed myself.'

'Well, he came off a lot worse.'

'Yeah, but he'll probably have somewhere to live in a couple of months.'

'Look, nothing's set in stone yet. It's still something we're considering. We'll probably stay in Cambridge for quite a few months yet. We're not going to kick you out without any notice. We'll make sure you have somewhere else to live. You could always move back in with your parents?'

Kartik shuddered at the thought. 'What a terrible idea. These are the people that named me Kartik. They clearly do not have my best interests at heart.'

They finished up their drinks, or what was left of them, and then Andrew got a call from Louise saying she was on the train home, which sadly put an abrupt end to the evening's festivities. They said goodbye to Cameron, who was walking back to her university accommodation, and jumped on their bikes. Before they left, Kartik looked back at the pub. Ryan was watching them from inside. He curled his hand in a loose fist and started swinging it from left to right in the universal symbol for 'wanker'. A wanker he may be, but he strongly suspected that he wouldn't have to pay for Ryan's dry cleaning.

CHAPTER SIX

Traffic shuddered to a halt in front of Ryan's car. There was the briefest of pauses, a time when Ryan almost felt calm. Then his ears filled with the sounds of blasting horns as frustrated motorists beeped at one another. For lack of anything else to do, Ryan joined in.

'Stop that. You're not going to help.'

'That prick in front of me just cut me off.'

'Language.' Ryan's wife, Anna, slapped him on the arm and then indicated to the backseat where their ten-year-old daughter, Arabella, sat. Ryan looked up in the rear view mirror just in time to see his daughter roll her eyes clandestinely at her mother. He smiled. She did have moments when she rather delightfully resembled her father.

'I'm sorry I said that word. I shouldn't use such language in front of Arabella.'

'I know what it means, you know,' Arabella said.

'Arabella!' her mother cried, as if her daughter had just turned her head one-hundred and eighty degrees and spewed demonic vomit on them both. Arabella giggled. Ryan nodded to her in the rear-view mirror.

'Don't encourage her,' Anna said.

'Well, it's not my fault people around here don't know how to drive,' Ryan said, turning his attention back to the road.

'Don't know how to drive? I'd much rather drive around here than London. It's a lot less aggressive.' They were currently heading south out of Cambridge towards Wandlebury, a park that had been recommended as a good place for kids by Philip. They had a picnic in the back and Anna had been itching to get out of the house and explore more of the local attractions as a family. However, on this particular Saturday, it seemed everyone in the city had the same idea, and now they were currently surrounded by Ford Mondeos and Renaut Lagunas packed with children and picnics, all probably destined for the same patch of grass that the Stanfields were intending to sit down on.

If Ryan were the sort to feel embarrassed, he would have felt slightly out of place towering above the modest family cars in his Range Rover Sport, but he didn't care. It was a far superior vehicle and he'd drive whatever he damn well pleased. Plus, the air conditioning in the car was superb, meaning that overheated, angry car journeys were a thing of the past. Well, the overheated part anyway.

'At least people in London drive with some balls,' Ryan continued.

'Ryan! Not in front of Arabella.'

'I know what balls are, mum.'

'Arabella! See what you've done, Ryan?'

`'Balls are like pricks,' Arabella announced.

'Not quite, sweetie,' Ryan correct his daughter. 'But you're in the right general area.' Arabella giggled again.

'For god's sake, Ryan. Do you want our daughter growing up to be a...' Anna took a quick glance at Arabella, covered her mouth with her hand so her daughter couldn't see, and mouthed the word 'slut'.

'I think she'll be ok.' He looked at his daughter in the rear-view mirror. 'Won't you, sweetie?'

'I'm going to be A-okay.' She put her thumb and forefinger together in a circle to back her statement up.

'That's my girl.'

After another twenty minutes of gridlock and a few more aggressive manoeuvres from Ryan, they finally pulled into the car park. Ryan unloaded the picnic from the boot, and the three of them walked into the park. They found a grassy area of the park with half a dozen families sitting lazing around. The sun was still high in the sky and patches of grass had turned yellow after the hot summer. It hadn't rained for weeks, and the last vestiges of summer remained, even as the leaves on the trees started to don their autumnal colours. The sound of the traffic on Babraham Road could faintly be heard over the trees that surrounded the park, but with a little imagination, you could pretend that you were in the middle of nowhere.

Anna was fussing with Arabella, who wanted to join a group of children playing with sticks in the woods nearby. There were about a dozen children, running around, climbing trees, and generally doing what children did when left to their own devices. Ryan could understand his daughter's yearning for that sort of freedom, especially from her mother. He often had a burrowing desire to escape when he was around Anna.

Ryan was laying down the picnic blanket and unpacking the food as mother and daughter argued.

'Why can't I go and play?' Arabella said, her face locked in a grimace of childish ostentation.

'We don't know them. It's not right to just impose yourself on other people's games.'

'But mummy,' her daughter protested. 'I want to play.'

'Arabella, put yourself in *their* shoes. Would you want

some strange child whom you have never met before to just join you without asking your permission?'

'Yes,' Arabella said. Ryan smiled to himself as his wife's reasoning tactics were derailed by a ten-year-old who was still young enough to not worry about social protocols and conduct.

'Well, you shouldn't. That's not how things are done. You need to introduce yourself and await invitation.'

'Oh, come on, Anna,' Ryan interrupted. 'She's not meeting the Queen. Let her play.'

'Are you deliberately trying to raise our daughter as some kind of social terrorist?'

Ryan sighed at his wife's utter lack of perspective. 'Look, I'll go over to that group of parents and see if it's ok for Arabella to play. Then we'll be able to get a "proper invitation."'

'Yay,' Arabella yelled as she grabbed her father's hand.

'I suppose that'll be okay,' Anna grudgingly accepted.

'Then we can relax, just the two of us for a bit,' Ryan kissed his wife with what he hoped felt like tenderness.

The two of them scurried over to a large group of parents sitting a few metres from the stick-wielding hoard. The parents, as expected, didn't have a problem at all with Arabella joining in. As soon as she was given the go-ahead, she dashed towards her new playmates with the alacrity of an escaped convict.

'Make sure you come and get some food before I eat it all,' Ryan shouted after her, but she showed no sign of hearing. Instead she was talking to the tallest boy—the one she had already identified as the leader—and was imposing her presence on him. *Clever girl. Even at an early age she already knew to get in front of the decision-maker.*

He watched her play for a while, a stick-gun in hand, already commanding a squad of her own, and taking aim at the group of the opposing team. She was a natural leader, and had the physical and mental ability to back it up. She was thin, but an early enrolment into ballet (Anna's choice) had given her body a strength and poise that defied her slender limbs. Last year she had also started playing football (Arabella's choice) and had joined the team of her new school. Although he had been too busy with the move and work to have seen her play in the flesh, he had heard that she was a naturally gifted footballer.

She had a pretty, round face, with large, curious blue eyes. Her mouth was currently missing some of her front teeth, as her milk teeth gave way to permanent teeth, which were slowly pushing up through her gums. She had straw-blonde hair, which was pulled back in a ponytail.

Her posture was strong and gave off an organisational authority that was rare among children that age. Most importantly, she made eye contact when she spoke. Ryan had noticed this was unusual among her friends, whose eyes were used to stare at a TV, computer, or mobile phone screen almost as soon as they learnt to talk. This resulted in many not being able to hold a conversation for more than a couple of minutes, or staring at their shoes, when they spoke. Arabella on the other hand, who had been taught the importance of good manners and social appropriateness (Anna's choice), always looked you in the eye when she spoke, and Ryan realised now that it gave her a powerful advantage over the other kids. Some of them may have been physically bigger, but none could better Arabella's social command.

'See? Not such a big deal,' Ryan said as he sat back down with his wife.

'You indulge her too much.'

'Maybe you try to control her too much,' Ryan replied hotly.

'I'm just making sure she grows up to the sort of person that people are going to want to be around.'

'If you had your way, there wouldn't be any people whom she was allowed to be around.'

'Don't be ridiculous. She had Lucy and Tiffany from down the road over for a playdate the other day.'

'Only once you'd checked with their parents and vetted their families for appropriateness.'

'I just don't want her getting in trouble again. I don't want her hanging out with the wrong crowd.'

'We're sending her to a £15,000 a year school, Anna. Not exactly the sort of place you are going to find the "wrong crowd", is it?'

'Yes, but then you just send her off with a bunch of children we've never met before. And look at them. They look, well, a little bit, common.'

Ryan looked up. Arabella was indeed a bit out of place in her blue and white checked designer dress, against the other children who had jeans stained with dirt or, even more worryingly for Anna, sportswear. 'If it makes you feel more comfortable, the parents were all very pleasant and middle-class. You're safe from your prejudices for now.'

'Can you stop being so...' Anna struggled, as if she couldn't quite pinpoint the specific criticism she had for Ryan among the plethora of faults that she saw in him. 'Superior,' she finally blurted out. If she understood the irony of using this adjective to describe someone else, she didn't show it.

'I'm not being superior. I just want our daughter to experience a bit of freedom.'

Anna filled up a plastic glass with wine and drank from it. 'I just don't get it. You seem so uptight, so controlling about everything. About the bills, about your job, about me. But when it comes to Arabella, well, it's like you just don't give a—' She looked around, and then mouthed the word 'shit' like she had done earlier. It was a habit that was beginning to grate on Ryan.

But she was wrong. He did give a shit. In fact, his

daughter was perhaps the only person he felt like he really connected with. Arabella was the only person for whom he didn't have to fake emotions, whom he could have a natural conversation with, and who didn't constantly annoy him with some kind of gross stupidity. She was ten years old, but she was already smarter than almost everyone he knew. He looked over to his daughter again. She was standing tall on the enemy base, the territory conquered, and her team was defending the flanks from the usurped former occupiers. She was more capable than the majority of his team at work.

'Look, I just think you're trying to mould her, trying to control her too much. She's got to see what life is like outside that protective shell that you've tried to build around her.'

'Oh, and how would you like us to do that? Why don't we take her out of her education and send her to a state school?' Anna spoke the last two words as if she was talking about a dirty infection. Jesus, he had gone to a state school when he was growing up in Birmingham, and he turned out fine. Anna had conveniently forgotten about that when she was scouring schools in Cambridge three months earlier. Anna had totalitarian single-mindedness when it came to making sure Arabella would have the best education.

So there had been a revolving door of meetings and interviews and tests for a wide range of exclusive education establishments over the past couple of months, which was a horrible strain on his work. They had been checked, referenced, cross-referenced, and examined in every way imaginable. By the end, the only surprise had been that none of the interviewers had pulled on a latex glove and asked them to bend over. Arabella, who had been having private home tuition immediately after the move, was put through even more strenuous examinations, with the advanced testing reducing her to tears on more than one occasion. Usually Ryan would be all for this sort of mental taxation—it would breed a stronger workforce in the future—but his daughter was a ten-year-old girl, not some post-graduate intern who had to be yelled at and overworked.

'Why does everything have to be so political with you?' Ryan asked. 'I just think it's good for Bella to have some friends that she's made on her own, not just a handful that you've preselected.'

'Please, don't call her Bella. Her name's Arabella.'

'For god's sake, it's a nickname.'

'It sounds cheap.'

Ryan threw his hands up in the air in frustration and then lay back on the grass. The sun was beating down on his face and his neck was resting just over the top of the blanket. He could feel the sharp, dried grass prick at the back of his head. He tried to push himself down even further, increasing the subtle pain running down his spine. He closed his eyes and tried to shut it all out. He could turn off the screams of the playing children, the gentle hum of traffic coming from the road, the sounds of birds in the trees, but try as he might, he could never block out his wife's presence as she scowled right next to him.

It'd been a tough week and his plan of spending a relaxing weekend with his family was already starting to unravel. His team at work were still underperforming, and at the rate they were going, he wasn't going to be able to justify taking on new employees that he could hand pick himself—not unless he was able to fire a couple first. He considered the notion of firing more people. It brought him a momentary sense of satisfaction.

Secondly, he still hadn't been able to get in contact with the elusive Cameron Fitzgerald. He'd sent her a few emails to introduce himself, but so far had nothing in return. Not even a polite acknowledgement of his efforts. He'd managed to find a picture of her on the internet, as she'd written a number of articles for *Varsity*, Cambridge University's newspaper. The articles were a feminist take on a recent student play. They were completely pointless, but very well written. The girl clearly had talent. She just needed to focus that energy on more tangible applications and not waste her time with feminist issues.

Lastly, he wasn't yet over the midweek incident with the little bugger that had poured beer all over him. He still hadn't taken his jacket to the cleaners yet. He felt his shoulders tense at the memory. It wasn't so much the act itself that annoyed him. He could have dealt with that idiot with a couple of blows and some strong words of advice. But it was the ignobility of having to accept the situation by the landlord, and being moved inside without any form of reparations from the disrespectful bugger. He had been paralysed by a stranger who had allowed him no satisfaction of retribution and he had been made a fool out of in front of his colleagues. They would forever remember that moment when he had been made to look like a fool by some kid.

Worst of all, he had recognised him. He couldn't place him. He knew he had seen him before. It wasn't so much the face, but it was… what was it? What did he recognise? The smell. It was the smell. That smell of stale smoke that was intrinsically linked with the dozy lassitude of a stoner.

'The barista!' Ryan suddenly said.

'What?' Anna said, looking at him over another glass of wine.

Ryan sat upright. 'That guy that started trouble with me the other day. I remember where I know him from.'

'Oh, not this again,' Anna said dismissively.

'I know where he works.

'I thought you had let it go.'

'This is great. He works in that coffee shop by Market Square.'

Anna's eyes had drifted off into the distance. She talked as if from a sleep. 'Really? And what are you going to do about it?'

'I could complain to his manager,' he said. Anna barely reacted. As soon as the words left his mouth, Ryan realised how ineffective they sounded. 'Or, I dunno. I've got to do something.'

'Of course you do, dear. Go and tear the place up. Show him who's boss.' Ryan gave up with his wife and lay on the grass again. He didn't know what to do, but he'd do something. He'd go in there on one of his lunch breaks next week and give him something to be afraid of. He had to. Honour was at stake. Or at least his dry-cleaning bill.

Arabella and her new friends had stopped playing their war games, and were now kicking a football around. Jumpers had been put down as goalposts, and the kids were chasing the ball around with the sort of enthusiasm only youth could harness. When she was able to get the ball, it was clear Arabella had talent. Her touch was soft, and she kept the ball close to her feet when she ran with it. Due to her size, she wasn't able to muscle her way around some of the larger children, so instead she would pick smart passes to her teammates.

After half an hour or so of playing, Anna called Arabella over for food and they ate the sandwiches and cake that had been prepared. Arabella chatted away with incessant enthusiasm, but Ryan and Anna said little. There was too much between them.

When they were done eating and Arabella had run out of things to say, they set off back to the car. Their daughter ran off ahead, arm in arm with one of the children she had been playing with earlier. Anna drew in a deep, worried breath, most likely because the girl her daughter was skipping with looked to be of Middle Eastern descent.

'I'm afraid she's going to have difficulty at school,' Anna said, breaking the long silence between the two of them. 'She was having difficulty at her last place. And it's going to continue.'

'I'm having difficulty at work. We're all adjusting.'

'But we've spent so much on her. I don't see why she can't be happy all the time.'

'She's been happy today,' Ryan said, pointing to their carefree girl twenty metres in front of them.

'But only because we've let her run wild. Whenever she's in school, or with her tutor, she acts out.'

'She's just an awkward age.'

'She talking about balls and pricks.'

'She's just doing it because it gets a rise out of you.'

'She said "A-okay" in the car. A-okay? We sent her to elocution lessons. Where is she picking up slang like that? She's watching too many American movies.'

'Yes, American movies from fifty years ago maybe. Kids don't say A-okay anymore. They say lol.'

'Lol?'

'Laugh out loud.'

'This isn't funny, Ryan.'

'No, it means... look forget it. A-okay is endearing. It's sweet. She's doing fine, our kid.'

'I don't want her getting detentions again. Especially at this new school. I want us to have a good reputation in the community, and I'm worried that she'll damage it.'

At times, Ryan just wanted to scream at his wife. To grab her, shake hold of her, and force herself to look in the mirror, to remind her there was more to life than Anna Stanfield's reputation. 'She's just independent. She'll have friends soon. Look at how she's doing now.'

'I wish you put as much work in with your daughter as you do with that bloody job of yours. If your employees started behaving like her, you'd get rid of them all.'

'Yes, well if my employees were behaving like her, they'd be filling in their time sheets in crayon. She's ten years old. Just relax and let her have some fun.'

Anna didn't relax. Anna was in a permanent state of

agitation. And she remained that way as Ryan navigated the traffic on the way home. Arabella sat quietly in the backseat. She had used up too much of her energy that day to be agitated. Ryan looked at her through the rear-view mirror. The serenity of his daughter's face was the only thing these days that made him feel calm. Even the VW Golf that cut him off at the roundabout couldn't take away from that momentary feeling of peace that he got from Arabella.

CHAPTER SEVEN

It had been a bad morning for Kartik. Just like every other morning. But today was especially loathsome. It had gone wrong from the beginning. His alarm had failed to go off on time, resulting in him being late. Gabor wasn't pleased to see him when he strolled in at quarter to seven, a full forty-five minutes later than he was meant to, and only fifteen minutes before the doors were due to be open.

After a rushed set-up they managed to get the place open on time. As soon as the doors were unlocked, the usual dead-eyed morning crowd fought their way inside so they would be the first to the complimentary copies of *The Daily Mail* or *The Times*. The regulars were in an unseasonably cantankerous mood, grumbling about the smallest and most insignificant trivialities from their lives. They would utilise Kartik and Gabor as confidents, moaning about whatever was bothering them that day.

'My roof's been leaking and the builders still haven't got round to fixing it.'

'My husband was snoring again last night.'

'I can't trust any of these politicians these days.'

Sometimes they would just look at the headline of the

paper, tut, shake their head, and mutter, 'What's the world coming to, eh?'

With every complaint, every moan, every issue shared, Kartik felt his will to live dissipate.

As he was going to sneak off around the back for a quick mid-morning smoke, Gabor got the phone call. His face was pale.

'Senior management are coming in,' he said as he put down the phone.

'Huh?'

'Senior management. Both area and regional. Are coming here. Today. Sometime this morning.' The fear on Gabor's face would have been comical if it weren't for the fact that it would directly affect Kartik's day as well.

From then on, work turned to panic mode. Gabor made sure nothing could be faulted: every table was cleaned, every coffee was quality-checked, every customer served with polite haste and a beaming, ear-to-ear smile. Kartik just about managed to plaster on a convincing smile, as he gritted his teeth and prayed for the end of the day.

They were joined by the area manager and regional manager a little after ten o'clock. Gabor was taken up into the office, where he no doubt got a horrendous grilling, and Kartik was left at the bar with an enthusiastic, but utterly useless newbie called Alison, who was barely able to spell latte, let alone make one.

Half an hour later, Gabor and the two managers came out of the office. The managers shook his hand, said a quick goodbye to Kartik and Alison, and then departed.

Gabor joined them behind the bar and helped Kartik serve the customers. Alison was told to focus her energy on her main talent: the monumentally intricate task of emptying and refilling the dishwasher.

'How was it?' Kartik asked, the false smile fading from his face as soon as their unexpected guests had left.

'Horrendous. They're very disappointed with the figures we are making.'

'They're always disappointed in figures. That's their job. To make us feel like we are barely treading water, so we work even harder, and drive up profits and their bonuses.

'That is not how they see it. They are thinking of bringing in a manager from another area to help out here.'

'To replace you?'

'Not to replace me. But they would supervise us both.'

'That's not good.

'And, they are looking to reduce our hours,' Gabor said.

Kartik stood frozen for a second. 'Reduce them? Again? Jesus, I'm only just earning above minimum wage as it is. As much as I loathe every second that I spend in this place, I need to be here at least forty hours a week just to stay alive.'

'I know. I tried to protect us all.'

'Look, I need to pay rent. And pay bills. And pay for food. You can't really do that if they keep cutting hours.'

'I understand, Kartik. But with the downturn and the economy, things are not looking good for us.'

'What the fuck are you talking about?' he said indignantly. Upon hearing his language, the elderly lady that Kartik was serving glanced over at him as if he had just defecated in her coffee. 'This is a coffee shop. We sell a semi-addictive liquid that people will still spend money on every single day, regardless of the quality of the product and customer service.' Kartik handed the large mocha over to the infuriated customer. 'That'll be £2.75, please.'

The elderly lady tossed him a five pound note in an obstinate display of displeasure. Kartik gave her a wide, false smile. She went to her table, took out one of the customer feedback comment cards that were next to every table and then started scribbling on it furiously.

'You see? You are complacent, Kartik. We cannot assume people will always be coming to us. If we are not showing great service to every customer, then they will go somewhere else. We are in close proximity of three Starbucks. Three! If you are swearing at customers, where do you think they will go?'

'I didn't swear at her. I swore at you and she heard me. Not my fault that she was within hearing range from me.'

'We are at work. Everyone is within hearing range from you.'

'Well, then they shouldn't be coming in here.'

'And then you would not get any hours at all,' Gabor said, his voice becoming louder as he became more exasperated. 'Because there would be no one to serve, you fucking idiot.'

'Hey, don't swear in front of the customers, Gabor,' Kartik said, faking indignation. He turned to the next customer in the queue. 'I'm so sorry for my colleague's language. I'll make sure it doesn't happen again.'

Gabor didn't look happy. Kartik patted him on the shoulder as an act of fallacious benediction. His manager shrugged and went back to work.

By lunchtime, Gabor and Kartik were no longer talking and Alison had even managed to mess up her dishwasher duties. Bubbly liquid was foaming from the bottom of the machine and she was fighting back tears. Gabor sent her on her lunch break while he attempted to fix the problem.

The customers kept coming, the world kept turning, Kartik's stress level kept rising, the job remained unrewarding. But it wasn't just the job that was getting to him. It felt like there was a pressure building somewhere behind Kartik's eyes. A throbbing ache that heightened every time the world dealt him another bit of bad news. Louise was going to kick him out so she could frolic around in London, his manager was going to cut his wages to satisfy some shareholders at the top, and there was no other company that would employ someone like him. Drop-outs like him weren't exactly in much demand.

For a moment, as the pounding blood rushing behind his optic nerve seemed to thicken and coagulate, he considered that if he had only focused a little more, if he had only been more determined to succeed, if he had cut back on the weed and the flippant responses to life's challenges, he wouldn't be in this mess. It was a downward thought process that was pleasantly broken when Cameron came in to see him.

'I'm going for lunch,' he announced to Gabor. The Hungarian grunted in response.

He made a couple of coffees—his usual shot and a half of espresso in his Americano, and a double-shot latte for Cameron—and they sat down in a quiet corner at the back of the café. He filled Cameron in on the events of the morning (although he decided not to go into details about how he should have perhaps taken life a little more seriously; it would give Cameron too much satisfaction in her rectitude). He then remembered something important.

'Hold on,' he said to Cameron. He went over to the small black post-box attached to the wall with 'Customer Feedback' written on it. Taking out a key from his pocket, he unlocked the box and took out the only comment card in it.

Scrawled in barely legible handwriting was: 'Bad coffee. Terrible atmosphere. Insulting staff.' Kartik closed the box and took the card to Cameron.

'One of my many fans,' he explained as he gave her the card written by the elderly customer earlier in the day.

Cameron briefly looked at the card but didn't seem to read what it said. 'That's nice,' she said.

Kartik took the card back from her and tore it up into little pieces.

'I've got something to tell you,' Cameron said once Kartik had finished destroying the evidence of his bad service.

'What is it?'

'I met someone.'

'Met someone?'

'Yeah.'

'A girl?'

'No, I'm back in the closet and dating guys again.'

'Really?'

'Of course she's a girl.'

'Right.'

'Yeah.'

'Cool.'

'It is.'

Kartik waited for Cameron to explain but there was a monosyllabic breathlessness to her answers, a certain childish excitement in her voice. This was unusual for someone who always seemed to have a well-considered response to everything.

'And? Who is she?'

'She's an engineering student. She's about to start at Churchill this year.'

'How did you meet her?'

'Well, you know how I've been doing some tour days for some of the new students? To give them a quick overview of the university before they formally move?'

'Ah, getting on the fresher bandwagon early, I see.'

'Kartik, it's not like that,' Cameron said. 'And, well, I know it's going to sound a bit weird, but I think we're in love.'

Kartik had to almost stifle a laugh. It had been under a week since he had last seen her during the incident at the pub, and in that time she had fallen in love? Under most circumstances, he would have thought it was some kind of joke, but there was a candour about her that made him think otherwise.

'Do tell all.'

'Her name's Rachel. She's starting at Churchill in October. And she's studying engineering.'

'You mentioned that already,' Kartik said, amused by her

forgetfulness. This girl had got her flustered.

'Sorry. Well, I had a group of about ten people to show around the college, the grounds, and some of the city. And she was really engaged. Like the whole time, asking questions, wanting to find out more, talking to me loads. So then, at the end of the day, all the others go their separate ways. But Rachel stays behind.' The words rushed out in a torrent. Cameron's eyes were focused on her gesticulating hands in front of her, but every now and again she would look directly at Kartik with dramatic intensity. Kartik kept his face straight, discarding the wisecracks that were coming into his head and listening to what his friend was saying. If he was going to be making changes to his lifestyle to reach his potential, he could start by taking Cameron seriously.

'We were chatting down by King's College. You know, just on the wall outside the chapel. Just the two of us.'

'Very romantic.'

'I find out she's from Edinburgh and she's staying the night in Cambridge before getting the train back the next day. And she says she wants to see a bit more of the city. And so we go to a pub.'

'The Maypole?'

'The Eagle.'

'Traitor.'

'She wanted to see where Watson and Crick worked.'

'Still…'

'And then one drink turns into two. Which turns into a lot. And then she ends up coming back to mine. And, well, then she stays for four days straight! And it's…' Cameron paused, trying to re-examine everything that she had just told him. 'I don't know. It's something like I've never experienced before.'

'So, you're in love?'

'She stayed for four days.'

'I've played PlayStation for four days straight before. Doesn't mean I love my PlayStation.'

'She's a person, Kartik. Not a games console.'

'I am aware of that. But, you don't think it's a bit soon to be in love?'

'Four days. She stayed for four days in a row.'

'I know. You keep saying that.'

'We were inseparable.'

'I was inseparable from *Grand Theft Auto*.'

'Kartik!'

'Sorry.'

'I know it sounds ridiculous. But yesterday morning, just before she left, we were talking and it kind of slipped out. I told her that I'd had a really good time, and that I couldn't wait to see her again. And then, almost by accident, I told her that I loved her. And I was so scared. For a few moments, I thought I'd messed everything up. That I'd scared her off, and I'd never see her again, and she'd go back to all her friends to tell them how insane and deluded Cambridge students are. But she said that she loved me as well. And she meant it. Well, I think she did. I meant it when I said it to her. I said it as an accident, but that's not to say I didn't mean it.' Cameron laughed. She was laughing at herself. Kartik couldn't help but laugh as well.

'Don't take the piss,' she said.

'I'm not. I think it's very sweet,' Kartik said. He was surprised to realise he meant it. 'I think you're insane. But that doesn't stop it being quite sweet.'

'Thanks.'

'When are you seeing her again?'

'I said she could come and stay with me before term starts. She said she's going to think about it.'

'So you're going to be living with each other?'

'Yeah. Do you think it's a good idea?'

'I don't know. I can't remember the last time you came to me for advice.'

'I know, it's strange. But if you met her, you'd understand. She's so cute, and interesting, and sexy. And, the sex is just unbelievable. She does this thing with her—'

'Good for her,' Kartik interrupted. He stirred his coffee to keep his mind from wandering.

For the rest of his break, Kartik listened as Cameron waxed lyrically about her new girlfriend. He listened diligently, asking appropriate questions, encouraging Cameron to talk about herself, and the future engineer who had had a profound effect on her in such a short space of time. Cameron was usually so entwined with studying, or worrying, or sorting Kartik's life out, that she rarely had time to just enjoy life and talk about herself. Sure, she would claim that she got a sense of pleasure from her work, but that was only through a method of rigorous, taxing, and often exhausting intellectual exertion. It felt like a breath of fresh air that she was finding pleasure in something purely emotional (and, by the sound of it, physical).

After Cameron had told him every tiny detail she knew about Rachel, she paused. She glanced around, looked down at her coffee, and then giggled like a child. She rubbed her forehead, almost in disbelief at what she was talking about. 'Sorry, I went on for a bit there.'

'Don't worry about it. It's good to hear. I'd like to meet her sometime.'

'We'll see. Maybe I'm just getting overexcited about nothing. Maybe it was just a bit of fun for her.'

'The way you talk about her doesn't make it seem like just a fling. It sounds pretty serious. Well, serious for a four-day-old relationship.'

Cameron was about to reply when a figure appeared next to them. For a second Kartik thought it was a customer interrupting his lunchbreak with a frivolous complaint. But when he looked up it was a face that he recognised. It took him a few seconds to place it.

His memory took him back to the previous week outside The Maypole and the face suddenly came into context. He remembered the angry fat man, red in the face, screaming something about having to dry clean his suit. The broad shoulders were the same, as was the slightly protruding belly and the pudgy face.

To Kartik's surprise, the man, instead of yelling at him, extended his hand.

CHAPTER EIGHT

As he approached the front doors of Café Ristretto on Wednesday lunchtime, Ryan wasn't sure if the stoner would even be working, but he knew he had to do something. It wasn't so much that his pride had been damaged, it just needed to be restored a little. He had to teach this kid about life's pecking order. If that barista thought he could get away with his behaviour without consequences, then he'd end up in even more trouble. If he continued to spill lager on people and ask them cheeky questions without any fear of reprimand, then one day he'd run into someone not as forgiving as Ryan and end up getting a right kicking.

So, it was in his best interest that he be taught a lesson. Ryan was a benevolent teacher, generously spending his free time helping the younger generation have more respect for their elders. He would help the lesser man with a dose of discipline.

He knew he wouldn't be able to shout at the barista, like he could at his own staff. That wouldn't go down well from the point of view of other patrons; there was a strange deference for those in the food industry from their regular customers. No matter how incompetent they were at their jobs, you weren't allowed to openly berate them these days. It was all part of the softening-up of youth culture.

Instead, he would have to deploy all his powers of persuasion to convince the kid that he'd been in the wrong for spilling the beer on his jacket. He'd have to get him to apologise and reimburse him for the dry cleaning. It would be a tough conversation; he'd have to be polite but firm, ostensibly measured but discreetly assertive. It was the sort of effectual conversation he was used to having in his line of work.

It was half past one in the afternoon when he entered the coffee shop and the place murmured with the gentle hum of lunchtime trade. There was a queue of four or five people waiting to be served by the two people behind the bar. One was a short, stocky man, whose forehead was furrowed with a stressed concentration that Ryan sadly didn't see enough of at his own office. Next to him was a girl who worked in a demented panic, her hands moving around at lightning speed, but not seeming to do anything productive. Neither was the person he had come to see.

He looked past this mismatched couple and saw whom he was looking for. He was, unsurprisingly, sitting down at the back of the café not doing any work. He was talking to a brown-haired girl, completely unconcerned with the fact that he wasn't helping his colleagues out. Ryan tightened his tie to make sure he was looking professionally powerful and made his way over to them. It was only when he was a few metres away that he realised whom the stoner was talking to. He recognised her face from her headshots in the *Varsity* articles. Ryan didn't believe in serendipity but if he did, this would be a good example of it.

In the space of the four or five steps that it took to walk over to the seated pair, he was forced to change his entire game plan.

Ryan arrived by the side of their table and reached out his

hand to introduce himself. 'Ryan Stanfield. I believe we met last week.'

The stoner looked confused at the offered hand, and then squinted suspiciously when he realised who was standing in front of him. The barista cautiously and weakly shook Ryan's hand. It was a terrible handshake, conveying no sense of respect or self-worth.

'Err… Yeah, we did.'

'I wanted to come in and apologise for my behaviour the other night,' Ryan continued. He put on the most genuine smile he could muster. It was hard to have to swallow his pride like this, especially on such short notice. But he'd done a rapid mental calculation and realised that appearing humble now would stand him in a better position with the girl.

'Right, well, thanks I guess.'

'Sorry, I should explain,' Ryan said turning to Michael Fitzgerald's niece. 'I had a bit of an altercation with your friend…' He paused, waiting for the stoner to fill in the gap.

'Kartik,' he eventually responded.

'I had an altercation with Kartik down the pub and I may have lost my temper a little bit.'

'I know. I was there,' Cameron Fitzgerald said. 'You acted like a dick.' She had a venom that her friend did not. Kartik would be all too aware that he was in his place of work, and the last thing he would do was swear in front of customers. His friend on the other hand wasn't controlled by any such constriction.

'I know. I'm sorry for the way I behaved,' Ryan said, putting his hand on his heart to convey sincerity. 'I realise now that it was an accident and that I should have let it go then and there. Can I buy you both a coffee as a way of apologising?'

'We've already got one, thanks,' the girl said curtly.

'And, to be fair, you don't really need to pay for coffee when you work here,' Kartik said, pointing out his name badge with the company logo above his name.

'Kartik. That's an… unusual name,' Ryan said, hoping to progress the conversation. He had been trained in situations like this to not come across as supercilious, no matter how superior you actually were. Affecting a tone of deference and humility was key.

Cameron rolled her eyes. 'Look, I've got to go back to the library.' She started to pack up her things.

'And what do you do?' Ryan asked, feigning ignorance.

'I'm a student,' she replied while putting a couple of books back into her satchel.

'At Cambridge?'

'Yes.' She closed the satchel and fastened the latch.

'Which collage?'

'Churchill.' She picked up her phone from the table and put it in her pocket.

'What do you study?'

'Maths.' She stood up.

'Really? That's interesting. Look, I'm the director of a recruitment consultancy. Well, we're more in the head hunter business. One of the best in the country. We only look for the most talented people out there.' Ryan realised he was quickly running out of time to impress her. He had to do a lightning fast elevator pitch. 'We're called Fusion Vision Recruitment. You may have heard of us?' Cameron shook her head. 'We work with the world's largest companies to source the best new talent and are always looking for bright young people such as yourselves.'

'So you can make a commission?' Cameron said dismissively.

'So we can help you find the right company for your future. Maths graduates from Oxbridge are in particular high demand and we've got the best connections in the industry.' Ryan reached into his pocket and produced a business card. 'It'd be good to touch base sometime soon for a follow-up conversation. No obligation. Just a chance to go through some of the clients we work with and see if any are of interest to you.'

Cameron took the card, and snorted in derision. 'I knew I recognised your name. You've been emailing me, haven't you? Look, I don't know how you know who I am, but I think it's creepy and intrusive. And I get quite enough careers advice from my university without messing around with someone who is only thinking about their own targets. You're nothing more than a glorified used car salesman. And I make a point never to deal with people who say things like "touch base."' She pocketed the business card and turned to her friend. 'I'll see you later, Kartik. Give me a call soon.'

'Bye,' Kartik said weakly.

Cameron marched out of the coffee shop, leaving Ryan standing in her wake.

'Sorry about my friend,' Kartik offered. 'She's quite... opinionated.' He was being diplomatic. Ryan took this as very good sign.

'No, it's no problem. I know I probably didn't make the best first impression the other night.'

'So, you work in recruitment?' Kartik asked.

Ryan felt a flash of excitement. Here was a spark of interest. If he couldn't find a direct way through to Cameron, what better way than through word-of-mouth marketing from a close friend?

'Yeah, are you looking for a job?'

Kartik looked around panicked for a second, and motioned with his hand that Ryan lower his voice. He then indicated the chair opposite that was until recently occupied by Cameron. He clearly didn't want his current employee knowing he was considering jumping ship.

Ryan sat down. The barista had smudges of coffee grounds on his apron and smelt of steamed milk. Ryan worried that the smell would creep into the fabric of his Saville Row suit or neatly combed hair. He leant back a little on his chair.

'Well, as you can imagine, working in a place like this isn't exactly what I want to do with my life.'

'What do you want to do with your life?'

'I'm not exactly sure yet,' Kartik said, almost apologetically.

'What's your background?'

'I studied English literature at university.'

'Great, a graduate. We've got a specialist team for graduate recruitment. It's a tough climate out there, but we've had some great recent successes. Where did you study? Cambridge as well?'

'Oxford,' Kartik said. He looked like he was about to say something else, but stopped himself.

Ryan smiled. It didn't matter what someone studied or how they got on. When you were booking candidates in for interviews, if they had Oxford or Cambridge on the CV that was what they were sold on.

'Excellent. How did you end up in a place like this?' He waved his hand around dismissively.

Kartik squirmed a little bit. 'I don't know. You kind of fall into these things don't you? I live in Cambridge, and after I was done with university I decided to move back to save a bit of money. But there aren't exactly many jobs around here.'

'You're right there. But we work with a lot of companies that don't advertise their positions. They only selectively headhunt. I'm in a unique position as well because I've got some excellent contacts with some of the most influential financial decision-makers in London. I've got some interesting openings in hedge funds coming up in the next couple of months. Have you ever thought about working in finance?'

'Not really. I was thinking more along the lines of... I dunno... the media?'

The media? Why did all young people think the media was the Holy Grail when it came to career options? Did they think they could stroll into glamorous jobs, and start rubbing shoulders with celebrities? Did they even know what they meant when they announced they wanted to enter the media industry? Did he not realise what a redundant and unrewarding life he would encounter if he pursued that dream?

'What part of the media industry exactly?'

'I don't know. Maybe radio? Maybe films?'

Films! He thinks he's going to work in films. As if he could just walk up on set and Scorsese would hire him on the spot.

'Do you have any qualifications?'

'What do you mean?'

'To get into that industry.'

'Well, not really. But do you need it?'

'You can't just stumble your way into the media industry. You generally need to know a specific skill and even then it's horrendously competitive. And you won't get paid for the first couple of years. Too many graduates like yourself are doing internships for free.' Ryan felt at this point it was right to be appropriately truthful. Telling people to 'follow their dreams', 'believe in themselves,' and 'do what they love,' was counterproductive and misleading. That was the job of parents and teachers. His job was to bring people's expectations in line with the current job market.

'Oh. Right,' Kartik said looking more than a little deflated. 'What other roles do you recruit for?'

'Well, I personally only specialise in finance. But my team covers a wide array of different industries and job descriptions: sales, marketing, communications, events management.' Kartik didn't seem too enthusiastic about any of these responses. Ryan decided to try a different approach. 'You know, it may help to find out what sort of thing you are interested in. What's on your CV?'

Again Kartik pulled a blank. *For an Oxford graduate, this guy sure did have a lot of empty space in his head.*

'You do have a CV, right?'

'Uh, yeah. Just working on it at the moment. I need to update it with my current circumstances.'

The two of them looked around their surroundings. Ryan nodded understandingly. 'Look, I've got to get back to the office. It's my lunchbreak as well. But I want to continue this conversation. Take my card and have a think about what you may want to do. Then drop me your CV when it's been… updated. Then we can have a chat towards the end of the week. How about that?'

'Sure,' Kartik said, looking relieved. This was not a man who did well under pressure.

'Kartik,' Ryan said. Kartik looked up. 'It is an unusual name.'

'Yeah, it's Indian,' Kartik said, somewhat wearily.

'But you're not Indian. Are you? Don't have a problem if you are. It's just, you're very... white.'

'No. It was my parents' choice. It's a long story.'

'Right, well maybe you can tell me about it next time we meet.' Kartik didn't seem too enthusiastic about that. But then again, he didn't look too enthusiastic about anything.

Ryan shook Kartik's hand again and then said goodbye.

He was in a good mood as he walked back to the office. Fortune favours the brave. It was one of his favourite sayings (he'd even had it printed out and pinned to the wall of his office), and it had certainly paid off this time. Too many people would have brushed off the incident down the pub as just one of those things that happens. But not Ryan Stanfield. He had been proactive. He had gone after the culprits. And he had confronted them. And he had got a result from this confrontation. Because not only did he possess enormous bravery, but he also had exceptional powers of instinctive manoeuvring, and he had come out with two promising contacts.

Cameron was definitely the main goal out of the two of them. There was something driven and determined about her that he liked. Even the way she had insulted him had shown intelligence and understanding. Not to mention guts. The only thing that bothered him was that idealistic streak, that holier-than-thou attitude that gave her an air of superiority. Who was she to demean his target-driven lifestyle? Without targets to aim for, you were just blindly treading water in the swamp of mediocrity. He supposed it was something to do with being a lesbian. He didn't consider himself prejudiced, but he always found gay people hard to work with. It was an 'us vs. them' mentality. But he was smart enough to utilise that, to control her, to get the results that he wanted.

Kartik on the other hand? That guy had the opposite problem. He had nothing to offer. Ryan struggled to understand how he had managed to get into Oxford, let alone complete a degree. But then again, he was more typical of his generation: lazy and entitled. *Work in the media? Ha!* Kartik could be given hundreds of brilliant opportunities, but would turn his nose up at them, as they weren't quite right. He was the sort that thought everything should be done for them, instead of doing things for himself. There was something wrong with young people. They'd never experienced any hardship in their lives, and they were so pampered neither the carrot nor the stick encouraged them anymore. Ryan had had no formal higher education, and was one of the most successful people he knew. Just because someone had their name at the bottom of some fancy certificate, didn't mean they were capable or useful.

But despite Kartik's flaws, he'd still have his uses. Without the barista, he'd never get through to his more talented friend.

A light rain had started to fall, the first for weeks, and perhaps a signifier that the Indian summer was coming to an end. Thoughts of his family came to his mind, a rarity during his working hours. Arabella would be going back to school soon, and Anna would have more time on her hands, meaning fewer arguments between them. Hopefully.

The weekend at the park had demonstrated the tension between them. Anna had suggested they go to counselling, but Ryan had dismissed that idea. He didn't need some overpaid shrink trying to get into his head and, more worryingly, his wife's head. Besides, counsellors were nothing but overqualified salesmen anyway. They convinced you that you had problems that didn't exist, and then insisted that you pay them one hundred pounds an hour to help you fix them. You could go in to therapy with a couple of minor marital squabbles, and end up a few months later with a full existential crisis and a bill for thousands of pounds. Then the only solution would be to spend even more money on sessions. They were clever, these shrinks. It was all a scam. An industry built on psychological dependency and addiction. They operated in exactly the same way as the tobacco industry, but at least a cigarette helped calm you down.

It was as he pondered the sneakiness of psychologists that he arrived outside the office. Aaron, the junior recruiter, was outside smoking and Ryan joined him.

'Can I borrow a cigarette?' Ryan asked.

Aaron automatically obliged, like a good little employee. 'I didn't know you smoked.'

'Every now and again,' Ryan said, taking Aaron's zippo and sparking up. 'How are things?'

'You know, not too bad. Not great, but getting there. How about yourself?'

'Good. I've been having some productive meetings. Look, Aaron, have you got some contacts within the university? Careers people and the sort?'

'Yeah, a few.'

'Have you made much progress there? I know they like to keep things as internal as possible.'

'It's tough. They don't really like external agencies. They think we're doing their job for them, and they get insulted when I offer to help.'

'They're arrogant, that's what it is,' Ryan explained. 'They know we're better than them so they feel threatened. Then they try to cover up their inferiority by being rude to us. And their own pride prevents them from using a service they would actually benefit from.'

Aaron nodded obediently.

'Look, there's a girl I want you to ask around about. Her name is Cameron Fitzgerald.'

'What do you want to find out?'

'I don't know yet. Just something that may be useful. She's a bit unresponsive.'

'You mean arrogant?' Aaron offered.

'Exactly. Nail on the head,' Ryan said. Aaron beamed as if he'd just been given a pay rise. He was one of the good ones in the office. He could be led by both the carrot and the stick. And the carrot didn't have to be big to have the desired effect.

'Thanks for the cigarette,' Ryan said, stubbing it out on the small metal ashtray secured to the wall. It had only been half smoked.

'No problem,' Aaron said. 'By the way, you had a call from a company called Encode Investments in London. A chap you used to work with.'

'Robert Keynes?'

'Yeah, that's the one.'

Ryan laughed. It'd been a while since he had heard from Keynes. Clearly, word had got out that he'd been moved to this parochial little town. Keynes was probably wondering when he was coming back to the big time. It wouldn't be too long now. He was turning things around slowly but surely. He'd be back in London within a year.

'Keynes, old man,' Ryan said enthusiastically once he was back in the office. 'How are you?'

'I'm good, Ryan. How are you?' The Northern Irish accent coming down the other end of the phone was sterner than Ryan had expected. If Ryan were the sort of person to flinch, he would have. But he took it in his stride. Keynes was probably just having a tough day. Working at a hedge fund could do that.

'I'm okay. I guess you know what happened to me?'

'I caught wind that they had moved you out of the City. I was surprised to hear you'd landed in Cambridge.'

'So was I. But they need someone reliable to work this patch. It's just a temporary thing. Should be back rubbing shoulders with you guys soon enough.'

'Hmm...' Keynes said. His old drinking buddy was clearly so bogged down with work he couldn't even muster the excitement of getting the boys all back together in the city again. 'How're Anna and Arabella?'

'They're well. Arabella is adjusting. But you know, she's at a difficult age.' Keynes didn't have any children himself, but he was bound to be able to appreciate the difficultly of raising one. In many respects, a business was like a child. The only difference was that bad parenting decisions didn't have as many destructive consequences.

'Well, I just wanted to touch base with you in your new office and remind you that we're still in business and we're always looking for the best talent.'

For Ryan, this was like telling a junkie you had a fresh syringe waiting. But Ryan knew he couldn't seem too excited. The recruitment game was poker and you needed to keep your cards close to your chest until you knew you had the winning hand. He levelled his voice, to let his old friend know that the frivolities and small talk were over. 'Anything in particular?'

'Not at the moment. But things come up all the time. Anything from entry-level all the way through to senior management. But just the best, understand?'

'You know I wouldn't deliver anything less.'

'Hmm...' Keynes said again. It was his new go-to phrase. 'Good to know. And in the meantime, if you've got anyone you think it worth us knowing about, then drop us a line.'

Ryan was about to mention Cameron but held himself back. Not yet. Now was not the right time. He needed to secure her first. He had been presented with the hook he needed and he just needed the right bait. 'Will do. Great catching up with you, Keynes, old man. And if I'm around your neck of the woods anytime I'll stop by. We can make a night out of it. The Square Mile crawl. Like old times.'

'Hmm... yeah. Good to hear from you, Ryan.'

'Yeah, you too,' Ryan said and then hung up.

So Robert Keynes was feeling the pressure. Gone was the banter. Gone were the jokes. Gone was the inside gossip. Ryan wasn't the sort to get worried about personal matters, but he couldn't help but feel a bit annoyed at how the conversation had gone. The two of them went back over a decade. It wasn't like he was some lackey who'd just started out in the business. One of the luxuries of being in their positions was the gentle ribbing of familiarity that could elongate business meetings into something bearable. What was the point of progression if you weren't allowed to mask social engagements under the pretext of work?

All things considered though, it had been a successful day. He now had both supply and demand. And with a bit of tinkering and planning on his part, he would be putting things together for his old friend. As long as he could get the rest of the office working as productively as he did, then things would be fine.

He felt a sense of contentment as he drove home that evening, a contentment that would be broken by the inevitable argument with his wife.

CHAPTER NINE

The next three weeks proved that any hope of an Indian summer was misplaced. The warm nights became scarcer and were replaced by an unwelcomed but inevitable drizzle and dark skies.

As the weather turned for the worse, Kartik felt his life was stuck in limbo. Andrew hadn't mentioned anything else about moving to London and he had, by this time, numbed himself to the drudging tedium of his work. His nicely balanced routine of sleep, work, PlayStation, and then back to sleep was only interrupted every now and again by the occasional pub visit or, less frequently, trips to his parents' house.

There had been a few calls from Ryan's dogsbody, Aaron, who had put forward the odd job opportunity. These had been politely batted away, usually citing vague personal issues as reasons for declining. The truth was that the jobs on offer were far more advanced than his capabilities. He realised this was because he had never fully explained what university he had specifically gone to, and had accidently omitted the fact that he had never actually graduated. Aaron kept asking for him to email his CV, but again Kartik evaded, as this would be a written confirmation of his deception. At the moment, Aaron's misconceptions lay in the fact that Kartik hadn't told the whole truth to Ryan. Kartik was fine for this knowledge to remain unknown until his pursuer got bored and sought worthier contacts.

And obviously by worthy contacts, he meant Cameron. A couple of times Ryan had gotten in contact directly with her to talk about his opportunities, and eventually she agreed to the briefest of phone conversations. Kartik didn't know exactly how it went, but there didn't seem to be much progression. It was unlikely she would open up to Ryan, despite his persistence. Cameron was the sort of person whose perception of a person was based almost entirely on the first minute of meeting them, and she would usually dogmatically stick to this opinion, unless something drastic happened to change her opinion. So far, Ryan had not offered her anything to change the original assessment

This approach generally served her well, as she was a good judge of character, but on the odd occasion it led her to make mistakes. For instance, Louise had been uncharacteristically nice to her the first time they met, and now Cameron thought of her as a pleasant, affable, ambitious woman making her way in the world, instead of the constricting Machiavellian that she actually was.

Another reason Ryan may have struggled to get through to Cameron was because it was clear at this stage that she was totally and completely crazy about Rachel.

Every conversation they had revolved around the library of text messages and emails they were sending every day, not to mention the hours they'd spend on the phone. For hours on end it would be: 'Yesterday Rachel did this…' or 'Today Rachel said this…' or 'Oh my God, Rachel just sent me the funniest picture. Look, look, look! Isn't it great?'

Kartik would nod along with quiet deference. Whilst it was definitely sweet, he couldn't help but think it was bordering on obsessive. Was it still madness if the person you were obsessed with was also as obsessively infatuated with you as you were with them? Kartik decided it was. It was a mutual madness, and every interaction was progressing the malady further.

It was in the final week of September that the Rachel-fever reached an all-time high. She was due to arrive in Cambridge on the final weekend of the month.

'We're bowling,' Cameron announced out of the blue.

'Huh?' Kartik hadn't been listening.

'Bowling.'

'What about it?'

'That's what we're doing.'

Kartik looked around him. They were sitting in the café in Churchill College. 'Are we? Now? I think you and I have very different ideas of what bowling is.'

'Not us, you idiot. Rachel and I. When she comes down. We're going to go bowling.'

'Bowling?'

'Right. Bowling. For her first night. I want to do something fun, but also something where we can get to know each other really well.'

'That's a great idea.'

'You think so?'

'Yes. If she's celebrating her fourteenth birthday.

'She's not celebrating her fourteenth birthday.'

'Then don't take her bowling. It's a terrible idea.'

'Really?'

'Really.'

Cameron, for once in her life, looked panicked. 'I don't know what I'm doing. I keep thinking of things, and then they seem like a good idea, and then I think it may be a rubbish idea, and I worry that Rachel won't like it, or I worry that I wouldn't like it, or we both wouldn't like it, and it will be terrible, and I'll ruin everything before we even get a chance to do anything together.'

A couple of other students around them had turned their heads as the outburst became faster and more frantic. Kartik held his hand up apologetically, like a driver who knows he's made a dangerous manoeuvre in front of another car. The café was quiet as most students were still on their extended holiday, but a couple of eager souls had returned early, either because they were really focused on their studies, or because their parents hated them. When it came to Cambridge students, neither explanation would have surprised Kartik.

'Do you know what you should do first?'

'What?' Cameron said, her eyes desperately large and hopeful that Kartik would have the answer to her panicked riddle.

'First, you need to breathe. And calm down.'

Cameron started taking more measured breaths.

'Then, you need to realise that she's probably just as nervous as you are. You know, like spiders.'

'What?'

'You know, spiders. People always get really worked up about spiders, but you have to remember they are far more scared of going on dates than you are.' Cameron just about managed a laugh. 'But why not just go for the classic? Go punting and then go for a meal.'

'But it's so clichéd. And unoriginal. And contrived. And she's going to think I'm just one of those snobby Cambridge types, and she won't like me, because she's not like that, and it'll ruin everything.'

'How can you be so smart, and yet so stupid?'

'Oh, I forgot about your infinite success when it comes to relationships, Casanova.'

'I'm not claiming to be an expert or anything. All I'm saying is that I bet she doesn't care what you do together. As long as she's with you. Do something relaxed. Do something where you can talk. But for the love of god, don't go bowling!'

'Okay. Well, she's getting dropped off by her parents tomorrow. So tomorrow night we'll know if I've completely ruined it or not.'

Kartik reached out his hand and clasped hers in what he hoped was a sort of platonic support. 'You couldn't ruin it if you tried.'

'Thanks,' Cameron said.

She leant back and breathed deeply. Then she reached inside her brown satchel for something. As she drew her hand out, a loose sheet of paper crept out of a notebook and floated to the floor next to Kartik's feet. He bent over to pick it.

'Stop!' Cameron said abruptly as Kartik reached down.

'What?' He was frozen in a half crouch, fingertips on the paper. 'What is it?'

'Don't move!' Her voice was strained.

'Ever?' His lower back was starting to hurt a bit. He could feel the cramps tightening the muscles around his spine. It was only now he realised how inflexible he was. Maybe he should take a yoga class.

'Just give it back to me. Don't look at it.'

He pulled himself up, lifting the paper with him. There was handwriting on the other side, in a neat column of short sentences. A sudden and terrible realisation came over him and he knew what he was looking at. It was more terrible than he could ever imagine. But just like motorists who slow down and crane their necks to see the wreckage of an accident, he couldn't help but look. With every word, the pain became greater:

All I wanted was to be Jesse to your Cerline.
  We'd walk around Vienna,

To everyone else unseen.
Before sunset, before sunrise,
Before midnight, before you,
I was lost, I was stuck,
I was trapped in glue.
But there is something that we've changed,
Something that we both know should be sung.
We've walked around this city for so long a time,
It's now that I can accept that we can never be undone.

Kartik tried to stifle a laugh. He failed miserably.

'I told you not to read it.' She snatched the poem from his hands, her face contorted in both embarrassment and annoyance.

'Cameron, you are many things: a mathematician, a scholar, a dear friend, and almost certainly the smartest person I know. However, one thing you are definitely not is a poet.'

'You don't think she'd like it?'

'I think we need to burn it as soon as possible.'

'I put a lot of work into this.'

'You did?'

'So I shouldn't show this to her?'

'Shouldn't show it to her? You shouldn't show it to *anyone*.'

'You're such a dick. You know that, right?' She snatched the poem back from him.

'Yep. Anyway, I've got to go.'

'You doing the late shift at work?'

'Nope. Got a meal with my parents this evening.'

'Good luck with that.'

'Thanks. Give me a call to let me know how it goes tomorrow.'

He gathered up his things and turned from the table. He

was only half paying attention when he slammed into something massive and solid. At first he assumed it was a misplaced Humvee, but it turned out to be a person.

'Watch where you're going,' came a posh voice from about half a foot above Kartik's eye line.

'So should you,' Kartik said, suddenly in an unwisely combative mood.

'Excuse me?' The voice sounded like a riled politician who had come under unexpected fire: the mixture of well-mannered, clipped restraint charged with simmering anger. It was impossible to take him entirely seriously, although the sheer size of the person in front of him was undeniably intimidating. For self-preservation's sake, he really had to stop bumping into people who were much larger than him.

The head sat on a thick neck, which itself towered above a broad chest and shoulders. From the collisions, Kartik could also detect that this bulk was sprightly muscles rather than podgy fat. Ever so slightly cauliflower ears suggested this physique was once used on the rugby field. The body was probably what Ryan's had been two decades ago. Behind him stood a second, slightly smaller student, who looked and dressed like a slightly inferior version of his friend, like a determined, but not entirely talented tribute band singing the hits of their idols.

'You should watch yourself as well, mate.' Kartik deliberately dropped some of the 'T' sounds from his response, so as to distinguish himself from his assailant's register, in the hope that he could use this difference as a weapon to his advantage.

The student was flustered for a second with this response, clearly not used to be talked back to. He glanced at his shorter friend, and knew he quickly had to regain his composure to save face. 'Do you know who I am?'

Again, it was an almost comical question, and Kartik felt this was going to be a repeat of the situation down at The

Maypole. Hopefully this new obstacle wouldn't be sending him job offers after their confrontation. Before Kartik could answer that he didn't give a shit, Cameron interrupted. 'Leave it out, Max.'

Max—of course he was called Max—looked down to see Cameron for apparently the first time. He sniffed dismissively at her and then turned back to Kartik. 'I wouldn't waste your time with this one, mate.' His tone had become belligerently advisory towards Kartik instead of openly hostile. 'She bats for the other team, if you know what I mean.'

'No, I'm not sure we know what you mean. Could you unwrap your sophisticated metaphor for us, Max?' Cameron's voice was now hard.

A large, powerful hand slapped down on Kartik's shoulder, seemingly to create a unity between them against Cameron, but in practice it was to demonstrate Max's strength. 'You won't get anywhere with this dyke. Will he, Ollie?' he said lowering his voice. Ollie giggled, like an Etonian goblin.

Kartik pushed Max's hand off his shoulder, and was about to proceed with a rather unadvised act of violence when Cameron spoke again.

'Careful Max. Remember that this dyke dated Alicia Kitson last year.'

At this name Max visibly tensed and his attention shifted to Cameron again. 'And she's got a bigger mouth than you might think,' Cameron continued, and then winked.

'I don't know what you're talking about.' Max took a step away from Kartik and almost bumped into Ollie, who now looked confused.

'What's she talking about, Max?' Ollie asked.

'Shut up,' Max commanded. 'Come on, we'll be late for practice.'

He swept past Kartik, giving him a half-hearted barge with the shoulder, more to keep face rather than as a statement of aggression. Kartik didn't react, secretly glad the man-mountain was leaving them.

Once the two had gone, Kartik turned bewildered to Cameron.

'What was that about?'

'That's Max Bellingham. He's a "big man on campus."'

'And who is Alicia Kitson? He didn't seem to like her too much.'

'She's one of the student counsellors. She's the person that students can go to when they want to talk about personal matters in confidence. I dated her for a few weeks last year.'

'And?'

'She had some interesting gossip on our friend Max.'

'Such as?'

'Why do you think he's so hostile to homosexuals?'

Kartik suddenly understood. 'Really?'

'Yeah, apparently he was *very confused* about the feelings he had for one of his rugby teammates in the changing rooms.'

'And she told you this?'

'She certainly did.'

'That's confidential. Isn't that, you know, unethical?'

'It certainly is.'

'But you don't mind using this against him?'

'I certainly don't. It's important to keep well informed in places like this. You never know how a bit of knowledge can help you out in a situation.'

'This isn't prison, you know?'

'Isn't it?'

'Anyway, thanks,' Kartik said. 'I owe you one.'

'Don't worry about it.'

He started to head for the exit when he stopped.

'And Cameron?' He turned to face her again. 'About the poem?'

'Yeah?' she said hopefully.

'Burn it! I'm serious!'

Her goodbye was unconventional as there was only one finger extended as opposed to five, but he knew she meant well.

Kartik cycled the short distance from Churchill College to his parents' house just off Histon Road. The mudguard over his back wheel had become slightly buckled and it rubbed against the tyre, emitting a muffled drone as he cycled. This meant he had to put in twice the effort to go half the speed. He resolved that later that night he would finally fix this. Then he remembered he had said that two weeks ago when the problem had first become apparent, and realised he could probably put off doing anything for a while longer at least.

He pulled the whining bike into the driveway of the semi-detached house and down the side ally where he left his bike.

He let himself in the backdoor and was immediately greeted by a blast of hot air and the smell of burning food. There were sounds of movement coming from the kitchen. They were not good sounds. They were the sounds of things going wrong. As he walked down the corridor, he heard his father's voice. 'Shit, shit, shit.'

'Well, this doesn't look good.' Kartik said as he opened the kitchen door. The room was thick with smoke and the work surface resembled the aftermath of a natural disaster. Food remains, utensils, pots, pans lay senselessly scattered everywhere. There was smoke coming from the oven, and the hob was overcrowded with pans and woks, most of which were bubbling past boiling point. In the middle of it all, his father rushed around trying to make sense of something that he hadn't quite got the measure of, like an incompetent conductor leading an orchestra of talentless musicians.

'Kartik, pass me those oven gloves,' his father, David, said as he tried to come to terms with the disaster he had created.

Kartik did as he was told and his father used them to open the grill, which resulted in even more smoke filling the room. 'I left the kitchen for five minutes and I've come back to madness.' A charred, blackened lump was all that was left of whatever had been in the oven. His father lowered his head in defeat. 'It's meant to be a Mughlai dish.'

'Looks great,' Kartik said, going over to the window and opening it.

'No, don't do that!'

'Why not?'

'The book says you're meant to cook the dish in conditions similar to Hyderabad's summer climate. That's why I'm keeping the heat in.' Kartik knew Hyderabad was a region of India but had never bothered to learn where.

Kartik looked at the sorry excuse of a meal that had just come out of the oven. 'Dad, you've cooked it in conditions similar to the surface of the sun. I think you're going to have to let this one go.'

'But I can still save the other bits.' He whirled to where the curry boiled over the edge of the pan and onto the electric hobs. He turned down the heat, stirred the ooze with a spoon and tasted it. David stood motionless for a couple of seconds, and then his face started to spasm.

Eyes bulging, he barged past Kartik to the sink and stuck his head under the cold tap and took large gulps to ease the flaming pain that was clearly now dancing in his mouth. Kartik took this opportunity to turn off the kitchen appliances that were still on, an act that was akin to closing the eyes of a fallen comrade in battle, giving them a more dignified passage into the afterlife.

Finally, his father's face appeared from the sink. His cheeks were red and his eyes had tears running down them. 'Too many chilies, I think.'

'I don't think that was the only problem.' They both looked in silence at the ruins which once was the kitchen.

'How about a takeaway?'

They abandoned the disaster zone in the kitchen and moved into the living room. His father was a shrinking man, someone Kartik remembered as being so tall when he was young, but somehow seemed to diminish in height every time he visited. He obviously took into account that he himself had grown taller since his teenage years. But it was impossible to avoid the fact that his father was getting shorter, which Kartik supposed was common for someone about to hit sixty.

David had a thin, sharp face that was covered by a greying beard and round glasses. He wore pale jeans, and a wrinkled navy shirt. The entire look made him look a bit like a scientist in an 80s science-fiction film.

As they walked into the living room, Kartik noticed his father was walking with a slight limp.

'You hurt yourself?'

'Just an old hiking injury,' his dad said sitting down.

For a moment Kartik froze, his fingers tense, his breath held, as he waited for the man in front of him to launch into a story about how he had been hiking around some part of India at some time in his life, recounting in mind-numbing detail every single aspect of the trip, and therefore completely forgetting to order the takeaway, meaning Kartik would be found dead two days later from starvation —or perhaps boredom— as his dad finished the story.

Luckily the story didn't come, and instead they sat in silence for a while, neither looking at each other.

'Where's mum?'

'She's at her yoga class. She'll be back soon.' Again there was silence. The room was adorned by souvenirs from countless trips to India that his parents had made over the years: incense burners over the fireplace, a Ganesh statue on the windowsill, an art silk rug under their feet, a large landscape painting of the lower Himalayas covering one wall, and a map of the entire country on the other. The map was dotted with countless pins, representing all the cities and areas that Kartik's parents had visited over the past twenty-five years or so. So far, Kartik had avoided joining them on any one of these expeditions. When he was younger, his parents had always insisted that he wait until he was older before he experienced Indian culture first-hand, as a young child 'wouldn't be able to see the country outside the blinkered viewpoint of a tourist.' This was a euphemism that Kartik understood to mean: 'We can't afford to take you with us.'

Now deemed old enough, and having grown up in his parents' own little forgery of the country all his life, he didn't have any desire to see the real thing. He knew this annoyed his parents more than they cared to admit, but not enough to fund the trip themselves. If they paid for the holiday, he'd definitely go, but as they wouldn't , he instead preferred to spend his money on more cost-effective European holidays with his friends.

'Did you see the football scores today?' his father asked.

'Not yet.'

'Cambridge United won three-nil.'

'Right,' Kartik said. His father was an avid supporter of his home team, and believed you should only follow the team in the closest proximity. However Kartik, having grown up in the glamorous era of the Premier League, had little time for local teams and instead supported his Chelsea.

This had been a bit of a failing for David, who had tried to encourage his son to see the wonders and delights of Cambridge United's Abbey Stadium when he was younger, dragging him along to the family stand, talking about all the great matches he had been brought to. His father had been aware of the growing seductive threat that the Premier League presented, and he tried his best to install a sense of loyalty and dedication before it was all too late. He had been like a boss worried about losing his most talented member of staff to a bigger firm, who tried forcibly imbedding an almost spiritual connection to their workplace.

But Kartik never felt any sort of connection with those cold, Saturday mornings in the Abbey's east stand, and when all his friends at school in the early nineties started announcing they were fans of Manchester United, Liverpool, or even Blackburn, Kartik realised it was time to pick a Premier League team, if only so as not to be left out on the playground. One of his close friends at school was a Chelsea fan, so Kartik decided he was one as well.

He was in good company supporting teams he had no connection with: Gabor supported Spurs, Andrew supported Liverpool, and Louise had some vague history as a Manchester United fan (however she didn't seem too committed to keeping up with the modern game; the only time Kartik had convinced her to sit down and play him at FIFA, she had immediately asked if Beckham was still playing for United). The only exception was Cameron who claimed to despise football. Whenever astronomical transfer fees were mentioned, she'd always be diligent enough to calculate the amount of aid or debt relief that fifty million pounds would be able to provide a third-world country.

On the odd occasion Kartik had convinced her to watch a game, she couldn't help get caught up in it. All it would take for her to go from an uninterested bystander to an expert pundit was one misplaced pass or defensive error. She would go off on a tirade, yelling at the screen in a litany of technical jargon, some of it accurate, most of it misappropriated. It was a lexicon borrowed from Kartik and Andrew's conversations, and she blurt it out, like someone just learning to swim. The execution wasn't particularly graceful or flowing, but the skeleton of the stroke was pushing her forward just enough to see the satisfaction of progress. She would get full-backs confused with wing-backs, suggest antiquated formations that hadn't been used in decades, or demand a red card for an innocuous challenge, and then throw her hands up in despair when one didn't materialise (this last trait wasn't at all different from the dyed in the wool dogmatism that was associated with people who identified themselves as true football fans). After these outbursts, she would then slink back into the background, as if the game hadn't affected her at all and start mumbling something about Abramovich being forced to send foreign aid to Afghanistan as punishment for owning a well-run football team. Football was to Cameron what musicals were to Kartik: something to be dismissed and derided when discussing them, but when watching a well-executed example of the art form, for the briefest moment, it was impossible not to get carried away with it all.

Thanks to his influence, Kartik liked to think that Cameron was a closeted Chelsea fan, even if she would never admit it.

'Apparently it was a good game,' David said, chewing over his team's result. 'Alex Warner from next door went down to watch it. Really exciting, determined football. Not like that lot at Chelsea who just play for their wages.'

'Well, those wages mean they're top of the league,' Kartik replied.

'Hmm...' his father said. 'How's the house?' he asked for a lack of anything else to say.

'Good. Everything is good.' He hadn't told his parents that there was a possibility the room wouldn't be there for much longer. He had a sneaking suspicion they thought he was a bit of a loser as it was, so he didn't want to have to admit his shit was so far from being together that he may find himself homeless in a matter of weeks.

'And how is work?'

'Work's fine. Busy. But fine.' They often found themselves in these stunted conversations from which there was little escape. David would struggle to think of engaging things to say, and Kartik would struggle to think of anything interesting to reply with.

'You mother saw a job in the paper for one of the exam boards.' His father picked up one of the papers that sat beside him, and started flicking through it aimlessly. If he was trying to find said advert, he didn't seem to be looking with much intention.

'Okay,' Kartik wasn't going to take the bait so easily.

'Well, it looks like it pays better than what you are doing now.' It was an obtuse way of approaching the subject. 'And it may make use of what you learnt at university a little bit more.' His father was disappointed that Kartik had failed to graduate and meant that he wasn't able to structure the sentence to say, 'make use of your degree'. Other parents with children Kartik's age were also struggling in the job market. But these contemporaries of David could also fall back on the knowledge that at least their offspring had managed to get through the required three or four years, and had a proudly framed piece of paper to prove it.

In an effort to avert his father's attention to the well-documented failings of his early twenties, Kartik said, 'I'm actually talking to a recruitment consultant. He's looking at a number of different roles for me.'

'Oh, really? What sort of thing?' He looked up from the paper, intrigued. As a parent, his father would be considered a laissez-faire, allowing his child to find his own way and make his own mistakes. But Kartik's ability to make every educational and career mistake in the book had been testing these liberal attitudes.

'A few things at the moment. I'm just having a look through. You know, to see if anything fits better.'

'I can't think of anything that would fit worse than working for almost minimum wage at Starbucks.'

'Café Ristretto.'

'Same thing.'

'Well, there are a few jobs around London. So I'm weighing up to see if I want to move away.'

'London? It's a big decision. But you're right. You need to do what you will feel is best for yourself.' He had quickly returned to his default, more acceptable liberal persona, perhaps embarrassed that for a second he had collapsed into what he would refer to as 'intrusive, pushy parenting.'

Before the conversation went any further, there came the sound of keys turning in the door, as Kartik's mother, Katherine, entered.

'Hello?' came her voice from the hallway.

'In here,' David replied, before she bounded into the living room with an unnerving energy. She was in a constant state of animation, which Kartik thought was inappropriate for someone who had passed her fiftieth birthday. She kissed David on the cheek and gave Kartik a rather perfunctory pat on the head.

'How are we all?' she said, dumping a gym bag on the floor and sitting in the seat next to her husband. She was still wearing trainers and her high-vis jacket. Like Kartik, she had arrived by bike. Unlike Kartik's, it had been a smooth, easy ride on an expensive, well-oiled, machine cared for with fanatical devotion.

'Good,' David said.

'Smells a bit in here.'

'Dad burnt dinner.'

'Typical.'

'It wasn't my fault,' David protested.

'Whose fault was it?' Katherine asked sardonically.

David didn't reply.

'We're getting takeaway,' Kartik offered. For a tiny, hopeful second, one of his parents may suggest Chinese, Middle-Eastern, or pizza, or fish and chips, or anything other than what he was certain would be ordered.

'I'll call Mr. Patel,' David said, pulling his phone out of his pocket.

No luck, it was to be Indian takeaway again. The well-rehearsed order rolled off his tongue like an automated answering system. It was an order that Mr. Patel on the other end of the line was so used to, he probably only needed to see David's number come up on the phone for him to start with the preparations.

Half an hour later, the doorbell rang and Kartik wearily went to retrieve the painfully predictable carrier bag of assorted Indian food that he had had a million times before.

'Alright, Kartik,' Mr. Patel's son, Iftaker, said when the door was opened.

'Alright, Iftaker,' Kartik replied, nodding.

'Same as always,' Iftaker said wearily.

'Same as always,' Kartik replied wearily.

Iftaker had been in the same school year as Kartik and they had been friends before slowly drifting apart when they went to different sixth forms. Back then, Iftaker had been a slim, athletic boy who excelled at both football (to Mr. Patel's dismay) and cricket (to Mr. Patel's delight). But working in his father's restaurant hadn't done much for his fitness, as every time Kartik ran into him, he seemed to be getting wider and wider. Behind him on the drive was his tiny moped. If Iftaker kept gaining mass at the same rate he was going, it was going to become dangerously heavy.

'You see Cambridge United won today?' Iftaker asked.

Why was everyone so concerned with Cambridge United all of a sudden? 'I heard. My dad said it was a good game.'

'Yeah, it was. I went down. Good atmosphere.'

'How much?' Kartik asked, reaching for the money his mother had handed him. He had tactically put it in his pocket before the door rang. This meant, in the likely event that it would be Iftaker delivering, it would appear that it was himself paying for the food and that he wasn't still sponging off his parents in front of his old classmate. Why was he concerned with not appearing to be surviving off his parents in front of a person who only had a job because his dad owned the restaurant? Kartik was a bit useless, but it didn't mean he didn't have pride.

'£25.95,' Iftaker said and Kartik handed over the money. 'Thanks.'

'No problem.' Kartik was about to say his goodbyes when Iftaker leant in and lowered his voice.

'I know it's a bit cheeky, but Ikram said you may be selling some weed again.'

Kartik was confused. 'Nah, not anymore.'

'Shit,' Iftaker said, shaking his head. 'You got any on you? I'm dying for a spliff.'

'Yeah, I'll just run upstairs, roll up a joint, and then we can smoke it out here, while my parents wait for their takeaway.'

'Sounds good.' As well as losing his physical fitness, Iftaker had also lost his ability to understand sarcasm.

'No, you idiot,' Kartik said, in a way that he hoped was a friendly taunt from a friend, but instead just sounded harsh.

'Oh, right, yeah. Sorry. Anyway, good to see you.'

'Yeah, you too, mate.'

Iftaker waddled off and Kartik closed the door on him. He didn't want to watch him trying to straddle the painfully small moped. There would have been too much of a sense of tragedy.

'Was that Iftaker?' his mum asked when Kartik returned. He nodded, and went about setting the dinner table.

'I always liked that boy,' she continued, presumably simply because of his ethnicity, rather than his former talents on the football pitch or his fondness for pot.

Kartik took the cardboard lids off the foil containers and poured the contents into a selection of plates that he then placed in the centre of the table, along with serving spoons.

David and Katherine came to the table. 'Well, this looks

lovely,' David said, as if it were the very first time he had laid eyes on the culinary skills of Mr. Patel and his dopey son.

The three of them sat down, and served their own portions in silence for a while. Eventually his mother asked, 'So, did you hear Cambridge United won today?'

Kartik did all he could not to slap his palm against his head in frustration.

The rest of the meal wasn't entirely unpleasant, but Kartik was glad when it was time to leave. That is, he was happy until he mounted his bike, and was reminded of the wonky mudguard. It was dark now, the nights coming unstoppably quicker as autumn gained momentum. There was a chill in the night air that hadn't been felt since spring. One or two of the trees on his route home were just starting to turn brown, and he felt a sense of mellow sadness around this time. Soon he wouldn't be able to sit on the grass, smoke weed, and waste away another day in a relaxed, content, hazy daydream. Cameron's workload would increase, so he wouldn't be seeing her as much, and it'd end up just being him and Andrew hiding away in the pub, trying to avoid the wrath of Louise. At least he still had that.

He cycled down Mill Road, across the railway bridge, and then right down a small street of terraced houses. He locked his bike in the small garden in the back, and then headed inside quickly through the backdoor and into the kitchen.

Andrew and Louise were in the living room, almost as if they had been waiting for him. Louise looked severe (the same as she always did), but Andrew looked worried.

'Hey,' Kartik said.

'Kartik, we need a word,' Louise said.

He obediently walked through the open arch that separated the kitchen at the back of the house from the living room at the front. Both his housemates were sitting on the sofa. A single dinner table chair had been placed in front of them, like an informal job interview. Kartik would have preferred to settle into the large, red, comfortable, worn-out armchair that faced the TV, but it was clear the solitary chair in the middle of the room was for him. He sat on it and looked at Louise. Louise was still dressed in her work clothes, a white blouse and a black pencil skirt. As he waited for the interrogation to begin he wondered, not for the first time, why Andrew was dating her.

Sure, she was fairly attractive. But she also had something hard and unyielding about her, both in personality and appearance. Her jawline was well-defined and precise, like it had been engineered with artful precision. Her eyes were dark and observant, monitoring and recording events with an unnatural attention to detail. Her blonde hair was also never out of place, dropping just below her shoulders, flowing into deliberate curls at the end as if to say, 'Sure, I'm a serious person, but that doesn't mean I can't have fun as well.' She was the sort of person who would arrange a party using *Microsoft Excel*.

The entire package left Kartik feeling slightly confused. She was pretty, but the factory-made quality of her features put him off. And to his credit, he had only ever tried to sleep with her once, when Andrew had been on a work trip and Louise and Kartik had got spectacularly drunk together. Mostly likely, this was why Louise rarely drank in his company anymore.

'We've got some good news,' Louise continued, her voice conveying as much warmth as a supermarket self-service checkout machine. Her facial expression had all the personality of a mannequin.

'We're moving to London,' she announced.

Andrew shifted awkwardly in his seat.

Kartik felt his life taking a brusque turn from bad to worse.

CHAPTER TEN

Ryan made an angry beeline for Aaron, who visibly shrunk as his boss approached. 'What have you got on Cameron?'

'Cameron?'

'Cameron Fitzgerald. The girl I told you about the other day.'

'I found some people at Churchill College. I tried to get in contact with one of her tutors, but no luck there.'

'But she's there? She's definitely at Cambridge?'

'Huh?' Aaron looked as if he had just been asked a question in Mandarin.

'She's a student, yes? She's definitely studying at Churchill?'

' Of course she is. Why wouldn't she?'

'Good. Fine.' A few people in the office were looking over at the exchange. Ryan stared back at them, as soon as he made eye contact they suddenly became very engrossed with their computer screens or fingernails.

'Is something wrong?' Aaron asked.

'No. It's fine.' Ryan adjusted his tie, which had come loose at some point between receiving the email that had made him lose his temper and yelling at Aaron. 'I want a meeting with those Cambridge careers people.'

'It's not that easy. I've tried. It's a closed shop.'

'Try harder.' Ryan turned to head back into the office, to confront the document that had affronted him.

'There is something interesting I found out about her.'

Ryan turned back to face Aaron. 'What?'

'She's a serious participant in this Eden's Bonfire thing.'

'Really?'

'Yeah. She goes under the pseudonym Manhattan Samurai on a few websites. And there's interest in her work and theories.'

'She's solved it?'

'Well, no one's solved it. But she's been responsible for finding the solution to some of the puzzles within the puzzles that make up a sequence. She's putting forward some interesting and controversial ideas. Look at this.' Aaron brought up an online message board on the screen.

'What am I looking at?'

'It's a dialogue between Manhattan Samurai and some academics. I did a quick search on these guys, and it looks like they are from MIT. They're courting her.' Ryan peered down at the computer's monitor. 'Look, I know I'm not the most experienced person around here, but I think this girl may be quite special. Like smart. Very smart. Top-of-her-class smart. You don't get top mathematicians from MIT asking just anyone for advice. I don't want to sound hyperbolic, but she sounds like a one-in-a-million find. The sort of person your friends would be very interested in.'

Ryan was impressed, both with Cameron's talent and Aaron's correct use of the word hyperbolic.

'Send this to me,' Ryan said pointing to the website, and then walked back into his office. His anger had been somewhat assuaged by this new information, but on his desk still sat the document that had set him in a rage in the first place. It was a document that was headed 'Kartik McNair', and it revealed the truth. This wasn't some brilliant but lazy Oxford graduate that was slumming it in a coffee shop. This was an ex-polytechnic drop-out who had ended up in a job that was suitable for his meagre qualifications.

The fucker had had the nerve to lie. To boast about achievements that he had never earned, and was too stupid to even comprehend. That was why Ryan had to double-check Cameron. That is why he never trusted what people said in casual conversation. Casual conversation was the death of fact, it was the primeval soup of rumour, myth and exaggeration. That's why he liked things in writing. Statements in writing made everything clearer. And it was clear that Kartik was a lazy fraud.

Not only was he a fraud, he had also caused Ryan to risk his reputation on him. Ryan had been told he had gone to Oxford. And whilst that was strictly true, there were much evidence to suggest otherwise. An uncomplete degree. From Oxford fucking Brookes! Ryan didn't waste his time with ex-polytechnics.

It wasn't because he was a snob. He hadn't even gone to university. There had been a time in his career when his job was to place anyone, regardless of their talent or lack thereof. But it was something that he didn't touch at his level. The mechanics of his job didn't warrant it. His responsibility here was to prove to the executive board of the firm that he was good enough to go back to London. He shouldn't even be spending time on a graduate like Cameron, but she was an exceptional case. But Kartik? Kartik was the sort of driftwood he would throw to Aaron. Well, not even Aaron anymore. Even Aaron was above this. This was a newbie's responsibility.

The ramifications could have been potentially dangerous. What if Kartik had looked into some of the suggested roles that he'd been sent over the past week? What if he had tried applying directly, without informing Ryan of his outstandingly dire professional record? Ryan's reputation was on the line. That's what happens when you put trust in someone based on their word alone. You need it in writing. Get everything in writing. Ryan had a good friend who was a solicitor and that was his mantra: everything in writing, no matter how trivial. One time, the solicitor had got his son's PE teacher to email him the starting eleven of the school's cricket team, so he wouldn't drop his son at the last minute. That was the sort of diligence you had to do in this world.

That was why he was so worried now about Cameron. Who was she? She seemed to be almost too good to be true. Aaron was talking about her. MIT were talking to her. The only problem was she was as responsive to him as Helen Keller.

Ryan looked up and was surprised to see Philip at the door. He hadn't even knocked.

'We're not knocking now?' Ryan asked hotly.

'It was left open.'

'You can still knock.'

'Sorry.' Philip tapped the door three times theatrically. Ryan felt his pulse quicken. 'What was all that about?'

'What was all what about?'

Philip closed the door behind him. 'All that yelling at Aaron.'

'I wasn't yelling. I was getting information.'

'You know, Mr. Underwood never used to get information like you did.'

'If you hadn't noticed, Philip,' Ryan used his colleague's first name deliberately and with force, 'I've got a different style from Mr. Underwood.'

'You'd have to be living under a rock not to have noticed.'

'It's those people out there that are living under rocks. It's like an office full of hermits. Listen.' Philip listened obediently. There was the soft hum of the air conditioning and the gentle tapping of keyboards from outside Ryan's office, but not much more.

'I don't hear anything,' Philip said perplexed.

'Exactly. Silence. Nothing. No one on the phones. No one making deals. No one talking to clients. It's like a graveyard. What the hell happened to this place? When I was starting off, we had to be on the phones from the moment we entered the office to the time we left. If we were going through a bad patch, we would have to stand on our desks until we closed a meeting or secured a deal. There was a sense of incentive. A sense of productivity. You lived and died by your call rates.'

'It's a little different here, Mr. Stanfield.'

'A little different?'

'And things have moved on. We're not in the era of the hard sale anymore. It's about being smart. About researching. About being targeted.'

'Philip, I respect you. You've been here a long time. I like you.' Ryan only considered one of these statements to be entirely accurate, but he ploughed on regardless. 'But we need some fundamental changes. You work in accounts. You're not one of the consultants. They need to be led by someone who can lead. To be motivated by someone who can motivate. Aaron aside, I don't rate many of those people out there.' Philip raised his eyebrows. 'And yourself, of course.'

Philip stroked a non-existent beard and took a deep breath. 'Look, Mr. Stanfield. I respect you as well. I know you've been in this game for a long time. And I know that you are a good leader.' Ryan knew all three of these statements to be accurate, but calculated that his colleague only considered one of them to be true. 'So, what we really need to do is clear the air, to brief the company on how you want things to be run. To give everyone a clear expectation of what they can expect from us, and what we can expect from them.'

Ryan didn't like how Philip had used a collective pronoun

to imply they were a joint entity, but he did concede the accountant had a point.

'Okay, you're right.' Ryan got up and walked around his desk, as a way of demonstrating there were no barriers between them. He then leant against the edge, with his arms folded, in a pensive, rather defensive manner. 'Let's have a Town Hall meeting. Get everyone together next week. You and I will draft up a presentation; our goals, our motivations, our targets. We'll get input from the office. And we'll move forward as a team. Plan?'

Philip nodded like a cheap, pseudo-sage. 'That's a good idea. We'll get thinking. I'll put some ideas together of where we've been. You look at where we're going. I'll also put an anonymous suggestion box at reception, so everyone can have their input.'

Now it was Ryan's turn to nod. He tried to mimic Philip's behaviour as much as possible. This was supposed to display a sense of empathy towards the other party, which could then be cleverly exploited as servitude. He didn't like the idea of the suggestions box—this was supposed to be a highly professional office, not Café Ristretto—but he had to make some concessions to get Philip on his side.

The two of them sorted out a few more details and they agreed Philip would draft the email on their behalf, explaining what was going to happen to the office. After they had concluded this bit of business, Philip turned to leave. Just before he turned the handle to the office he turned once more. 'Oh, and I know you're excited about this Cameron girl. But your main focus is running this place, rather than getting directly involved in the hiring process. She's good, but she's young and she's got to make up her own mind. She's just a graduate after all.' He signed this off with a smile and a nod and then departed.

The sense of suppressed rage once again smouldered within Ryan. He hated Philip's smugness. The been-there-done-that sense of scholarship. Even when he was offering friendly advice, he came across as superior and condescending. Ryan knew that Cameron wouldn't be worth as much as some other high-level appointments, and it wasn't like he was forgetting about all his other work. But he wanted to demonstrate that he had a keen eye for talent. That he hadn't lost his spark. And the fact that Cameron was doing her damned best not to be found only made him want to try harder.

It meant he wasn't going to go down the conventional route. He would have to try something different. He looked at the shoddy CV in front of him, and an idea started to form in his mind.

CHAPTER ELEVEN

The past two days had been strange for Kartik. He had been looking for other places to rent, and it was clear his wages from Café Ristretto weren't going to get him much more than a cupboard under the stairs. Louise may be a nightmare of a housemate, but the house was always clean because of her (or her insistence that Andrew keep it clean) and his rent was heavily subsidised.

This meant he would have to get a better paid job, unless he wanted to move back in with his parents; an outcome that in some ways would be worse than living in a cupboard under the stairs. How many conversations would he be able to have about Cambridge United before going completely insane?

And so his thoughts had turned to Ryan, right around the time that Ryan's number had popped up on his phone.

Kartik had half-expected that he would never hear from the recruitment consultant again, once he realised how dismal his CV actually was. However, he was surprised to find Ryan was understanding about it, even apologising for the misunderstanding.

Ryan asked if Kartik was still interested in getting a job

and the barista explained his recent housing situation and how this turned out to be the perfect timing.

'I know how hard it can be to receive news like that,' Ryan said. 'So, I want to help you out.' They had both agreed that the roles that had been sent over so far had been too high a level for Kartik at the present time. Ryan suggested the two of them meet again, along with his colleague Aaron. He then suggested something Kartik didn't expect. 'We'll meet you down The Maypole on Friday.'

'The Maypole?'

'Yeah, why not? I owe you a drink, remember?'

'Yeah, but I thought I owed you a suit?'

Ryan laughed. 'Don't worry about it. We'll forget all about it. If you can do me a favour?'

'What's that?'

'Your friend. The girl.'

'Cameron?'

'Yeah, Cameron.'

'What about her?'

'Bring her as well.'

Kartik could be slow sometimes, but even he could see through this ruse—somewhere a little more casual would be easier to assuage Cameron's hostility. 'I don't know if she'll like the idea. I mean, no offence, but I don't think she's your biggest fan.'

'Look, I see that. But it'd be good to have a chance to make amends. As you've seen, we work with a lot of the big financial institutions. They'd bite their arm off to get hold of her. And I know everyone in the business, so I'll be able to negotiate her the best deal.'

`'I'll try.' Kartik knew Cameron was stubborn, but he had to admit that Ryan seemed to know what he was talking about.

'Just get her out for a drink. Don't tell her what it's all about. And then we can go from there.'

Over the next two days, Kartik had received emails from Aaron with suitable job offers. He had even been productive enough to do some rudimentary research, which should have made him feel good, but instead made him feel intimidated—even these entry-level jobs seemed out of his league.

Luckily, as he was finishing his Friday morning shift, he got a call from Camilla. She had said she had a new wardrobe that she needed help putting up and her husband wasn't around to help, and wouldn't be for the next few hours. For a moment he worried that his DIY skills weren't up to scratch, before he realised what this really meant.

He had jumped on his bike and began riding into the headwind towards Camilla's house feeling confused, anxious, excited, and aroused.

He was so deep in his thoughts that he didn't see the blue Toyota reversing out of its driveway on Granchester Street until it was too late. He swerved sharply to avoid colliding with the back of the car, but this took him into the path of a white Ford Transit coming in from the opposite direction. Simultaneously the driver of the Toyota and the van honked their horns, and the shock caused Kartik to lose control of his handlebars. The van driver slammed on his breaks, as Kartik veered toward him. In a blind, gut-wrenching panic, he yanked the bike to the left. As he did so, the fabric of his jeans became entangled in the bike chain. There was a tearing sound, which Kartik hoped was his jeans and not his skin, before his right leg snapped back towards his back wheel. The bike came to an abrupt halt, tossing him over the handlebars, like a cartoon character, mercifully away from the path of the van. He hit the tarmac elbow first, and a sharp pain shot up his arm. He felt friction burns as his body skidded across the coarse, black surface. He eventually came to a stop a few metres behind the blue Toyota, the driver of which was still honking her horn.

The van driver wound down his window and yelled

angrily at his prone body, the verbal abuse mostly consisting of non-politically correct accusations of mental disabilities. When the driver was satisfied that he had got his point across, he drove off. The Toyota driver, who was of a milder temper, wound down her window and enquired if he was feeling okay. 'Just my pride that's hurt,' Kartik lied as he struggled to his feet. Satisfied that he wasn't seriously injured, the Toyota driver also accused Kartik of being an idiot (although her language was much milder than the van driver's) before driving away.

Once on his feet, he examined the damage. His jeans had a long tear in them where they had caught in the chain. Unpeeling the material of his jeans revealed a shallow cut that was black with grease. A further examination of his body revealed deep grazing on his elbow and the right side of his stomach. Some of the grit from the road had embedded itself into his skin.

He dusted himself down, wiping the grazes with the back of his hand to dislodge the gravel. He tried to make himself look as presentable as possible, which wasn't easy for someone who had just taken part in his own Charlie Chaplin slapstick, and then got back on his bike.

Pushing down on the pedals was easier than he had expected, and the wheels moved with an unusual ease. He looked back at his rear wheel and was pleasantly surprised to discover his mudguard, as a result of the impact, had shifted away from the tire, no longer causing an obstruction.

Every cloud and all that.

He continued down into Newnham with a new formed sense of freedom to go along with his fresh wounds. He swung the bike into the gravel driveway of the large, white house. The driveway was big enough for three cars, and there was a garage door wide enough for another two, but there was only one in sight: the small, black, sporty Mazda. It was a car that when driven gave the feeling of vitality and youth.

Kartik suspected Camilla used it much the same way she used him.

He locked up his bike at the side of the house—he had been informed this was the least likely place Camilla's husband would look if he were to unexpectedly come home—and then phoned. She didn't answer, but this signified that he had arrived. He had been instructed not to knock on the tall, wooden door in case there was someone else in the house. Her face appeared between the curtains on the third-floor bedroom.

He waved to her. She disappeared back behind the curtain. Then, a few moments later, the door opened. She stood behind the door as it was opened, so it wasn't until he was inside that he saw her. The door was quickly shut behind him.

He turned to face his host. She was wearing a long, white silk dressing gown and had her hair down. She was leaning against the wall, doing a bad impersonation of a femme fatale in a film noir—a pantomime of seduction. It didn't quite work because of her awkward pose. She had to half lean over the small table where the keys and mail were kept. Her hand rested on an unopened bill from a water company and her foot stood on a slightly muddy doormat that had 'Home Sweet Home' printed in a garish pink.

'Hi,' Kartik said.

'Shhh.' Camilla raised a finger to her lips before moving towards him.

'Sorry,' Kartik said instinctively. He hadn't realised greetings were off-limits.

She pressed up against him and wrapped her arms around his neck biting his lip. He pretended it didn't hurt.

Her arms started to explore his body. She took his coat off and discovered the graze on his arm. 'What happened to you?'

'I came off—' Kartik began, but was interrupted by Camilla again raising her finger to her lips.

'Shhh,' she repeated. He felt this was a bit unfair considering she had asked him a question, but he didn't bother arguing.

'It doesn't matter,' she whispered. 'I'm here now.' She unbuckled his belt and forced her hand into his jeans. 'Does your wife know you're here?'

This statement confused Kartik terribly. He wasn't good under pressure at the best of times, let alone when he was getting a hand job, so this strange inquisition stumped him. But Camilla had asked it with such a forceful intensity that for a moment Kartik did indeed wonder if his wife knew he was seeing another woman. He was about to respond when he also remembered he was bound to a code of silence.

He shook his head, playing along to Camilla's fantasies. She grinned. 'Pity. It would have been so much hotter.' She increased the intensity of her hands' movements. 'You want me more than her, don't you?' she asked.

Kartik nodded helplessly, and Camilla let of an audible gasp of pleasure, even though Kartik was doing nothing more than holding her.

'I hate that whore,' Camilla continued as she licked his neck. Kartik couldn't help but feel a bit defensive of his imaginary wife. Sure, he was willing to admit that Camilla was more attractive than her, but he found it insulting that she was considered of such moral disrepute, especially when she wasn't the one cheating on him.

Camilla stopped licking his neck and looked at him. 'I see Penelope looking at me sometimes. I think she suspects something.' So his wife had a name.

Kartik's t-shirt was swiftly discarded by Camilla, which was an impressive test of skill considering her right hand was still firmly in his jeans. How much backstory had she attributed to this? It was getting a little bit creepy, but not enough for him to want to stop.

'You know what I'd love?' she whispered.

Kartik shrugged his shoulders.

'I'd want her to watch. I'd want her to be here. Be here now, watching me get you off. Watching you enjoy it. Knowing I can give you pleasure in ways she never could.'

Poor Penelope, Kartik thought. *Has she really done anything to deserve this?* He was a bad man to give into such temptation when he had such a lovely girl at home.

'Imagine her there, watching us.' Camilla pointed down the hallway. Kartik turned, but could only see a grandfather clock and the open doorway into the kitchen. If his wife was there, she was keeping herself well hidden.

'Do you think she's jealous of me? Jealous of this?' Camilla removed her hand from Kartik's jeans and untied her dressing gown, letting it drop to the floor. She was wearing nothing underneath. Kartik couldn't help but stare.

'What do you think she'd say if she saw this?' Camilla asked, drawing her arms up and down her body.

The only response he could muster as his mistress took off his jeans and boxer shorts was a soft, low noise that was little more than a whimper.

'Shhh.'

He refrained from moaning again.

Next thing he knew he was being pushed to the floor and Camilla was on top of him. He felt the coarseness of the rug underneath him as she guided him inside her.

It was over in a matter of minutes. Camilla barely looked at Kartik as they fucked, but instead stared at a fixed point somewhere down the hall, presumably where she imaged Penelope was standing. When she came, she snarled at her imaginary foe. When Kartik came, she slapped him hard on the chest.

It was only when it was all over, and they were lying

sprawled on the hallway floor in a mess of limbs and exhaustion, that Kartik considered how insane the whole thing had been.

They eventually rose from the floor, Kartik stroking his chest where he had been slapped. A painful red mark had already appeared, adding to his cycling injuries. Camilla had quickly thrown her robe around her—much to Kartik's disappointment—and then had run upstairs saying she was going for a quick shower and he should make himself at home.

It was always a vague instruction, 'make yourself at home.' What did it mean? If he was to truly make himself at home, he would be rolling a joint on the kitchen work surface in his pants, with crap daytime TV on in the background. That clearly wasn't an option in a place like this, so after putting his clothes back on, he slowly meandered through the rooms, not focusing on anything in particular.

There was something about the house. The smell was familiar, but it wasn't an altogether pleasant or welcoming scent. He passed the large grandfather clock in the hallway and was almost surprised when he didn't find his imaginary wife, Penelope, hiding behind it, her face a mess of tears and rage. Beyond the grandfather clock was the archway that led into the kitchen. It was bright, new, and expensive. Black marble covered all the surfaces, all spotlessly cleaned. It was unlikely that Camilla did any of this cleaning, and her husband seemed so non-existent that it was even less plausible that he was responsible either. The answer was found on a note attached by magnet to the unnecessarily large fridge door. It was headed, 'Iwona's to-do list,' and below was a litany of instructions written in the most perfunctory language possible: 'Clean toilet. Empty Bins. Clean Out Rabbit's Cage.' Nothing polite about it, just instructions. It was like someone was coding a computer program. Kartik imagined Iwona: some diligent Polish girl getting paid cash in hand for less than the minimum wage, who tries her best to hide the resentment she feels for the people that employ her. It was funny, that the richer someone became, the greater they were at finding ways to avoid parting with their cash. Any loophole that they could exploit, they would, just for the sake of having a little bit more than everyone else. It was a hoarder mentality. They sat on vast properties in nice parts of town, safe in the knowledge that prices were inflating, and at the same time, they cooked up schemes that would allow them to live an easy life. They may not be doing much with their assets, but they certainly weren't prepared to use them to help someone else. After the financial crash, the only thing that mattered was that you were still demonstrably richer than the people around you.

Kartik tried not to be envious, but it was hard. He wanted to think that if he ever found himself in the same financial position, he would be industrious enough to not hire a cleaner or, if he did, he would be generous enough to pay her reasonably. But again, he did a reality check, and conceded to himself that he would probably do the same as Camila.

At the back of the kitchen were large windows that illuminated the sweeping garden beyond. It drifted so far back that Kartik couldn't see the end from where he currently stood, partly obscured by the miniature orchard that was located beyond the well-kept patio and expansive lawn that followed.

On the mat by the patio door, were two small muddy pairs of shoes. A set of blue trainers and a pink pair of wellies. They were too small for adults, and Kartik was reminded of the time he had seen the scooters in the hallway from his last visit. He tried to push the thought of Camilla's children from his mind, however this time he wasn't able to focus on anything else but the thought of tiny feet filling those shoes, running around outside on the damp grass, shouting, and laughing, and yelling with their parents. Or maybe this was

Iwona's job as well —to play surrogate parent to children of a physically absent father and an emotionally absent mother.

Both pairs were a feminine design, so Kartik surmised that Camilla had two little girls (she certainly wasn't progressive enough to allow any son she had to run around in non-gender appropriate footwear). For the first time, Kartik felt guilty about what he was doing, about the confusion and suffering that would be inflicted on the kids if their affair was found out.

He looked away from the muddy trainers, a way to nullify the sense of guilt, crossed the kitchen and headed for the living room. Naturally it was large, clean, and lacking any sort of personality. The eye was first drawn to the massive TV and sound system that took up a good proportion of the room. It was an exquisite piece of kit, fifty-one inches by his estimation, and as thin as paper. Kartik was tempted to pick up the remote to test the picture quality but felt like he would be actually making himself at home, which was unacceptable behaviour for someone who had been told 'make yourself at home.' On either side of the TV were metre-high speakers, built into mahogany wood frames. Kartik was aware that, spiritually speaking, you weren't meant to covet material possessions, but owning a TV like this would be as close to pure happiness that he imagined a human being could feel. How could Camilla be dissatisfied with anything when she had something as perfect as this to come home to?

Maybe the answer lay in the positioning of the furniture. Other than have the two white leather sofas and armchair facing the TV, which any sane mortal would do without hesitation, the furniture was placed in an open-ended rectangle, so that only one of the sofas had an optimal view of the TV. It was a layout that looked clutter-free, without being suitable for living. It was the layout of a furniture catalogue rather than the layout of a family of four living their lives.

As he studied the room's layout, an unpalatable wailing

descended from the second floor. Camilla was singing again, this time to Frank Sinatra's *My Way*. There was a swatter graph to be drawn that would directly correlate the intensity of Camilla's sexual intensity with the awfulness of her post-coital singing. Today, the mark would be high on both axes.

Camilla bounded into the living room with the energy of a teenager, arms out wide and she reached the crescendo of the song. She had her eyes closed in a state of emotional abandonment, which was fortunate as she missed Kartik flinch.

'What do you think?' she said when she had finished.

'Lovely,' Kartik replied.

'My husband hates my singing,' she continued. Kartik felt he was being backed into a corner but Camilla didn't wait for a response. 'But fuck him.'

'Right…'

'Sit down, Kartik. You look uncomfortable.'

He sat on one of the large white sofas. Camilla sat next to him, spreading her arms along the back, like a bird stretching its wings.

'How do you feel about this situation? Be honest with me, Kartik. Do you think it's right?' Her lightly made-up face didn't betray any sort of emotion that could be reasoned to be human.

'Well, it's getting a bit strange, isn't it?'

'Why?' Camilla's response was so quick that it caught Kartik off-guard.

'Well, you are married.'

'So?'

'So… it's not just the two of us to consider.' Kartik nodded towards the kitchen as he spoke, thinking about the pink wellies.

'You want to know about my husband?'

'Not really.'

'Well, I'll tell you one thing. He's having an affair.'

'With Penelope?'

'How do you know her name?' Camilla seemed genuinely confused and concerned.

'You know. Just now. What we were doing. You said her name. A lot.' This time Kartik nodded in the direction of the hallway, and Camilla was able to follow.

'Yes, but that was just a fantasy. Completely different from real life.'

'But her name is Penelope?'

'Coincidence.'

'It's a coincidence that the woman you've created as a voyeur of your affair, just happened to have the same name as the woman your husband is having an affair with?'

Camilla didn't say anything. She rubbed her hands together and licked her lips. And then she started crying.

It started slow at first, her eyes starting to well up, and then the tears started to run down her cheek. She didn't try to hide her emotions. She didn't wipe the tears away or bury her face in her hands, or turn away. Instead she looked directly at him and wept, as if it were the only course of action she could take. He didn't know if she wanted consoling or if she wanted him to leave. She just sat there, her arms still spread like a composed seductress, but the illusion shattered by her visible, deep misery.

'Do you want me to go?' Kartik said, feeling increasingly uncomfortable.

'Do you want to go?' The tears rolled into her mouth as she spoke.

'I don't know. I don't know what this is. I don't know what you want, Camilla. I'm genuinely confused by all this. And it's not a good time for me to be confused. There are a lot of things happening right now in my life, and this is a situation that doesn't seem to be helping either party.' It was a relief getting this off his chest and momentarily he felt lighter.

Camilla didn't respond in any obvious way, and the tears kept rolling down her cheeks in a steady trickle.

'So you *do* want to leave?' she asked.

'I don't know what I want. I want something. I want things to be easier. I want things to be different. But I don't want to change anything.'

'You want the sexual gratification without the complication.'

'Yes,' Kartik answered honestly.

'Well, you're young. So, I'm going to pass on the one bit of knowledge that I know to be absolutely true. It's impossible to have sexual gratification without complication. Those two go hand-in-hand and can never be separated. No matter what you want, or what happens to you, that is one of life's constants. Water's wet, the sky is blue, and sex ruins everything.' Her make-up had smeared down her face. 'Kartik, you are the worst kind of person there is. You're exhausting. And you're stupid. My husband may be a bastard, but at least he's not useless. I don't think you've ever done anything in your life that has any kind of merit. You've never done anything good or bad. You just exist. You're just someone that gets in the way.' She wiped her eyes. 'Now please, get out of my house.'

Kartik left the house, jeans still torn, and his leg still sore. The worst part of Camilla's words wasn't the fact that they were true, but that she had him figured out even though she knew very little about him. He was useless and he was easy to read.

But at least the mudguard on his bike wasn't stuck anymore.

CHAPTER TWELVE

Ryan wasn't one to be pessimistic, but he started to doubt himself around the second pint. Aaron and Philip were next to him, talking about the upcoming autumn international rugby fixtures. Ryan had once mentioned he used to play the game, and now Aaron, being a keen fan, brought it up as much as he could, even though his boss had lost almost all interest in the game. When England had won the 2003 World Cup, Ryan knew his nation had reached its peak, and so he had started to drift away from following the sport he had once loved as a teenager. Work simply didn't allow him time to indulge so many hours in something he had absolutely no control over. Why get stressed about something you couldn't directly contribute to? Work, his marriage, his car—these were all things he had some direct control over, and could therefore take an interest in. But a group of athletes he'd never met, playing against another team he knew nothing about? Why get involved? At best, you will only ever feel a distanced, undeserved, and vicarious thrill from their triumph, and at worst, disappointment in their defeat.

But it wasn't Aaron's rugby talk that was causing Ryan to

be pessimistic. It was the fact that they'd been sitting outside The Maypole for almost an hour and there was no sign of Kartik or Cameron. He knew the barista was unreliable, but he thought that at least the offer of getting him out of that café might galvanise him to turn up that night. If not, the promise of free beer should have helped. It was past seven o'clock on Friday evening, and he could be spending time with his family instead of wasting his time, waiting in a pub for two people who might not even turn up.

And it was because of this agreement that Philip was there. Ryan would have preferred it if the accountant hadn't joined them, but Philip had a way with words. Ryan suspected why Philip wanted to meet the girl, but it still seemed like an inconvenience. It was hypocritical of his colleague. Though he had warned Ryan not to spend too much time on one candidate, here they know sat, three members of the Fusion Vision Recruitment team, spending their Friday night waiting for the girl.

But by the end of the second pint, this seemed to be one particular girl that wasn't even going to show up. It was especially frustrating that he was sacrificing time away from his daughter. Arabella had continued on a streak of lonely recklessness and was struggling in school as a result. She had friends there, but she was convinced that none of them liked her. She was also starting to talk about boys. Anna had convinced him that one of the benefits of having Arabella go to an all girls' school was that any complications caused by relationships would be postponed for as long as possible. He thought he'd at least have a few more years before it became an issue. But at ten years of age, she was already attracting attention from the adjacent boys' school (they were technically the same school, run by an overarching independent body, but the girls' school was on one side of the road and the boys on the other. Anna considered that a good proportion of the money they paid each term should be spent on keeping this distance as wide as possible).

Ryan had picked her up that afternoon—justifying that he could bunk off early from work as he'd be working later that evening down the pub—and she had been talking to two boys. They were both a couple of years older and he immediately recognised the ritual as amateurish and undeveloped flirting from all three parties. One of the boys—the taller one—was being cruel about Arabella's backpack, and his friend was laughing along. Arabella was reacting by pushing the boy and telling him to leave her alone, but without much conviction. The attention was enough for her, even if it was malicious, and the taller boy knew exactly what he could get away with. The shorter boy, probably not the quickest-witted, was just happy to be in the company of a girl.

Ryan's immediate reaction was anger, followed by dismay. Where were these boys' parents? And why were they being allowed to cross the road into the grounds of his daughter's school? And why was Arabella alone with them? Didn't she have her own friends?

All through his own teenager years, and for a good proportion of his twenties, he had used these bullying tactics to pick up girls, chipping away at their self-esteem so they felt that they had to redeem their self-worth by making themselves available to him. When he recognised this tactic being employed on his daughter he felt sickened. At least he had the decency to only start doing this from about fifteen onwards, rather than when they were all still in primary school. It was true what the papers were saying: kids were growing up too quickly these days.

He had taken his daughter's hand, quite forcefully, and had quizzed the two boys on where their parents were. The slow-witted one immediately became sheepish and apologetic, but the taller responded with righteous indignation. The boy claimed that his parents hadn't arrived yet, and he was entitled to go anywhere he wanted in the school grounds. Ryan had remonstrated, saying that the boy was wrong, and he should be on the other side of the road. His adversary had then pointed out a group of boys with hockey sticks, playing on the field nearby in an organised game in full sight of all the teachers, and said if those playing hockey were allowed in the school, then he was as well.

It was clear the kid was going to grow up to be the worst kind of smug politician and Ryan couldn't argue any further. Instead, he whisked his daughter in the direction of the Range Rover.

On the drive back, he tried not to show his annoyance, but he struggled to contain himself. She had complained that her dad had dragged her away from her new friends, and now she was embarrassed and they would never talk to her again.

'But I thought you wanted me to make friends?' Arabella yelled loudly from the backseat. She had thrown her open backpack on the seat next to her, scattering the contents all over his car. She sat next to a small mountain of wayward textbooks, stationery, and expensive gadgets that were meant to assist with her education, but were primarily used to play games on. If she had caused this mess on purpose, she seemed rather satisfied with the result.

'Friends, yes. But not those sorts of friends.'

'Why? I like them.'

He hadn't been able to counter his daughter with a satisfactory response, and had driven home with exasperated intensity that seemed to be a default setting for his emotional state these days.

When they had arrived home he researched the school's rules for whom is allowed on the school grounds at any time. Boys under eighteen were forbidden, except in the case of sports when facilities weren't available on their own campus, or had already been booked up. He cursed himself for not working this out at the time, effectively making him lose an argument to a twelve-year-old. He lodged the knowledge away in his head, in case the situation came up again.

He'd stayed in a bad mood for the rest of the afternoon and early evening, and things weren't being helped by the fact that he was being stood up by a couple of kids barely recovering from the other end of puberty. Since when did young people get this entitled, this lazy? When he had been their age, if he had been expected to turn up somewhere, he fucking turned up early—not an hour late, not thirty minutes late, not on time, but ten minutes early. That was what a bloody professional did.

The conversation between Aaron and Philip was getting strained now, since the rugby conversation had all but dried up. Despite his best efforts, Aaron didn't have enough to say to someone in their early forties to keep the conversation alive and Philip appeared to be looking for the first excuse to get home early. Unlike Aaron, he didn't consider getting drunk on a Friday night to be the ultimate zenith of each week. If anything, once you've passed the forty mark, the entire thought of Friday night drinks becomes an obstacle to be dodged, rather than an activity to be pursued.

It was with some relief that Kartik finally turned up to the pub, with Cameron and another girl that Ryan didn't recognise in tow. The new girl was hand-in-hand with Cameron.

The three of them came over and, rather awkwardly, said hello. Ryan had saved two seats at their table under the outdoor heater, and now he had to stumble around for a bit, fetching a third chair for Cameron's girl.

'Kartik, Cameron, it's good seeing you both again,' Ryan said, placing the newly acquired chair in front of them. The three of them sat down, uncertainly, as if they were walking into a trap. 'This is Philip. And this is Aaron.' Ryan singled out his colleagues respectively. 'I'm sorry, I don't know you name.'

'Rachel,' the girl said. She had a soft Scottish accent but didn't extend her hand. She barely made eye contact. Ryan was struggling to respect her already. But he didn't let it get to him. He wasn't about to get side-tracked with wishy-washy introductions.

'Would you like a drink?' Ryan offered.

'Lager would be good,' Kartik said affably.

'Same,' Cameron said. She may be guarded, but wasn't above a free drink or two.

'Yeah?' Rachel said. It was neither and answer nor a question.

'Aaron, get them three pints,' Ryan dictated to his subordinate. Aaron looked like he was about to remonstrate, but didn't quite have the courage. He disappeared and Ryan turned to manage the situation. 'So how are we all?'

'Yeah, good,' Kartik said. 'Hope it's okay that Rachel came along. She's new to the city. Just started at university. Thought it'd be good to introduce her to the most important places first.' He spread his arms, to suggest that The Maypole was some kind of Valhalla.

'It's a great place,' Ryan said to Rachel. 'I mean the city as well as the pub. University's not bad either, eh?' He smiled at this and Kartik joined in. Rachel did likewise but only out of politeness. Cameron's lips barely moved. Philip didn't seem to be paying any attention. 'How are you finding it so far?' he continued.

'Yeah, it's good,' Rachel said. 'I'm very busy already.'

'I can imagine. I never went to university myself. Sometimes wish I had,' he lied. 'You know, see what the fuss is all about, eh? What are you studying?'

'Engineering.'

'Great subject. Lots of opportunities there. Very

employable. At Fusion Vision we work with a lot of firms and there is a massive demand for engineers.'

'That's good to know,' Rachel said. Her hand was planted firmly in Cameron's lap, as if she required protection.

Looking at the two girls, he struggled to see what Cameron saw in the plain engineer. Comparatively, she wasn't much to look at. Cameron was easy on the eyes. Good-girl-with-an-attitude looks. But Rachel? Meh. There was nothing distinctive about her. Her face was too round, like she had never grown out of her puppy fat, and her ginger hair was flat and drab. She wore minimal make-up that could somewhat disguise her bad skin, drained and lifeless, with a small smattering of just visible acne scars around the chin. Her body was round in the wrong places, and not round enough in the right places. She tried to hide it with clothing that was much too baggy and a bit masculine: jeans, an old band t-shirt, an ugly brown hoodie. She was the sort of girl that Anna would describe as not putting in the effort to deserve any attention.

Aaron returned with the round and the six of them sat in silence for a while. The early October evening was getting cold, but they were close enough to the orange glow of the outside heater for it not to be encroaching.

It was Philip who broke the silence. 'So, how's Eden's Bonfire going?'

Cameron's head snapped towards him. 'Huh?'

'Eden's Bonfire. Made any progress recently?' Philip said. He was enjoying the confusion that was breaking over Cameron's face.

'How do you know about Eden's Bonfire?'

'I dabble a bit. You're Manhattan Samurai, right?'

Cameron's pint had lodged itself halfway between the table and her mouth. She had temporarily forgotten about it. 'Umm… Yeah.'

'Dr. Radiowave's Transmission,' Philip said, pointing to himself.

Cameron was quiet for a second and then smiled. It was the first time Ryan had ever seen her lips contort in this manner. It was a brilliant and unashamed smile. 'Really?'

'Yeah.'

'I see why Ryan brought you now.'

'Ryan didn't bring me. I wanted to come along.'

'You know each other?' Kartik asked, always a couple of paces behind.

'We're both members of an Eden's Bonfire online forum,' Phillip explained. 'We've been messaging each other recently. Cameron's the real expert, so I wanted to meet the person behind Manhattan Samurai.' For all the frustrations that Philip could cause, Ryan felt these were exactly the extra-curricular activities that made him valuable to his team, even if the superhero-esque pseudonyms were nothing short of ridiculous for a grown man with a wife and kids.

'I wanted to talk to you about your ideas of Chapter 13,' Philip continued.

'This thing has chapters now?' Ryan asked. Ridiculous or not, this had the potential to be the catalyst for organic, unforced conversation between the two groups.

'Maybe,' Philip said, looking to Cameron for a more fleshed-out explanation.

'It's a theory that the sequence the puzzles appear in is organised by chapters,' Cameron said. 'And if you can find the text that corresponds to each separate chapter that would be a clue to finding the answer.' For the first time, she wasn't speaking like a monosyllabic teenager. Next to her, Rachel was hanging on to her every word as well as her arm. The clinginess would have been adorable if it weren't so cloying. 'You've got to compile all the information gathered into suitable and coherent chapters, sort them into a logical order, and then find the right text to give some kind of workable conclusion. It's complicated by the fact that a lot of the information so far could be wrong, more is still missing, and the whole chapter hypotheses could be complete bollocks anyway.' Cameron smiled at the confusion on Ryan's face and then returned to converse with Philip. Soon they were discussing equations, and riddles, and theories, and themes, and a bunch of other nonsense that sounded as if it came straight out of a cheap science-fiction film.

'How's Café Ristretto?' Ryan asked Kartik so the laymen had something to discuss.

The barista's face fell, like all the joy in the world had been sucked out into the vacuum of space. 'How do you think it is? My regular customers are a horrible mix of the painfully stupid, the perpetually impatient, and the remorselessly picky. It's run by the compulsively underachieving. And it's owned by the morally vacuous. I've got a jobsworth manager, who is so scared of senior management, that he'd rather make us all do the work of five people each, rather than admit he needs to hire more staff.'

'Not scared of a little hard work, are you?'

'I don't mind hard work,' Kartik said, his eyes darting away to his right. 'I just don't like hard work when you're on the road to nowhere. And I'm so underemployed that I'm pretty sure some species of chimp are soon going to be moving up the career ladder faster than me.'

'Well, they are good at climbing,' Aaron said. Ryan and Kartik both looked at him, heads slightly tilted. 'You know, because they're monkeys,' he explained, not ready to give up on his joke quite yet. 'And they like to climb.'

Silence ensued.

Ryan and Kartik turned back to each other, pretending the interruption had never happened. 'Well, look, I know you've seen some of the offers that we've put together, right?'

'Yeah, I had a look.'

'What do you say we set up some interviews?'

The barista swallowed and then drew himself upright, as if gathering courage. 'Yeah, okay. Let's do it.'

'Excellent. Anything in that has taken your fancy? There are a couple of media sales jobs that look quite promising.'

Kartik shook his head. 'I've got a friend who works in media sales. And from what I gather, it's not something he's really enjoying.'

'What's the company?'

'Works Word Media.'

'That's why. They're a horrible place to work. Small time. Dying industry. Stuck in the nineties. Never evolved. Couldn't keep up when the recession hit.' As Ryan spoke, Aaron was nodding along by his side like one of those toy dogs in the back of cars. 'There are much better companies out there. In fact, the best places to start are in London. That's where the lion's share of the hiring is taking place.'

'London?' Kartik said sceptically.

'You ever thought about making the move? Lot more going on there. I worked there for over twenty years. Greatest city in the world. A lot of start-up companies are springing up all over the place.

'I've thought about it. A couple of my friends are about to move there. But I like Cambridge. Every time I visit London, well, it's all a bit... overwhelming.'

'It's exciting,' Ryan corrected him.

Fucking hell, Kartik was hard work. Here he was, being offered every opportunity in the world, even though he had a CV most recruiters wouldn't touch, and he was dragging his feet like some leper. If he wasn't connected to Cameron, he would literally have zero redeeming features. Hopefully Philip was building enough of a relationship with the girl for him to be able to dump the deadweight and start getting her in front of the hedge funds. He had the contacts ready, all he needed was some enthusiasm from her end. 'Look, just think about it. Aaron, if you drop some info to Kartik on Monday morning, then you guys can touch base and see if we can find something we're all happy with.'

This was agreed and Ryan started relax a little bit. Another round of drinks was purchased and conversation started to flow more smoothly. Kartik and Aaron were soon on the subjects of girls, football, films, and music, and thankfully they seemed to have a lot of common ground. With Philip and Cameron still engrossed, the only person left for Ryan to talk to was Rachel. Out of everyone at the table, it was the person he was least happy being lumped with, considering, at this moment, any interaction with her offered him few practical advantages in the short term. However, Ryan was a long-term strategist, and he saw opportunity in any situation presented to him (this was a line he had used in every job interview he had been in, and while hackneyed, it was something he believed in). The girl had loosened up her grip on her girlfriend's arm after the first pint, and had even had the courage to stand out from the rest of the group by asking for a gin and tonic.

'So, how long have you known Cameron?' Ryan asked Rachel after he had returned with the drinks.

'Just over a month,' Rachel replied. She played with her ginger hair as she spoke. 'We met when I came down for an open day to look around the college.'

'Moving quickly, eh?' Ryan nudged her. She didn't seem to understand, or if she did, she didn't respond. 'So which college are you studying at?'

'Churchill.'

'Same as Cameron.'

'Yeah.'

'Where are you from?'

'Scotland.'

'I figured that,' Ryan smiled, hoping the conversation would move away from the induced stunted awkwardness.

'Edinburgh.'

'Very nice.'

'I guess.'

Ryan felt his left leg tense.

'It must be pretty exciting to be starting university?'

'A bit.'

'That's not the most convincing response…'

'Sorry.' She looked down into her drink and then put her hand in her girlfriend's lap again.

The stunted conversation rattled on for a while longer. Ryan found out that she had spent some time in Berlin that summer, doing work experience before starting university. She also hoped to join the college rowing club, but wasn't too confident in her prospects to get into one of the teams.

All the information was delivered in short, clipped sentences, conveying the least possible information for Ryan to work with. It wasn't that she was unwilling to talk to him, she just didn't seem to have the skill-set to cope with a free-flowing conversation. She never asked him any questions about his life, and when he ran out of things to ask her, she would just sit there, playing with her hair, waiting for him to pick up the ball and throw it in her direction again.

Ryan couldn't work her out. The other two were easy: Cameron, though sceptical and openly hostile, could be engaged with someone with a common interest; Kartik was lazy but deferential, and just needed someone to give him a bit of motivation. But what was he meant to do with this Rachel? Her personality was a mixture of crippling awkwardness, lazy entitlement, with a side dish of nagging self-doubt. After forcing conversation for the best part of an hour, he turned his attention to the others in the group.

'Right, who's up for heading somewhere else?'

CHAPTER THIRTEEN

Kartik's head was spinning by the time they entered the nightclub, but not yet in a bad way. He almost tripped as he ascended the stairs to the main dancefloor, but managed to grab hold of Aaron who steadied him. They then made the final climb arm in arm, talking about some girl they had seen in the queue ten minutes before. They were intent on finding her, but Kartik suspected that he wouldn't remember what she looked like now.

The nightclub was on the second floor, perched above a Superdrug and a TK Maxx. It was far too small, and far too crowded on a Friday night, but that didn't stop the bouncers from cramming as many people in as they could physically manage. Brushing past someone, you could feel the sweat on their exposed skin.

With some expert navigation on Kartik's part, they arrived at the bar. He turned, counted four other members of their party, and for a second thought they had lost someone on their climb. It took a couple of moments to remember that Philip had left several hours ago, and their motley crew had been reduced in size. Ryan barged his way past Kartik and immediately purchased five tequilas and five bottles of beers.

A young patron to Ryan's left tried to protest that he was next to be served, but a quick, dangerous look from the older man finished any debate before it could really begin. The shots were finished as quickly as they were purchased. Kartik felt his stomach turn. He fought off the sickly feeling by taking a sip of his beer. The beer was served in a plastic bottle, which was a smart idea as people like Ryan could do a lot of damage with a glass one, but they didn't make a satisfying clink when they all said cheers for the one-hundredth time that night.

They made their way to a corner of the club, and tried to find somewhere to regroup. Aaron was yelling something about a time he had sex with some girl in an elevator, and Kartik just grinned at him, not hearing, understanding, or caring about the story. He was more concerned with the fact that his stomach was performing biological gymnastics. Every time he blinked, he felt the world do a backflip. He was at a fixed point in the universe, and everything else was twisting on an axis in ways that should not be allowed by the standard model of physics. The laws of motion were broken, science had collapsed, and if he didn't concentrate his eyes would quickly become blurry.

Ryan had grabbed Cameron by the hand and was taking her to the dance floor. He was moving with the lack of coordination of someone who had been punched in both ears, dancing to music repetitive enough to be used as a torture device by interrogators. Strangely, Cameron didn't seem to mind, and if anything, she looked like she was enjoying herself, something Kartik thought would be impossible. Ryan moved with all the grace of a concussed walrus trying to keep its balance on a treadmill. Cameron danced like the girls in Jean Luc Goddard's films. The dance floor was crowded, but because of Ryan's size, he managed to fashion a space with sheer bulky intimidation. His unstable movement meant that he could careen in any direction at any time.

Through squinting eyes, it almost looked like they were

related: a father and daughter on the dance floor at a wedding. Except someone was getting married in a sweatier version of hell, and the father had a habit of putting his arm around the daughter in a slightly inappropriate way.

Kartik blinked and Cameron was gone. In her place, Ryan had managed to find a new girl to dance with. How long had the blink lasted? It was impossible to tell. The new girl, a thin, brunette girl of a similar age to Cameron didn't seem to be as keen on being in such close proximity of her new dance partner. He kept trying to move close to her, to whisper in her ear, to gently touch her shoulder and lean into her personal space. The girl tried to move away to a group of her friends, but Ryan followed like a naive but obedient dog following its owner. As she turned away from him, his hand dropped and grabbed her backside.

The brunette recoiled in shock, turning to see Ryan's stupid, drunk face break into a teenage-like grin. The grin was knocked off-kilter by a surprisingly powerful hand swinging open-palmed at his chubby, wet face. His neck snapped sideways, and you could see the moisture fly from his hair, like the slow-motion replay of a well-placed punch in a boxing match. Then he was laughing, and holding his cheek, and not really giving a fuck about regaining his composure. The girl walked away, grabbed Aaron, who had somehow wandered into the sea of people, and thrust him into the path of his boss, creating a human barrier between the recently slapped and the recently molested. Aaron was the sort of person who made a good human barrier. Not in a hard-as-nails-bouncer type of way, but as a general nuisance and obstacle. The girl was not to be seen again for the rest of the night.

Where had Cameron gone during this commotion? She would have helped sort everything out. But she had disappeared somewhere. Kartik was about to go and look for her, but instead he blinked again, and when he opened his eyes again, it was very clear a significant amount of time had passed.

Some guy was yelling at him that he couldn't sleep in the club. That he had to go. That he was too drunk. Kartik protested that he couldn't be asleep because he was standing up. However this argument didn't hold up to scrutiny, as the yelling man, who was dressed in black and had the nasty look of someone who is hired to kick drunks out of clubs, quickly pointed out that he was sitting down. He couldn't remember sitting down, but all the evidence pointed to the fact that he had at some point.

He got to his feet, in a way he hoped suggested he wasn't at all drunk, and then picked up a bottle from the table. Was it his drink? Hell, if he knew. He drank from it. The yelling man forced him to put it down. He put it down.

He scanned the club. Rachel was hurrying over to him, but the creepy dad and the human barrier were gone.

'Kartik, are you ok?' Rachel asked, as she barged past the man who was still yelling at Kartik.

Seeing Rachel would have been a relief but he was acutely aware he was feeling very sick. He needed to empty the contents of his stomach somewhere. He just about had the willpower to signal that he needed to head outside. Rachel nodded and helped him. The yelling man would have looked pleased with his exit, except the nasty face was incapable of displaying joy, and only existed to emit anger, intolerance, and the threat of a server kicking.

They stumbled down the stairs and out of the club. There was no queue outside anymore, and it was clear more time had passed than Kartik had realised. Without thinking, he ran into a nearby alleyway and threw up.

Then he stopped, retched and coughed. Then he threw up some more.

This pattern repeated itself several times until there was a substantial mountain of foul semi-liquid, semi-solid matter covering a discarded copy of The Sun. He had thrown up on a story showing a picture of the Leader of the Opposition, David Cameron, meeting factory workers somewhere. Underneath was a picture of Gordon Brown looking glum.

Rachel was behind him, rubbing his back. 'Are you okay?'

'Doing better than David Cameron.'

Rachel didn't seem to understand that he had projectile-vomited on the poor sod.

'Do you know where the others are?' Kartik asked when he was sure he had got everything out of his system.

'Just got a text from Cameron. They are coming our way now.'

Kartik straightened himself up, and was amazed how much better he felt already. The world had stabilised, the axis had stopped spinning, physics had finally got its shit together again. 'Sorry about that,' he said, trying not to motion to the mess he had just made. He was surprised he had managed to avoid getting any on himself.

'Don't worry about it. Would you like some gum?' Rachel produced a packet from her pocked and Kartik took a piece. Not only had Rachel helped him exit the club, she was also now exercising the sort of lifesaving philanthropy usually reserved for saints.

'Thanks,' Kartik said, realising nothing he said would fully convey the gratitude he felt for getting the taste of bile out of his mouth.

As he started to chew, three familiar shapes came bounding down the road. Aaron threw an arm around Kartik, laughing and saying something about him being an 'absolute legend' or something. Kartik smiled back at him.

Ryan was talking to Cameron. No, talking wasn't the right word. Scheming—that was what they were doing. They were scheming. But about what?

'Right guys, we've got a plan,' Ryan announced. It was clear the night was not over yet.

They were led from the city centre down past Gonville and Caius College, towards the river. Kartik's legs managed to function well enough to complete this trek.

They came to a shallow jetty next to a foot bridge where numerous punts were anchored. The spot was secluded, dark and quiet, like it was hiding from the hordes of the night, praying not to be used. There was no one else around, as other people were smart enough to steer clear of jetties at this time at night. Ryan dug around his pockets and produced a set of keys. 'Now, which one of these fuckers is it?' He proceeded to clamber on the boats, inspecting the padlocks that chained them to the shore. 'Company's punt,' he said.

Ryan finally found the boat he was looking for and unlocked it. The keys were then tossed to Aaron. 'Get some stuff out of the outhouse.'

Aaron unlocked the door to a small outhouse to their right that Kartik hadn't even noticed before now, as it was half covered in ivy. He came out with a punting pole, a few blankets and a bottle of whiskey. 'Always keep the place well stocked,' he said, smiling to his boss, who had taken the poll and had set himself up as their chauffer for the night.

They clambered ungracefully onto the boat, steadying themselves as they rocked on the dark water. Cameron and Rachel sat together huddled under a blanket, and Kartik sat opposite. Aaron was at the front of the punt, using the small paddle to help steer them out of the jetty. Ryan was punting them from the back. After a couple of false starts, they were soon heading southbound towards the Mill Pond.

Ryan, even in his state of inebriation, was a proficient punter and kept them at a decent speed, while maintaining a straight line. He didn't talk as they went upriver, and had the look of someone who had finally found a small amount of contentment. There was a sense of purpose to his strokes , a stoic deliberateness in the way that he lifted the pole above his head, before plunging it down into the dark water, pushing them with an aggressive but careful diligence to wherever their destination may be. They were relying on his guidance, and he enjoyed the calm confidence of his abilities. The soft lapping of the water against the side of the boat added to the sense of serenity.

The bottle of whiskey got passed round, and Kartik figured now was the best time to roll a joint. In normal circumstances, he wouldn't have been reckless enough to start smoking in front of people whom he didn't really know, but Ryan and Aaron were clearly reckless enough not to care.

They passed the gardens of Trinity Hall and Clare College on their left-hand side, The Backs running alongside on their right. Kartik had never seen the river this quiet. Year-round there was a steady flow of boats making their way up and down the river. In the summer months, it became a floating traffic jam, so congested that you could barely see the water beneath the flat-bottomed boats filled with tourists, and families, and lovers, gawping at buildings, taking photos, and generally getting in the way. There was a sense of serenity to know they were the only people on the water that night. For a while they would have the historic dark passage all to themselves.

The joint was passed around, and everyone took a hit apart from Ryan who stayed dedicated to his self-appointed role. By the time they were passing under the Mathematical Bridge, everything had become a bit fuzzy to add to their drunkenness.

Ryan took them a few metres further and then pulled them to a stop under Silver Street Bridge, which gave them cover from any passers-by. The older man jammed the pole into the soft sediment as a temporary anchor, securing the punt against the underside of the bridge.

'Right,' he said sitting down and taking a swig of whiskey. 'You can do anything. Anything at all. And you know you can't fail. What do you do?'

Kartik, Cameron and Rachel looked at each other blankly.

'Just one thing. It can be anything. Regardless of ability, qualification, or realism, you can do it. What would you choose to do?' Again, there was no response.

'We use it at work when talking to candidates.' Aaron said as way of explanation. 'It's a recruitment trick.'

'It's not a trick, Aaron,' Ryan said with restrained disparagement. 'It's a tool. A way to get to know someone. To find out what truly motivates a person. Then you can use that knowledge to help them on their path.'

It would be playing fast and loose with the word 'philosophical' to attribute it to someone like Ryan, but there was something almost comforting in the way he was sitting at the head of the boat, bottle in one hand, cigarette in the other, not looking at anyone directly, but not looking away either.

'What do you do?' His eyes scanned the motley crew of fellow boaters, waiting patiently for someone to offer an idea.

'Scarlett Johansson,' Aaron offered.

'Huh?' Ryan snapped out of the dreamy daze.

'If I could do anything, and knew I couldn't fail, I would do Scarlett Johansson.'

Even though they were drunk on a punt at three o'clock in the morning, Ryan still managed to give Aaron a reprimanding look. Aaron laughed to himself, pleased with his contribution, and then lay down at the front of the punt.

'Anyone have anything a bit more substantial to offer?'

'I'd like to go into space,' Rachel said.

'That's certainly more admirable,' Ryan nodded. 'Why space?'

'I just think it'd be cool. Only a handful of people have done it. And the space program is one of the only projects where technology has been used to bring people together instead of dividing them. I've always wanted to be an engineer on the International Space Station. If you look at the history, twenty years ago, no one would have thought Russia and The West would be building something together in space. But when we got past our ideological and political difficulties, we've been, as a species, able to do amazing things. We've sent people to the most inhospitable environment we know, and people can now live there for months, experimenting, learning, and contributing—the single most expensive and advanced object mankind has ever created.'

Rachel looked around at her fellow boaters. It was more than any of them had heard her speak, except for Cameron. In the darkness underneath the bridge, it was impossible to tell, but Kartik suspected she was blushing. Cameron had her arm tightly wrapped around her girlfriend and looked happier than Kartik could remember her ever being. 'Sorry for rambling. I guess I took this a bit too seriously.'

Ryan passed the bottle of whiskey to her. 'Don't apologise. That was very inspiring. I wish I had some contacts at NASA for you.'

Rachel thanked him. Then she turned to Cameron. 'What about you?'

'What would I do?'

'Yeah. Remember, you can't fail.' Rachel looked over to the originator of the game who nodded sagely, happy that his message was getting through to his disciples.

'I don't know. It's hard. I want to do so many things.'

`'Come on,' Rachel said, kissing Cameron. 'You must be able to think of something?'

'I dunno. Eden's Bonfire?'

'Really?' Rachel said, slightly sceptically.

'Well, I've spent so much time on it already. It would be a waste if I never get to the end of it.'

'Maybe it's not about finishing it though,' Ryan offered. He was staring into the dark water of the River Cam, a village elder, summoning the spirits and knowledge of the planet. 'I mean, I've talked to Philip, and he's not sure there is an ending. No ultimate solution. It's just something that's going to keep on going and going. He thinks the whole point is to see what people do with the material they are presented with. Maybe the reward is actually the work you are putting into it now.'

'Maybe,' Cameron conceded. 'But, I'd be pretty annoyed if that was the case. I want to finish the bugger.'

'I believe in you,' Kartik said, mainly because he hadn't said anything for a while.

'Thanks, Kartik. What about yourself?'

Kartik had expected this and had prepared a parrying defence. 'What about Ryan? Sitting up their like Budda. What do you want?'

'What do I want? I want my daughter to grow up, be successful, and be happy. And I want to move back to London.'

'I thought you were only allowed one,' Cameron said.

'It's my game. My rules.' Whatever spirituality may have possessed Ryan up to that point had evaporated, and the head-hunter was back, bending the world to shape his needs. 'Now, Kartik, your turn.'

Kartik's mind went blank. As blank as he could ever remember it being. It was a void, a black hole, and a vacuum completely devoid of thoughts or substance. Try as he might, he just couldn't think of something that he wanted.

'Come on,' Cameron nudged him.

'I don't know,' he said.

'You can't cop out like that,' Cameron said.

'She's right,' Ryan agreed. 'Think. You can do anything. You can't fail. What do you do?'

He looked out onto the river, the moon reflected on its surface. A light mist rose from the water, and with the colleges in the background, it was like something out of a dream, or a painting, or…

'A film,' Kartik said with a clarity of mind that was so sharp it almost sobered him.

'A film?' Ryan asked.

'I'd like to direct a film. I mean, I'm pretty good at watching films, so maybe I'd be good a directing them.'

Ryan smiled, and was about to comment on this revelation, when an alarming sound came from downriver.

'Oi. What are you lot doing under there?' The voice left them all temporarily confused. This confusion was heightened when a bright light started shining into their eyes.

Two policemen were standing on the docking station of the Mill Pond, twenty metres away from their hiding place.

'We're fine, officers. Thanks for your concern.' Aaron waved to the men, expecting this was a significant explanation.

'Shut up,' Ryan said, hiding the bottle of whiskey under a blanket and standing up. He removed the pole from the sediment of the river bed and pushed them towards the officers. They pulled up alongside them, and were eyeballed suspiciously. Kartik was suddenly aware of how drunk he was.

Luckily Ryan had a remarkable gift for talking his way out of troublesome situations. He managed to rationally clarify how they had ended up in the boat, just by telling the truth (with a few omissions). He produced a business card, explaining that the punt belonged to Fusion Vision Recruitment and he was the manager there. He explained they had had a few drinks for a work social, and then taken the punt. The officers took some details from Ryan, and explained that they would need to do a follow-up call on Monday to check the details. Ryan agreed, and then said he'd chain the punt at the Mill Pond dock, to further appease the officers.

There they were, five people, standing in the darkness, slowly sobered by the encounter with the law, growing increasingly aware that the night was colder than any of them had realised. There wasn't much left to say, and the energy they shared on the boat had somewhat waned since they had set foot on dry land. It was all a bit real again. Kartik looked down at his watch. It was close to four in the morning.

'Well, ladies and gents,' Ryan concluded, rubbing his hands together to get the feeling back. 'It's certainly been an illuminating night. But perhaps it's best if we draw it to a close.'

This certainly seemed to be the best course of action, so after some brief goodbyes, Aaron and Ryan departed looking to see if they could flag down a taxi.

'We're heading this way,' Cameron nodded across Silver Street Bridge to the other side of the river.

'I'm this way,' Kartik said, pointing in the opposite direction. He would have to walk all the way back to The Maypole where his bike was chained up.

'Well, it's been an interesting one,' Cameron said. She still had her arm wrapped around Rachel, keen to get out of the cold morning air.

'Yeah,' Kartik agreed. 'It was nice meeting you,' he said to Rachel. If there was one thing to take out of the night, it was that she made Cameron happy, and that was all that really mattered.

'You too,' Rachel said. They shook hands in a mock-professional way.

Then they were off, arm in arm. Kartik felt a pang of jealously that he was walking himself home alone.

It took him just under an hour to get back to the house, the creeping sunlight breaking the darkness when he fell into his bed.

CHAPTER FOURTEEN

A cyclist swerved in front of Ryan's Range Rover as he turned right off Brookland Avenue and onto Hills Road, forcing him to break. Ryan responded by driving as closely to the irritating cyclist as possible, forcing him closer and closer to the kerb as they simultaneously crossed the railway bridge. The cyclist, aware of the deliberate aggression, showed him the middle finger, before being forced to apply his brakes and allowing Ryan to overtake again. It was another satisfying moment in a week that had already had a few highlights.

Cameron had agreed to have an initial conversation with some of Ryan's contacts about her movements after she graduated. The early scepticism had thawed and a trust was beginning to develop. She was still looking at other options for continuing in academia—there were conversations with the elite universities in America—but even Cameron wasn't immune to some of the starting salaries that the world of finance would offer someone with her talents.

'Word is you've got a bit of a budding prodigy,' Keynes had said over the phone. 'I hear she's one of these Eden's Bonfire geeks.' This hadn't been an insult; the puzzle was well known in the City, as many of its component parts had strong links to the world of finance. Even in this moneyed world where salaries were in the hundreds of thousands, bonuses could reach millions, and deals weren't worth talking about unless they had nine digits, there were still people quietly obsessed with this bizarre riddle.

'I've got a small team working on this myself,' Keynes continued. 'They've mentioned this…' He paused and he could be heard shuffling things around, 'Manhattan Samurai is fairly astute.'

Keynes couldn't admit it, but this clearly meant that Cameron was far more advanced than the team he'd put together, something that would be gently driving him nuts. 'If you can get her in for an interview, I'd love to meet her,'

'I'll see what I can do,' Ryan had said, playing it as cool as possible before hanging up.

Even in a recession, there was still a ridiculous amount of cash to be made by the most capable of people. In fact, the environment meant that the City had cut back slightly on the nepotism hiring that had dominated the past twenty years—a system that had helped breed stagnation by employing those with family contacts rather than skills—and the focus had shifted slightly once again to people who could actually do the job (although having the right surname was still a significant factor).

It wasn't a pleasant analogy, but someone with as much talent as her would be subject to a bidding war. She would be treated like a lot in an auction, which Ryan supposed was slightly dehumanizing, but also boded well for him.

Admittedly, Philip had been a massive asset in winning over Cameron. It had been the accountant who had lain the ground work. He'd given her assurances that the world of finance wasn't all just an old boys' network of boozy lunches, and that her skills would be appreciated. Like all young people these days, validation of her abilities seemed to be as much of a motivator to Cameron as cold hard cash.

The accountant had a gentle way with people that Ryan was beginning to realise was almost as much of an asset as his own bullish single-mindedness. It wasn't easy to admit, but there were elements of his working method that could perhaps be modified in the new financial climate. But hey, you always had to keep growing, to keep improving, to keep swimming in the right direction, or otherwise you'd be eaten by a bigger fish.

And on top of this, Aaron had also managed to find Kartik a couple of half decent clients that were willing to have him in for an interview. Nothing outstanding—a couple of admin roles, an entry-level sales position. The only problem was they were all based in London, and Kartik, a man who didn't so much drag his heels but anchor them down, was dithering on whether he would want to make the move. Fortunately, his housing situation was finally forcing him to make a choice.

'I'm getting kicked out of my house,' Kartik had told Ryan rather solemnly two days previously when he had stopped in for a coffee. 'I need to find somewhere new for January.'

'What about London? Hasn't Aaron sent you over a couple of ideas?'

'Yeah. Maybe. I don't know though. I like it here.'

'Really?' Ryan had asked, gesturing to the interior of Café Ristretto.

'Well, not exactly here. But my parents live here.'

'Jesus, it's forty-five minutes on the train. You'd be living in London, not Lahore.'

But even someone as lazily complacent as the barista would get itchy feet sooner or later. The next day, Aaron had confirmed to Ryan that Kartik had agreed to one of the interviews for an entry-level position in a financial events marketing company.

As he drove towards his destination, he thought back to the night on the punt the previous month. Usually, Ryan would have been a lot more cautious around people he was working with. The morning after he had worried that he had revealed a bit too much, been too reckless, a bit too unprofessional in his approach. But instead it had helped break down some of the barriers, and he now saw Kartik and Cameron on a semi-regular basis in Café Ristretto. He had even warmed up to Rachel, realising there was more to here than her initial awkward shyness suggested.

For the first time since leaving London, he suspected that he had developed friendships with people. Was friendship too strong a word? Perhaps. The end goal was still work-related. Even so, he wouldn't stop by for his double espressos nearly as much if he didn't somewhat like talking to the barista.

However, if his work and social life were on the up, there was something rotten in the state of Demark when it came to the family.

He was driving to Arabella's school after some kind of incident that Anna hadn't explained fully on the phone. Whatever it was, his wife was terribly upset by it, and it was something that the school wasn't taking lightly. When Anna had spoken on the phone, her voice had been accusatory, as if whatever had happened was more his fault than that of their daughter.

It was becoming a familiar tone that she had adopted over the past few months, as if everything that went wrong was somehow due to his incompetence. He didn't like being talked to this way, especially as he was anything but incompetent. Everything from the neighbours' front garden not being tidy enough ('If you don't say something to them, it's going to start affecting the price of our house') to the fact that the Conservatives weren't leading the polls by a margin she deemed suitable ('Why aren't you talking to your old clients about what will happen if Labour stay in power for another five years? They need to be speaking to the media more').

It had become exhausting, and Ryan was looking for any kind of excuse to get away from the house. This naturally led to more frequent lectures from Anna about how she was having to raise a child on her own. She would exaggerate that Ryan's absence was creating a monster, believing that their daughter was going to turn into, 'one of those grubby kids from the estates back in London who ruin perfectly nice areas of the city.'

He'd left work early, but the light was already fading from the day. Autumn had given way to winter, and grey, spitting skies accompanied Ryan as he pulled into the school car park. Anna was standing beside her car as Ryan parked the Range Rover next to her. She was smoking, a new habit that he knew she didn't really enjoy, but something she did to demonstrate her irritation. She was all surface.

'What's going on?' Ryan asked as he got out of his car.

Anna stubbed out the cigarette and ground it into the asphalt aggressively. She folded her arms tightly. 'She's been acting out.'

'Acting out' was Anna's polite euphemism for everything bad that Arabella did. They started to walk towards the school entrance.

'What do you mean "acting out?"'

'What do I mean? She has been swearing at her teacher. And she's been swearing at the head-teacher. She'd been making a complete and utter spectacle of herself in front of all the other children. And you know what's going to happen?' Anna turned on her husband like a journalist ready to grill a politician. 'Those children—all those *well-behaved* children— are going to their parents to tell them what a terrible family the Stanfields are. We're going to be pariahs. And all because you've been encouraging our daughter to talk like an effing builder.' The irony of this statement was lost on Anna, and Ryan suspected pointing this out would just enrage his wife further.

It was going to be a long afternoon.

They headed inside. The automatic doors swung open for them and they approached the receptionist, Anna immediately swapping her scowl for a look of apologetic embarrassment. She could camouflage her emotions quicker than a chameleon could change its skin.

'Hi. We're the Stanfields. We're here to see…' She paused for a moment, a quick flash of panic on her face as she searched the vast emptiness of her mind, before she was able to conjure the names she was grasping for. 'Mrs. Dowling and Mrs. Scott-Howell.' She lowered her tone and in a hushed tone continued, 'It's about our daughter, Arabella.'

They were pointed down the corridor and entered the office of Mrs. Scott-Howell, the head-teacher.

Arabella was sitting on a plastic seat on one side of the office. Mrs. Dowling, her teacher, was standing behind the desk, along with the proprietor of the office, Mrs. Scott-Howell, who was sitting. Arabella was looking at her feet, which didn't quite reach the floor, her shoe swinging in an obdurate rhythm. She looked up when her parents entered, her face red from recent tears. Her eyes started to water again when she caught the glare of her mother.

There was a quick, awkward introduction between the adults, and the Stanfields were ushered into the chairs in front of Mrs. Scott-Howell's desk. Ryan was immediately drawn to Ms. Dowling. She was in her mid-twenties, wearing a tight green dress, which quickly drew attention to her figure. He reminded himself that he was there to discuss his daughter's progress in school but realised it was going to be quite a challenge to focus on the issue at hand.

Mrs. Scott-Howell, or Carol as she introduced herself, started the proceedings.

'Thank you for both coming in. As you both must be aware, we are starting to get a little bit worried about Arabella's recent behaviour.'

Anna looked over at her daughter. Tears had started to run down her cheek. Ryan looked over and smiled supportively, but his wife glanced at him and he tried his best to flip his supportive smile into a look of concern. He failed.

Mrs. Scott-Howell then ran through the events that led them to this moment. Earlier in the day, Arabella had been caught on her mobile phone in class. When Ms. Dowling had asked her to put it back in her bag she had refused. Ms. Dowling had then tried to confiscate the phone, and had been greeted with a curt 'fuck off' (Mrs. Scott-Howell had censored the exact phrase by explaining, 'Arabella then declined to relinquish the offending item by using the f-word.').

Her teacher had then tried to get Arabella to leave the class, which had erupted in noise from the other students. Arabella had then proceeded on a foul-mouthed rant as she was led out of the class and into the head-teacher's office. It was only when Mrs. Scott-Howell announced that her parents were coming, that Arabella finally let up her tirade and had burst into tears.

'Today's incident isn't the first time Arabella has displayed anti-social behaviour. However, it is by far the worst outburst,' the school's matriarch concluded. 'In fact, I'd say it's one of the worst displays of behaviour that I've seen from any student in this school in my fifteen years here. Needless to say, this is not something I wish my staff to be subjected to.' Ms. Dowling shifted uncomfortably where she stood, her small fingers subtly pinching the material of her dress around the waist. Ryan tried not to stare.

'I can't believe it. I just can't.' Anna's tone was somewhere between outrage, anger, and deflected blame, keen to absolve herself from her daughter's actions.

'Sadly, action is going to have to be taken.'

'Yes, yes of course,' Anna hastily replied. 'She'll be grounded from today for a month. No phone. No TV. No seeing friends. Just doing homework and going to school.'

Arabella looked like she wanted to protest, but Ryan signalled with his hand not to say anything, a gesture hidden under his chair from the other adults.

'I'm afraid this is something that is going to be handled by the school as well,' Mrs. Scott-Howell said sternly. 'Arabella will be suspended for a week while we work out whether she is going to be welcomed back at all.'

There was a sharp intake of breath from Anna, like her head had just been released after being dunked into an ice bath. Ryan started doing some sums in his head. This was the most expensive school in Cambridge—at least there was a possibility of saving some money if she wasn't welcomed back.

'Please, can you let her stay? We will do anything to ensure her behaviour improves,' Anna pleaded. She too was now on the verge of tears. They were tears for her own tattered social reputation as much as her daughter's lack of private education.

'That is a matter for the school to decide,' Mrs. Scott-Howell said. 'Ms. Dowling is going to write up a report of the incident and then we will have an official review.' Once again, Ms. Dowling shifted awkwardly where she stood. Ryan tried not to let himself get distracted and to maintain his look of serious concern. 'Only then will we make a decision to Arabella's future.'

'I'm so sorry that this has happened. She's usually such a good girl. We raised her well. And we're a good family. I don't understand,' Anna continued, not able to resist defending her parenting ability.

'I understand. But clearly something is going wrong,' Mrs. Scott-Howell said sternly in her Victorian manner. 'Is there anything we need to know about that may be causing these outbursts?'

Ryan felt the head-teacher's piercing eyes on him. She was judging them, assessing their abilities as parents, looking for a hint of any cracks in their foundations. *How much did she know?* For a second, Ryan worried that she was telepathic and that she knew everything.

The eyes then shifted to Anna and she swallowed, not fully able to hide her delicate fear.

'No, everything is fine,' Anna said in a voice that was a little too high-pitched. Mrs. Scott-Howell's eyes narrowed.

'Well, it's not always easy readjusting to a new city. To a new school,' Anna continued. 'It's a lot to take in at her age. I think Arabella is just having a little problem settling in.'

'Mrs. Stanfield, this is more than just a "little problem". This is a serious incident.'

'I understand, I understand. We'll make sure we do everything we can to help fix things. We fought hard to get Arabella into this school. We know your reputation. We know that it is one of the best. We know how hard all the teacher and staff work.' Mrs. Scott-Howell barely reacted. Flattery will get you everywhere, unless you are flattering a humourless, authoritarian head-teacher plucked straight out of the pages of a Charles Dickens novel.

Anna ploughed on regardless, determined to get her point across in as many breathless, rushed sentences as she could muster. 'And that is what we want for our daughter. We know what it means to her. We'd feel terrible if this opportunity was taken away. We'll do whatever it takes to make things better.'

'I can see how much this means to you, Mrs. Stanfield. And it is good that you feel so passionately. But as I said, it is all subject to the outcome of our review. That is our process here, and we must follow the guidelines.'

The two parents nodded in agreement and then were

made to sign some paperwork to confirm that the meeting had taken place, and they understood the rules of next week's evaluation.

'Thank you for your time, Mr. and Mrs. Stanfield,' Mrs. Scott-Howell said, rising from her desk for the first time and reaching out with her small, bony hand. 'I will contact you once we have completed our investigation.'

'Thank you,' Ryan said.

'If you need anything else from us, anything at all, let us know,' Anna said pleadingly.

They then turned to Arabella who was still sitting on the plastic chair.

'Let's go,' Anna said to her daughter. Arabella, head lolled, stood up and started for the door.

'Aren't you forgetting something?' Anna asked.

Arabella turned to look at her mother, a look of confusion on her face.

'You're going to leave without an apology?'

'I'm sorry Ms. Dowling. I'm sorry Mrs. Scott-Howell,' Arabella mumbled to each of them in turn. 'It won't happen again.' She didn't make eye contact with either of them.

You may not have the chance, Ryan thought to himself.

They led Arabella out of the office, Ryan chancing one last look at Ms. Dowling, who was now busy sorting out the paperwork that Mrs. Scott-Howell had gotten them to sign. Anna marched her daughter swiftly past the secretary and out of the building.

Once the three of them were in the car park, Anna exploded.

'I can't believe what you've just put me through. I've never been so humiliated in my whole life. Who do you think you are?'

'It wasn't my fault,' Arabella said, the tears coming fast again.

'Wasn't your fault? Wasn't your fault? You swore at your teacher. How could it not be your fault?'

'She was trying to take away my phone.'

'And you think that's a good reason to swear at her? A good reason to make a spectacle of yourself? Do you think that is how you were raised?' Anna pulled her daughter's arm, trying to yank an answer out of her.

'Mummy, you're hurting me.'

Ryan was aware that they probably weren't out of earshot of the school offices yet.

'Let up on her a little,' he said.

'And don't you start,' she snapped. 'This is just as much your fault as it is hers. You wonder where she gets this language from? Who? Who could possibly be encouraging her to swear like this?'

'Anna, let's wait until we get home to have this conversation.'

'Don't you dare tell me what to do! Not now!' She pulled Arabella to her car. 'Get in,' she commanded. Arabella did as she was told.

'Go somewhere else tonight,' she said to Ryan softly. 'I don't want to see you.' She didn't look him in the eye as she got into the driver's seat and pulled out of the car park.

Ryan kicked at the gravel and got back into the Range Rover. The leather seats that were usually so comforting to him after a hard day now seemed hard and unforgiving. He turned on the heater but he didn't feel much warmth.

Suddenly, all the positivity that had been building up over the past week, the progress he had made at work, with Cameron, with his friendships, seemed far away and distant. He knew clearly, that his marriage was breaking down, and he was failing as a father.

CHAPTER FIFTEEN

Kartik was nervous. Really nervous. Beads-of-sweat-dripping-down-his-forehead nervous. Hands-trembling-when-he-lifted-his-glass-of-water nervous. He was so nervous he had lost control of the movement off his pupils and couldn't focus on anything. He kept trying to snap out of it, but he didn't know where to look. Eye contact with the three people in front of him was terrifying. He tried to look the woman in the face, who was smiling in a perfunctory way, but he couldn't concentrate. Behind the smile was something harder, firmer, and smarter. If you ripped the skin of her veneer you'd see the all-consuming lifestyle of the corporate ladder. Her face reminded him of Cameron's if she were to become infected by an unyielding hardness and distain. He tried to channel a sense of professionalism. *What would Ryan do in a situation like this? Be professional, act like Ryan.*

Flanking the woman on either side were two men, bored and stern, easily dissecting Kartik with years of experience of judging people. Both men sat rigidly and haughtily, as if they wanted to be seen as the most senior, but there was no doubt that the woman controlled the room. She was the one who had led him into the frosted glass-walled office, who had directed him into the uncomfortable seat that he was now sweating in. The room was both too cold and too hot at the same time. He was directly under the air-conditioning unit, icy, stale air blasting him from above, and at the same time the large glass windows were magnifying the afternoon sunlight, turning the rest of the room into a corporate greenhouse.

To add to the discomfort, his shirt felt too tight around the collar. With the top button done up and tie on, it squeezed his Adam's apple every time he swallowed. The shirt had been hastily purchased the day before when he had realised he had no suitable interview attire. In his rush, he had not done up the top button in the fitting room, an oversight he was now massively regretting. In fact, he was regretting coming along to the interview at all. It was, in no uncertain terms, going tits up.

'So *why* exactly did you drop out of university?' the woman asked, more an accusation than a question.

He had rehearsed this answer with Aaron two days before. It was bound to be one of the things that was brought up, and he needed to deal with it smoothly and calmly, as if failing in his degree was a proactive choice to better himself, rather than a proactive choice to avoid doing work.

'Well, you see, I didn't feel like I was getting the um… relevant experience from university. Like, it wasn't preparing me for work in any way. And it wasn't an easy decision. But I felt that by using that time more effectively I would be able to get ahead of, you know, my peers.' The use of the word 'peers' was something Aaron suggested. There were certain words and phrases that he believed should be shoehorned into any interview. They made you look more professional. Kartik had already used 'enthusiastic' and 'self-motivator' and was now looking to use 'dynamic' and 'forward-thinking' in the conversation.

Sadly, Aaron's recommended lexicon didn't seem to be

having the desired effect. In fact, the only reaction he received from those sat opposite him were scepticism and boredom.

'You studied for over a year and a half, doing...' She looked down at the under-populated CV in front of her, 'An English literature degree before realising it wasn't for you? Were you not able to come to this decision sooner?'

Fuck. A follow-up question. Aaron hadn't told him what to do in this situation. He'd have to freestyle it. 'I wanted to, you know, get a feel for it. To see what would come up. Anything that would be, like, you know, useful...' He trailed off. Evidently freestyling was not his forte.

'Right. And since you've left, you've been working as a barista?'

'Yes, that's right.'

'And serving coffee was what you had in mind when you wanted to get ahead of your *peers*?'

Was she was sneering at his use of the word 'peers'? It sounded like it. That wasn't meant to happen. Aaron said nothing about this kind of condescension. Kartik felt uncomfortable and realised he needed to go to the toilet. He also wanted to drink water to help with his increasingly croaky voice, so was stuck in a catch-22. He decided to forgo the water, as pissing himself would create a much worse impression than having a hoarse voice.

'Well, that is why I am here now. As you understand, the financial crisis has meant that it is becoming increasingly difficult to get your foot in the door. However, I wanted to prove that I am still proactive, dynamic (*yes, there it was!*) and not afraid of putting in a shift while I search for something more fulfilling.'

These were Aaron's words almost verbatim, who had explained how important it was to appear busy at all times. 'People in these jobs haven't taken a break from work for decades,' Aaron had explained before he had left for the interview. 'You don't want to come across as a dosser. Any work is better than inactivity. Even if you had been shovelling shit for the past ten years, it is important to highlight that you were digging with enthusiasm and consistency, and getting paid for it. Everything else is just transferable skills.'

Kartik looked back up at the three figures in front of him. 'And I think it's more important to have the desire, and determination to do the work. Then, the relevant skills you will be able to pick up on the way.'

'Don't you think it's rather optimistic that you will just "pick up" skills on the way?' This time it was the man on the right who spoke, the one who looked slightly less bored. He sat forward in his chair for the first time. He was only a couple of years older than Kartik, but wanted to impose himself on his interviewee to ensure he came across as superior. He had thin, blonde hair, which had been aggressively gelled backwards to cover what Kartik suspected was a premature bald patch at the back of his head. 'I'm not being funny, but this is a fast-paced job. You will be expected to come in at an entry-level with a certain degree of competency. Looking over what you've done so far, I just don't see that.'

This sort of aggressive honesty was something he had been told to expect, but it still put him on the back foot and he couldn't find the words to turn the negative into a positive. This was completely different than when he had interviewed at Café Ristretto, when he'd winged the completely undemanding interview and fallen into the job more by accident than by design.

He mumbled something about transferable skills and hard work and being results-driven, but he knew his audience was lost. The man on the left hadn't even spoken since he'd entered, and now it wasn't entirely obvious if he was awake or not.

The rest of the interview petered out as Kartik struggled for words, and concluded with the woman walking him to the door. As he was pushed out of the door, he was aware how light-headed he felt, and how pressing his need for the toilet was.

There was the briefest of handshakes, Kartik's sweaty palm against the woman's steely grip, words exchanged—she said they'd be in touch if he was selected—and then he was back in the reception area. Not able to think of anything else, he asked the receptionist where the toilets were, and was pointed down the hallway. He half ran into one of the cubicles, and locked the door, cherishing this momentary privacy. He propped himself against the wall as he peed, his body flooding with relief, weakness, and a spinning light-headedness. When he finished he lowered the toilet seat and sat down, empty and anxious, trying to keep himself from passing out. He undid the top button of his shirt, put his head between his knees and took some deep breaths.

Spots had started to dance around his eyes and, for the first time in his life, he realised how much trouble he was in. All the messing around, all the missed classes, all the half-assed exams, all the days he'd lain on the grass and pretended that he could put off the future—all of that was catching up to him now, and he wasn't even able to get the most rudimentary of roles, some entry-level non-sense at a company that organised financial trade exhibitions. He wasn't even entirely sure what the role he had meant to be interviewing for was or what would have been expected of him.

And now he was trapped in central London, sweating, depressed, and a significant train journey away from his bag of weed that he had tactfully decided not to bring. He had even missed out his morning joint for fear of messing up the interview, which may have actually been detrimental. Maybe that was why he was so uneasy now; sobriety was both stark and disorientating.

His vision was coming back again and his palms had

dried slightly. He used some disposable towels to dry the sweat under his arm pits.

He was buttoning up his shirt again when the door to the toilet opened and two men entered talking. He recognised one of the voices as the slightly less bored looking man from his interview.

'Honestly, I've never seen anything like it. It was ridiculous. I felt embarrassed for him. It was so awkward. I think we all felt uncomfortable.'

The two men were standing by the urinals. 'I hate that. What a waste of your time.' Kartik didn't recognise the second voice.

'I know. I've got twenty other candidates to see, and we've got to fanny about with some idiot that looked like he'd borrowed his suit off his little brother. It didn't even fit.'

'Really?'

'Yeah, it was too tight. It was like he was being strangled. He spoke like this: *I've got transferable skills.*' The man put on a croaky voice that Kartik had to admit was accurate. '*Serving coffee is the same as working for you guys. Everything else I'll just wing it…*'

The two men laughed. Kartik prayed that they didn't realise he was there, the pathetic moron with the croaky voice, now trapped in a toilet cubicle. Things couldn't get much more humiliating than this.

'How did he ever get it?'

'I did it as a favour for Ryan Stanfield.'

'Ryan Stanfield?'

'Oh, you remember him. Works in recruitment for Fusion Vision. Fat guy. Unnecessarily aggressive. General twat.'

'Oh, yeah. Didn't he try to hit on Alice at the Christmas dinner a few years ago?'

'Yeah, that's the one. Another embarrassment really. But we go back a few years, so I thought I'd at least entertain this Kartik guy. I didn't think he was going to be that bad though.'

'Ryan's still around? I thought he would have been the type to get the chop after the crash.'

'He's not in London. Working in their Cambridge offices. From what I've heard, the company wants him out. He's a dinosaur but Fusion can't find a justification to get rid of him. So they demoted him and shipped him off to the provinces in the hope that he would leave. But the divvy cunt didn't get the hint and now he thinks he's on some crusade to save the ship from sinking. Keeps talking about some protégée that he's fished up from the university or something. Talking like she's going to be his resurrection.'

The other man laughed. 'A student is his resurrection? What are they smoking down there?' They moved away from the urinals and to the taps.

'He hasn't realised the landscape has changed these past two years. You can't just bulldoze your way through the industry. People like him are finished. He'll end up teaching GCSE Business Studies for the next twenty years before having a heart attack.' They headed for the door. 'I'm not going to be picking up any calls from him again.'

The two men left and Kartik could breathe again. In the worst kind of way, overhearing the conversation made Kartik feel a little bit better. At least he wasn't the only one that was completely fucked.

Checking the corridor was clear, he left the toilet, and got out of the building. London rushed around him: men and women with sharp faces and determined looks pushed past him, getting to wherever the hell people who wear thousand-pound suits and sharp haircuts go to at 2.30pm on a cold Tuesday.

He headed across the road to a Starbucks and got a coffee. He was reluctant to admit the quality of baristas there were better than Café Ristretto, but he would be lying to himself if he didn't acknowledge there was something impressive in their work. They moved with a mechanical efficiency, the same sort of conveyor-belt mentality that drove the entire city. He sat in a quiet corner, or as quiet as can be found in central London, and phoned Ryan.

The head-hunter was in a foul mood when he answered, so Kartik softened the report on his piss-poor performance. He told him that it had gone okay, and that he would wait to hear back from them. He omitted any mention of his eavesdropping in the toilet.

'Good. Good,' Ryan said. 'I'm down in London now. Let's go for a drink and talk through it all.' It was a command rather than a suggestion. Kartik got the name of a bar in Islington, hopped on the tube and a few minutes later he was sitting opposite Ryan, recapping his interview, trying to put a positive spin on it. Ryan seemed to be only half listening—something that was happening a lot recently when Kartik was talking. He wished he was on the train back home, to get away from everything, but Ryan had something on his mind. It wasn't clear what, but Kartik sensed this wasn't a quick drink to discuss work.

The bar was in a quiet afternoon lull and the sky outside was already darkening. The nights were drawing in ever quicker as October slowly was coming to a close. It hadn't been staggeringly cold yet, just wet and grey. It was going to be a long winter.

A young guy with a beard and a red lumberjack shirt was drinking coffee by a table by the window with a MacBook in front of him. Every now and again he would type some words, sigh, stroke his beard, and then look out the window. The writing-to-looking-out-the-window ratio was split around 90:10 in favour of the view.

Sitting at the bar was an older man, half a pint of lager in hand, the newspaper's racing pages in front of him. He was circling the odd name here and there. He seemed more proactive in his leisure than the young guy with the MacBook.

Ryan was wearing a suit that cost about ten times as much as Kartik's. The collar fit him perfectly.

'What brings you to London anyway?' Kartik asked.

'Had a meeting with the head office. Looking over my performance review.' His voice was flat and it was impossible to know if it went well or not.

'Good…?'

'Some of it. Not good enough though.'

'Really?'

'Thought we'd at least start talking about moving back to London. I didn't expect it to be overnight. But I thought there'd be a plan in place. Six months, twelve months, something like that. But they didn't mention anything. Nothing.'

Kartik automatically squirmed, but disguised it by taking a sip from his coke. Ryan was on his second pint. He debated bringing up what he had overheard in the toilets, but thought that would probably just aggravate things further. No one wants to find out that they are shit, do they? The events of the afternoon had solidified the belief that ignorance was bliss. Many people had called Kartik a bit shit: Cameron, Andrew, and most recently Camilla. But they were all messed up in their own way. You couldn't take criticism seriously from someone who cheated on her husband and had sex with you in a hallway in front of imaginary mistresses. That'd be like taking feedback on your personality traits from Charles Manson. But finding out that you are shit from a board of clinical, rigorous, successful professionals? For some reason, that was the sort of judgement that bore weight. And he didn't want to subject those judgements onto Ryan right now, especially considering there was something else on his mind. *If I've just gone through the horrible process of finding out just exactly how little I'm worth, then I'd be a bad person if I were to condemn a friend to a similar judgement*, Kartik reasoned.

He didn't say anything. He sat there, and hoped that there

was a place in the world for people whose only talents were smoking weed and serving coffee.

'How's Cameron getting on?' Ryan asked.

'Yeah, she seems to be doing well. Business end of term right now. Very busy with things. But you know her. Always been busy.'

'Yeah, that's why I like her. What about that girl she's with?'

'Rachel? Yeah, they seem to be getting on well. I thought they may have jumped in too quickly. But they are making it work.'

'Hmm... What about you? How's your love life?'

'Not much really. There was this girl that I was kind of seeing. But I don't know if it's still happening. It's all a bit up in the air.' Kartik had only seen Camilla twice in the past month, and that had been another round of perfunctory sex. She didn't seem to be taking any pleasure in it anymore, but just like a smoker reducing the number of cigarettes, she couldn't quite get out of the habit to stop it entirely. 'Nothing really serious. Just like, you know…'

'Sex?' Ryan said bluntly.

'Yeah.'

'Nice. Get it while you can. Do it all when you're young. No point in settling for one woman when you're what, twenty? Twenty-one?'

'Twenty-two.'

'Twenty-two. Best age, mate. Loved my twenties. Back when I was living in London, the boys and I would be out all the time. Going to bars, meeting women, it was great. I miss it. I did that for almost a decade.' Ryan sighed. He was at his most nostalgic and romantic. 'Things seemed to have changed. It seemed easier back then. There was money moving around, you could get on the property ladder. I used to have a flat in Brixton and the girls wouldn't come to mine because they thought it was too far away and unsafe. They only wanted to date guys who lived in West London. But look at it now. Trendy people moving in, making it all respectable. The house prices around there are through the roof.' Ryan was lost in his memories as he pushed back the rest of his pint. 'Don't get me wrong, I wouldn't want it to be in the state it was in the seventies or eighties. But it was a nice middle ground in the nineties. Exciting without being stale. And you could afford to buy a bloody flat. I remember the first time I took Anna there. She bloody hated it,' he laughed. 'And then suddenly, the wild nights seemed to get scarcer and scarcer and I got more and more serious with her. No more random women, fewer binges, things adjusted. And then Arabella was born, and everything changed irreversibly. I was finally an adult.'

'How did you two meet?'

'At some work event. She had some ceremonial job running an art gallery in Chelsea. Something her dad her set her up with. She came from money, see. I had to work for it. And her dad thought she'd be able to run a business, so he was like, "Here you go, here are the keys, sell some art." And she tried, bless her. But she wasn't very good. Didn't really have a mind for making money. Just spending money,' Ryan laughed to himself, in a way that almost displayed some affection for her.

'Anyway, we were doing some networking event at her gallery. Tracey Emin and that crowd were around. It was a few years after she had got famous with that bloody bed thing—never got it myself. So Anna and I are looking at this sculpture—some fucking modern art monstrosity that looked like a giant cock. It was bright orange, and curved like a dick, but instead of balls, it had these square boxes that looked like tiny houses. And these were blue. And there was some writing on it, some Chinese, or Japanese, or Koran letters on it, probably translated from a takeaway menu or something. And I'm pretending to know about art, describing its reflection on the nature of humanity and how we turn everything into a commodity or something. And Anna is nodding along, also pretending to know what the fuck she was talking about, asking if I could imagine it in my bedroom. Can you believe it? She was trying to sell me this hideous thing.'

He shook his head. 'In the end, it was her that ended up in my bedroom that night, and we've been together ever since.' Ryan lifted up his pint glass and swirled around the dredges, for the first time perhaps seeing the complete passage of time with his wife. 'Some guy ended up buying that sculpture that night for twenty grand.' They both laughed.

'But as I said,' he continued. 'There was money to burn back then, so people spent it on dumb things. Things are different now.' Ryan's wistful remembrance had taken a back seat to melancholy now and Kartik was starting to wish he had been born twenty years earlier. And that he would have made something of his life with that extra time.

'Anyway, let's get another,' Ryan said, already on his feet.

'I was thinking about heading home,' Kartik said.

'Don't be like that. Get a bloody pint down you at least.'

'I don't know. I'm thinking about saving money at the moment. The whole moving out situation and everything.'

'Don't worry about it. I'm buying. Let's make a proper day out of it. When was the last time you had a night out in London?'

'Went to a couple of gigs at Brixton Academy when I was a teenager. Punk and ska and things like that.'

'Not like that. Like a proper night. Bars and clubs. Not chasing after teenage girls with their heads shaved and safety pins in their jeans.'

'Never really have.'

Ryan's face distorted into astonishment. 'Right, let's change that.' Before Kartik could protest any more, Ryan was at the bar getting more drinks. It was going to be a long night.

CHAPTER SIXTEEN

They were in the fourth pub of the day. Maybe the fifth? Ryan couldn't remember. Things were busy now, people coming from work and getting into some serious midweek drinking. The masses were packed tightly around tables, the queue at the bar was endless. They were near Moorgate station, the excitement of the City palpable. He had been drawn towards it, like a moth to a flame, desperate to feel the atmosphere again. He hoped he would run into someone he knew. He longed for the old city talk: the rapid-fire conversation that zig-zagged between important shop talk, light-hearted banter, and the casual objectification of female colleagues and/or bar staff.

But though he recognised the faces, the suits, the watches, and the atmosphere, there was no one there that he actually knew. Kartik was talking to some girls as he queued for the next round (with money Ryan had given him, like he was his bloody son or something) but it didn't seem to be going particularly well. They were probably the same age as him, but there was something about him that seemed very young still. Maybe it was the shirt. It didn't even bloody fit.

No, it wasn't just the shirt. It was the lack of confidence. His approach had been tentative, first making awkward eye contact, and then some terrible small talk, asking if they came to the pub often. It was like he had learnt to talk to women from a badly written TV show.

One of the girls was humouring Kartik, smiling politely, engaging in small talk, but the other was desperately trying to make eye contact with the barman so they could get served and get away.

When Kartik returned, he had a smile on his face. 'See that?'

'What?'

'Chatting to those girls over there.' He pointed to the two girls who were now sitting on the opposite side of the pub.

'Nice work,' Ryan said, trying to shield his drinking partner from his cynicism. 'What are they called?'

Kartik looked at him blankly.

'Got their numbers?'

Another blank look.

'Nothing?'

'The blonde works in finance.'

'We're in the Square Mile. Everyone here works in finance.' Ryan shook his head and sipped his drink. What was this? His sixth? Seventh? It was all going down very well. He was capable of drinking heavily when he needed to, and now seemed like a time when he needed to. Kartik was a couple of pints behind him, but was acting like he was a couple ahead.

'Look, I'll give you a bit of advice,' Ryan said, putting a paternal hand on his protégé. 'You need a bit more confidence. A bit more assertiveness. Don't do that dopey nice-guy thing. No one really buys it or cares. Act like a bit of a prick. Not too much of a prick, just enough to get you noticed.'

'Right,' Kartik said.

'And stop smoking so much weed. Jesus, that shit rots the brain,' Ryan said. Kartik looked uncomfortable. 'Weed's great if you're some surfer or musician on a beach in California, passing your time one hazy day to the next. But here, it just makes you look like you've never grown up.' He finished his pint in a few large gulps. 'Come on, let's go somewhere else.'

CHAPTER SEVENTEEN

Kartik was drinking a pint of water, whilst Ryan knocked back yet another lager. *How did he manage to keep drinking?* Ryan was drunk, but he wasn't collapse-in-your-own-piss-and-vomit kind of drunk. Kartik would have been if he had kept up the same rate.

They were somewhere in Soho now. Ryan had bundled him on the tube at Bank, and then yelled at him a few stops later to get off. 'There's a fucking great place just down the road from here,' he said. It was close to eleven, and they had been drinking solidly since the afternoon.

Shortly after their arrival, Ryan bumped into someone he knew, and Kartik listened whilst they caught up. He had to steady himself by leaning against the wall. Ryan's old acquaintance was wearing an ultramarine suit, which, if anything, made Kartik feel even more nauseous, although he was aware this probably wasn't the man's intention. It was at this point he had decided to take a break from the pints, and move on to water. Ryan had called him a pussy, but he simply could not stomach any more alcohol in his system.

The man in the blue suit appeared less interested in the conversation than Ryan was, who kept slapping his back enthusiastically and trying to bring up anecdotes about the old times. 'You won't believe what this guy used to be like,' Ryan would say to Kartik, as the man shifted restlessly, his feet pointed to the door, like he was about to make a bolt for it any second. 'This man, this man,' Ryan continued, his words starting to slur slightly. 'He was a monster. A fucking animal. You should have seen him with the girls. Some of the girls we used to get…'

The old friend nodded and smiled and engaged in perfunctory conversation, but didn't elaborate further on his days as an animal. It was almost as if he found it embarrassing to be a man in his forties boasting about chasing girls half his age.

Finally, the man had made an excuse to leave—something about a wife and kid—and Kartik was left alone again with Ryan talking about the good old times.

As Ryan spoke he reached into his jacket pocket and pulled out a small plastic bag. 'Fancy some coke?'

'Huh?' he said. He hadn't really been listening.

'Want a line? I'm going for a bump now.'

'No, I'm fine thanks.'

'You sure? It'll be like the good old days.'

'I wasn't around for the good old days,' Kartik insisted, getting a little bit fed up with Ryan's fascination with them. *Had it all really been as great as he made them out to be?*

'Well, you're currently living through your good old days. Never a better time like the present.'

'No, really, I'm good,' Kartik insisted. Ryan shook his head and headed for the toilet. He returned a few minutes later looking more alert, and even chattier.

Kartik decided to go to the bar, because this level of one-way conversation required a drink to get through it.

The bars were getting a bit quieter now. Eleven on a school night was a bit too late for all but the most hard-core drinkers in whatever part of town they were in. He got two more pints, and also decided to get a couple of shots with them this time. He was still spending Ryan's money, but he figured his companion would appreciate the sentiment. He wasn't wrong and Ryan threw back the shot with enthusiasm. Then he continued, 'Kartik, can I talk to you about something? Something personal?'

'Umm…okay?' He felt like this was the entire reason Ryan had invited him out. This was what had been weighing on his mind since that first pint back in Islington. This was what he had been waiting to say.

'This goes nowhere, right? Nobody knows. No one at work. None of my friends. No one. Can I trust you?'

`'Yeah,' Kartik said.

'You can't tell people. Not your friends. Not Cameron. This doesn't go anywhere,' he reiterated.

'No problem.'

'Are you sure I can trust you?'

'I'm sure.' He wasn't sure at all.

'I'm…' Ryan hesitated and scratched the back of his head, a rare sign of indecisiveness. 'I'm having an affair.'

'What?'

'An affair. I'm having an affair.'

'Really?'

'Yeah.'

'Shit.' It didn't surprise Kartik that he was, but it was a surprise he would talk openly about it with him.

'It's been going on for months. Maybe even a couple of years. You lose track of time with these things. I can't help myself. That's why I'm in London today. I was meant to meet up with her tonight. But she cancelled.'

'I'm assuming Anna doesn't know?'

'I don't think so. But I think she must suspect. She may have been a shit art dealer, but she's not stupid.'

`'Don't you think you should, you know, stop it?' Kartik

said, knowing that this thought process had obviously already crossed Ryan's mind.

'I try to. And she's married as well. And we always tell each other when we meet that it will be the last time. That we won't do it again. But for some reason we can't help ourselves. There's something about her. We used to work together. She's younger, so much more exciting than Anna.'

As Ryan talked, a terrible thought was building in the darkest recesses of Kartik's mind. Something terrifying. *It couldn't be...*

'What's her name?' Kartik asked.

'Huh?'

'The girl. What's her name?'

'Penelope Sandler. Why?'

Penelope? Fuck. 'No reason.'

'We both know it's wrong. But it's worse for me. She doesn't have kids. I've got Arabella. I feel guiltier about being a bad father than I do for cheating on Anna. And it's been building up inside for so long. And like I said, I think Anna's starting to catch on. Besides, you know what the worst thing is? I think Anna may be having an affair as well. Kartik, are you listening?'

'Yeah.' *Anna was Camilla. Camilla was Anna. This couldn't get any worse.*

'What do you think?'

'I think it's time we get more shots.'

PART TWO

CHAPTER EIGHTEEN

The sun was rising outside and the sound of the early morning traffic could already be heard: street cleaners, early morning commuters, perhaps a few revellers only just getting in. Ryan's face was still numb and his nose was blocked. Both nostrils were completely clogged up, like two collapsed caves. He could only breathe through his mouth.

He checked on the girl. She was asleep now, and would have looked peaceful if she didn't look like such a mess. They hadn't even got under the bed sheets, and now she lay naked and exposed, curled up in a ball. He put a duvet over her. His first, and likely last, charitable act of the day.

Sleep was an impossibility for him. He had been trying, but every time he started to nod off, he automatically tried, and failed, to inhale through his nose, waking himself. The clock by the bed said six o'clock. It was going to be a long, long day.

Throwing on his boxer shorts, he dragged himself to the en-suite bathroom and looked at himself in the mirror. He'd aged about ten years in one night. His pupils were small and unfocused, dancing in bloodshot eyes. His eye sockets looked like they had fallen down into the multiple bags below them.

His nose was red and blue with veins. He was fat, he had too many chins, and his skin was a mess. Spots had started to break out on his forehead. He had a gut, and recently he found walking both painful and exhausting. He was in the very slow, but very real, process of falling apart. Ryan was what decay would look like if you threw it in nice clothes, gave it a haircut, and stuffed it into an office.

The bathroom was small but clean. He felt out of place in it.

Pressing his index finger against his left nostril, he blew hard through his right. There was a disgusting sloppy sound as a mixture of yellow and white semi-liquid was launched into the sink. He looked down at the horrible combination of snot and cocaine.

He splashed his face with water, cleaned the mess from the sink, and headed to the small living room with an adjoining kitchenette. There was another body on that sofa. It had half-crawled out of a cheap suit and had covered itself in pillow to keep warm.

He went to the kitchen tap and drank two glasses of water, one after another. On the fridge was a picture of Penelope and one of her friends on the top of Kilimanjaro, kept in place by a strawberry-shaped magnet. His depression deepened.

The flat belonged to Penelope, but the girl in the bed wasn't her—just some random girl that had taken an interest in him when she noticed he had coke on him. Originally, he had tried to set Kartik up with her—she was the same age as him after all—but the kid was too drunk and incoherent to flirt, so he'd decided he'd keep her entertained instead. After a few more drinks and a few more lines (Kartik abstaining from the latter like a priest) the three of them had jumped into a taxi towards Old Street, and to the flat that they all currently occupied.

Although it belonged to Penelope, Ryan thought of it like it was partly his. He had a spare key that she had given him, so it made it easier for them to meet. This is where they had conducted their affairs. This was their base. This was what they really meant when they had told their respective partners that they were on an overnight work trip. This was where they had spent some of the best nights of their lives, rarely leaving the bedroom, forgetting their commitments, forgetting the responsibilities of family and work. They would spend hours in bed together, making love for hours, only resting to catch their breath. Together they constructed their own universe: a mess of bedsheets, wine bottles, and cigarettes. They would talk about a life somewhere without traffic, without emails, without phones ringing in their pockets every five minute, a feudal kingdom with a population of two. This was where they had come to forget the world existed. This was where they came to get lost in oblivion. But those days seemed to be coming to an end.

She was with her husband somewhere now, at a country retreat for a long weekend, a chance to focus on her faltering marriage. It had been a surprise excursion, hurled on her by her husband. That was why she hadn't been able to tell him about it until the last minute. That was why he had ended up roaming the streets of London with Kartik and sleeping with a twenty-something year old girl rather than Penelope. Before she had left she had told Ryan that she needed to get away from him, that he was a poison, that he was ruining her chance of happiness.

So she'd be in some Cotswolds country-house, trying to re-establish a connection with the husband—a backbench Tory MP in a seat so safe he'd barely even talked to his constituents in the past five years. Next year, when the election came, he'd campaign for about a week, and still gain a majority of 30,000 votes. In the meantime, the prick was denying Ryan time with Penelope. The thought of them together made him sick. Thinking of Penelope being with someone else, even her husband (especially her husband) made him madder than the thought of Anna having sex with another man.

The heap on the sofa behind him stirred a bit, but didn't wake up. Ryan felt envious of Kartik, at least he was able to sleep off his hangover. The kid would be feeling bad when he awoke, but it was doubtful he would be consumed by the all-encompassing sense of doom that only a night railing lines of coke could produce.

The flat felt cramped and busy and messy, so he headed downstairs to a shop across the road. The city was already warming up the motor of its productivity engine. Some of the brightest and most proactive commuters were shuffling out of the tube station to their offices, cup of coffee in one hand, laptop in the other. The Old Street area had seen a radical shift in the past few years. It had been a perpetual building site for a while, with new offices and flats being constructed at lightning speed. And as soon as these new buildings were complete, they would be swarmed by tech start-ups, a few bearded programmers in flannel shirts and horn-rimmed glasses desperately coding away, dreaming (hoping, praying?) of becoming the new Jobs, or Zuckerberg, or Page, one skinny flat-white at a time. The agile start-up scene had been dodging and weaving its way to semi-prosperity. At the same time the City, only a few hundred metres down the road, had been delivered a sucker punch in the form of the financial crisis.

He went to the closest corner shop and picked up the morning paper and a bottle of water, not because he wanted either, but just because he had nothing better to do. He crossed back over the road and re-entered the flat. He tried to read the paper, but couldn't focus on any of the words. He just stared at the pages, failing to take any of it in.

There was something about David Cameron attacking Labour's handling of the economic crisis, a story that Ryan felt he had read a million times before. The election was only seven months away, and things were getting tense. Every day, Gordon Brown looked more and more haggard, like a man who knows he is headed for defeat. Anna always complained that he shouldn't have been there in the first place, that there should have been a snap-election the moment Blair stepped down, so that all the liars and freeloaders of the Labour party could be cleansed by the supposed purity of the Conservatives. Whilst Ryan didn't share his wife's belief in the infallibility of the Tories —they were politicians after all— they were at least on the side of free-flowing capital. His preference was always money over politics, and Cameron at least sounded like he was on the side of the markets, unlike the restrictive Brown and his cronies. 'Bolshevik Brown' was how he was known within the Stanfields' circle of friends.

Political thought was a bit too much for him in his current state, so his mind wandered back to last night, and the girl in his bed. He thought about waking her up for morning sex, but he didn't have the motivation. He didn't have the motivation to do anything, not even sleep, so he crawled back onto the bed, drifting in and out of consciousness for the rest of the morning, images of Penelope and her Tory husband swimming in his head.

When he awoke again, at eleven in the morning, both the girl and Kartik had vanished.

CHAPTER NINETEEN

It all started to go very wrong when Kartik tried to get through the ticket station. He was in no state to try and navigate the complex task of boarding a train, and the man in the uniform in front of him wasn't helping in the slightest. Not only was the man not helping him, but he was being a downright obstruction.

'That's not the right ticket, mate.' The small, round, bald head sticking out the top of the uniform said. He was a big lad, the sort of person who could make a statement like that sound like a threat.

'What do you mean it's not the right ticket?'

'It's not a ticket. It's a receipt.'

Kartik looked down at the small orange and cream cardboard rectangle in his hand. He had tried to feed it through the ticket gates twice, but both times it had flashed red instead of green. When it came to security gates, a red light was not a good thing. It meant something bad. Even Kartik knew that. Green was good, red was bad. A five-year-old knew that. And Kartik knew himself to be at least a little bit smarter than a five-year-old, even when running on very little sleep and suffering an almighty hangover. But even though red was bad, Kartik didn't really understand why it was going red. That had prompted the bald man in the uniform to come over and try and sort out his mess. A few people behind him were muttering at the hold-up.

'It's the only thing I've got,' Kartik said, still looking at what he had thought up until recently was a ticket.

'Well, if you don't have the ticket, you're going to have to buy a new one.'

'But I got a return,' Kartik protested. It was a pretty feeble excuse, like a scolded child wailing 'that's not fair'.

'Move away from the gate and go buy another one, mate. You're blocking the way.' The bald man in the uniform didn't look like he was going to debate the subject any longer.

Kartik moved away from the ticket gate and back into the main concourse of King's Cross. He had five minutes to get on the train, or it would be a forty-five-minute wait for the next. Not the longest wait in the world, but he was feeling like someone had released a pack of rodents inside his skull, so any delay, no matter how minor, was most unwelcome. He was still in his suit from the interview yesterday, which was creased and untidy. His hair was a mess. He looked, and felt, like the end of the world.

In the end, he missed the train he was meant to get on, so he bought a ticket for the next one before sitting himself down in a stymied heap on one of the public benches. He closed his eyes and whatever was left functioning in his brain kicked into gear. *Anna was Camilla. Camilla was Anna.* It all made sense now, in some horrible, twisted, terrifying way. He'd been sleeping with his friend's wife.

Wait. Wait. What? What did you just say? Your friend's wife? Your friend's wife?

Were they really friends? That was an odd thing to contemplate. *You've only known the guy for a few weeks, and for all intents and purposes the only reason Ryan spent any time with you is because he wants access to Cameron.*

Ryan was a parasite. He used other people for his own needs. He feeds of the talent off others. All he wants is the link to Cameron. You're a bridge. And he's walking over you. Not a particularly well-constructed bridge, mind. You're that ropey old wooden bridge from the end of Temple of Doom. Soon your limbs are going to snap and you're all going to fall into a river full of crocodiles. And you're going to bring down Cameron, and Rachel, and Ryan, and Camilla, and Arabella, and everyone. Somehow, without particularly doing much, you're going to ruin everyone's lives around you.

That was his thought process and he closed his eyes and drifted into a state of welcomed oblivion.

'Rough night?'

Kartik snapped back to the real world.

'Huh?'

'Did you have a big night?'

A girl was sitting in front of him, a small smile on her face. How much time had passed? Had he fallen asleep?

'Yeah, a little bit,' he said, wiping away what he hoped wasn't drool from the side of his face, and shaking images of bridges, and crocodiles, and ruined lives from his mind.

'I think you dozed off. I didn't want you to miss your train. It's leaving in a few minutes.' The girl nodded towards the timetable board on the wall. The train he had a ticket for left in seven minutes.

'Oh, thanks,' he said, straightening up his suit and praying he didn't smell. To his surprise, the girl got up with him.

'Come on, I'm on the same train. You look like you need some help today.' She picked up his bag for him. They made their way over the barriers, and to Kartik's great relief, the light flashed green and the gate swung open. He was Moses parting the Red Sea. A smug smile towards the bald man in the uniform, who was still presiding over his small station of the world, was returned by a barely recognised look of disdain. Kartik had conquered the

Pharaohs of Egypt. The Jerusalem of carriage 3, seat 47 awaited.

'I saw your argument with that guy earlier,' the girl said as they walked down the platform.

'When I saw you fall asleep I didn't want you to miss another one.'

'Thanks. That's very kind of you,' he said sincerely as they walked down the platform.

'Nice suit,' she said, looking him up and down.

'I had a job interview yesterday,' he replied.

'I see. Well, by the state of you this morning I'd guess it either went very well or very badly.'

'Which do you think?' Kartik asked.

'Well, you seem like a very respectable, likable young man, so I'm going to go with the former.'

'I wish those in the interview yesterday had such a favourable opinion.'

'So it went…'

'Badly,' Kartik confirmed. 'Astronomically badly.'

They boarded the train together and sat at an empty table. She was short, with very dark, raven-hair that fell just beyond her shoulders. She spoke with a northern accent, maybe Yorkshire. She had a sharp, angular nose, and large brown eyes. Below the right eye was a small patch of scar tissue, like that of a burn, which gave her face an intriguing asymmetry.

'I'm sorry to hear that.'

'Oh, well. I don't think I really wanted the job anyway.'

'What was it for?'

'A financial events company.'

'Sounds exciting. And what were you to be doing at this financial events company?'

He answered with a shrug.

'I feel as though we've found the root of your problems right there. It's important to know what you would be doing at a company before going to an interview.'

'I think I went along to make myself feel productive.'

'So what do you do now that makes you feel so unproductive?' She looked at him smiling, a glint in her eye.

'I make coffee.'

'A barista?'

'Yep. Nine months.'

'And are you a good barista?'

'I'm not sure my heart is in it.'

'I read a quote somewhere. It said that whatever you do, you must do it to the best of your ability. So if you're a heart surgeon, save as many lives as possible. And if you work in Burger King, you should strive to be the best burger flipper in the world.'

'You think I should apply for a job at Burger King?'

'I don't think you're quite following.'

'Sorry, I was being facetious.'

'Right.'

There was a pause in the conversation, and Kartik felt like he might be messing things up.

'What do you do?' he asked.

'I'm a programmer for an independent cinema.'

'And are you the best programmer working for an independent cinema in the world?'

'I'm trying to be. But I'm trying to move into filmmaking as well.'

'Really?' Kartik said, genuinely interested.

'Yeah. I'm working with a director down in Brixton at the moment, trying to get a short film off the ground.'

'That definitely sounds more interesting than working for a financial events company. What's the film about?' Kartik asked as they sped through the urban expanse of north London.

'It's a comedy about a pair of passive aggressive neighbours fighting over the hedge line in their back garden, with both parties slowly encroaching on what the other believes to their rightful property,' the girl started explaining, going into full pitch mode. 'Slowly they both start to go insane, and decide the only way to solve it is to destroy each other's gardens so there is no longer anything to fight over, and they can get on with their lives.

'Like the Cold War?'

'Yes, but with more visits to Homebase. We're working on the script and have just got the funding approved. Next, we need a cast and some locations and we should be ready to shoot. All being well, we'll have something finished early next year.'

'How do you get into something like that?' he asked.

'You just have to go after it,' the girl said rather nonchalantly. It was the sort of unspecific advice that Kartik would have usually found irritating, but from this girl felt like the most brilliant wisdom.

'That's the sort of thing I think I'd enjoy doing,' he said. 'Sure sounds better than the stuff I've been looking at.'

'I don't know. I'm thinking about packing it all in and working in a non-specific role at a financial events company.'

'Well, the interview process isn't very pleasant.'

'Why were you even interviewing there in the first place?'

Kartik filled her in on the situation with Ryan, and his attempts to entice Cameron, and how he was being used as a makeweight in the meantime. He was careful to omit any mention of Camilla, or Anna, or whatever she was meant to be called.

'It doesn't sound like this Ryan guy knows you very well.'

'He's a recruiter. He sees everyone as a number or a quota or something.'

'And he's your friend?'

'Yeah, I guess so.'

'Sounds like an odd friendship to me.'

'You've got no idea.'

The girl twisted her hair a little bit. 'It sounds to me like he's taking advantage of you. Or using you.'

'Yeah, maybe. I think he's using Cameron even more. But she's smart enough to know what she's doing.'

'And you?'

'Me? I'm the guy that couldn't even board a train at King's Cross.'

The girl smiled and then gazed out the window for a while, looking at nothing. They passed gentle rolling hills, small commuter towns, bored sheep and endless fields of wheat.

'You seem close to this Cameron. Is she your…?' For the first time the girl didn't look one hundred percent sure of herself.

'My…?' Kartik could have helped her out, but a sudden thrill of controlling the situation came over him. Make her ask about it. Have her poke her head out of the foxhole first.

'Girlfriend?'

'No, nothing like that. She's got her own girlfriend.'

'Oh, right,' the girl said, seemingly satisfied with this response. 'So do you…?' Again the question hung around her lips like an autumn leaf stubbornly refusing to fall.

'Do I what?'

'Do you have a girlfriend?'

Kartik had a flashback of Camilla in his head, and almost made the mistake of saying 'not really' but managed to stop himself and said, 'Not at the moment.'

'Okay,' said the girl. Kartik, developing a long-dormant sense of self-confidence, couldn't help but feel that what she actually wanted to say was 'good'.

They looked out of the window for a little bit longer. Then the girl excused herself and headed to the bathroom. When she had disappeared at the other end of the carriage, he sat back, and mentally high-fived himself. He couldn't help but think he had somehow managed to turn around what had started as an abjectly dismal couple of days into a more productive narrative.

When she returned, any lingering awkwardness she may had had about the girlfriend comment had faded and they were back to talking about films, and their lives, and all the other small things that make the world go around.

For the next half-hour the conversation flowed easily and smoothly. There were no awkward pauses, or looks of embarrassment, or a sense of regret at sitting next to each other. He talked about his job, his friends, his family, without feeling nervous about coming across as a loser. He played down the casual drug use and kept avoiding any mention of Ryan's unfaithful wife, but apart from that, he was surprisingly honest.

The simplicity of conversation came from the girl. She had an affability about her that Kartik rarely encountered. She was twenty-seven, five years older than Kartik, a fact that for some reason put Kartik at ease. The more they talked, the more he enjoyed her company. It was only as the train headed past the small town of Royston that he realised he didn't yet know her name. He made a mental note that this was an item of significant importance that he should not forget to ask.

They pulled up at Cambridge still deep in conversation. The girl pulled a large cream coat around her and Kartik gathered their bags. They left the train and headed outside.

The sun was already low in the winter sky, a streak of red sunlight piercing through thin clouds. They stood by the taxi rank next to the station and looked at each other.

'So,' Kartik said.

'So?' The girl responded.

'So, what are you doing now?'

'I'm going home.' She pulled the coat tight around her to shield against the creeping cold. Kartik only had his blazer over his wrinkled shirt and he could feel the biting winter winds that were both refreshing but, because of his hangover, made him feel slightly sick.

'I thought youmight want to go get a drink?'

She looked him up and down. 'I didn't think you'd really be in the mood for a drink.'

'I think maybe I'm getting a second wind.'

'It's a nice offer. But I think I'm going to have to decline. This time.'

'Just this time?'

They shuffled forward as a middle-aged businessman got in the taxi in front of them.

'I'm not completely ruling out seeing you again,' the girl said gently nudging her shoulder into his.

'Oh, really?'

'Well, it hasn't been entirely unpleasant.' She pulled out her mobile and they exchanged numbers.

Kartik was about to add a contact into his phone book when he looked up. As if telegraphing him, the girl extended her hand, 'Freddy.'

'Freddy?'

'Yes.'

'Really?'

'It's short for Frederica,' Freddy said instinctively and wearily.

'I'm Kartik.'

'Kartik?'

'Yes.'

'And you had the nerve to question my name?'

'Good point.'

'Isn't that an Indian name?'

'Yes.'

'But you're... you're white?'

'Yes?'

'Why do you have an—'

'Look, why don't we meet up at some point next week

and I'll tell you all about it,' Kartik interrupted, not wanting to spoil the moment.

'We could.'

'We could? Does that mean we should?'

'We should.'

'So we will?'

Freddy laughed. 'Yes, we will.'

They stood there, gently swaying, neither entirely sure what to do next. Their thoughts were interrupted by the irate voice of the taxi driver. 'Oi, you getting in or what?'

'Call me,' Freddy said as she went for a kiss on the cheek. There was a deliberate last-minute tilt of her head, resulting in the edge of her lips meeting his. Then she glided into the Hackney Carriage and drifted off into the dark winter afternoon, leaving Kartik in a mixed state of anticipation , confusion, cold, and soft elation. A second taxi pulled up next to him and the driver signalled him to get in. He waved it on and went to the cycle rack where the occasionally trusty steed was locked up.

The bike swung onto the road, and for the first time in a long time it didn't feel like there was anything wrong with it. The pedals felt secure and the wheels turned without friction or buckling. He rode with the wind behind him, preventing his eyes from watering. The cars around him felt like objects of little consequence, and he zig-zagged between them with an irresponsible nonchalance that made him feel more relaxed than he had felt in months. He passed Foster's Mill, abandoned and decayed and soon to be turned into commuter-belt flats, and headed in the direction of the cycle bridge that would take him over railway tracks and towards Mill Road. Down the other side of the bridge cars were dodged, red lights run, and potholes avoided. His shirt, now untucked from his trousers, flapped out from behind him, cracking like a whip every time it got caught in the wind.

And as if things couldn't get any better, he managed to

sneak in before Louise had gotten back from work (no doubt working hard by downing several large Gin and Tonics with clients), so he managed to fit in some productive hours destroying Andrew's Liverpool with Chelsea on FIFA. As Didier Drogba scored his third goal and clinched the game, Kartik relaxed and felt a long way from the ticket gate debacle at King's Cross.

CHAPTER TWENTY

November Rain was playing on the radio, and November rain was falling outside Ryan's office. It was a miserable day. He didn't want to go home, but he couldn't avoid it. Such was life. There are some things in life that you can side step forever: the slight pain in his back? Yeah, he could ignore that for a bit. The throbbing on the side of his temples? He was pretty sure that had been a constant for the past twenty years. He had no problem shrugging that off. But his wife? And his child? It was very tough to dodge those commitments.

The week of Arabella's suspension had been the worst. Anna had been forced to stay at home, which she had agreed to do with reluctance. Ryan had managed to restrain himself from pointing out that she didn't have any other commitments anyway, and the only thing she would be prevented from doing were her coffee mornings and shopping sprees with her friends during the day. Staying at home had put her in a foul mood, and her relationship with her daughter was at an all-time low. Arabella actively cowered from her mother now, petrified to put a foot out of place. It was good in a way, because the fear had resulted in an unparalleled streak of good behaviour: she was quiet, clean, studied from home, and towed the line like a well-drilled soldier.

But for all the positives that came from the good behaviour, the girl was missing something. Her bright eyes had dimmed slightly, her smile rare, her laughter non-existent. She had been systematically and psychologically programmed by her mother into a life without happiness.

Obviously, in Anna's eyes the blame for Arabella's behaviour and suspension lay directly at Ryan's feet, so now when he came home, he had to face a woman that hated him as well as a daughter that was a shadow of her former lively self.

And on top of this, he was more certain than ever that Anna was having an affair. It was the smell that gave her away. On certain days, when he came home from work and she was being particularly evasive, there was a masculine taint in the air: a light whiff of cheap aftershave or deodorant that was at odds with the flowery scent that Anna usually suffused their bedroom in. He admitted to himself that this was not an exact science for detection, and his methods were crude at best. However, every time he suspected he was just being paranoid, the scent would suddenly return. And besides, if he was immoral enough to conduct a long-term affair, then why wouldn't Anna be as well? In many ways, she was more manipulative and sly than he was.

It had been three weeks since Arabella had been accepted back into the school and since Arabella's return, Ryan was certain the masculine smell in the bedroom was more noticeable than ever.

Still, he had no idea how to approach the topic, or even if he wanted to bring it up at all. He didn't know the extent of Anna's knowledge about Penelope, and the entire situation could unravel if he tried to point blame, especially if he was wrong in his assumptions. He had picked up a few stones, but for the moment he had managed to resist tossing them around his glass house.

He reluctantly switched off his computer and headed out of his office. He passed the monthly quota board on his way out; at least things were going well at work. The board was covered in numbers written in green, which indicated a value above the required target. There were only a couple of numbers still in the red, but these were far outnumbered by the green. He had got through the process of getting rid of most of the underperforming employees, and only the more capable ones were still around. It had also helped that the company had just signed a massive advertising deal with a major Premier League club, resulting in unprecedented exposure and the largest influx of inbound clients and candidates that Ryan could remember. As a result, his team, bar one or two employees, were smashing their targets. For a country still deep in recession, and companies bitterly unwilling to take on new staff, it was a small miracle that they were making such impressive numbers. Revenue, productivity, profit, growth, for Fusion Vision they were all up, even in a country that was slowly sinking to its knees. Briefly he allowed himself to feel a bit of happiness as he nodded towards Philip, an acknowledgement of the hard work he was putting in. No, wait, it was in acknowledgement of the hard work *his team* were putting in. It seemed the more messed up his personal life got, the better things got at work. His work/life balance was a seesaw, with a big, diabetic fat kid on one side, and an anorexic, bulimic supermodel on the other.

Driving home in the dark, he tried to muster a positive attitude for his family. He'd be agreeable, relaxed, and would treat Anna with deferential respect. He wouldn't give her any excuse to find fault with him or Arabella.

It was a game-plan that lasted for a monumental thirty seconds after his arrival. He forgot to take his shoes off at the front door, and had to face the wrath of his wife. He did his best to placate her, but he felt like whatever he said, whatever he did, she would just get angrier. It was like trying to hold together the San Andreas Fault with duct tape.

Once the shoes were removed and the muddy footprints mopped up, Ryan evaded his wife's gaze and headed to his daughter's bedroom.

The door was decisively shut, and he gave a tentative knock.

'Come in,' came Arabella's cautious voice.

He gently pushed the door open and stepped into the bright pink room. She was hunched over her desk, her laptop and the text books, which had cost a small fortune, in front of her. Her eyes didn't look up from the books. She was making a deliberate effort to show how studious she was.

'How's it going?' Ryan navigated his way around the stuffed horses, bears, and what seemed like most of the animal kingdom that populated her room. He sat on the bed next to her desk.

'Fine,' came the monosyllabic reply.

'What are you working on?'

'Science.'

'Any particular science?' Ryan leant over Arabella's screen. There was a cross section diagram of a planets leaf.

'Biology. Photosynthesis.'

'Always a favourite of mine.'

'Do you know what leaves use to absorb light energy?'

'Well, if I told you, then you wouldn't learn on your own, would you?'

'So, you don't actually know?' Arabella said, turning toward him for the first time. She was trying not to smile.

'Well, of course I know. But you need to go through all these books and learn for yourself,' Ryan said tapping the text books.

She turned back to her pink laptop, hammered the keys quickly and then turned back to the bed. 'Chlorophyll.'

So much for the expensive text books. 'You know, when I was young we didn't have Google to help with our school work.'

'What is the name of the cell that absorbs light and that contains chloroplasts?' Arabella asked, ignoring Ryan's wistful stroll down the memory lane of a pre-internet age. For her, it was probably like trying to image a world without gravity.

'I have no idea,' Ryan admitted. This all sounded like advanced science for a ten-year-old. At least he was getting his money's worth when it came to the quality of education the school provided.

She chewed on the end of her pencil and screwed up her face in concentration. 'It's the palisade cell,' she announced, pronouncing the cell's name slowly and deliberately. She hadn't used Google this time. After Ryan's gentle taunt, demonstrating her powers of recollection without the laptop was important now. She had a point to prove.

'And what type of sugar is produced by the planet as a result of photosynthesis?'

'I know this one,' Ryan said, surprised at himself. 'Glucose.'

'Correct,' Arabella said, clapping twice. 'You get a gold star.' She had a page of golden stickers in one of her files. She peeled one off and stuck it to his shirt collar. 'Only the smartest people in my class get a gold star.'

He squeezed the star onto his collar to ensure it would stick. In a strange way, it felt better than all the green numbers on the sales boards. His daughter was facing her desk again, tiny fingers flying over the keyboard like it was an extension of her body. For her, using a computer was as natural as breathing. He remembered when his own father had gotten their first home computer, a Macintosh 128k, in the mid-80s.

He had been around thirteen or fourteen, and using the keyboard and the monitor in tandem had felt completely alien. He had to keep his eyes locked on the keys below him, frantically searching for the next letter to press. There were no arrow keys, and no numbers, and the letters were arranged in some kind of bizarre act of randomness with no planning or design. A typed and printed thousand-word report on the D-Day landings had taken him four hours. If he had had Arabella's typing speed, along with the small help of an internet search engine, he would probably have finished it in a matter of minutes. He admired the efficiency of the modern world sometimes. It was just a pity so many of the people in it were so lazy.

He looked down at the star on his collar. 'Thank you, sweetie.'

'I didn't think you liked helping me with my homework.'

'I always like helping with your homework. Why do you say that?'

'It's usually mum that helps. Well, Iwona, really. But mum helps sometimes as well.'

'Well, I'm very busy with work at the moment.'

'Then you should stop going to work,' Arabella stated, as if this were not only a feasible, but the expected thing to do. 'Then you would have more time to spend on the biology homework with me. It's better than work.'

'It certainly is. But I need to work in order to buy you nice things. And you need to do your biology homework so you can get good grades, so you can get a good job and then you will be able to buy yourself nice things. Then I can retire.'

'What does retire mean?'

'It's when you don't work anymore.'

'Oh, retire. That sounds good. I want to retire. Can we retire together?' She practised the new word, experimenting with the sound, pronouncing it slightly differently both times to see which would fit better.

'I would love to,' Ryan said, putting his arm around his daughter. Her small frame was slightly trembling, even though the room was warm. Her arms were bony and slender, and for the first time in years, Ryan was reminded how fragile his daughter could be.

'So, are you going to help me with the rest of my homework?' Her eyes looked up at him expectantly.

'Sure I will.'

'Are you going to help me with my homework every night?'

'I probably won't be able to do every night. But I'll try to help out when I can. How about that?'

Arabella nodded animatedly.

'Looks like I'm turning over a new leaf, eh?' Ryan waited for the laughter to come from his daughter. It didn't.

'You know, a new leaf,' he repeated, pointing to the picture of the leaf on the computer screen and nudging Arabella's shoulder. 'Get it? Turning over a new *leaf*.'

She fixed him with an unimpressed stare. 'That's not funny.'

'It is a little bit, though.'

'No. No it's not.' The statement was definite and unyielding.

'Okay, maybe it's not. What's the next question?'

For the next hour, the two of them worked their way through several chapters of biology, before moving on to a bit of maths. Ryan found he was more useful on the latter part of the homework than the former but realised that as long as he threw himself into the project with enthusiasm, Arabella was able to take care of the actual answers.

When he had left her room, he had not only gotten her ready for the following day at school, they had managed to finish her assignments that she had due for the following week. She was then transferred into the care of Anna, who helped prepared her for bed. His wife even gave him a rare smile when she saw how much homework she had done, a sure-fire way for the Stanfields to get back in the good books of Mrs. Scott-Howell.

As he headed into their pristine bedroom, Ryan questioned why he had wanted to avoid his family earlier in the day. All he had to do was put a little effort in, show a bit of kindness, do his duty as a father, and he would be able to turn this ship around.

A wave of positivity washed over him as he brushed his teeth in the en-suite. His face in the mirror still looked haggard and tired, but there were muscles operating there that had been dormant for quite a while. The tissue on his cheeks was pushing upwards. He was smiling a genuine smile. Maybe things weren't so bad?

He spat out the remaining toothpaste and rinsed his mouth out. The tube of toothpaste was finished so he pressed the foot-pedal that opened the lid of the bathroom bin and tossed it in. The lid did not fall again. It stood rooted upwards just like Ryan. The mounting positivity drained from him. His eyes were fixed on something small jutting out under an empty bottle of mouth wash and loo roll. It was well hidden, but the corrugated edges, the half silver, half luminous pink design was unmistakable to anyone over the age of fourteen.

He hadn't used a condom with Anna for years. What the hell was a wrapper for one doing in his bathroom toilet?

CHAPTER TWENTY-ONE

If it wasn't for the fact that it stank of cigarette smoke, the interior of the car would have been lovely. Firm leather seats, sleek dashboard, high ceiling, plenty of room for his feet. Above the dashboard a screen displayed the internal workings of the vehicle as a 2D cross-section. When they pulled away from the kerb, you could see the engine relaxing into second, and then third gear in real time. He had two cup holders on his side door. Two cup holders? What sort a passenger would be travelling with multiple open beverages? The Range Rover was not short on luxury.

Yet the issue still remained that the place stank of cigarette smoke. And the driver, Ryan Stanfield, was not looking too great either.

Kartik picked up a cigarette butt that had fallen onto the edge of his seat. It had burned into the upholstery. Ryan looked down at it, shrugged at its superficiality, and continued driving. A distinct smell of booze was mixing with the tobacco smoke, which would explain why Ryan's diving could be described as erratic at best. He only had one hand on the steering wheel. The muscles on his forearm tense, the fingers, clasped tightly around the wheel, white. The other hand was repeatedly stroking his chin. His eyes were attempting to focus on the road, but kept wandering with a will of their own, causing the car to wobble inside the lane.

'Are you okay?' Kartik asked. He wasn't scared. Not yet. But the situation had potential.

'Fine,' Ryan grunted. Kartik didn't know much about what was going on. He had been at work when he had received a text from Ryan saying he needed to speak about something urgent. Kartik had agreed to meet at 5pm when his shift ended. Ryan had insisted that he meet him somewhere he could be picked up by car. Upon finishing work, Kartik had walked down King's Parade, past the looming outline of King's College, and met Ryan who was parked close to Mill Lane. They had pulled out of Mill Lane and then down Silver Street, crossing the river via the same bridge they had drunk under the night they had gone punting. To their right was the Mathematical Bridge, to their left were rows of chained punts, bobbing by the Mill Pond, all but abandoned in the dark November nights.

He had assumed that Ryan had wanted to talk about job opportunities. Kartik had unsurprisingly not heard back from the financial events company, and it had been a few weeks since he'd had any contact with Ryan or Aaron. In fact, he hadn't heard from Ryan since the night after the interview when they had both gotten incredibly drunk. But this had suited Kartik for two reasons: he had been spending most of his free time with Freddy in the initial stages of a relationship that had accelerated so quickly it had already become semi-serious; and because Kartik was terrified that Ryan would discover his wife's indiscretions.

But it was clear this was not about job opportunities. This was something different. This was something worse. Something much worse. Flashbacks of being sprawled out in an airy corridor, Anna Camilla Stanfield yelling nonsensically on top of him, appeared in his mind. He cleared his throat, partly to get away from the thick smoke, partly because he couldn't clear his mind.

The car rolled forward, in an uncontrolled manner. It stalled at a set of lights.

'Bugger,' Ryan muttered, putting the car back into first gear. His hands clawed over the silver gearstick, not able to find it at first. It was the sort of blind grappling of a learner driver still adjusting to changing gears without looking down.

'Are you sure you're okay to drive?' Kartik asked again. Ryan grunted in response. They headed past Darwin College and towards Newnham Common. Illuminated by portable floodlights, a group of students were working through a cross-fit session on the muddy grass.

'So, any word on where we are headed?' Kartik could already guess the answer.

'I thought we'd go and pay my wife a little visit,' Ryan said. He snarled at the mention of his spouse like a dog, his grip tightening on the steering wheel.

Fear washed over Kartik, and he was pretty certain his heart stopped for at least three or four beats. He felt off-balance despite the fact he was sitting down, as if he could slip off his seat and roll under the moving wheels of the vehicle. Momentarily, he thought this wouldn't be such a bad way to die. He struggled to focus and he felt his eyes cloud over, a white mist, like that of an early autumn morning, hung in his field of vision.

'Remember what I said about Anna when we were in London a few weeks ago?'

Kartik swallowed. 'What about her?'

'Don't play dumb. You know what I'm talking about.'

'Yeah, I think so.' Kartik felt that there was still the slimmest possibility that his friend was talking about something else, so he avoided mentioning the word 'cheating'. That would have been the final nail in his coffin.

They were driving down the residential roads of Newnham now, a route that Kartik knew only too well. He rubbed his knee unconsciously as they passed the point he had come off his bike a couple of months before. He was pretty sure he still had the ripped pair of jeans lying around somewhere, a souvenir of his stupidity. A stupidity that was now catching up with him.

Just before they arrived at the house, Ryan pulled the car over and switched off the engine. It was a poor attempt at parking, the back end of the Range Rover sticking out into the road at an awkward angle, but Kartik decided not to mention anything. They sat in silence, Ryan staring at the gravel driveway that lead up to his house. From their positioning, fifty metres or so away, they couldn't see directly into the house. Could Kartik make a run for it? To disappear? To immigrate to South America and never be seen again?

He realised he wasn't supposed to know where Ryan lived. 'I'm assuming one of these houses is yours?'

Ryan didn't take his eyes off the driveway. His breathing was heavy, and he wasn't paying attention to anything but what lay directly in front of him.

'There! See that?' Ryan suddenly exclaimed.

'What?'

'Look!' Ryan pointed towards the house. Through the foliage that covered the front of the house could be glimpsed a light. Kartik wasn't sure if it had always been there or if it had just been turned on. Was there movement inside? Impossible to tell.

'Come on.' Ryan stumbled out of the driver side door, with a total lack of grace and coordination. Kartik followed, feebly protesting that this may not be the greatest idea in the world. But his friend was not listening. He marched on with a single-minded determination. Terror was still rushing through Kartik's body, but for some reason he followed, as if dragged on by a self-annihilating curiosity.

When they got to the edge of the driveway, Ryan crouched by a bush and yanked Kartik down by his side. The street was quiet and there was no one else around to see them acting like criminals. They had a better view of the illuminated window now. It was on the third floor and a silhouetted figure was moving around behind the curtains. Kartik knew this to be Ryan and Anna's bedroom.

'Do you see anything?' Ryan whispered.

'I see two people about to get arrested.'

Ryan turned around bemused, and then realised that Kartik was referring to themselves. 'We're not going to get arrested. This is my house. And that,' he pointed to the figure, 'is my wife. The question that we've got to ask ourselves, is who is that?'

A second silhouette joined Anna's outline in the window. The second figure embraced the first, and from an outside perspective, it seemed like the two had become one, a dark shape enveloping each other, twisting and turning, a demented shadow puppet framed by the large windows.

The single-minded intensity had gone somewhat from Ryan, and instead a sense of calm practicality had come over him, a veteran soldier under fire. No panic, just calm calculation. For a moment Kartik's tension eased, and his mind turned towards inquisitiveness. There was someone else involved: another person who was the reason for this mission. He wasn't out of danger yet, but he wasn't the immediate target.

'Let's go around back.' Ryan snuck low across the driveway, surprisingly light on his feet, creating minimal noise on the gravel. Kartik followed.

They headed down the side passage where Kartik would have usually locked his bike, and into the large back garden. Dew had already settled on the grass. It would start to frost over in the next couple of weeks. But not yet. Important things were to pass before autumn finally succumbed to winter.

Ryan moved to the back door and inserted the key. Before he turned it, he paused, as if paralysed. Kartik realised this may be his last chance to talk him out of whatever plans he had.

'Ryan, what exactly are you going to do?'

'What?'

'When you get up there. What are you going to do?'

'I don't know yet. I haven't planned that far ahead.'

'Maybe we should take a moment now to think about what we are doing.' Kartik remembered a book that Cameron had lent him one time that said using collective pronouns was a good way to persuade people to do what you want.

'Well, we're going to go into the house, and then we're going to find out who my wife is fucking, and then we'll probably beat the shit out of him.' Ryan ran through the course of action, counting off the finer points of his plan with his fingers as he went.

'Don't you think that's a tad hypocritical?'

'What do you mean?'

'You know, you're cheating on your wife with Penelope. Not to mention that girl that you brought back to your place in Old Street last month.'

Kartik was surprised by the speed at which he was grabbed around the collar by the bigger man. His face was yanked towards Ryan's snarling teeth. 'If you fucking mention Penelope again around here I'll rip your fucking face off. Do you want that to happen?'

'Do I want you to rip my fucking face off?'

'Yes. Do you?'

'Not really.'

'So, do you know what you're going to do?'

'Not mention Penelope again?'

Ryan tightened his grip, pushing his large knuckles into Kartik's windpipe.

'Sorry,' Kartik said, his voice hoarse from the strain. 'I won't mention a certain person again.'

'Good,' Ryan said, releasing his grip. Kartik managed to restrain from coughing as he massaged his throat. They were still kneeling by the door and Kartik's knees were getting sore in the cold.

The key was turned in the lock, and they heard the bolt snap back. Ryan reached for the handle and was about to turn when Kartik reached for his hand to stop him.

Ryan turned and Kartik flinched, thinking his was going to get assaulted again. 'What now?'

'What about Arabella?' He knew he was risking the wrath of his friend's short temper again, but it was a subject that needed to be addressed.

'What about her?'

'Won't she be at home?' Kartik hoped the thought of his daughter might be able to suppress Ryan's rage.

'You think my wife's that stupid?' Kartik didn't dignify this with a response. 'Arabella's having a sleepover with one of her friends. Anna thinks I'm on a business trip in London. She thinks she's got this all wrapped up in a nice little package.'

'Okay, well, you go ahead,' Kartik said, finally accepting that there was no way he was going to stop Ryan from going inside. 'I'll keep watch out here.'

'Like fuck you are. You're coming inside with me.'

'Why do I have to go inside?'

'I may need backup.'

'Backup? This isn't the Sweeney.'

The door was pushed open and Kartik was pulled inside the small extension that poked out the back of the house. Inside was a tumble dryer, a coat rack, and miscellaneous shoes. Opposite them was the door that led into the kitchen.

In the darkness, Kartik kicked something over by his feet. He looked down and saw the two pairs of wellies that he had seen on his previous visits. They had been knocked over by his clumsy entrance and now lay sprawled out on the ground. He'd assumed that Anna had two girls. He hadn't been bright enough to realise that a girl may own more than one pair of wellies. But then again, he hadn't been bright enough to realise that sleeping with a married woman would come back to haunt him.

The door to the kitchen was opened and Ryan held his finger up to his lips in an unintentionally comic fashion, imploring his accomplice to be silent. They listened, but heard nothing from the bedroom on the third floor.

'Take your shoes off,' Ryan whispered to Kartik.

'What?'

'Your shoes,' Ryan said, pointing to the ground as if he were the first person to make Kartik aware of what was on his feet. 'They're dirty.'

'So?'

'Anna hates it when mud is brought into the house.'

Kartik didn't respond for a second, preferring to think that Ryan had now gone completely insane.

'Anna doesn't like it when people wear shoes in the house? The woman who's very likely to be…,' he cleared his throat remembering the thick fingers that had been around it moments earlier, '…being intimate with another man at this very moment? And you're worried about her preferences on house-appropriate attire?'

'Just take your bloody shoes off.'

Kartik did as he was told and left his trainers next to Ryan's brogues. His socks were slightly damp—it was uncertain if from precipitation or sweat—but he hoped not enough to mark the floors. They went through into the kitchen, passed the grandfather clock, and into the hallway where Camilla had once pushed Kartik to the ground. He half worried that there would be some evidence of their liaison, some physical remnant of their affair, that until then had gone unnoticed by Ryan, but which he would notice and use to expose Kartik. Luckily, it seemed Camilla kept her house too clean to have to worry about post-coital detritus being left in the hallway.

The stairs were next. For a moment, it looked like Ryan wasn't going to ascend. He paused for a second and surveyed the situation, like a dog sniffing its new surroundings. Only when he was satisfied with whatever he was trying to sense did he start up the stairs. Kartik reluctantly followed.

What was he going to do? What were they going to say? It all seemed too crazy to make sense of. On the wall that ran up by the stairs were ascending family pictures: Ryan, Camilla and Arabella posing, smiling, their best clothes on, a masquerade of happiness. With each step up, the pictures took them back in time. He couldn't remember if these pictures had been on the wall on his previous visits. He doubted it, or otherwise he would have noticed and put two and two together much quicker. She would have taken them down when other men came to stay, but for whatever reason she had left them hanging this time.

At the bottom of the stairs was a picture of Arabella in a neat, navy-checked dress, her hair in a bow, and a big grin on her face, a couple of her milk teeth missing. By the time they reached the landing, Arabella was a baby again and Ryan was around fifteen kilos lighter. Camilla somehow managed to look the same, only her haircut—straightened, shorter, darker, curled into a bob at the ends—was different.

But it was the images of Arabella's face in the various stages of her life that troubled Kartik. She was the real victim here, her gap-tooth smile oblivious to the mess that her parents had gotten into.

At the top of the stairs, Ryan stopped again, holding out his palm to indicate Kartik do the same.

Kartik stopped.

They were crouched down now, leaning close to the banister, as if they were hiding behind a bulkhead as they stormed the beaches of Normandy. A fat, old captain and his lazy, semi-willing officer, attempting to expose the adulterous Nazis upstairs.

He almost laughed at this mental image, when they heard it: a slow, rhythmic, squeaking. A low murmur followed by giggling. A headboard slapping the wall. The unmistakable audio indicators that people in close proximity were having sex. And judging from the quickening tempo, it was becoming increasingly enjoyable for those participating. The sounds were almost comical in being so clichéd. He could have closed his eyes and it would have sounded like he had turned the volume down on his laptop and was listening to porn through a muffled speaker. However he was far too petrified to do this. Vicious fear gripped over him. There would be a time in his life when he wouldn't be terrified, when he would look back on this and laugh. But the all-consuming terror of the situation seemed, at this point, endless.

Ryan's face hardened at the sound. His breathing became heavier, but he still managed to keep his voice low. 'Right, let's go.'

'What exactly are you planning to do?' he repeated.

Ryan started to rise, but then stopped halfway, and was left paralysed for a second by the question, hovering halfway between crouching and standing, like he was sitting on the toilet. 'I don't know yet. I'll make it up as I go.'

Kartik decided this was his last chance to stop this madness. He gently put his hand on Ryan's forearm. 'Look, let's not do this. Let's just get out now. You don't want to do this.'

As he spoke, he saw something that surprised him. Ryan's eyes were watering. For whatever reason, he never imagined that sadness was an emotion the older man was capable of. His earlier anger had been understandable and expected. But for him to be upset was at odds with everything Kartik knew about Ryan.

'I'm going up.' The melancholy in his eyes twisted back to determination. 'And you're coming with me.' He was a terrorist who was ready to go down in a blaze of gunfire, dragging his hostage down with him.

He stood up and headed for the stairs that led to the top bedroom. He moved with a surprising speed, silence and grace. Kartik just about kept pace as they went up the cream-carpeted stairs. The door to the bedroom was almost ripped off its hinges by Ryan as they bundled inside.

CHAPTER TWENTY-TWO

Now there were four people in the room. Previously there had been two, but now there were four. This was a problem. Four people was too many. Three were drunk. Two were naked. All of a sudden, none of them wanted to be there.

No one was sure what to do. Who was going to make the first move? What should you do in a situation like this? What do you say?

It was the naked man—the person who had perhaps the least to lose in the long term, but who was in the most immediate danger—who made the first move. He started to roll slowly off the naked woman, whilst at the same time pulling up the duvet to cover his modesty. His wide eyes didn't know whether to look at the two men who had interrupted or not. He was a much slender build than the larger of the two men who had barged in, and it was clear he wouldn't stand much of a chance if it came to violence. He was also acutely aware that if it came to a fight it was a two-against-one situation, although he wasn't aware how little the younger, dopier-looking intruder wanted to get involved with any of this.

'Don't fucking move,' the larger, older, fatter intruder shouted. The naked man froze halfway on top of the woman's naked body, who was also trying to use the bedsheet to cover herself.

'Ryan? What the fuck are you doing?' the woman shouted. She had just managed to pull enough duvet to cover her left breast, but her right was still exposed. In some ways, it didn't really matter, as everyone present in the room had seen her naked already, although only fifty percent of those people in the room were aware of this fact.

'What the fuck am I doing?' the intruded replied. 'What the fuck am *I* doing? What the fuck are *you* doing?' He hadn't stepped into the room any further than his initial incursion, so he stood just a couple of feet inside the doorway. This left the younger intruder behind him, neither in nor out of the room. It looked like he was trying to hide behind the body of his accomplice.

'I didn't think you were going to be home until tomorrow,' the woman said, fear visible in her face.

'And that makes it okay to fuck someone?' The first intruder took a few steps into the room, towards the side of the bed that the naked man was laying on. As he stepped around, the woman noticed the younger man for the first time, a puzzled look mixing with fear on her face. As the older man stepped towards the bed, behind his back, the younger man shook his head and mouthed, 'he doesn't know' to her, indicating a code of silence between them was to be maintained. The woman was confused, but acquiesced.

The naked man, on detecting the approaching threat from the larger man, was now scrambling by the side of the bed, desperately trying to find some clothing, but so far had only managed to pick up one of his socks. The larger man approached the side of the bed, grabbed him, and forcibly yanked him out of it by the throat. The naked man did his best to flail away from his aggressor but to no avail.

'Ryan!' cautioned the accomplice.
'Let him go!' yelled the woman.

As his victim was starting to choke with his hand around his neck, the large man let go and took a couple of steps back. The naked man was now fully exposed, and suddenly the initial aggression from the larger man was gone. There was the sense from the aggressor that it was perhaps unsportsmanlike to hit a naked opponent.

They all paused.

Time stood still.

The naked man reached for his boxer shorts.

The intruder took this as an opportunity to break his nose.

CHAPTER TWENTY-THREE

'Jesus Christ!' Kartik yelled. The bone-on-flesh thud of the punch brought him back to reality again. For a moment he had felt like he was watching other people's lives unfold on a stage. Now he was back in the room.

The naked man had fallen to the floor, blood pouring from his nose. He was holding his hands up to his small, almost girlish face, trying to stem the flow. Ryan stood over him, fists clenched, unsure whether to follow up with a couple of swift kicks to the stomach or to admit he may have done enough already.

'Alan!' Camilla screamed as the naked man held his hands to his face.

'Who is he?' Ryan turned to his wife, who was now cowering from her husband under the sheets.

'He's no one,' Camilla said.

'Really? Doesn't look like no one.'

'Please, Ryan. Let him go. It's not his fault.'

'Damn right it's not his fault. It's your fucking fault.' Camilla winced, thinking she may be next to face physical retribution. Instead, Ryan threw her a dressing gown that had fallen off the edge of the bed. 'Put some clothes on.' She did as she was told.

The naked man, Alan, whoever he was, gingerly stood up, still holding his nose, his hands covered in his blood. Kartik could see some crimson handprints on the cream carpet. He hoped it didn't stain, creating a constant reminder of the events that were taking place at that moment.

He was also aware that he wasn't out of immediate danger either. If she wasn't quite so petrified, she would be questioning why he was there. All it would take was one hint of familiarity between himself and Camilla for their secret to come to light. He could only hope that Ryan was so focused on the naked man that his own affair with Camilla could be kept concealed.

Ryan, face shaking with rage, advanced on Alan again, who was doing his best to cover his modesty with one hand whilst holding his broken nose with the other.

'Ryan, stop,' Kartik insisted. Ryan turned, and Kartik noticed an unmistakable sadness beyond the frenzied wrath. 'Bloody hell, let him put some clothes on at least.'

The naked man looked like he was trying to nod, appreciating this sentiment, but he may have just been shaking in fear.

'Put something on,' Ryan said, kicking a heap of clothes next to the bed towards Alan. There was a hesitation, a confusion, a catch-22. Alan, realising that his nakedness was also his shield as Ryan was unlikely to strike again whilst he was so vulnerable, was reluctant to get dressed. But at the same time, there is nothing quite as humiliating as being fully exposed in front of complete strangers, even more so with a broken nose. He warily put his clothes on, starting with the boxer shorts, then a pair of jeans, and what had previously been a crisp white shirt, which was now smeared with blood. He looked like a survivor from a zombie movie. He didn't have time to do up all the buttons before he was grabbed by

Ryan again and hauled towards the doorway, like a drunk being removed from a nightclub by a bouncer.

Alan wriggled free from Ryan's grip and darted towards the door. Annoyed that his prey had pulled away, Ryan picked up the nearest thing he could find—the copy of Ayn Rand's *Atlas Shrugged* on the bedside table—and threw it at the intruder. The thousand-page book struck him on the back of the head and he let out a pained yelp before crashing to the ground again.

Ryan bounded across the room and hoisted Alan to his feet and forced him out of the door. The two men disappeared down the stairs, leaving Kartik and Camilla alone in the room for the first time.

'What the hell is going on?' Camilla cried, streaked mascara running down her face.

'Look, he doesn't know about us,' Kartik said quickly and quietly when he was certain Ryan was out of ear shot. 'I just know Ryan from his work. I had no idea that you two were married.' Camilla looked dismayed and sceptical, almost as if she suspected that Kartik had been the one that had set this entire thing up. He knew he only had a few moments to communicate with Camilla on his own, and as self-preservation was his top priority, he ploughed on quickly. 'Look, I'm serious. This is a fucking crazy coincidence. He got drunk and forced me to come along with him. But he's got no idea about us. I don't know who the hell that other guy was, but if we keep things quiet between us, then we may be able to minimise the damage.'

The mention of damage limitation certainly played well with her, and she nodded.

'I'm going to go now. I'm going to make sure Ryan doesn't do some serious harm to the guy.' He picked up the man's blazer, heavy and charcoal grey, with the intent of returning it.

'Don't let him hurt him anymore. It's not his fault.'

'I know.' Kartik turned to leave the bedroom. He heard Ryan yelling his name from downstairs. He turned and looked at Camilla one last time. She suddenly looked so young, so fragile, so pitiful. She was almost twenty years older than him, but he felt like a father figure in a family that had been turned upside down. 'I'm sorry all this has happened.'

'Please, just leave.' She couldn't bear to look at him anymore, her eyes fixed on the mattress of her bed. Every moment he stood in that room, her indiscretions were magnified.

He ran down the stairs, his heart pounding. He no longer felt panicked—he believed Camilla would keep quiet about their affair—but the adrenaline of the night's events had put him on a high.

He reached the bottom floor just in time to see the man thrown out of the front door, accompanied by a long litany of expletives pouring from Ryan's mouth. He had no shoes on, and he didn't seem to be too bothered about the blazer Kartik was carrying, his only aim was to evacuate the building as soon as possible. They watched him hurry to a silver Audi across the street and drive off with a screeching sound. Then there was silence apart from both men's heavy breathing.

Ryan closed the door and then leant against it, face in his palms.

'Are you okay?' It was a silly question to ask, but he couldn't think of anything else to say.

'What do you think?' Ryan's voice sounded like it was reaching him from a long distance away. His words were slurred, and he appeared drunker than he had during the confrontation. The violence of the evening had sobered the older man temporarily. Now that was over, the alcohol was taking over again from the adrenaline. He stumbled as he tried to regain his composure.

'Do you know who he was?' Kartik asked.

'Never seen him before.' Ryan took his hands away from his face and started to rearrange his shirt, tucking it back into his trousers. 'What were you saying to my wife?'

'Huh?'

'When you were upstairs. Just now. Before you came down. What was she saying?'

Kartik tried to keep his voice level. 'Nothing, really. I was just trying to calm her down. I think she's quite scared.'

'That was all?' Was there mistrust in Ryan's voice?

'Yeah.'

Ryan walked down the hallways into the kitchen and Kartik followed. Ryan propped himself against the table, looked up at the ceiling, his eyes flickering.

'Look, don't stay here tonight. You're not in the right state of mind,' Kartik said.

'Don't tell me what to do.'

'This is shit. I know. I can't imagine what you're feeling right now. But this isn't the time to confront her. Let's get you in a taxi. Stay in a hotel for tonight. Sleep off the drink and the rage.'

'Fuck off, Kartik. What the fuck do you know? You're just some kid.'

He let the insult slide. 'I know you're hurting. But we need to get you out of here. Before you do more damage to someone else. You could already be in legal trouble for what you did to that guy.'

'Legal trouble? Let him try and sue. I'll rip his fucking head off if I see him again.'

'Look, let's just get out of here. You can crash at my place if you really need to.' Kartik didn't think Louise would be particularly happy with this, but he was feeling morally responsible for the wellbeing of both his friend and Camilla. Ryan was a danger to both as long as he stayed in the house.

Suddenly, as if awoken from a trance, Ryan stood up from the table, pushed Kartik aside and opened one of the kitchen cupboards. His arm reached in and he came out with a bottle of whiskey. Kartik could see from the label it was the good stuff: a thirty-year aged bottle from the Isle of Skye. The older man then went to put on his shoes and headed to the front door.

'Good idea,' Kartik said, putting on his own shoes and then following. 'I'll call us a taxi.'

Ryan was swigging straight from the bottle. He left the house, crossed the gravel driveway, and walked across the street towards his Range Rover.

'Hey, Ryan! Look, mate, it's probably not a good idea to drive,' Kartik said as he walked alongside.

Ryan pulled out his keys and the lights of the car flashed as it was remotely unlocked.

'Seriously, you're drunk.' Kartik tried to pull Ryan away from the car. 'It's not a good idea to…' He was cut off as Ryan shoved him away with his powerful arms. Kartik had to steady himself to avoid being pushed to the ground. He watched helplessly as Ryan entered the car and started the ignition. The Range Rover pulled away from the kerb with an unrestrained lurch barely avoiding the parked car in front, did a U-turn mounting the pavement on both sides of the road, and disappeared down the road they had driven up twenty minutes earlier. For Kartik, standing there alone and disorientated in the darkness, this all felt like a lifetime ago.

The light from Camilla's bedroom had gone out, and the only source of illumination was from the almost full moon that hung in the clear sky. A taxi didn't seem appropriate, so Kartik started the long walk back to his house. It was only as he started to walk that he realised he was still holding the charcoal blazer, a memento passed on from one adulterer to the next.

CHAPTER TWENTY-FOUR

His head was against the steering wheel.
This was not usual.
This was not good.

His temples were sore and his mouth was dry. He was painfully thirsty and he didn't understand why he was in his car. He wasn't meant to sleep in a car. He was meant to sleep in a bed. Why was he asleep at the wheel of his car?

His head snapped up, panicking that he had been in an accident. He was relieved to see there wasn't another car in sight. He was in a semi-gravelled, muddy car park somewhere. In front of him was a bush that looked a little too close. He looked behind and saw a familiar field. He wasn't far from home, just a few hundred metres down the road at the Newnham playing fields.

He knew he had gotten drunk last night, but it was still a bit hazy as to why, and he couldn't remember how he had ended up there. As he got older, alcohol did a better and better job halting his ability to create memories. When he was a kid, first going to pubs underage back in Solihull, he would be able to remember every aspect of his nights out, no matter how much he drank. Even sitting in the cold car now, he could remember going to the back rooms of pubs to see his mate's terrible bands. They would sneak in a bottle of vodka and clandestinely knock it back in the crowd, as his friends struggled to find any rhythm in even the most basic three-cord punk. His friend's band, Point Mental Museum, had distributed their songs via cassette to the school before their gigs. Even now Ryan could remember the entire set list they played on their debut night, even after getting through half a bottle of vodka, and a couple of pints bought by Adrian's charitable older brother.

The opening song, rather imaginably called The System Sucks, got a raucous response and it seemed like half his school year turned up for the show—although admittedly there wasn't much else to do, as a sixteen-year-old on a Friday night in Solihull in 1985. Ryan could still recall the smallest detail of the night: the gig room's peeling purple paintwork damp with condensation; the distinctive smell of piss and sweat and vomit of the pub's terribly maintained toilets; the moment that Sophie Lewis, barged into him on the way past to lock lips with the captain of the rugby team. Alcohol soaked memories from twenty-five years ago that were clearer and more distinctive than the memories from last night.

Despite the fact that he couldn't recall the night before, he was certain they were not going to be good memories. There was already the onset of early morning doom: a mixture of regret, worry, and loathing for what he had done and everything that he was. Something had happened with his wife. And he was certain Kartik had been there as well. And his knuckles hurt, which was never a good sign.

To avoid thinking about things, he decided to inspect the front of his car. It was worrying how close to the bush in front he was. The branches were enveloping the front of the bonnet, the leaves reaching towards him like tiny green hands. He opened his door, and as he stepped out, his foot kicked something hard and round and hollow. The bottle of whisky further confirmed that whatever had taken place last night, it wasn't going to be positive. It was an expensive bottle, and it was empty.

He stepped out of the car and for the first time since owning it, he thought how inconveniently high off the ground his Range Rover was. Why the hell hadn't he purchased a more practical car?

The front of the car was indeed too close to the bush. And not just the bush, but a low tree stump that had been obscured by the high view from the driver's seat. As a result, the stump had imbedded itself into the grill of the Range Rover. The licence plate was cracked, a neat line down the middle splitting it in two, and there was a shallow dent in the body work. He couldn't have hit it at much more than five miles an hour, but he was still going to take a nasty hit on his insurance. Along with the whiskey, this was already adding up to be an expensive morning, and that wasn't accounting for any emotional damage that he may have caused. The mounting costs, mixing with the excesses of last night, caused him to be violently sick next to the stump. It was a small miracle he avoided getting any on the car itself, although his shoes weren't quite as lucky. He wiped them on the grassy verge, succeeding in removing most, if not all, of the recent contents of his stomach.

On returning to the driver's seat, he examined the bottle in more detail. It was a thirty-year-aged Tallisker that had been an anniversary present from his father-in-law. He'd just ejected five hundred pounds worth of single malt from his stomach.

The memories were coming back now. It was the anniversary gift that had promoted his recollection to kick into gear. The reason he was here was because of his wife. He remembered breaking into his own house, seeing the two of them together. He half remembered a punch and blood and screams. Why had Kartik been there? Who invited that idiot?

Fuck! Kartik! That wasn't good! Now it would all come out. Instead of keeping this mess between the three active participants, he had invited along a spectator, someone who was fully capable of telling the world, or more worrying, of acting as a witness. He knew he had hit the guy with a clean punch, and the cracking sound had implied that the bridge of the man's nose had been broken. Given what he could recall, Ryan would struggle to defend himself against an assault charge if the man was morally repugnant enough to press charges after nailing his wife. He'd be able to seek mitigation considering the circumstances, and a good lawyer would be able to spin it that he had shown restraint but there would still be a hefty fine at best, and a short jail term at worst. Either way his position at Fusion Vision would be compromised and he'd never be allowed back into the City, no matter how great his performance.

The feeling of doom deepened. He knew he had to take practical steps to fix things, but he didn't know what to do or what to fix. Was his marriage irreparable now? Would he even consider staying with Anna? He couldn't see it, but the reality and logistics of the situation was that they still lived in the same house and they were raising a daughter.

Divorce was too big a thing to think about in that moment. He needed to start fixing the small things first, and then he could work on the bigger things. He checked his phone and noticed a lot of missed calls, mostly from work. He jumped into his inbox and saw assorted questions from Philip, Aaron, and others. It was Friday and he wasn't in. He hadn't gone in yesterday either, but at least he had made an excuse. He looked at his watch. It was half ten in the morning, and he was on radio silence. He sent a quick email to explain he was sick again. That was one problem solved, and he had done it with just a few taps on his Blackberry. It gave him a tiny sense of accomplishment but was still dwarfed by the mountain range of doom.

The next stage was getting to Kartik. Damage limitation was of upmost importance. There were still some blanks in his memory, and going through it all again would clear his mind. He'd also look to get some stories straight in case the naked man tried to get the police involved: he was under extraordinary pressure at work, he was caught unaware causing emotional stress, the man looked like he was going to attack him first. They could play up the diminished responsibility card together.

Unfortunately, as he went to phone Kartik, his phone had the audacity to switch itself off. The battery was flat.

He'd have to do it in person.

He turned on the engine and turned up the heating, which made him feel nauseous, but the cold car was almost unbearable after a night in the exposed November night. He slowly reversed away from the tree stump and drove towards the city centre.

He left the Range Rover in the multi-story car park next to The Maypole and purchased a bottle of water from the vending machine on the ground floor to try and wash away the taste of vomit. Then he made the short walk to Market Square. Trinity Lane was relatively quiet, only a handful of Japanese tourists and some bleary-eyed students walking down the cobbled streets. He almost had to make a quick detour down one of the side streets to be sick again, but he managed to keep his composure.

The café was similarly quiet, which was a welcomed relief. The morning rush had dispersed, and there was only a small smattering of elderly regulars, characters that Ryan was starting to recognise from his visits over the past three months. However, there was no sign of Kartik. He didn't even know if he was scheduled to work that day. He had just assumed that he was perpetually making cappuccinos when he wasn't getting drunk in The Maypole or messing up job interviews in London.

A short, muscular man with a military crewcut and a slightly wonky nose was arranging the cake display in lieu of having any customers to serve.

'Hi there,' Ryan said. His voice strained and the words came out crackly, like they were being broadcast on a radio with a faulty antenna.

The man looked up, a forced smile beaming on his face. 'Good morning, sir.' He had an Eastern European accent, but Ryan couldn't tell which country he was from.

'Is Kartik working today?'

The smile faded slightly, but not entirely. He still had to be polite to customers, but probably less so to the friends of employees. He also took in Ryan's dishevelled clothes and made a mental assessment, not at all positive.

'No. Kartik is not at work today. He is in tomorrow.'

Ryan nodded and then pointed to the menu board above the barista's head. 'Just an Americano then.'

'What size?'

'Hmm?'

'What size would you like?'

'Just regular is fine.'

'Medium?'

'Yes, sure, whatever.'

'Eat in or take away?'

'To have in,' Ryan said, ignoring the fact that he wasn't going to be eating.

'Would you like milk?'

'Yes, please.'

'Hot or cold milk?'

'It doesn't really matter.' Ryan shuffled with impatience. It'd be nice to order coffee without having to do a quiz beforehand.

'I'll use hot milk.'

'Fine.'

The coffee was made and Ryan headed upstairs where it was even quieter. He was about to sit down when he heard someone call his name from the back of the room. Cameron was sitting behind her laptop. He headed over.

She was against the back wall of the room, with a pile of papers and books occupying the vast majority of two tables. It was an environment that suited her best, surrounding herself with the defences of academia. She had set up her perimeter, perhaps to guard herself from the short man sat drinking a double espresso a few tables away from Cameron. Ryan had seen him on previous occasions hovering around Cameron when she was sitting in the café doing work. He had small beady eyes, with an unconvincing look of self-importance. They were of similar age, but Ryan had seen him flirting very badly with some of the café's staff who were half his age. The man was lonely, but he was probably doing better than Ryan at this present time. He shrank away as Ryan approached, obviously disappointed that Cameron had acknowledged his presence from across the room.

She made space at the table for Ryan to put his coffee, stuffing a couple of books into her brown satchel before placing it on the floor. Even though it wasn't cold in the café, she was wearing a navy bobble hat. On the back of her chair was a grey duffle coat that on any other girl would have looked geeky and dumpy, but when Cameron wore it, it gave her an air of Parisian chic.

'You've looked better,' she said as he sat.

'I've felt better.'

They didn't say anything for a while. *Did she know about the night before? If she did, she wasn't letting on.*

'Do you want some muffin?'

'Sorry?'

'Some muffin?' Cameron lifted a plate that had been hidden behind her laptop. 'It's blueberry.' On the plate sat the semi-intact baked item. The tears in the top of it suggested fingers rather than teeth—she had been tearing off small pieces before nibbling them. There was something quite childish about eating that way; Arabella would tear small bits of her food and then nibble them rapidly, like a rabbit chewing lettuce. She looked adorable doing it. Maybe Cameron looked the same. Maybe that's why the leery man with the small eyes watched over her.

'I'm okay, thanks.' He was starving, but it didn't seem appropriate to accept this offering at this time. Not before he knew how much she knew. 'I was looking for Kartik.'

'He's got the day off.'

'So I've heard.' They were playing a tentative game of chess, both waiting for the other to make the first move.

'He's with his girlfriend.'

'He's got a girlfriend?' This was news to Ryan.

'Yeah. He met her on the train after your wild night out in London last month.'

'Oh, yeah. That night.' *Jesus, how much did she know? Everything?* He had revealed too much that night as well. He was completely exposed, and there was no reason why the girl in front of him, the studious young thing with the brilliant brain and the half-eaten muffin, didn't know all the terrible moments that made up his life.

Before, on the night when they had taken the punt out, Ryan had worried that his behaviour had come off as unprofessional. That she would think less of him as a headhunter, that he may have dented the reputation and the seriousness of his firm. But now he was worried about something new, something different. The cold emptiness of the morning had made him realise that he didn't care if Cameron didn't like Fusion Vision, or if she passed up on the offers that he presented her. But rather he didn't want her to like him less as a person. *What was that look she was giving him? Was it pity? Was it disgust?* All he wanted now was for her to like him, for her to validate his existence as a human, not just a suit.

'Are you making a habit of it?'

'A habit of what?'

'Of wild nights.'

'I did something very silly last night.' The use of the childish adjective changed the tone of the conversation. He had no pretence of control over the situation now. He remembered how Arabella had sat in Mrs. Scott-Howell office the day she had sworn at her teacher. How her little legs had swung under the chair because her feet didn't quite reach the ground on the adult's chair. He remembered how hard it had been for her to make eye contact. 'Kartik was there. That's why I wanted to talk to him.'

'I know. We met up last night after you disappeared. He was worried.'

'So you know?'

'Yeah. I've got my ear pretty close to the ground.'

'I don't really know what to do.'

'Maybe start from the beginning. Talk through it all. Try and make sense of it.'

'To you?'

'Do you have any other friends that would listen?' She said it with a gentle, tilt of the head which suggested she was joking, but it was a bit too close to the bone to completely avoid inflicting pain.

'I suppose not,' he accepted. Her tilted head turned to sympathy.

'Well, I picked up Kartik last night,' he started. 'I was drunk, so I don't remember everything that happened. But then we drove to my house…'

'Wait,' she interrupted with a surprising forcefulness. 'Start from the beginning. Not from last night. But when this all started.'

'What do you mean?'

'The beginning. The beginning of it all.'

'Sorry, Cameron, it may be the hangover, but I don't really understand what you are talking about.'

'How did you end up here?'

'I drove.'

'Not literally.'

'Then what?'

'Why are you here now? What got you here? Start at the beginning, Start with your marriage.'

And he finally understood. And he started from the beginning.

He started from when he met Anna. He talked about falling in love, about when she had been full of energy instead of bitterness, excitement instead of suspicion. He talked about having a child, about how that had changed everything. With every year that Arabella had grown, Anna had become more distant. How work had taken over his life. How he started to neglect the family. He described how he had met Penelope. How he had created a fantasy world from their relationship that he knew was impossible. He talked about how when he was with Penelope, it was the best escape from a life that was delivering him so little joy.

When the markets had crashed the previous year, everything got tossed away. Everything from global economic stability, to his last real efforts with his wife. The markets plunged downwards as he plunged into the unsustainable fantasy world with Penelope and their small flat together in Old Street. That had been when Arabella's behaviour really started to change. For years she had been quiet, reserved, demure and polite. But as her parents' relationship hit the proverbial fan, she started to act up. She became louder, aggressive, argumentative. She learnt what annoyed her parents—especially her mother—and she exploited their reactions with her small acts of rebellion. The negative attention from Anna was at least attention, and so she kept picking the scabs of her mother's strict social etiquette. Ryan had encouraged this in a way, enjoying some of the boisterous traits he thought would sever her well in the real world. What he didn't realise was that he was only encouraging her into swearing at her teacher and almost getting herself kicked out of school.

'And I suppose that brings us up to the events of last night...' He trailed off. He had been talking nonstop for a long time, Cameron only interjecting with the odd question to make his timeline clearer for her understanding. He hadn't been looking at her much, instead staring blankly at his left hand, which had been twirling and gesturing against the table as he tried to make sense of his marriage. When he had looked up, he had been greeted with eye contact that was both unwavering and comforting. It was the first time he had noticed the streaks of blue running through her left eye.

'You've got heterochromia,' he said, surprising himself with the observation. He had a childhood friend who had the same condition and the technical term had always stuck with him.

'Very good.'

'I never noticed it before.'

'Kartik never was able to remember how to pronounce it.'

'That doesn't surprise me.'

'Well, I'm impressed.'

'Really?'

'Well, by your knowledge of my iris pigmentation, rather than some of your life decisions.'

'Bit of a low blow.'

'Well, I don't really know what to say. I'm not sure if I have much sympathy. You've been cheating on your wife, so is it a surprise when she cheats on you? You've been the master of your own downfall. And it's hard to empathise.'

'Then why did you ask me to go through it all?' He felt betrayed.

'It wasn't for me. It was for you. How I feel is irrelevant here.'

'No it's not. I don't want you thinking I'm a sack of shit.'

'Why? Because you don't want me to go to MIT but take one of your offers instead?'

'I don't care about that. Go to America if you want. It's not about the work. The office will survive fine. It's about, well, it's about… I don't know the right word for it. I want you to like me because…' He struggled with the dryness in his throat. 'Because I admire you, I guess.' He drank his coffee and looked at the cheap wooden table. He wasn't sure what his intentions were at the moment. He felt like for the first time in his life he didn't have a safety next under him, and he wanted someone to make sure he didn't fall. 'Look, I never spent much time with nice people. The sort of people I grew up around, well we were selfish, and greedy, and out for ourselves. And it's refreshing talking to you. It makes you feel a bit better about the world. And I'd quite like it if you liked me.'

'It's like you're looking for salvation.'

'Yeah, maybe.'

'Well, that's a little bit out of my jurisdiction, I'm afraid. But it's okay if you're going through a hard time at the moment. As long as you can feel it. *Scars have the strange power to remind us that our past is real.*'

'That's a quote or something, isn't it?' Ryan said, the synapses of his brain firing.

'It's from *Cormac McCarthy's All the Pretty Horses*.'

'I've never seen it.'

'It's a book.'

'Well, in that case, I've never read it.'

'You have to accept the pain you feel and the pain you've created. And then we all need to work on our own redemption,' she continued. 'It's not something someone else can grant you. That'd be too easy. That's the fundamental flaw of The Bible. All you have to do is to ask for forgiveness and it will be granted and you will be accepted into Heaven. The real world doesn't work like that. You've got to work and behave every single day in a manner that you are comfortable with. Otherwise, you're fucked.' Cameron shrugged. 'That's where the Bible got it wrong. You know, that and claiming the world was created in just under a week.'

Ryan laughed. 'You think God paid himself overtime for working that Saturday?'

'I assume he got at least time and a half. Maybe came in for a half day the following Monday.'

'So what happens now?'

'I don't know. I was working on Eden's Bonfire,' she nodded to the pile of papers, books, and the laptop. 'Philip's been helping me out on it. We've been working on it together. Sharing ideas. He's got an interesting take on things.'

'Dr. Radiowave's Transmission and... What was your pseudonym again?'

'Manhattan Samurai.' She turned away as she said this, the faintest hint of pink on her cheeks, as if she was embarrassed at the childish nature of the alter-egos.

'Dr. Radiowave's Transmission and Manhattan Samurai. Quite the duo. So, is he a genius like you?'

The reddening on her cheeks intensified. She knew the praise was genuine, and she was struggling to acknowledge it for some reason. He hadn't known her to be coy before. 'He's very smart,' she said eventually.

'I never realised. Maybe I should give him a raise.'

'Maybe you should. He deserves it.' She slammed a book shut, driving attention away from herself. 'But that's enough of one riddle. Let's try and solve the puzzle of your life.'

'Stick to Eden's Bonfire. It's more straightforward.'

'Shall we get in contact with Kartik?' The collective pronoun was comforting. As much as she eulogised that his mission to find redemption was something he had to handle on his own, she was already putting herself forward to assist him.

'If he's with his girlfriend, it's probably best not to disturb him. Let him get on with his own life. It's good he's finally got a lucky break. He needed it.'

'That's a very kind thing to say. Probably the nicest thing I've ever heard you say.'

'Taking tiny steps closer to redemption.'

'It may take a bit more than that.'

'True. What about you and Rachel? How are things?'

'Look, you don't have to try and be interested in my life because of what we've just talked about.' No matter how much he thought he was getting to know Cameron, there was always a reflexive level of defensiveness that kicked in at surprising moments.

'I'm not asking for the sake of it. I genuinely want to know.'

She scratched the back of her neck and took a sideways glance to her left. The leery-looking man diverted his gaze, pretending that he hadn't been watching them the entire time. 'It's going well, yeah. She's nice.'

'Just nice?' He raised his eyebrows. 'That's a very mundane description for someone as intelligent as yourself.'

'Yes, she's more than nice. She's, well she's, err…' Now it was her turn to stare at the table as she spoke, perhaps to hide the fact she was still blushing. It was the first time he had seen Cameron struggle for words. 'I think I'm in love with her.'

'You *think*?'

'No. I *am* in love with her,' she said defiantly. 'And I'm worried.'

'Worried about what?'

'Next year.'

'About going to America?'

'Yeah. I don't want a long-distance relationship. And I

don't want to break up with her. And that's why I've been looking at your offers.'

'What about doing a post-graduate at another university? Or what about doing it here? I'm sure Cambridge isn't too shabby when it comes to further education.'

'I've lived here twenty-one years. I feel like it's time to move somewhere else. But then, I don't want to leave Rachel here.'

'What about London? LSE? Imperial?'

'Your solution to everything is to move to London.'

'Greatest city in the world.'

'You really want me to stay in education? Wouldn't that mess with all your plans and targets?'

'I'm just making suggestions. At the end of the day, it doesn't matter what I want. It's not for me. It's for you. How I feel is irrelevant.'

Cameron smiled. 'You're a keen student of my ham-fisted attempts at philosophy?'

'Do whatever you think will be best for you and Rachel.'

'Thanks.'

'I know you'll be able to work it out.'

'I'm sure we will.'

The coffee had gone cold. Ryan felt like he had delayed the inevitable for too long. He was going to have to go back home. 'Look, I'm going to head back. I've got a lot to work out with Anna. And I've got to make sure Arabella is okay.'

'Good idea.'

'I'll leave you with your puzzle. And your admirer.' The leery man looked away again as they both looked over again.

'I hope it goes okay,' she said.

'Thanks. And a quick favour?'

'Sure.'

'Can you keep what I've said to you today quiet? And ask Kartik to do the same as well?'

'No problem. '

'Thanks.'

'Good luck.'

He gathered himself—his entire body felt heavy, but his mind seemed a little less murky. He may not have been able to solve any problems with Cameron, but he felt like he had a greater idea of what his problems were.

As he left he made a deliberate move in the direction of the beady-eyed watcher. Ryan stared at him as he walked past, attempting to look as intimidating as he could—which wasn't hard considering the height and bulk advantage he had over the smaller man. Panicked, the man scrabbled up his things, and made an observable effort to show he was about to leave, avoiding looking at either Ryan or Cameron.

When he got to the stairs, Ryan turned around to see Cameron smiling at him as the voyeur shuffled away.

One small step towards redemption at a time.

CHAPTER TWENTY-FIVE

'So what's the plan for today?'
'Well, I've got a meeting with Sanjay about the locations at three.'

'I think we can skip that.'

'I absolutely cannot skip that.'

'Why not?'

'Because it's very important.'

'But what we're doing right now is very important.'

'Kartik, we're not doing anything right now.'

'Exactly. Doing nothing is one of the most important things in life.' He pulled Freddy closer to him. 'And we're also naked while we're doing nothing, which is the best kind of nothing possible.' He pulled the sheets off them, to highlight just how naked they were, in case she had forgotten.

'We can't spend all day in bed,' she protested. Her slender body rose and fell in shallow breaths, her ribs very slightly visible when she arched her back. On her neck was a small pattern of five moles, which resembled a constellation of dark stars on a milky white sky. He followed the line of her neck with his gaze up to her face, to the barely visible scar tissue under the right eye. He kissed her on the nose.

'Yes, we can.'

'No, we cannot. It's time to get up.'

'It's too early to get up.'

'It's ten in the morning.'

'Exactly. Far too early.'

'If you don't move soon we'll be late.'

They were lying in Kartik's bed. Freddy pulled away from him, but not particularly far. She didn't bother to pull the bedsheets over to cover herself. She started to roll out of bed, but Kartik grabbed her by the arm. 'No, let's stay in bed a little longer.'

'I'm not going to lie in your bed all day. I've got better things to do.'

'Really?'

'I'm sure all the other girls you've had in this bed were content to idle around all day, but it's not for me.'

'If only these walls could talk,' Kartik said wistfully.

'And what would they say?' Freddy said with an accusatory glance.

'They'd probably say, "this guy really doesn't get laid much."' Freddy laughed. 'So let's stay here for a little longer. For the entertainment of the walls if nothing else.'

'No, I'm putting my foot down.' Her right leg glided out from under the duvet and touched down against the floor, making her statement literal as well as figurative. She pulled herself out of the bed graciously and pulled on black lace underwear and a matching bra. Even though they had spent many nights together already, Freddy always made an effort to wear good underwear 'Life is too short to wear granny pants,' was her way of putting it. Kartik appreciated this, and mirrored her by going out and buying several pairs of Calvin Klein, which set him back more than he would usually spend on boxer shorts, but felt it was appropriate.

He rolled to her side of the bed and clasped her wrist gently. She had thin arms, freckled like her neck. Her hands were long, and her fingers were a pale shade of red, as if they were constantly exposed to cold, even though she never complained about the temperature.

She tuned to look at him. 'Get up.'

'Why?'

'Because we're looking at the location today,' she said firmly.

Freddy was meeting the director who was making the short film about the neighbours fighting over hedgerows. Over the past two months, the script for the film had been finalised and the cast assembled. Now, in early December, the locations were set and they were close to shooting. Freddy had recommended Cambridge to the director, as they would require houses with large gardens, and it was much harder to convince London's residents with big gardens to open up their houses and let a dozen semi-professional filmmakers waltz through.

This turned out to be both convenient for Freddy as well as Kartik, as he had somehow managed to secure work as a runner on the production in-between shifts at the café. It was unpaid, but at least it was something, and he was quite excited about it.

She pulled away from his grip. She then turned and grabbed his arm with both her hands, trying to pull him out of the bed, but didn't have the strength to budge Kartik's deadweight. She started to laugh in frustration, as he pulled her back towards him. She landed on the bed, half her body on top of his, her legs still off the edge. With a deft manoeuvre that later he would feel quietly proud about, he reached behind her and removed her bra with one hand as she tried to pull away from him. She slapped him on the chest playfully, to suggest that she disapproved of this sort of behaviour.

They weren't to reach the kitchen for another half an hour.

It was two months since their meeting on the train. Their easy-going conversation on the train had transitioned easily to their first official date. From there they picked things up quickly and easily, seeing each other as frequently as they could. As they only worked a few minutes down the road from each other, they would often drop in to see the other at work, depending on the shift allocated.

And so Freddy had been introduced to Cameron and Rachel, Andrew and Louise, Gabor and Café Ristretto. She got on well with all of them, slipping into social circles like she was slipping into a pair of well-worn jeans.

There was also an introduction to The Maypole, a pub she had never visited since she had moved to Cambridge from Rotherham five years before, a fact Kartik, Cameron and Andrew still found shocking. Louise on the other hand had considered this perfectly normal, and was more shocked at the amount of time her boyfriend spent at the pub. Rachel didn't have an opinion on the correct amount of time spent in The Maypole, but instead was just happy to be anywhere that Cameron also was.

Freddy had even met his parents, which Kartik had been initially sceptical about, but the meal they had had together had gone surprisingly well. Nine years previously, during her gap year, Freddy had spent some time travelling around India by train, which had delighted both his parents. The stories of exotic locations, foreign cities, local cuisine, and fascinating people seemed to go on forever, and Kartik did a fantastic job of zoning out for the most part. If this wasn't enough on its own to make a good impression with the McNairs, she scored extra brownie points with his father with tales of lower league football.

Although she hadn't been to a game for almost fifteen years and at this point in her life had no interest in football, her own father had taken her to Rotherham United games as a child and was able to please David with the importance of supporting your hometown's team. At this point Kartik got a quick glare from his father, as Chelsea were steadily marching their way towards the top of the Premier League and were favourites to win the 2009/10 title, whilst Cambridge United were languishing somewhere in League Two. So after surviving a verbal tour of the entire Asian subcontinent for a couple of hours, Kartik was to endure tales of standing in rundown football stands, with cold pies and bad tea, cheering on a bunch of semi-skilled footballers hoofing long balls across badly maintained pitches.

His father was pleased that Freddy had never migrated to following one of England's major clubs, and seemed to glaze over the fact that she didn't follow football anymore—to lose interest altogether was better than supporting Arsenal, Chelsea, Liverpool, or, heaven forbid, Manchester United.

'She's a perfectly pleasant young lady,' had been his mother's assessment after the night. 'She's got strong roots,' had been his father's. This as strong an endorsement as you could hope for.

Somewhere in the middle of this two-month upturn in Kartik's life there had been the incident at the Stanfield's house. All in one night he had been an accessory to home invasion, adultery, and assault, and the rug had been threatened to be pulled out from under him. There had been the initial worry that Ryan would find out about him and Camilla and come after him, breaking his nose in the middle of a shift at Café Ristretto, but this never happened. Camilla had kept their secret, and the only after effect had been Ryan disappearing entirely from his life, which he adapted to quickly.

Cameron had mentioned that Ryan had come looking for him the next day. But rather than being angry, he had been remorseful and full of guilt. Since then, Cameron hadn't heard from the recruitment consultant either.

When Kartik and Freddy eventually made it downstairs, Louise and Andrew were already up and in the kitchen.

In the kitchen Kartik was roped in to cooking breakfast

with Andrew—bacon, eggs, and fried mushrooms on toast—whilst the girls made coffee. Louise's and Kartik's friendship had become both better and worse since Freddy had entered the scene. She liked the fact that Freddy seemed to be having a positive influence on his life; he spent less time lounging around playing FIFA, fewer nights dragging Andrew to the pub to get drunk with Cameron, and he had stopped smoking weed.

The weed had been surprisingly easy to stop, although he had done this more by accident rather than design. Freddy wasn't opposed to him getting high, and she didn't pressure him or suggest that he stopped. She didn't smoke herself though. The more time he spent with her, the less time he could dedicate to getting high, and so he gradually made the transition from being high every day to being almost completely sober.

However, Louise didn't seem so keen on having yet another person in a place she very much considered *her* house. It wasn't something she made obvious, but the tiny shifts in her behaviour suggested that she felt her world was being constricted, her life overcrowded, like the underground she had to squeeze into every day for work. For Louise, Freddy was another commuter, pushing onto an already crowded train, taking up too much room, exhaling into her personal space, snatching glances of her newspaper over her shoulder. She was pleasant enough to the newcomer, but never entirely relaxed around her, always treating her with a professional distance—don't get comfortable, you're not here for long.

Louise and Andrew had a moving-out date now. They were to move down to London in mid-February, so Kartik had a couple of months to find somewhere else to live, or to otherwise face the fact that he might have to move back in with his parents, a prospect that no member of his family would be particularly thrilled about. The problem remained that he was getting incredibly cheap rent living with Louise and Andrew, meaning if he moved into another place, he'd almost certainly have to pay more, which would be very hard to cope with on his tiny salary. Since losing contact with Ryan he hadn't spent much time looking at alternative employment, and because he was spending his spare time working on the film, he didn't have time to spend job hunting.

He had talked to Freddy about this, and she had seemed to think that a move back in with the parents wasn't such a bad idea, as long as it were temporary, and he didn't fall into yet another comfortable rut. She had picked up fairly quickly that the direction of life followed that of least possible resistance—the easier the route, the more likely he was to trundle down it, regardless of the final destination.

To counter this, she had a keenness about her that looked to prop him up, making sure he didn't fall by the wayside, carefully navigating his existence into something greater that it had been in the past. In that regard, she was a little like Cameron, although less direct and more sympathetic, an encourager rather than a director, someone who had questions herself, rather than someone with all the answers. She never seemed to be too bothered that he was a little slow off the mark when it came to life. There was no bluffing, no façade, no masks, no mirrors, or pretence; she seemed to just exist effortlessly, and that in turn made things around her move smoothly. The fact that she was in her late, rather than early, twenties contributed to this. She was more comfortable within herself and with the people who were around her. Most importantly, she had never looked him dead in the eye and asked:; 'So, what exactly are you going to do with your life?'

But for now, breakfast was on the agenda, and Kartik and Andrew did a decent job of knocking up a good one. Radio 2 was on (Louise's choice. Andrew and Kartik would have settled for TalkSport and Freddy would have opted for BBC 6 Music) and the atmosphere was pleasantly communal. Louise spoke about the previous night's agency meeting, which involved a lot of fancy food and gin and tonics in bars and restaurants that the other three weren't familiar with, but she spoke of like they all knew like the back of their hands.

Her anecdote was habitually punctuated with the phrases 'oh my god, we were so drunk,' and 'we drank so much' and sometimes, 'I've never been that drunk with a client before'.

Of course, this was all allowed in Louise's eyes, as it was work-related. If Andrew had started talking about getting drunk in a pub, he would have been rebuked by his girlfriend. Even these double standards didn't dampen the mood for Kartik, who was still feeling slightly euphoric from his morning activities. He even found Louise's stories more bearable now he knew there was to be a limit on how much longer he was going to have to suffer through them. He was like a prisoner finding his cell more accommodating as his release date approached.

After Louise had finished, they talked about the film, and Louise sunk back into her hangover, listening with polite disinterest, although Andrew seemed genuinely engaged.

After breakfast, Kartik and Freddy were due to meet with *The Line's* director, Sanjay Bhatt, in the small village of Comberton, where they had secured a location to shoot the film. They were to run through some rehearsals with the actors in their scenes.

He had met Sanjay a couple of times already with Freddy. He was a hugely excitable man of thirty, with boundless enthusiasm for everything. The first time Kartik had met him, he had run through the plot of the film—aiming at around thirty minutes in length—acting out every scene and line of dialogue himself. He knew it all by heart. If it had been logistically possible, he probably would have played every part himself, as well as done every job behind the camera.

Sadly, his endless enthusiasm was only matched by his lack of funding. The entire project was scraped together with borrowed money, equipment, and favours—the sole reason Kartik had managed to get a position on the crew was because they couldn't afford to hire someone to do the numerous menial tasks that make up a film shoot. And it didn't seem like there was any business plan for release after it was completed, so Kartik wasn't entirely sure how it was supposed to make money to pay back the loans. Freddy assured him that this wasn't an unusual situation for small films, and very few made any money at all.

'What's the point then?' Kartik had asked after they had left Sanjay's flat in Brixton a few weeks earlier.

'It's not about the money. It's about creating something,' Freddy replied as they walked down the damp streets of Brixton Hill towards the underground station. 'It's about being part of something.'

'Yes, but how can something survive if there is no income involved? You can't just go on borrowing money for your projects and throw Hugh Grant in the lead role.'

'Hugh Grant? Really? That's your cultural and financial reference point?'

'You know what I mean.'

'Not everything works in a straight line like that. A lot of films lose money. Especially independent films. We inhabit a world where hopefully some of the ludicrous amount of money that comes off the back of Hugh Grant's smug smile gets redistributed into the smaller projects. It's a constant battle between individual creativity and some executive worrying over spreadsheets.'

Kartik had liked this idea; that their small gang were a bunch of renegade visionaries doing something outside of the system (even if this was because of necessity rather than choice). But he did occasionally worry that the enthusiastic director was pumping more money than he could afford into this tiny project. Where was the money coming from? Banks? Loan sharks? Would some East End gangster turn up mid-shoot with unpleasant intentions involving a cricket bat and their kneecaps?

Once breakfast was finished, Freddy and Kartik left the house to drive to Comberton. Freddy owned a 2001 blue Ford Ka, which sat outside Louise's house. Kartik had got insured on it as a second driver, not because it was necessary but just because he found a certain simple thrill in driving, and couldn't afford a car himself. It was an automatic, which had surprised Kartik the first time he drove it, when he unconsciously went to push down on the clutch to change gears, and slammed on the break instead, almost causing a VW Polo to slam into the back of them. He had to think back to the times he went go-karting as a kid, and suddenly the two pedals instead of three started to make sense again.

Freddy tossed him the keys as they walked to the car, knowing that driving regularly was somewhat of a novelty for him. The day was wet—every day seemed to be wet this time of year—as he pulled the car onto Mill Road. Cyclists crawled past their left-hand side and Kartik felt a certain liberation from being propelled by a combustion engine rather than pedal power for a change. There was a satisfaction from being in a dry, heated, enclosed space, rather than ploughing through the light rain and wind that would have been slowing him down if he had been on two wheels.

They took the route past Parker's Piece and across towards Fen Causeway. As they passed the turning to Newnham, Kartik took a cautionary glance down the road that led to Ryan's house. He hadn't told Freddy anything about Ryan and Camilla, beyond what he had mentioned on the train during their first meeting. It seemed easier to pretend the entire affair had never happened, to start afresh with his relationship with Freddy untarnished.

'I like it around this part of town,' Freddy said reflectively as they headed out of the city. 'It looked nicer a couple of months ago though, when all the leaves on the trees were golden.' Winter had stripped the trees of their colour, and the calming, rich autumnal tone had given way to bare skeletons of bark.

'Yeah, I never really come out here.' Kartik felt like he had to put some distance between himself and his surroundings, but worried that his denial came across rushed and suspicious.

The road took them past Wolfson, the postgraduate colleges, and then past the sports grounds of various college. A mile from the edge of the city the M11 cut through the countryside.

The road was clear in front, so Kartik put his foot on the accelerator as they crossed the bridge, over the motorway, spray picking up on either side of the car. There was a steady stream of cars coming in the opposite direction, inhabitants of Cambridge's quiet and affluent surrounding villages heading to the city centre for a day of shopping, eating, and queuing up in coffee shops, being surprised and annoyed in equal measure that everywhere they went was busy. How many of those going past would end of in Café Ristretto, tutting at Gabor for not being able to serve the streaming hordes with the swiftness that they unrealistically expected? As Kartik swung the car around a roundabout faster that he perhaps should have, he felt a sense of elation for not having to work on a Saturday for a change.

They turned off the main road, and headed down country roads for a few miles until they arrived in Comberton. It was a low, flat, gentle village that was almost entirely surrounded by farmland, the fields ploughed into brown mud for the winter.

'Just up here,' Freddy said, pointing right at a crossroads. He was directed to a small bungalow with several cars parked outside already.

Sanjay greeted them at the door with his usual unshakable energy, grappling both of them in a tight bear hug, before leading them into the living room.

The room had already been mostly taken up by the cast and crew, with a dozen or so people milling around with equipment: cameras, tripods, boom mics, props and costumes. Near the wall, squeezed into a corner that looked a bit too small, were an elderly couple, in their late seventies who were smiling politely to mask the utter bewilderment that they were clearly feeling.

'This is Mr. and Mrs. McGarry,' Sanjay said introducing Kartik and Freddy. 'They own the house and have agreed to let us shoot here.' Their hosts waved sheepishly and Freddy and Kartik nodded in response. They were doing this very much pro bono.

'Right, so there has been a change of plan,' Sanjay continued, turning to them again. 'As you can see, we're all here and we're all a little early. Which means we can start shooting today.'

'Start shooting today?' Freddy was more than a little surprised.

'Everything's ready, we're good to go.' Sanjay was already ushering people into the garden to start setting up. Kartik didn't really understand what his role in all this way to be, but followed anyway. Three people in the group he recognised as the principal actors, the rest he assumed were the other crew. They went out back into a long garden and started setting up positions. It was clear everyone present had had more training and a better brief than he had, with the exception of Mr. and Mrs. McGarry who gingerly followed them all as they automatically floated into positions that appeared relevant.

'Right, we've only got a few hours of good light, so let's make some progress today,' Sanjay announced.

The actors took their places, their movements and actions well-rehearsed, and Sanjay went over to work with them.

For the first hour or so, the equipment was set up and Sanjay fiddled with the cameras, the lighting, the sound equipment and the actors. The actors went over their lines and movements with Sanjay hovering nearby. Freddy joined in with the bustling activity smoothly, checking off items with the team, asking technical questions, finding solutions when people had questions for her. She was a joy to watch, slotting in without missing a beat. There was something about her unwavering, emotionless professionalism that made him almost more attracted to her than he had been when she had been naked beside his bed this morning—almost, but not quite.

He did little aside from moving some boxes and running cables into the house. It wasn't exciting, but at least he wasn't spending his Saturday making coffees for strangers. And he did a damn good job moving those boxes.

'Kartik, right?' Sanjay said, as he took a break from the whirlwind activity that had surrounded him since they had started in the garden. There was a sense of satisfaction with the progress of the set up so far. It was a little after midday, and the day was going according to plan.

'Yeah,' Kartik said, keen to show he was eager to work.

'How are you finding the day so far?'

'Yeah, it's great. Do you need anything from me?'

'Well, we're just about to take a break before we start rolling the camera in thirty minutes or so.'

'Cool.' Kartik was half expecting to be asked to get behind the main camera, the weight of expectation suddenly heavy on his shoulders.

'So, is it possible to fix the crew with a quick round of coffees?' The request was delivered with an expecting grin. 'I would ask the McGarrys, but they've been so kind to let us use their house in the first place.' Kartik turned toward the

McGarrys to hide his sense of deflation. They were wisely in the comfort of their living room, watching out the window with a hazy sense of curiosity at the circus unfolding in their garden.

'A coffee round?'

'Yeah.'

'No problem,' Kartik said as he marched into the kitchen, to a routine he found more than a little familiar.

CHAPTER TWENTY-SIX

'Max Bellingham came out.'

'Huh?'

'Max Bellingham. He came out of the closet.'

'Who is Max Bellingham?'

'The guy from Churchill who almost beat you up a few months ago.'

'The rugby player?'

'The first openly gay captain of the Cambridge rugby team,' Cameron said reading from the front page of the Varsity newspaper. They were sitting at a table in Café Ristretto. Kartik was on his break.

'Good for him.'

'No, it's not good for him.'

'It's not?'

'No. It's not. I don't know why everyone is making such a big deal out of it.'

'I would have thought you'd be more supportive?'

'Why? No one gives a shit when thousands of people come out every day. No one gave a shit when I told everyone I was gay.'

'I gave a shit,' Kartik said.

'Only because you fancied me at the time.'

'That's not true,' Kartik said. Cameron fixed him with a look that suggested she knew better.

'Okay, maybe a little bit. But that's beside the point. Isn't it good that he can talk about it? That your newspaper covers it like this.'

'No, it's not good,' Cameron said. 'They're fawning over him like he's the chosen one. Just because everyone knows he's gay doesn't mean he's not a dick.'

'But it will probably mean he will get more dick.'

'Can you take anything seriously?'

'I'm taking a lot of things seriously actually. I've got a lot of responsibility on the film.'

'Kartik, you carry boxes and make the coffees. You're not Hitchcock.'

'Thanks.'

'You've got a new hobby. It's not like it's a career path.'

'I thought you'd be happy that I was doing more with my life than working here?'

'I am. But what happened to following things up with Ryan? See if you can get more interviews?'

'Ryan's gone dark on us. And that's not exactly a bad thing after everything that's happened. Besides, I'm actually enjoying working on the film. It's nice being part of something that will have a tangible product at the end.

'It's good your girlfriend has roped you into her little project, but don't forget you need to earn money at some point in your life.'

'Little project? You can talk. What about Eden's Bonfire? You've been working on that for months and no one is any closer to knowing what the hell it is.'

'That's different.'

'How?'

'It just is.'

'Good argument.'

'I'm sorry. I'm in a bad mood. I guess I'm just annoyed about this sycophancy for Max. Why does it have to be the front page of the student newspaper? Some people are just put on a pedestal because of their name or background, not because of what they've achieved.'

'No need to get jealous,' Kartik said, perfectly aware that he was being abrasive. 'I think you need to be more supportive of other members of your community.'

'My community? He's not part of my community. Let's get out of the mentality that just because two people are of the same sexual orientation they have common ground.'

'Okay, you don't like him. I get it. But, you know, progress and all that.'

'Progress? Max Bellingham is as progressive as a puddle.'

'Fine. Whatever. I'm going back to work,' Kartik said, even though he still had a few minutes. For the first time in years, it felt like there was something coming between him and Cameron. It was also perhaps the first time he had ever cut short his lunchbreak. The times they were a-changing.

CHAPTER TWENTY-SEVEN

Over the next two weeks, what became apparent was that filmmaking was boring. Very, very boring. Ninety-five percent of Kartik's time was spent waiting around, hoping that someone would ask him to do something to stop him from gnawing his own hand off out of sheer tedium. He would watch as the actors rehearsed, he watched as Sanjay instructed the crew, he watched silently when they were doing takes. Then, after he had become numb with boredom, there would be some orders barked at him, which would be followed by a frantic few minutes as he was galvanised into action, moving equipment, running cables, or arranging the next round of tea and coffees.

Gabor had been good about giving him flexible shifts at Café Ristretto, so he could spend half his time shooting. In the Hungarian's mind, he was working on a big budget blockbuster, and Gabor wanted to do everything in his power to allow Kartik to have this opportunity.

'In Hungary, English films are very popular,' Gabor said one time as they switched the shifts on the rota to allow Kartik an afternoon of film work. 'James Bond is the best action film. Everyone loves it.'

'Well, it's not quite a Bond film,' Kartik replied sheepishly.

'Yes, but you start here, then in few years, if you are lucky, you will work with Daniel Craig.'

'And if I'm unlucky I will work with Roger Moore.'

'Don't joke about Roger Moore. He is very respected in my country.'

Kartik also half-suspected that part of Gabor's encouragement for the film was to get Kartik out of the café more so they would have a better chance of getting the coveted Gold Star Store of Excellence Award.

And so, with a favourable rota, he was able to work the two jobs, which seriously dented the time he could allocate towards playing FIFA or going to the pub. Only Andrew seemed to have a problem with this.

As a producer, Freddy wasn't required to spend every day onset, so a lot of the time he would drive down to the location alone. For the first couple of days the crew were patient with him, but always seemed to be a few paces ahead. It was like trying to enter an Army unit without going through basic training. He messed up twice on his first day without Freddy: once for dropping a tripod, and again for coughing in the middle of a take, resulting in one of the principal actors throwing a strop about reshooting.

The reprimands he got from Sanjay were gentle but patronising, and the next day he was relegated back to doing the coffee runs. He therefore got to know the McGarrys quite well instead. They were a gentle, gracious couple, who were enthusiastic, if somewhat befuddled by the process that was taking place in their garden and their living room. They both still had the had good mobility that sometimes leaves people by the time they reached their mid-seventies, and Kartik couldn't help but see a version of his parents, twenty years in the future, whenever Mrs. McGarry helped him prepare a tray of biscuits, or Mr. McGarry asked how to run malware software on his slowing and aging PC.

They had both been involved in the arts in one form or another for almost all their lives. Ian McGarry, tall, slender, with a hawk-like face, had been a lecturer in medieval literature at Aberdeen University from the seventies until the late nineties when they had moved to Cambridge to retire. He still wrote articles and papers in his spare time, and was worried that hackers would still these articles from his hard drive if he didn't act quickly. Kartik had to explain it wasn't individual hackers trying to get at his work, but the malware was automated, hidden within downloads and updates, which damaged his computer. Mr. McGarry claimed that he understood what this meant.

Vivian McGarry, short, round, and homely, had been a theatre actress in the late fifties and early sixties in London, but had drifted out of the profession when the couple moved up to Aberdeen. She had been the one whose idea it was to respond to the advert for locations, a way to vicariously relive her days in the spotlight by hosting the talent of tomorrow.

Whilst they were both excited to be part of the artistic process, one thing they had not expected was the mess the film crew dragged around. As a lot of the shooting was done in the garden the crew would often leave muddy footprints in the house as they stormed through foraging for a new camera lens or lightbulb. Kartik used some of his downtime to clean up his colleagues' debris. This won him special brownie points with their hosts and resulted in Mrs. McGarry bringing out 'the special biscuits'. On the third day on set, he purchased a few large sheets of plastic coverings from B&Q, which he put down in the living room and kitchen. Mr. McGarry decided this effort was worthy of the special whisky at the end of that day's work.

Getting to know the crew was harder than the hosts, but their coldness slowly defrosted as he became more competent and comfortable on set. Jack, a hulking, bearded boom mike operator in his mid-thirties, taught him how to handle his equipment to pick up the actor's dialogue the best and minimise background sound. Sanjay introduced him to the principle actors, two jobbing thespians in their forties who, you couldn't help but think, should have had a bit more on their resume to command the distinctly superior attitude they displayed to the people around them. It was an aloof arrogance reserved for everyone except Sanjay, to who they showed unwavering dedication. Professional in their approach, but dismissive to the little guys, it reaffirmed what Kartik had sometimes assumed about actors.

Regardless of the haughtiness of the thespians, by the third week he had worked his way into the fold enough to run lines with one of the actors, Margaret, between takes. The dialogue mostly revolved around her character berating her counterpart over an overgrowing wisteria plant. There was a metaphor in there somewhere, but it was lost on Kartik.

'How's it going?' Freddy asked when she visited the set at the end of the third week of shooting.

'It's going well,' Kartik replied as he moved framed pictures from the hallway walls. The day before Jack had knocked a painting off the wall with his boom mike, cracking the frame so Kartik had decided to remove the remaining pictures to avoid further mishaps. Mrs. McGarry had promised him some of her new 'special Assam tea' as a reward for his fairly obvious response.

'You're well ahead of schedule,' she said, surprise in her voice. The rest of the team were in the living room, finishing up the last few takes of the principle photography, a full week before what Sanjay had planned.

'Blame Sanjay, not me,' he replied as he put a picture of the McGarrys' children into the storage box.

'He says you've been very helpful. Very proactive.'

'Aren't I always?'

She laughed and kissed him on the cheek as he took the box of pictures into the spare bedroom.

Freddy slid into the room and talked with Sanjay for a while. Kartik went into the kitchen. Mrs. McGarry was there, not doing much other than staying out of the way.

'Hi.' She patted a seat next to the kitchen table for him to sit at and poured him a cup of tea. He had drunk more tea since meeting the McGarrys than he had in his whole life.

'You're almost finished, aren't you?' Mrs. McGarry asked, nodding towards the noise coming from the living room, where they were setting up Margret's close-ups. There was a hint of sadness in her voice.

'Yeah, just a couple of shots to get and then we'll be out of your hair.'

'Well, I've quite liked having you all around. It's been very exciting. All this movement and energy. I like watching creative people work. Reminds me of when I was working.' She picked up a tray of biscuits. 'I was saving them for the rest of them to take a break, but as you're here you can have first pick.' She nodded knowingly, as if this clandestine transaction was a secret that had to be kept just between the two of them. 'They're all the way from Belgium.'

'I though the Belgians did chocolate.'

'They do very good biscuits as well. We went on a trip to Antwerp in the summer. Have you been?'

'No. How was it?'

'Oh, it was wonderful.'

The biscuit was indeed good and would give him sustenance as Mrs. McGarry started to detail her week in Belgium in minute detail. Starting from the short plane ride, to the state of the hotel, the places they visited, and the people that they met. It wasn't necessary to listen too intently to this story, as an occasional nod and 'oh, really' would be sufficient to pass as interested.

At some point at the security gate in Stansted (Mr. McGarry was getting questioned by 'aggressive' airport staff because he kept setting off the alarm, which was ridiculous because 'he doesn't even look like a terrorist') his mind started to wander back to the last time he saw Ryan. What was that twinge in his stomach? Was it guilt? Did he feel partly responsible for the whole unravelling of his friend's marriage? He looked out of the kitchen window, which faced on to the barren, brown field. The field slopped very gently upwards over across about half a mile, before disappearing into the edge of the sky. Cambridge, five miles beyond the field, was hidden by the ridge. Somewhere there, Ryan was going about fixing things. Or so he hoped.

Was it a marriage that could be repaired? Camilla was a psychopath, there was no doubt about that. He doubted he was the first person she had cheated on Ryan with. But would the naked man be the last? Who had he been? Another disposal stooge like Kartik had been? Why had she taken down the hallway pictures when he visited her, but not the naked man? A mistake? Something deliberate?

He was very aware that she had used him during their liaisons but he really didn't care; she had received attention from a younger man and a chance to get back at her cheating husband, and he had got laid. It had been a happy little economy they had operated in. But then the stock market had crashed, and the names of other investors were revealed.

Several times in the past weeks he had wondered if he should get in contact with Camilla, but had always refrained from it. Why put himself in a position where he could be exposed as her former lover? All it would take was one small comment to her husband, and he'd be on the receiving end of one of Ryan's right hooks. The only upshot of this theoretical, but plausible, event would be at least it was more than likely he would be clothed at the time.

There was a blur of motion across the field outside the house, but it was too far away and too quick for Kartik to determine what it was. It could have been a hare. Were they around this time of year? Did hares hibernate? He had no idea about these sorts of things. It would have been the right size for a fox, but they were nocturnal, weren't they? The only time they came out during the day was when they were being chased by horses and hounds at the command of people that sounded and acted like Camilla. He could picture her on a cold, foggy morning, dressed up in Hunter wellies and a Barbour jacket, ready to enjoy watching her friends on the hunt, or ready to go shooting, or to cause harm to some small animal for pleasure. It was her right as someone with a large inheritance and the right family to be able to cause physical suffering. He could almost see Ryan there as well, but he was fuzzier in the picture. Dragged along rather than enthusiastically cheering, politely smiling at the blood sports instead of getting his hands dirty. He was an urban man, someone who had started life a little richer than he pretended, had flourished in a career that allowed him to put money before people, and eventually married into an even greater pile of wealth. The landed gentry weren't his sort of people, but he was only a second country home and a membership of a decent golf club away from purchasing his way in.

The streak of movement disappeared as quickly as it had appeared. It had probably just been someone's cat.

'...and that's where I got these biscuits. The same place that we had run into the Italian man! Can you believe it?' Mrs. McGarry's laughter at her own anecdote brought him back into the room.

'Right, yeah.' He obliged with a laugh of his own. He had no idea what Mrs. McGarry was talking about.

He was thankfully saved when Freddy re-entered the room.

'You've got crumbs on your jeans,' she pointed out to Kartik. Carefully, he swept them into his hand and transferred them into the bin.

· · ·

A day later, on the 20th December, the film's principal photography was completed. The crew disappeared from the house, the plastic was lifted from the floors, the photos were put back on the walls, they said their goodbyes to the McGarrys, and then went their separate ways for Christmas. Kartik had let Sanjay know that he would be available if he needed anything done in the post-production stage, although with the editing taking place in his Brixton flat, it seemed unlikely.

CHAPTER TWENTY-EIGHT

'He's coming.'
'No, he's not.'
'Yes, he is.'
'Why?'
'Why what?'
'Why is he coming?'
'Because I invited him.'
'That's the worst idea you've ever had.'
'He's got no one else.'
'He's got friends.
'Does he?'
'Philip? Aaron?'
'Philip's got a family. And Aaron's probably got friends his age he's going to spend New Years' Eve with.'
'Do you want to know what other people are also Aaron's age? We are. We are literally the same age as Aaron. We have friends Aaron's age. So why the hell are we accommodating Ryan for *our* New Year's Eve celebration?' Kartik looked over at Cameron from the counter of Café Ristretto. He hoped that his face conveyed the exasperation that he felt.
'Because he's your friend.'

'I haven't spoken to him in over a month.'

'Well, he phoned me up and he doesn't have anyone else. So I invited him to join us.'

'Why didn't you make some excuse? You're busy. You're out of the country. You're having a triple-heart bypass. Anything would have done.'

'Because I'm not the sort of person who lies to my friends.'

'He's not our friend, Cameron.'

'He's a good person.'

'Since when have you thought *he* was a good person?'

'Look, he's set me up with a couple of very good interviews with very prestigious hedge funds in January, so I thought I owed him one. It's the least we can do.'

'You've been talking to him all this time, haven't you?'

Cameron look uncomfortable for a second. 'Yes. We've been talking.'

'You've actually been engaging with him? After what he did to me?'

'What *he* did to you? What about what *you* did to him? You fucked his wife, Kartik.'

Racked with guilt, Kartik had finally told Cameron about the Anna Camilla Stanfield situation. She hadn't reacted positively to the news. 'I didn't know that at the time.'

'You accidently fucked his wife. Still not great, is it?'

'So, you're going to work in finance after you graduate?' Kartik said, keen to move the conversation away from himself.

'Yeah. So?'

'What about staying in education? Going for your PhD? Keep working on Eden's Bonfire?

'I can still do that after a few years' experience of real work. Education is always something I can come back to. But the positions that are being talked about, and the salaries they offer! These opportunities won't come around too often.'

There was a queue forming by the counter as Christmas

shoppers, weighed down with bags, took a break from hunting and fighting over gifts for a quick coffee. Most were carrying at least three bags, with quite a number with much more. There may have been a recession on, but that wasn't going to stop people throwing what little money they had to win the affection of a child, or a lover, or a colleague. How many of the presents in those bags would end up unused, unloved, or returned?

'Kartik, can you jump on a till?' Gabor called over as he took an order from a disgruntled and damp customer.

Gabor and Alison were struggling to keep the hoard at bay, but Kartik was too concerned with this recent news to even consider the possibility of doing his job. *How is one supposed to work when someone had dropped such a bombshell?*

'One second,' Kartik said dismissively to Gabor. He turned back to Cameron. 'You're starting to sound like him. I didn't realise that you would be so quick to sell out.'

'For god's sake, Kartik. Getting a good job doesn't mean you've sold out. And besides, hedge funds are changing. It's not an old boys' network anymore. They need people like me who knows how numbers work. Right now, there is a window of opportunity for a technocracy to evolve,' Cameron said. Kartik was eight-five percent sure he knew what a technocracy was. 'But in a few years, when things recover, it'll go back to bankers employing their nephews and people with the right surname,' she continued. 'The recession means I've got an opportunity that may never come up again.'

'You've bought into his lies.'

'I'm being a realist.'

'A realist? You'll sit in a suit, and crunch numbers, and turn into part of the machine.'

'Oh, stop pontificating this demagoguery, you myopic prick.'

'Huh?'

'Don't be such an anti-establishment hero. Because you're not. We can't all have artsy-fartsy jobs like your girlfriend.'

'Kartik, stop talking and give us hand,' Gabor shouted. But Kartik was now too incensed to respond.

'Oh, so this is about me and Freddy?'

Cameron pulled back from the bar, perhaps shocking herself with what she had just said. 'What? No! This has nothing to do with you and Freddy. This is about me. Stop being so self-important.'

'I'm self-important? Listen to yourself! Listen to how you've changed.'

Cameron tried to calm herself. The conversation had become personal, and neither party wanted to be mad at each other. 'Can we not do this here?'

'What's wrong with doing this here?' Kartik said.

'Well, you've got a queue to serve for one thing.' Cameron pointed to the irate customers waiting for their coffees.

'Don't tell me how to do my job, Cameron.'

'Well, don't tell me how to lead my life. If I want to take this opportunity, I'm going to.'

'Sell-out,' Kartik muttered.

'I don't care,' Cameron said.

'It was a mistake to invite Ryan.'

'He's not a terrible person.' Kartik looked her dead in the eyes. 'Okay, well maybe he's not the best person in the world. But he needs some friends. And he's helping me out.'

'How exactly am I going to explain Ryan's sudden appearance to Freddy?'

'Oh, I don't know: *Hi Freddy. This is my friend Ryan. Ryan, this is my girlfriend Freddy.*' She acted out her little farce, like it was going to be the most natural thing in the world.

'You were the one that told me not to tell Freddy about the Ryan incident with his wife.'

'Maybe I did. And maybe that's something that comes up. And then it's just something that we will deal with.'

'Something we'll just deal with? Cameron, you can't just deal with things. That never works. In the fantasy world you live in, there are problems, you take action, and then the problems magically go away. That's not how the real world works, Cameron. Dealing with things doesn't work.'

'Do you know who you sound like?'

'Who?'

'You sound like yourself. But from a few months ago. Before you met Freddy. When I didn't respect you much.' The personal barbs were out again.

'What?'

'Look, go and work, we'll talk about it later,' Cameron said.

'No, wait. What did you say?'

'About what?'

'About not liking me?'

Her eyes rolled with frustration, but Kartik wasn't about to let this go. 'It's not that I didn't like you. It's just that over the past couple of months, there's been a change in you. With Freddy, with the film—you just seem to be happier. But I also feel we've been growing apart. It's like, the happier you've become, the less we get on. And I don't want us to have a falling out here.'

They were on uncomfortable ground now. Both angry at each other, but both desperately wanting to make amends, but trying to do so without conceding their point. They were saved by an angry shout from a few feet away.

'Kartik, now!' Gabor's raised voice alarmed the customers he was serving.

'Okay, fine. He can come,' Kartik said before heading over to the till and trying his hardest to politely address the lady in the front of the queue.

And so it was devised, by Cameron's design, that Kartik and Ryan were set to meet each other again for the first time since the night of the incident with the naked man.

CHAPTER TWENTY-NINE

In a pile in front of him lay the label to his beer. He had torn it into small pieces and tried to arrange them into a pattern, but he lacked the artistic merit to do this adequately. So instead he just pushed the scraps into a pile and stared at them for a while.

'You know, they say it's a sign of sexual frustration.'

'Huh?'

'When someone picks at the label of their drink. It means they're sexually frustrated.'

'I'll move onto pints, I think.'

'Are you sexually frustrated, Kartik?' Louise looked at him. She was never this blunt around him.

'I'm fine.'

'Are you sure?' She nodded towards the bar of The Maypole where Freddy was standing.

'Excuse me?' Unintentionally, he had raised the pitch of his voice to an indignant high, which sounded more ridiculous than he had intended.

'Nothing.' Louise looked around the bar. It was already filling up for the New Year's festivities. It was early evening and the front room was full of good natured chatter and post-

Christmas cheer. Kartik, Freddy, Louise, and Andrew were the first of their group to arrive—they were still waiting on Cameron, Rachel, and Ryan. Kartik still held out hope that the latter wouldn't turn up.

'So how was your Christmas?' Louise asked turning back to face him. Her face was without expression and the question was purely perfunctory. They hadn't seen each other since before Christmas as Louise had spent the holiday skiing with her family in France.

'Yeah, it was okay,' he said. 'To be honest, I spent most of it working at Ristretto or on the film. I had Christmas Day off though, which was nice, I guess. Just spent a quiet day with the parents, watching TV, eating too much, and killing time with Scrabble.' He didn't mention that he lost every game, and his dad always won. The only break from this pattern was a quick visit from Freddy, who rather brilliantly broke his father's winning streak in her first game. Kartik still came a miserable last.

'How was skiing?' He didn't really care about Louise's holiday, but he felt it polite to ask. He had only gone skiing once himself, on a school trip to Switzerland when he was fifteen, and he had been more concerned with trying to take advantage of the continent's lax underage drinking laws and chasing after Swiss girls, than wasting much of his time throwing himself down a cold mountain with sticks on his feet.

'Yeah, it was great,' Louise said, happy that it was her turn to talk again. 'We went to Chamonix. We go every year. It was amazing. There was a big dump of snow just before we got there so it was perfect conditions.'

'Hmm…' Kartik replied.

Thankfully, Freddy and Andrew soon returned from the bar and they were able to distract themselves with alternative conversation.

At eight o'clock they were joined by Rachel and Cameron.

Louise welcomed both with an unusually warm embrace, especially Rachel, whom she seemed to squeeze a bit too tightly. She then proceeded to move chairs so she could be closer to Rachel, and they quickly started talking with an alacrity that was unusual for both.

Kartik caught Andrew and Cameron raise eyebrows at this, both caught off-guard by this friendship that was previously unknown to the group. Was there a sliver of jealousy in Cameron's eyes? Usually she was the only one that ever got any of Rachel's attention, and perhaps this new dynamic vexed her. Maybe because of this, or maybe because of a myriad of other factors, Kartik struggled to relax.

'You look tense,' Freddy said quietly to him as he drank from his pint.

'I'm fine.'

'Is it because Cameron's invited this head-hunter guy?'

'It's a lot of things.' He had told Freddy about his disagreement with Cameron, and she'd suggested that he ride it out, letting any tension dissipate with time. She was fantastically diplomatic which was probably why she was good at working as a producer. Kartik had tactically decided not to mention Cameron's comment about her 'artsy-fartsy job', as he didn't want a rift to develop between these two. He felt his life was on the edge of a seismic shift, and he didn't want to be pulled in two different directions by the two women who he was closest to. Celebrate ignorance and you celebrate a peaceful existence.

The night wore on, nothing much happened for what seemed like a long while. Drinks flowed, music played, people danced, stories were told, memories of 2009 were shared—the highs and the lows—and plans were made for how 2010 was going to be different, enjoyable, successful. When Kartik spoke about his plans, he made a vague promise that he would use his experience working with Sanjay to work on more films. He didn't know how he would go about it, but specifics didn't seem too important at this time. This response seemed to please both Freddy and Cameron, and there was a pleasant, knowing smile between them as he talked.

When it came to Kartik's round to buy drinks, Andrew offered to help him out, leaving the girls alone at the table. They had to wrestle their way to the bar, as the queue was already three deep, the bar staff already exhausted by the relentless cheer of the crowd and their ability to drink themselves into a stupor.

Though he spent a lot of his time in crowded pubs and bars surrounded by other drunks, on this night he felt on edge as strangers nudged into him, shouted in his ear, and generally got in his way. There was an emptiness in his stomach that translated into a weakness in his legs, as if they would collapse under the weight of the room's collective inebriation. The short-tempered barman did nothing to alleviate this uncomfortability. His order was barked back at him for him to confirm, a frown chiselled on the barman's face.

So this was how the year would end; not with a bang or a celebration, but with a creeping, undefined feeling of worry and anxiety.

It was as the barman frostily placed the first of the drinks on the bar that he felt a large hand on his shoulder. It was a grasp he immediately recognised, the thick fingers digging into his collarbone. He immediately tensed up.

'Hello, mate. It's been a while.'

'Hi, Ryan,' Kartik said turning. Kartik held out his hand for a handshake as Ryan went in for a cumbersome hug. They compromised with an inelegant pat on the shoulder at a difficult angle that didn't fulfil the criteria that either party had initially intended. 'Do you want a drink?'

'Yeah, pint of lager,' Ryan replied. The drink was added to

the order as Andrew and Ryan greeted each other. They opted for the safety of a handshake.

The three of them collected the drinks and they headed back to the table they had reserved for the night, Ryan introducing himself with a confident 'hello' to the girls. Cameron beamed at him. Rachel waved, her movements betraying a hint of nervousness. Louise's greeting was operational, one professional to another.

The final introduction was the one Kartik feared the most. 'Freddy, this is Ryan. Ryan, this is my girlfriend, Freddy.' He realised he had worded it exactly as Cameron had suggested before Christmas.

'Freddy?' Ryan said, leaning over and shaking her hand, planting two kisses on each cheek.

'It's short for Frederica,' she replied, one step ahead.

'Right,' Ryan said.

And then they sat down, and that was that. It had gone exactly how Cameron had predicted. An introduction had been made, two people who had vaguely heard about each other had now met face to face, and whatever inexplicable terror Kartik had expected to happen, had somehow been avoided. The night could continue, and everyone could bloody well relax.

An hour later Kartik found himself at the end of their table with Freddy and Andrew. Louise and Rachel were chatting away on their own, and Ryan was at the bar with Cameron. They were both tipsy, and Cameron looked like she was trying to be his wingman. They were talking to two women in their mid-forties, heavily made-up and dressed to impress. The women were humouring them both, but didn't look too interested, no matter how many times Cameron mentioned that Ryan was 'a really great guy that any straight woman would be lucky to have.'

'About Ryan?' Freddy said, looking over at his attempt at flirting.

'Yeah. He's a character,' Kartik said diplomatically.

'He seems interesting,' Freddy said inquisitively.

'I'm not sure if interesting is the best word to use,' Kartik demurred. At the bar Ryan had pulled up his shirtsleeve and flexed his bicep. Cameron squeezed the muscle in a mock display of amazement, and then tried to get the two women to do the same. Neither did.

'He reminds me of someone. I'm not sure who. He's like a character from *La Nouvelle Vague.*'

'What's that?' Andrew asked.

'It's a film movement,' Freddy explained.

'Is it foreign?'

'Really?' Kartik raised an eyebrow at his friend.

'The clue's in the language, Andrew,' Freddy said patiently.

'French, right?'

'*Tres Bien.* The French New Wave.'

'I don't really know what that means,' Andrew said. His favourite film of all time was *Rush Hour 2.*

'There's a film called *A Bout de Souffe.*'

'A boot da what?'

'The English title is *Breathless.*' Freddy said. 'There's a character played by Jean-Paul Belmondo. There's something about Ryan that reminds me of him.'

'Is that a good or a bad thing?' Kartik asked.

'I don't know. He seems like a bit of a loose cannon.'

'Sometimes,' Kartik agreed, suddenly feeling that the room had risen a few degrees in temperature. Freddy was fishing. It was like she knew there was something in the murky waters of his past, but wasn't entirely sure what lay beneath. He decided he needed to put some distance between her suspicions and his past. 'But he's a good person. He's good with his family. Well, his daughter anyway.'

'And his wife?'

'Well, not everything is perfect.'

'How come?'

'Is this really the right time?' Kartik said sharply.

Freddy pulled back slightly. 'Sorry. I didn't mean to pry.'

'Louise doesn't like him,' Andrew said.

'Louise's doesn't like anyone,' Kartik said, a little too loudly.

Louise looked up from her conversation with Rachel. 'What was that?'

'Just wondering if you wanted another drink,' Kartik said.

'I'm fine thanks,' Louise said, before turning back to Rachel.

'Idiot,' Andrew said, hitting Kartik in the arm.

At the bar, the two women were making a swift move for the exit. Cameron and Ryan were yelling after them, promising them a wonderful night if they stayed. When the girls got through the throng of the crowds and disappeared into the night, the wingman and her prodigy burst out into hysterics. At least Cameron seemed to be unreservedly enjoying Ryan's company.

'So how have you been?' Kartik asked a couple of hours later, as he and Ryan stood outside smoking. The night had been a whirlwind of musical chairs, as people went to the bar, talked to different people and swapped positions. Ryan had spent most of his time with Cameron. They had continued their wingman routine for a while, flirting with any girl who came into the pub. Rachel had occasionally looked over with a stabbing look of jealousy in her eyes. Since Ryan had joined them, a clear asymmetry had blighted the group, three couples infiltrated by someone only tenuously linked to them, whose absence of a plus-one was known about by all, but talked about by none.

'Yeah, not bad,' Ryan replied. 'Been getting back into shape.'

He did look better than he had when they had seen each other last. Even under his parka, it was noticeable he had lost weight; the protruding beer belly no longer hanging so far over his belt, his jawline more prominent as excess fat had receded from his face. His nose was absent of visible veins, and he was clean shaven. He had carried his conversations through the night in a controlled manner, and there was a measured pace to his drinking. He was probably the least drunk of all of them, the exact opposite of what Kartik had expected when he had walked in.

'Yeah, you look good.'

'Thanks.'

Silence. They watched as the smoke from their cigarettes rose into the clear winter air. The temperature had dropped dramatically since Christmas Day, with daytime temperatures no longer getting above freezing, and the New Year expected to be welcomed by temperatures approaching minus-five. It had snowed the day before, which had camouflaged the black ice that had terrorised pavements and roads for the past few days.

Kartik decided to take the plunge and address the elephant in the room. 'Do you want to talk about, you know, *that* night?'

Ryan exhaled. 'How long have you got?' He took another drag, but his cigarette had gone out. Kartik reached into his pocket and pulled out his lighter. He was wearing a long grey coat that Freddy had got him for Christmas. Around his neck was a maroon cashmere scarf, also a present. His girlfriend was making a conscious effort to dress him better. Ryan took the lighter and relit his cigarette.

Kartik looked down at his watch. 'Well, we've got fifteen minutes before the clock strikes twelve.'

'I don't think that's going to be enough time.'

'You haven't thrown a thousand pages of neo-con propaganda at anyone else, have you?'

'Huh?'

'*Atlas Shrugged*. The book that you threw at the naked guy. Don't you remember?'

'I threw a book at him?'

'Yeah. You hit him right on the back of the head with it.'

'I don't remember that. Was he hurt?'

'Well, it's a very heavy book. Luckily it wasn't a hardback.'

The two men looked at each other, and then burst into laughter. In retrospect, there was something hilariously surreal about that night's events.

'Well, no, I haven't thrown a book at anyone recently. Not that I know of. But I'll give you the paraphrased version of what's happened since.' He sighed, as if he was struggling to remember a long-forgotten memory. 'Well, Anna has moved out of the house. She's moved in with her sister on a temporary basis. She said that, "things weren't working", which is her euphemism for "I've been fucking other men."'

'Other *men*?' The use of the plural scared the crap out of Kartik.

'Yep. Apparently there were others. I didn't want to find out who they were, or how many. There's only so many shocks that someone can take, you know? Besides, it's not like I was any better.'

'Yeah, she knows about Penelope.'

'What do you mean she knows about Penelope?'

Shit. Fuck. Bollocks. 'No, it was a question. She *know*s about Penelope?' He added an upward inflection to mask his mistake.

'I don't know. Probably. Again, she didn't want details. So that was that. She's moved out and I imagine the divorce paperwork will start piling up sometime early next year, once all the lawyers come back from their Christmas holidays in the Caribbean.' He was speaking very plainly, without bitterness, as if instructing someone how to change a tyre. 'So, I've just been pottering around the house, keeping up with work, keeping my mind off it. Working with Cameron to find a few options.'

'Yeah, she mentioned.' Kartik didn't repeat his opinion of this to Ryan.

'And I started going to the gym for the first time in years. Got a personal trainer and everything.'

'Money well spent.'

'Yeah, but my trainer would be pissed off if he knew I was smoking.' He chucked the butt of his cigarette. 'Plus, I'm not meant to be drinking beer. Did you know it's the same number of calories as eating seven slices of bread?'

'I did not know that.'

'It's true. I've got a new diet and everything. Since Anna's left, I just wanted to get healthy again.'

'What about Arabella?' Kartik asked.

It was the first time the calm in Ryan's voice wavered. 'She's living with me in the house. We both agreed it was better for her to stay in the house. But she's confused. She was smart enough to know things weren't going well for a long time. But that's the worst thing about this whole situation. She's the one that gets the worst deal. Me and Anna? We're adults, you know? But Arabella? Shit, she's just a child.' He paused. 'I just want to make sure that when the monstrous paperwork comes through for the settlement, we both get a fair share of her time. I'm not getting locked out of seeing my daughter grow up.' There was fire in his voice as he talked.

'So, she'll stay with you in the house?'

'Maybe. That's just a temporary solution. It gets complicated when it comes to the house. A lot of it was paid for by Anna's father, so we could afford Arabella's private education. We've been living outside our means for years. It looks like it could be catching up with us now. Maybe a downsizing will do me good.'

'Downsize the gut, downsize the lifestyle,' Kartik summed up.

'Then all you need to do is downsize your ego, and you may become a decent person.' They turned to see Cameron standing by the door, three tequilas on a tray, accompanied by salt and lemon slices.

'Thanks. You're making me feel all warm and fuzzy inside,' Ryan said.

'That's her speciality,' Kartik said. He pointed to the tray of drinks. 'What are those for?'

'To stick up your arse. What do you think they're for?'

'Oh no. I'm alright,' Ryan said.

'I agree you're alright. Nothing special, just alright,' Cameron said with a smile. She was drunk and thought her responses were cleverer than they actually were. 'Now, drink your medicine. The others inside have already had theirs.'

Ryan attempted to protest again, but with some gentle nudging, and some good old-fashioned peer pressure, they eventually persuaded him.

'Hold on. What are we drinking to?' Cameron asked.

'To Eden's Bonfire,' Ryan suggested.

'To Arabella,' Kartik put forward.

Cameron looked at Ryan and Kartik. 'To a very unusual friendship.'

'We drink to Eden's Bonfire, Arabella, and a very unusual friendship,' Ryan concluded, before they all raised their glasses and threw the shots down.

'And on that note,' Ryan said, as he held his fist over his mouth, 'I'm going to be sick.'

He rushed inside, cheeks already swelling.

Kartik and Cameron stood alone, the empty tray of shots on the table next to them.

'So?' Cameron said.

'So?' Kartik replied.

They hadn't spoken much for the past few hours, nor since they had had their disagreement in Café Ristretto. When they had talked, they had both tactically avoided any mention of Ryan's situation, Cameron's interview, or Kartik's relationship with Freddy. They were taking part in an amicable Cold War, with principles, rather than politics, at stake.

'About the other day in Ristretto,' Cameron began.

'Don't worry about it.'

'I do worry about it. I worry about what I said. I didn't mean it.'

'You did mean it. And you were right.'

No one said anything for a few moments. This wasn't what Cameron was expecting. She wrapped her arms around her body, protecting it from the cold.

'I just want you to be alright. I'm sometimes worried for you. You're my best friend and I need you to be okay. I don't want to be lying on Jesus Green in twenty years' time, having the same conversations.'

'I'm fine, Cameron. You were right. Freddy, the film, doing things, I am feeling better about life, I guess.'

'And us?'

'And us, what?'

'Are we okay?'

'Cameron, twenty years from now we'll be sitting on the grass on Jesus Green, laughing at all this, thinking about how far we've come.'

Her arms unwrapped from her body with lightning speed, and were thrown around his body. She pulled herself towards him. He hugged her back, and they stayed there for several moments, the hint of sweet alcohol on their breaths, swaying in the soft light of a Cambridge pub, the sound of laughter drifting through the window.

Cameron sniffed. With her head still buried in his body it

was impossible to tell if it was from the cold or from tears, but he felt he had a responsibility, in this tiny instant that was so insignificant to every other person in the entire world, to protect her from both.

He stroked her hair, and she curled her arms around him tighter, as it started to snow. Flakes of snow were landing in Cameron's soft brown hair. Kartik started to pull away, but Cameron pulled back into him. 'Just a few more moments,' she whispered. He brushed the snow from her hair. They were moments Kartik would never forget.

The door to The Maypole opened. 'Hey, you two,' Andrew yelled. 'You're going to miss the countdown.'

The embrace finished as quickly as it began, Cameron unpeeling herself, and dusting some flakes of snow from her shoulders. Andrew looked like he was trying to work out what's going on, but was luckily distracted by a not particularly unusual weather phenomenon for this time of year. 'Oh, wow. It's snowing again,' he exclaimed, head craning to the sky.

'It certainly is,' Cameron said.

'Well, forget the snow,' he said, snapping out of his momentary daze. 'The countdown is coming up.'

'Fuck the snow indeed,' she agreed.

'And we need to find Ryan,' he said looking around. 'He's gone walkabouts.'

'Try the toilets,' Cameron suggested.

Which was exactly where they found him, head over the bowl, looking like he was regretting the entire evening already.

'Come on, let's get you up,' Kartik said to the back of his head. With some difficulty, and a fair bit of protesting from Ryan himself, they hoisted him up and got him out of the toilet, and back in the bar. He found no difficulty in acquiring another pint for himself.

The volume on the TV above the bar was turned on and

the view of Big Ben filled the screen, the second hand ticking unstoppably towards 2010.

'Ten,' the pub yelled.

'Nine.' Cameron squeezed next to Rachel.

'Eight.' Andrew raised his pint.

'Seven.' Freddy glanced over at Kartik and smiled.

'*Hic*,' Ryan said, before turning his attention back to his pint.

'Five.' Louise forced Andrew to lower his arm as he was spilling beer on the floor.

'Four.' Rachel took hold of Cameron's hand.

'Three.' Andrew looked like he was going to raise his glass again, but thought better of it.

'Two.' Kartik looked around at his assembled team, in a state of pleasant drunkenness. It was a good lot.

'One,' they all yelled in unison again.

'Happy New Year!'

The pub burst into an explosion of cheering, clapping, and yelling. The three couples, Andrew and Louise, Rachel and Cameron, and Kartik and Freddy, turned to their partners and kissed. Ryan finished off the rest of his beer, and was already storming towards the barman for his next.

As Kartik's lips parted from Freddy's, they looked at each other long and hard, drinking in each other's' gaze. Her long, cold fingers stroked his forearms.

Well, for better or worse, they had all made it into 2010.

CHAPTER THIRTY

Four tracks of footprints made their way through the snow, winding drunkenly, erratically. The snowfall was heavier now than it had been when the clock struck twelve, the falling flakes illuminated by the Victorian lamps that stood to attention every twenty metres or so.

The figures made their way across Jesus Green with no plan or purpose, other than to keep the night going for as long as possible. It was four in the morning, and only Kartik, Freddy, Cameron and Rachel survived. Louise had dragged Andrew home an hour after the New Years' bell. Later, they had rolled Ryan's barely conscious heap into a taxi. His parting words came tumbling out of his mouth in an incomprehensible mess; 'Iloveyouguysandhaveagoodnewyearandrememberthatnextyearisgoingtobegreat.'

So now only the two couples remained, sharing a bottle of red wine they had snuck out of the pub. They were walking along the path at the back of the park, next to the small stream that separated the public space from the towering spectre of Jesus College in all its Tudor glory.

'The stream,' Rachel exclaimed. 'It's frozen.' This shouldn't have been such a revelation given the current temperature and weather, but all present were amazed by this.

'It's like something out of bloody C.K Lewis,' Kartik said.

'C.S Lewis,' Freddy corrected him.

Cameron picked up a branch that had been half buried by the snow and tossed it onto the stream. It bounced on the solid ice, and skidded to a halt near the opposite bank.

'It's impenetrable!' Freddy said. 'Bloody impregnable!'

'I bet I can skate on it,' Cameron said.

'No, Cameron, don't,' Rachel said, a sudden shrill in her voice.

But Cameron was already making her way down the steep bank. 'Don't worry. I took ice skating lessons when I was younger.' She took a sip from the bottle of wine and then placed one foot tentatively on the ice.

'Yes, but we don't want you falling through,' Rachel said.

'I'll be fine.'

'I agree with Rachel,' Freddy said. 'I don't think it's the best idea. What if it's not that thick?'

'It's a tiny bloody steam. It's only two foot deep. I'll be fine.'

The stream was shallow and if the ice did break it would be near impossible to drown. Kartik felt somewhat reassured, yet he could still feel his muscles contract with nerves.

The ice supported Cameron's right leg. Gently, slowly, she shifted her weight and eased her left leg onto the stream, her whole body now supported by ice. There was a second when it felt like everything stopped, even the snow took a moment to pause from falling. Then Cameron took another step and the world was able to breathe again.

'See? It's fine.'

There was no cracking sound, no disappearing into the ice like they had all feared. She started to half walk, half shuffle across the surface like a baby penguin just learning to walk.

'Impressive ice skating,' Kartik called out.

'Thanks. Think I could make the Olympic team?'

'I'd pick you.'

'You'd better, Coach McNair.'

As she became comfortable with her balance, she started to take, long, gliding steps, only slightly less graceful than if she had blades on the bottom of her shoes. She elaborately flung her arms in long arcs, mimicking an ice skater, gradually gathering momentum, the wine bottle still in hand. When she was a few meters away, she sharply twisted side on, causing her to come to an abrupt halt. She twisted off the top of the bottle of wine and drank from it. The three figures on the bank celebrated with cagey applause.

'Very good. Now get back,' Rachel said like a worried mother.

'But I am only just beginning my routine, my love.' She shifted her weight onto her left leg, and with her right, she pushed off the ice in a circular motion, causing her to spin. She complimented this by raising her arms above her head to create a badly performed pirouette. The bottle of wine in her left hand tilted uneasily. Red wine splashed onto the translucent ice, like specks of blood.

'It's a perfect ten from me,' Freddy said holding up an imaginary scorecard.

'I'm afraid it's just a seven from me,' Kartik said. 'On account of the spillage.'

Cameron feigned disappointment. 'And what about you, my love? Will it be enough for the gold?'

'Yes, it's ten out of ten,' Rachel replied. 'Whatever it will take to get you off from there.'

'Not fair!' Kartik protested. 'That's biased. You're sleeping with one of the judges. It's another example of Olympic corruption.'

'Maybe you would like to have a go yourself?' Cameron said skating back towards them. 'Let's see how well you do.'

Bottle still in hand, Cameron skidded to a halt by the bank. She lifted her right leg to clear the small drop that separated the ice from the grass, but as she did, she lost her balance and her left leg flew out from under her. Suddenly everything went by in slow motion and for a moment her body was floating in the air, attached to nothing, a look of confusion on her face. Her legs were tossed upwards as her head rotated downwards. Cameron let out a small, panicked gasp but didn't have time to twist as the forces of gravity pulled her down. Instead it was her temple that made contact with the ice first, a horrible, cold, thump powerful enough to leave a crack in the ice. It was a noise Kartik would never forget for as long as he lived. Then the rest of her body came crashing down, and she lay motionless. There was a moment of utter paralysis as the three figures looked on, the wind completely knocked out of them by the sudden, violent fall.

The bottle had smashed where Cameron's body had landed, the red wine running out of the shattered container. Then it was joined by another, thicker, scarlet liquid appearing from under Cameron's hairline.

CHAPTER THIRTY-ONE

Ryan wished he had access to a car other than the Range Rover. As he pulled into the small car park, he was all too aware how bulky and inappropriate it was. He squeezed past cars half its size as he reversed into the last remaining parking space. He was late, but hopefully not too late. He squeezed out of the driver's door, only opening it slightly to avoid hitting the Nissan Micra to his right.

Once out he straightened his black tie and tried to compose himself as he looked towards the east chapel of the Cambridge crematorium. There was a small group huddled near the entrance, clad in black, their breath visible as they talked in low, sad voices. There were a lot of people he didn't recognise, family mostly he assumed, but he was relieved to see there were familiar faces among the crowd.

Hard gravel crunched underfoot as he approached. The snow still hugged the slanted roof of the chapel, and the grounds that surrounded the building was hard with ice. The ground had remained frozen for the past week, and Ryan couldn't help but hate every frozen puddle, every icy path that he saw. Without a rational antagonist to take his frustration out on, he had instead decided that the weather, the cold, icy winter was to blame.

He saw Freddy, Andrew, and Louise among the mourners and greeted them quietly. They smiled back weakly but said little. There wasn't much to say. Seven days still wasn't long enough to think of anything appropriate. It wasn't long enough to process what had happened.

It had been Freddy who had phoned Ryan to tell him the news, and later sent him the details for the funeral. The call had floored him. For the first time in her life, Arabella had seen her father cry.

'Where's Kartik?' Ryan asked. He hadn't seen him since New Year's Eve.

'He's inside with Cameron's parents and Rachel,' Freddy explained.

Ryan nodded, and they waited.

After ten minutes of vague discomfort, the doors to the chapel opened and they were ushered inside, a minister on one side of the double doors and Kartik on the other. Ryan deliberately dithered for a while to ensure he would be one of the last ones in, and could take up a position near the back. Some part of him felt like a tourist, someone who had only jumped in on the last few months of Cameron's life, and didn't deserve to be near the front, where those that knew her best would be. Another part of him knew he was a coward and this was a delicate situation; he didn't want to be too near anyone during the service, as he didn't know how he should best react. Even through his grief, he couldn't hide his new-found social anxiety.

He nodded supportively to Kartik as he walked past, but wasn't acknowledged with a response—his friend's dark eyes were intent on looking right through him.

He squeezed down the back bench on the right-hand side of the hall and was surprised when Freddy joined him. Andrew and Louise took up seats opposite on the other back bench. The rest of the mourners had settled into their seats, and a melancholy hush descended on the room. The room was warmer than he thought it would be, the heaters working overtime to counteract the January cold outside. The room was dignified, roomy, and devoid of any symbolism of faith, a humanist ceremony rather than religious.

At the front of the room was the raised casket. It was made from tasteful, solid, dark wood, with little ornamentation. It seemed almost impossible that the vibrant girl he had done tequila shots in the snow with just a week before now lay motionless inside. Her personality, her life, her enthusiasm, her charm, her ability; it all seemed too big to be trapped inside six feet of wood.

He looked towards the front row, where a dark-haired couple in their late fifties sat next to a young teenager with sandy brown hair. The family resemblance was strong between Cameron and her parents, although the boy, who he assumed was her brother, less so. Cameron's mother eyes were already damp with tears. Several others in the room were also crying.

On the row opposite from the parents was Michael Fitzgerald, the logistics manager who had first put him on Cameron's trail. He looked thinner than he remembered. Everyone looked thinner these days. If he had never met Michael would any of this have happened? If he had changed the trajectory of his life, maybe her fate would have been different. Maybe she would have never gone onto the ice.

On the other row, four benches directly in front of him, he could see the back of Kartik's head. Next to him sat Rachel. He thought back to the lack of acknowledgement at the door, and his apprehensions of not being welcome grew. Freddy glanced at him, and smiled supportively. Did she feel like an outsider as well? Moral support for Kartik rather than her own friendship with Cameron? She had known Cameron even less time than he had. The only time he had seen them both together was that night in the Maypole, and from what he had gathered, there had been an odd sort of tension between the two girls. Had Freddy been suspicious of Cameron and Kartik's friendship? Had Cameron resented having a new person sweep into her best friend's life? He remembered how hard it had been for Cameron to accept his own presence at first, that cold, sarcastic demeanour that had taken months to breakdown. She had not been a girl that let people in easily. With the exception of Rachel, she did not let people disrupt her highly tuned world in which she lived and Freddy must have known this.

It looked like the ceremony was about to start when a late-comer arrived through the door. A couple of heads turned as the man closed the door behind him, and slipped into the bench next to Freddy. Ryan smiled at the newcomer.

'Philip?' he mouthed silently, as his colleague nodded at him before facing the front. Ryan had forgotten the accountant had known her. He felt good that Cameron, defensive and quick-witted on the outside, had grown such a large and varied group of friends.

When it was apparent that there would be no more late arrivals, the minister took the stage and started the proceedings of the ceremony. The minister read from a selection of passages that Ryan didn't know, and kind words of support, remembrance, hope, delivered with a sober dignity that only someone who deals with the difficulty of death on a daily basis could achieve. Cameron's mother and brother were both in tears now, but her father was focusing intently on the back wall of the chapel, blinking furiously, the strain of keeping composed evident.

It was Cameron's father himself who took the stage next. He stood up and purposefully walked towards the small podium and laid a piece of paper in front of him. His movements were slow, deliberate, and careful, as if he were trying to absorb the feelings of the entire room. He was a small man, with a fragile figure, the events of the past week no doubt exaggerating these features. He tried to start his speech, but couldn't get his words out. He cleared his throat and tried again.

He spoke without pause for the next ten minutes. He talked about Cameron's past, how quickly she had been to grow up, her maturity, and her strength, and her ties to her friends and family. He eulogised her uncompromising nature, how she only allowed those that mattered into her world, and how glad he was to see so many people that had been involved in her life paying tribute today. He admitted that she could be difficult at times, which was met with a low, soft laugh; the saddest laugh that Ryan had ever heard in his life.

He thought back to his father's funeral. He remembered trying to hide from the pain that it had caused him. He had tried to protect himself from his grief by distancing himself from the entire proceedings, to pretend he wasn't even there or that his father wasn't really gone. Every time someone had spoken about him in the past tense, he had pretended they had been talking about someone else, as if he'd wandered into the wrong room.

Now he realised it had been the wrong way to approach death. To deny its power, its impact, its inevitability, all he had achieved was to transfer that burden onto another aspect of his life. It was one of the reasons he was so single-minded about work. The months and years following his father's death he had thrown himself into his company, channelling a singular intensity to improve his own standing with a reckless disregard for the wellbeing of others. In doing so, he became one of the most successful head-hunters in the city. But it was only now he realised it had cost him his family. As he sat in the warm chapel, he was determined not to do the same here. There would be no ignoring or zoning out of these proceedings. He hung onto every word Cameron's father said, absorbed every detail about Cameron's life that he didn't already know. He tried to picture her as a child, as a teenager, and finally as the young adult he had known. He closed his eyes and he thought of Cameron and he thought of his father. As the speech came to an end, Ryan had an overwhelming urge to see Arabella, to hold her close, to never let her out of his sight.

After Cameron's father finished his speech, the minister took the stage again who thanked him for the moving speech.

Ryan was surprised by the next person to speak. The minister turned to Kartik and asked him to come to the podium. Kartik stood up and walked to the front of the room. He was holding a sheet of paper with some words prepared. His hands were shaking, but his face was stoic. He looked as if he had aged ten years in the past week. No longer was it a dopy, vacant twenty-two year old slacker in front of them, but a purposeful adult, someone determined to get things right.

'I don't think I am able to produce such perfect words as Nigel has in paying tribute to Cameron,' he began, nodding towards the family on the front row. 'I'm not even sure there are words that can capture truly what a wonderful person she was, and what a great friend she was. She had convictions and beliefs that gave her a great sense of moral spirituality. She believed in friendship, and those close to her were lucky to have her in their lives. I don't think there was a person that she met that she didn't enrich in some way.

'Along with friendship, the thing she also treasured was knowledge. She was also the most well-read person I had ever met, From Russian epics, to Greek tragedies, to romantic poets, to economic textbooks, to the comics in the newspapers, it seemed there was nothing that she hadn't read. And she always tried to encourage me. I wish I had remembered more of what she had taught me. But I do remember she went through an Emily Dickenson phase a few years ago, and I thought her poem *Because I Could Not Stop for Death* would be suitable for her.

. . .

'Because I could not stop for Death,
    He kindly stopped for me;
    The carriage held but just ourselves
    And Immortality.

We slowly drove, he knew no haste,
    And I had put away
    My labour, and my leisure too,
    For his civility.

We passed the school, where children strove
    At recess, in the ring;
    We passed the fields of gazing grain,
    We passed the setting sun.

Or rather, he passed us;
    The dews grew quivering and chill,
    For only gossamer my gown,
    My tippet only tulle.

We paused before a house that seemed
    A swelling of the ground;
    The roof was scarcely visible,
    The cornice but a mound.

Since then 'tis centuries, and yet each
    Feels shorter than the day
    I first surmised the horses' heads

Were toward eternity.'

'I don't think I'm smart enough to truly understand everything about this passage, but I'm sure Cameron did.'

Kartik finished with a little nod, and then returned to his seat. Ryan couldn't help but be impressed. He had been composed and calm, and had got the tone exactly right.

The ceremony continued, a few more eulogies and readings. And then they were told to stand, as the casket was lowered, and eerie silence descending, watching as the body of the young girl was carried to oblivion. In all, it had taken about forty-five minutes, but Ryan had felt like they had all been in there for a lifetime. They were all destined to leave fundamentally different people.

After the casket had descended they were led out of the chapel, this time it was Cameron's family guiding them out of the double doors, thanking the guests for coming and being consoled on their loss.

The fresh, winter air felt good on Ryan's face when he stood outside. He felt he could breathe again after being suffocated by the heat and the sorrow of the chapel.

He stood next to Philip, slightly away from the rest of the congregation. 'It was a lovely ceremony,' the accountant said.

'It was,' Ryan agreed. 'I didn't realise you were coming.'

'Yeah, I feel terrible about being late. I'd been working with Cameron on Eden's Bonfire for a few months. Ever since that night you all went out on the punts.'

Ryan smiled. 'She told you about that?'

'She had fond memories of it. She said that's when her opinion of you changed, that maybe you weren't all that bad.'

'I'm glad I could prove my moral rectitude by drunkenly high-jacking a punt and being stopped by the police.'

'You impress different people in different ways.'

They looked over at the rest of the mourners. Freddy was holding Kartik, comforting him, giving him strength.

'Was she close?' Ryan asked.

'Close to what?'

'To finding a solution?'

'To Eden's Bonfire?'

'Yeah.'

'She was. Very close. MIT were stunned with the progress she was making. They had a small army of PhD students working on it, and they weren't even close to what Cameron had done. Jesus, Ryan, we all knew this girl was smart, but it turns out she was extraordinary, even when compared with the intellectual elites.'

'Really?'

'Yes. And believe me, they weren't very happy that you had convinced her to explore her options in the City. They really wanted her. And they were offering some very generous grants to get her over.'

'She turned them down?'

'It seems like you're better at your job than I would have suspected.' Philip gave him a friendly pat on the arm. 'Anyway, we seemed, well… Cameron seemed, to be going in the right direction. There was some speculation that it was a coded interpretation of the financial crash. Everything that came before and since; the economic bubble, the subprime mortgage crisis, the recession, Lehman's Brothers, Northern Rock, the bailouts, quantitative easing, the Eurozone crisis, Eden's Bonfire covers it all, from start to finish. That's why it's so hard to find an end to it. Because the puzzle gets infinitely more complex with every market shock that takes place every day.'

'Surely it couldn't have been that hard to work out. I mean, once you recognised the patterns, you could see what it was about.'

Philip gave a tiny snort of derision that he tried, but failed, to cover up. 'The problem was that all the metrics are encoded. But they aren't a mathematical code. That would be too easy. It wasn't a case of breaking an enigma. The codes were to be found in an obscure passage of some Ancient Greek tragedy, or the symphony of a composition, or the coordinates on an antiquated map, or the editing rhythms of a Stanley Kubrick film. Whoever designed this was trying their best to make sure it could not be solved by an individual—the range of disciplines was too great, the breadth of knowledge required was too extensive.'

'But that was also the problem with the puzzle. The logic and progression to move from one stage to another required a certain single-mindedness, a lone train of thought away from the distractions of a collaborative effort. It was designed so the indecisiveness of a committee would prevent you from moving in the right direction.'

'Which is why the team at MIT has been struggling…' Ryan added.

'Exactly. Too many cooks spoiled the broth.' Philip agreed. He looked as animated as Ryan had ever seen him. 'That is why Eden's Bonfire has proved to be so elusive. It's created so that it is hindered by both an individual working alone and a group working together. That's what was so remarkable about Cameron's progress. She was perhaps one of the only people on the planet who had both the breadth of knowledge and the problem-solving capabilities to put this thing together.'

'You think she realised this?'

'I think so. That's why maybe she was reluctant to accept the offer to go to America. As bizarre as it sounds, she was worried her work would be watered down by the inferiority of group collaboration.'

'And because she was so familiar with the history of economics, she thought her talents could be used in finance?' Ryan suggested.

'Maybe it goes beyond that. Eden's Bonfire may be even more than just the recent history of boom and bust. If completed, it could map out the present and the future. Simply put, cracking Eden's Bonfire means a solution to all future financial models.'

'She wanted to use it to play the markets? To become rich?' Ryan was sceptical. Cameron hadn't been the sort of person with such shallow goals.

'Maybe. But by looking at her notes, she seemed to have a loftier goal'

'Like?'

'Fixing the economy.'

'Fixing the economy?' Ryan's eyebrow raised.

'Right. Fixing it for good. An end to boom and bust economics. A robust failsafe that could be implemented into the financial markets of the world.'

Ryan couldn't help but laugh in disbelief. It all seemed too much to be true. Cameron had been good, but solving all the world's financial problems? Philip had clearly turned to hyperbole as a way of coping with her death.

'So what happens now?' Ryan asked, trying not to sound condescending to Philip's delusions of grandeur.

'Well, I've got a significant amount of her work. I'm trying to piece it together from here. The Americans want it. I guess I'll start sending everything she had over to them.'

'But wouldn't that ruin her work? The dilution of collaboration and all that?'

'I don't have much choice. I'm not smart enough to work on this on my own. Maybe Cameron had got far enough that they can just pick it up from there.'

'She was one of a kind, wasn't she?'

'She certainly was.'

They both looked over to her family. The mourners had started to disperse now, disappearing into cars.

'Are you going to the wake?' Philip asked.

'Yeah. I want to catch up with Kartik. Are you?'

'Yeah. Do you need a lift?'

'No, I've got my own.' He nodded over towards the towering Range Rover, again embarrassed about how it soared over the cars around it. Philip didn't seem worried about the excruciating behemoth. Or if he did, he hid his feelings well.

Ten minutes later and he was manoeuvring his cumbersome vehicle out of the car park. The tiny Nissan Micra was still there, so it was a squeeze both getting into the car, and getting the car out of the parking space. He rattled past the last remaining mourners and headed down the A14 towards the small village of Histon where the Fitzgeralds lived. There was no room on the street outside the house so he parked two streets away.

He headed inside the semi-detached house and found Freddy.

'Where's Kartik?'

'Just over there,' she pointed towards the living room.

'How's he doing?'

'I think it'd be good if you asked him yourself. I'm sure he wants to see you.'

They passed through the room, which was tightly packed with mourners, Freddy leading the way to Kartik.

'Hi, Kartik.'

Kartik looked up as Ryan approached. His face hardened but he didn't reply.

'How are you?'

'Not great. Next stupid question.'

'I thought your reading today was very good.'

'Thanks.'

'Cameron would have liked it.'

'What do you want, Ryan?'

'Kartik, please.' Freddy said, trying to play peacemaker.

'What?' Kartik said, turning on his girlfriend.

'I just want to make sure you're okay,' Ryan said.

'Well, I'm not,' Kartik snapped. Two people nearby turned to look at them. 'And I don't think someone like you is going to make me feel any better.'

'Lower your voice, Kartik,' Freddy said, levelling him with a stare that made him shrink somewhat.

Ryan resisted the baiting nature of his accusation. 'I'm here to pay my respects to Cameron.'

'Good for you,' Kartik said.

'She was my friend as well,' Ryan said.

'Really? She was your friend?' Kartik said, sceptically.

'Yes.'

'Whatever.'

And with that, Kartik walked into the other room, a blank expression on his face.

'I'm sorry,' Freddy said after Kartik has left.

'Is he going to be ok?'

'I don't know. He's struggling.'

'I've never seen him like this before.'

'It's not been easy for him. She was his best friend. They kind of relied on each other. I'm worried that if he was lost before, it's going to be even harder now.'

'Well, he's got you.'

'Yeah, I know. But I've only known him for a few months. He'd been friends with Cameron for years. Things feel different now between us. Fragile. I'm going to be here for him, but I can't fill the gap that's going to be left by Cameron. I'm not that person.' She looked tired as she spoke. He couldn't image anyone had got much sleep the past few days. 'Did you know her well?'

'Not really,' Ryan admitted. 'Not as much as I would have liked. We were working on something together. I was helping her out with some options for what she was going to do after Cambridge. But I can't help but feel like a bit of an imposter.'

'You're in good company then,' Freddy agreed. 'I feel the

same way.' They looked around at the faces in the living room, not recognising any. The other people they knew at the funeral were elsewhere.

'I'm not very good at funerals, I'm afraid,' Ryan said. 'I'm never sure what to say.'

'Just show support when it's needed.'

'Well, I tried, but Kartik didn't appear to need my support.'

'Give him time. Do you know the Fitzgeralds?'

'I never met Cameron's parents. You?'

'Me neither. Shall we introduce ourselves? Offer our condolences?'

'That seems like a start.'

'We'll stick together. It'll be easier that way.'

'I don't think we're meant to be making things easy for ourselves here, Freddy.'

'It was just a figure of speech.'

Ryan nodded. They headed into the other room and introduced themselves to Cameron's parents. Mr. Fitzgerald nodded earnestly as they delivered their clichéd comforts. Mrs. Fitzgerald looked a million miles away, not looking either of them in the eye. After a couple of minutes, they shuffled on, their sympathies having been met with an earnest thank you and a look that suggested they had no idea who they were.

Feeling he couldn't do much more, he said goodbye to Freddy and asked her to let Kartik know he would be around if he needed to talk. She thanked him and then he drove back to his house, now large and empty.

CHAPTER THIRTY-TWO

It was just past four in the afternoon when he arrived home. As he had been at the funeral, Anna had agreed to pick up Arabella from school and would drop her off at the house. The divorce was officially underway now. When he wasn't at work his life was a mountain of paperwork and lawyers and clauses. It had become clear early on that he would not be able to keep the house, so he was enjoying staying there as much as possible for as long as he could, before being forced into some bachelor flat somewhere.

For some strange reason, as soon as the divorce was decided, Anna and Ryan had started getting on better. It would be too much of a stretch to say they were friendly, but at least they were being rational. They had both agreed that divorce was the best possible solution, accepted it, and were in the process of making sure things moved along as swiftly and economically as possible. No longer did they fight and argue over the smallest things, or cause conflict for the sake of it.

The main issue had been Arabella. Ryan had suspected that this would be where Anna would become possessive and determined, keeping his daughter away from him as much as possible. But she had been surprisingly pragmatic, acknowledging they both had the right to spend time with her. It was agreed Arabella would stay in the house in Newnham to prevent her life being disrupted any more than it already had, which meant she would be staying with Ryan for most of the week, but with Anna at the weekend.

Another unpredicted side effect of all this had been how Anna had become so much more involved in Arabella's life. There was no aspect that she was not jumping into with alacrity; homework, school runs, playdates, days out, spontaneous presents. Ryan had suspected she had thrown herself back into motherhood because of guilt; presents and attention almost a worthwhile substitute for a nuclear family. Arabella was smart enough to realise this as well, but she wasn't about to give up this chance to be showered with attention and gifts.

Christmas had been the hardest time, with Arabella staying with Anna and her parents on Christmas Day out in the Surrey countryside, and then spending Boxing Day with Ryan in the house, trying to fill the empty hallways and rooms with festive joy. In the end, it had fallen flat, and Arabella had spent most of the day sitting on the sofa and playing with her phone, texting friends, looking for any excuse to spend less time with her father.

However, since Cameron's death he had put the divorce proceedings on the back foot. Again, surprisingly, Anna had been affable about this delay, and had even consoled him when he had received the first phone call from Freddy to tell him the news.

He wandered aimlessly around the house for a while, thinking of what Philip had told him, and of the hostility that Kartik had shown.

He opened up his laptop and checked through his email and responded to some semi-urgent work-related items. One was from Robert Keynes, the financial recruiter who had been very interested in Cameron's CV.

'Hi Ryan,

We just heard about the news. All of us here are very sorry to hear about Cameron's passing. As you know, we were keen to talk to her, and it's a terrible tragedy that such a bright young woman's life has been cut short. We checked up on her CV and she was very talented. It looked like she could have achieved brilliant things with us.

Anyway, I hope you're holding up well. If you've got any more like her, don't hesitate to send them our way.

With condolences,
    Robert Keynes'

He resisted the urge to slam the laptop shut. The opportunistic little shit. 'Any more like her?' He wasn't sending his condolences; he was casting out a fishing line. Ryan stood up, paced around the room, and then sat down again. He felt agitated, but not because of the insensitivity of the email but because he knew he would have sent the same email if he had been in a similar situation a few weeks ago. In fact, he had done it on a few occasions in the past; 'I'm sorry to hear about the loss of Mr. Whatever in your office. Let me know if you need someone talented to replace them.' They were all just a bunch of scavengers, who preyed on redundancy, misfortune, and even death.

He was interrupted from scolding himself by the sound of a car pulling up the driveway. A few seconds later he heard the front door open and the patter of feet and Arabella scurried up to her room. Anna found him in the living room.

They exchanged a muted greeting.

'How are you?' she asked with genuine concern. She was wearing an expensive navy coat that Ryan had bought her for her birthday two years ago. It was designer, but for the life of him he couldn't remember which one, Alexander McQueen? Stella McCartney? It had seemed so important when he had bought it, but now it couldn't be any less significant.

'Yeah, I'm fine,' he answered.

She took off the coat slung it round the back of the chair opposite him. 'Do you want a drink? Coffee? Wine?'

'Don't you have that thing this evening?' Just like the coat's brand, he couldn't quite remember what Anna's engagement was, although he knew she had mentioned she was busy that evening.

'It's not until later. I can stay for one glass.'

'Wine it is then,' Ryan nodded.

She brought a bottle of red from the kitchen with two glasses. They clinked glasses. 'Cheers,' they said in unison.

'How was it?' Anna asked.

'Well, it was a funeral, so you know, not the greatest.'

'What was her name, again?'

'Cameron.'

'Strange name for a girl.'

'You should meet some of her friends,' Ryan reflected.

'Do you want to talk about it?'

'Anna, look, you don't have to do this if you don't want to. With everything going on...' He didn't know where he was going with this. He didn't know if he wanted to talk about anything or to anyone.

'I understand. We don't have to talk if you don't want to. I just want to make sure you are ok.'

Why was she being nice? Did she have an ulterior motive? He couldn't help but feel that everyone had an alternative agenda these days. The world he had inhabited for the past twenty years had left him cynical, untrusting, and borderline paranoid.

But maybe it was possible for people to look out for others without any ulterior motives. Maybe he should trust her. Maybe he could trust himself to talk about it. To talk about something real for once. Maybe, if he searched hard, if he really tried, he could remember what it was to talk about people as humans and not as numbers, or targets, or opportunities. Maybe this was one of his small steps to salvation.

And so he talked. He started at the beginning, from his first encounter with her to his last. And as he spoke, he went back to the places he had spent time with her. He was back at the Maypole, yelling at Kartik for spilling beer on him, Cameron in the background, a half-amused grin on her face. Then he was on the river, drunk in a punt, discussing life, the universe, and everything. And then he was talking to her in Café Ristretto, telling her his life story after waking up alone in his car. And finally he was in The Maypole again, his arm around her as they watched 2009 roll into 2010.

It was only as he spoke that he realised the first place he had met her was also the last place he'd seen her. Life is nothing but cruel little circles.

Anna leant in as he spoke, her body still and composed. Her hands were usually hyperactive little missiles, forever fidgeting, playing with her hair, caressing her arms, stroking her chin, and most commonly, reaching into her bag to play with her phone. But now they were unmoving, the fingers patiently wrapped around her glass of wine that she rarely took a drink from.

Upon finishing, Anna did something wholly unexpected. She got up from her chair, walked to his and put her arms around him. It was a hug that was devoid of romance, but filled with support. It was exactly what he needed at that moment.

'I'm sorry,' she said as she parted.

'Thanks.'

'Are you going to be okay?'

'I think so.'

'Do you need anything?'

'To be able to restart the year?'

'I don't think I can do that for you, Ryan.'

'Okay. Then just stay here a little longer.'

They said little after that, and instead finished their drinks in a comfortable silence, the grandfather clock ticking in the background.

Not long after Anna had to leave for her engagement so he took her to the door. They embraced once more at the door before she disappeared into the cold night.

It was as he was closing the door that the second unexpected event of the evening happened. A text came in through his phone. 'Meet me where she died at eight,' Kartik had sent.

CHAPTER THIRTY-THREE

Ryan stood looking at the little stream. The thick ice had melted, now only a small patchwork of small thin sheets remained. The water was a dark, dirty vein, slicing off the public park of Jesus Green from the private grounds of Jesus College. No more than four-hundred metres in length, a metre and a half wide, and barely half a metre deep. He'd barely even noticed it before. It was strange how such a small thing could change all their lives.

He looked down at his Omega. He was ten minutes early, and there was no sign of Kartik. He shuffled on the spot, shifting his weight from leg to leg to try and keep warm. The new black Oxfords he'd bought for the funeral weren't worn in yet, and the sides cut into his toes. The right foot suffering more than the left for some reason. It would take a few more wears before the leather stretched into something resembling comfort. The only thing that took his mind off the pain in his feet was the biting cold, and the only way he could ignore the cold was to think about the throbbing in his feet.

Life's cruel little circles.

He looked down at his watch again. It was eight.

And then eight-fifteen.

But still no Kartik. Ryan tried phoning but it went straight to voicemail. He followed this up with a text. He was starting to get worried. Had something happened?

Behind him came footsteps, and he turned in time to see a jogger rush past him. He was dressed head to toe in luminous yellow sportswear, topped with a Cambridge United woolly hat. A brave individual to be running in this cold. Even though Ryan had a new fitness regime, he didn't like exercising outside. Gyms were designed so you could get fit away from the exposed elements and, more importantly, away from the judging eyes of the public who may find some amusement from an out of shape, middle aged fat man attempting a five-kilometre run.

Eight-thirty came and Ryan was about to head home when a figure appeared from the opposite side of the green. It walked with a stagger stride, the movements both determined and uncoordinated. There was a bottle in the left hand, which seemed to drag the entire body down, twisting the shoulders, and making the figure zig-zag as he walked. The right hand was illuminated by the small burning glow. The glow was raised to his lips periodically, and the smell of weed grew as he approached.

'Hello, Ryan,' Kartik shouted when they were ten metres apart. His voice carried but there was no one else braving the cold to hear him; the jogger was long gone.

'Kartik,' Ryan nodded when the figure had taken a few steps closer. 'How are you?'

'Me?' Kartik lifted the half-drunk bottle of vodka. 'I'm drunk. How are you?'

'Sober, I'm afraid.'

'Have some.' The bottle was thrust just inches away from Ryan's face. It was cheap, store brand vodka, rather than the good stuff.

'I'm fine.'

'Have some,' Kartik repeated, a tiny hint of impatience in his voice.

'I can't. I'm driving,' Ryan replied, nodding over towards the multi-story car park next to The Maypole, which was just about visible in darkness.

'Too bad. More for me then.' Kartik took a sip and then pulled a face of revulsion. 'This is disgusting. You want a drag?' He offered the joint, which was damp and badly rolled.

'I'm fine, thanks.'

'What about a drink?' Kartik asked, as if for the first time.

'Maybe you should put it down.'

'Maybe. Maybe not. Maybe you should drink too.'

Kartik had exchanged his black suit jacket for a grey V-neck jumper and had lost his coat at some point in the day, but apart from that, he was wearing the same as he had been at the funeral. If he hadn't been so drunk, he would have been freezing. Ryan was wearing four layers, including a large overcoat, and he could feel the cold wind trying to wrestle its way to his skin. 'What do you want, Kartik?' He needed to move the conversation on, so he could move Kartik to somewhere warmer.

'This is the spot,' Kartik said with a look of disgust at the stream. 'Well, not exactly here. I think we were a bit further down that way. Or maybe that way.' He pointed one way, and then the next. 'I don't know. We were drunk. That was the problem.' He took a drag from the joint and then threw it away. He knew Kartik hadn't been stoned for months now. He had slowly been getting his shit together, working on that film, getting a girlfriend, not getting high. Everything was derailing now.

'So, what happened?' Ryan didn't know if it was a good idea to open this wound, but he had an insatiable need to learn the truth. He still didn't know all the details.

Another sip of vodka was taken. 'You really want to know?'

'Only if you want to talk about it.'

'I want a joint. Where's my joint?'

'You just threw it away.'

'Hmm… do you want a drink?'

'That's the third time you've asked that.'

'Really? And what were your responses the first two times?'

'No.'

'Okay then. Then let me tell you a story instead.'

And so the story began. The four of them together, Kartik, Freddy, Rachel, and Cameron. How they had walked down from the pub, how they had all been together, having fun, enjoying the early hours of the New Year. Cameron had decided to skate on the frozen stream and no one had even attempted to stop her. Kartik faltered as he tried to describe her fall, an inelegant attempt to climb off the ice, a violent slip, the sound of her skull connecting with the ice.

At this point Kartik's voice fell flat, the slurring of words stopped, and his voice became clear, as if he had entered a trance. When Cameron had fallen, the three of them had panicked, in their drunken state unable to form a coherent plan. Rachel was in tears, and Kartik was unable to do anything but watch the pool of blood slowly spread out across the ice. Had the delay been costly? It was clear that Kartik considered himself almost entirely responsible as he told the story.

Eventually Freddy had called an ambulance, and Kartik gingerly shuffled down to the stream to lift the prone body onto the grass. The warm blood had started to melt the ice, and Cameron's damaged head was covered in cold water. Once she was on the grass, he had wrapped his scarf around the wound. It had barely stopped the blood from flowing. Rachel was shouting at Cameron, trying to get her to respond, but her eyes were closed and her body was completely limp and unresponsive.

Kartik had found a very faint pulse, and tried to reassure Rachel that it was going to be okay. Her screams must have drawn attention of some members of the public, and shortly there was a worried crowd surrounding them. He didn't know how long it took for the ambulance to arrive, time seemed to stand still and speed up all at the same time. All he could do was sit on the ground, Cameron's head cradled in his lap, soaked with blood, his scarf as tight as possible to stem the flow, stroking her head trying to get a response.

Two paramedics broke through the crowd and took over, their expert and calm attitude offering a false sense of reassurance to the onlookers; maybe things would be okay after all. The paramedics wrapped the wound and tried to get a response, but when that didn't work, a stretcher was brought over and Cameron's body was moved to the back of an ambulance parked on Lower Park Street. Rachel rode in the ambulance, and Kartik and Freddy called a taxi.

The taxi driver had given Kartik a look of shock, his midriff and upper thighs dark with blood. The driver then refused to let them in the car, so they had walked to the hospital, four miles away. They had walked in agitated silence, eager to get to the hospital, but terrified as to what they may find. It had started to snow again on their way, and by the time they arrived at six in the morning, they were covered in white powder. The cold walk sobered them but it was nothing compared to what had happened when they finally arrived at A&E.

They were ushered into a small room, and a sombre looking doctor arrived. He asked if they were family, and Freddy had explained they were friends. Kartik knew at this point what the doctor would say; that they had done their best, but there weren't able to save her. She had died ten minutes before they had arrived.

'That fucking taxi driver!' Kartik spat before taking another swig of vodka. 'If only he had picked us up. Maybe I could have seen her one last time. Maybe something would have been different.'

Ryan didn't really know what Kartik's presence would have changed, but he kept that to himself. Kartik continued telling him how the doctor had calmly and professionally explained that the impact on the ice had caused massive internal haemorrhaging, and they weren't able to stop the bleeding. The doctor's words were a perfect balance between clinical description and sympathetic understanding, a variation on a speech he had no doubt done dozens of times before. It was a speech that gradually coaxed you to accept what a few hours before you wouldn't have been able to believe. He would let Rachel know that they had arrived. She had been hysterical through the night, so the nurse had given her a tranquiliser to calm her down.

After the doctor left, Rachel entered the room. There was a subdued blankness on her face, and her eyes barely acknowledged them. She slumped down in to the spare plastic chair and Freddy put her arm around her. They sat for the next hour, the three of them in anesthetised silence. On the wall opposite Kartik was a poster explaining what to do if you suspected an elderly relative of having a stroke. His eyes fixed on that until Rachel fell asleep and the sun came up.

'I'm sorry you had to go through that,' Ryan said. He tried to put an arm on his shoulder, but Kartik brushed it aside aggressively.

'We're all sorry about something. I'm sorry for killing my friend.'

'You didn't kill her, Kartik. It wasn't your fault.'

'Her parents think it was. Her whole family hates me now.'

'I don't think they do. Why would you have done that reading at the funeral if they hated you?'

'I don't know. To punish me, I guess'

'There's nothing you could have done.'

'I could have told her not to go on the ice. I could have stopped her. I could have acted quicker. I'm the reason she's dead.'

'It was a freak accident. No one could have predicted it.'

'We could have all gone home. We could have all jumped in a taxi when you left. We shouldn't have been out there.'

'Kartik, thinking like this is just going to tear you apart.'

'Good. That's what I deserve.'

'Have you talked to Philip?' Ryan asked. The memory of the night wasn't doing Kartik any good. He was swaying wildly now in the glacial wind.

'No. Why would I?'

'He was working on something with Cameron.'

'Eden's Bonfire?'

'It seems she had got further on it than anyone suspected. From what Philip said, it looks like she was close to unwrapping it all.'

'Well, now she's dead so you can stop getting excited about using her to impress all your old friends.' Kartik's voice was low and hard.

'Kartik…'

'You know they thought you were a joke?'

'Who did?'

'Your *friends* in the City.'

'What are you talking about?'

'Remember that interview you set me up on? I overheard them talking about you afterwards. They were laughing at you, calling you a dinosaur. You're a joke to them. You're useless.'

'Kartik, I know you're mad right now—'

'I'm mad? I'm not the one that should be mad. You should be mad. You would be if you heard what they were saying about you. Mad and depressed. You think you were sent to the Cambridge office to save it? Like you're some kind of hero?' Kartik looked like he was going to take another drink of vodka but then changed his mind. 'You genuinely think they transferred you for your talents, don't you? They were trying to get rid of you, you idiot. You're an antique and they want to modernise. But they didn't have any grounds to fire you, and they didn't want to pay the massive redundancy fee you would no doubt negotiate out of them. They hoped that by transferring you to some shitty little town, they would force you to quit. But what they didn't anticipate was how incredibly dense and self-important you are. Don't you see the irony? They tried to kick you out the door, but you ended up embarking on a rescue mission!' He laughed wildly when he finished talking, hideously delighted at this turn of events.

Ryan's anger seethed just under his skin. *It wasn't true, was it? It couldn't be.* The problem was, it all sounded plausible. If true, he was less annoyed at the board's cruelty, than at their two-facedness. He understood business; he had been part of the ruthlessness for two decades, and if they thought he was outdated, then they should have told him so. But instead they had uprooted his family, forced him to change his life, and sent him on a collision course with divorce. Worst of all, it had also resulted in him getting wound up in Kartik's untidy life. What added insult to injury was the glee with which Kartik was relating this news. Well, at least he had something to be happy about. It was probably the first time he had laughed all year.

'I don't care about any of that anymore, Kartik,' he said, trying not to be provoked. 'Cameron's work is more important than me or you. She was on to something. She was so close to an important discovery. I don't want to sound hyperbolic, but she can live on through her work. It would honour her memory.'

Kartik stopped swaying for a moment and locked his eyes on Ryan. For a moment, he thought his friend was going to engage with him, to want to find out more, to ask him about her findings. But then his face fell into a sour nastiness. Even in the dark, Ryan could see a stern brutality to his brown eyes.

'I fucked your wife, you know?'

Ryan stopped. He felt like the inside of his lungs were frozen. For a moment, he felt paralysed by shock.

'What?' Ryan said. He was aware of the pain in his feet again, as the sides of his new shows dug into his feet. Kartik had said it so simply, so coolly, that it seemed impossible to not be true.

'Your wife. Remember her? Pretty blonde? Big tits? A taste for infidelity? Yeah, you remember her.' Kartik smirked nastily as he spoke. 'I fucked her. Several times.'

'Kartik, you're drunk,' Ryan said, trying not to shake with anger. 'You don't know what you're talking about.'

'Anna Camilla Stanfield. That's her full name right? She always calls herself Camilla with her lovers. That's why I didn't realise she was your wife for so long. She tries her best to keep you separate from the other men in her life.'

'Kartik, stop it.'

'Five foot seven. Thirty-eight years old. Great in bed. Even better in the hallway,' Kartik continued.

Part of Ryan wanted Kartik to admit he was lying and that this was nothing more than a stupid, malicious, drunken invention. But he also knew some part of him wanted to be presented with evidence that proved it was all true. 'Why are you saying this? What do you want to achieve?'

'I want you to know the truth.'

'You're just making it up. None of those things prove anything.'

'She sings *Moon River* after sex,' Kartik said.

Ryan felt his body tense.

'Sometimes *The Sound of Music*.'

Ryan's fist curled up in a ball. He had flashbacks of the night they had caught Anna in bed with Alan.

'She's terrible at both.'

His right arm shot out with a mind of its own. Kartik instinctively tried to move out of the way but was too drunk. The punch caught him awkwardly on the side of the neck. He stumbled backwards, and Ryan followed up, catching him with a left hook on his jaw. The second punch floored Kartik, his body collapsing on the grass.

Nothing happened for several seconds. Kartik lay prone on the ground, not defending himself. Ryan stepped back, trying to assess the news. In practise, it changed little; he was still getting a divorce, Cameron was still dead. But for Kartik to do that to him? Why? And why tell him now? He had been praying for violent retribution. Punishment for his sins.

'Get up, Kartik.' Now it was Ryan's turn to snarl. The body didn't move. 'Kartik, get to your feet now.'

Slowly, reluctantly, the body rolled over in the frosted grass, and in unsteady movements, got to its feet. Kartik faced Ryan again. The jaw was already starting to bruise. He drunkenly looked on the ground for the vodka bottle, which had gone flying when he'd been hit. 'Where is it?'

'Why did you do it?'

'I don't know. I dropped it when you hit me.'

'Not the bottle, you idiot. I'm talking about Anna.'

'I don't know. I don't know anything anymore.' To Ryan's surprise, Kartik had begun to cry. But he had no sympathy left to give. He was tired of Kartik. He was beyond tired. He hated and pitied him with passion.

He grabbed Kartik by the neck, and squeezed his fist into his Adam's apple. 'You're a fuck-up, Kartik. You always will be. And if I hear you've been near Anna again, I'll kill you.'

Kartik could do nothing but give out a muffled grunt, somewhere between a cry for help, and a sob of remorse.

'You're coming with me,' Ryan said, as he shoved Kartik

in the direction of The Maypole. Although he hated him, he was so drunk it would be easy for him to fall asleep and be exposed to the elements for the night. He didn't want to have to attend a second funeral this early in the year.

Ryan marched them across the green, Kartik not willing or able to resist. When they arrived outside the pub, Ryan recognised one of the bar staff standing outside smoking a cigarette, who looked surprised at the sight of them.

'He's had too much to drink,' Ryan said to the barman. 'Make sure he gets home.'

The barman tried to protest, to claim that it wasn't his responsibility, that Ryan had to take him home.

'He's got nothing to do with me anymore. He's on his own from now on.'

And with that, he walked away, leaving the backstabbing mess to find its own way in life.

PART THREE

CHAPTER THIRTY-FOUR

Waverley Station was a nightmare in the summer months. Tourists, both national and international poured in and out in a never-ending torrent. Unlike London, where the chaos was spread around several main hubs—King's Cross, Euston, Paddington, Victoria, London Bridge—Edinburgh seemed to have all its major traffic networks enter the gorge in the centre of the city. Arabella looked out of the window in wonder as the train pulled into the station. The busyness excited her despite the five-hour journey on the overcrowded train. They had had to travel economy, rather than first class. Money didn't quite stretch as far as it used to. It was never a struggle, but some of the little luxuries had evaporated since the divorce. They had reserved the window seats over a table, and had been joined by two teenage boys. The teenagers had pulled out can after can of Carlsberg during the journey, even though they looked too young to be drinking. They were both Scottish and had discussed gigs, girls, and football for most of the journey. Arabella had spent most of the journey on her phone.

Ryan missed the relative quiet of first class, especially when Arabella put her phone on the table after a particularly prolonged texting session. Upside down he read, 'On train now. OMG boys sitting next to me so cute' followed by a heart emoticon. She had turned eleven in March, but the events of the past year or so had seemed to mature her at a much faster rate than the other girls in her school. She seemed exclusively to be friends with girls from the year above, and she projected a sense of self-reliance so often missing in children these days. But this maturity, her desire to look and act like the girls who were several years older had consequences, especially in her attitude towards boys. The speed at which she was growing up was scary.

Hormonal texting aside, Arabella had behaved exceptionally in what Ryan would have once dismissed as cattle class. On the rare instances that she took her eyes off her phone's blinking screen, she would stare out the window, watching as the east coast of the country rolled by. This part of the world was new to her, and it clearly held an instant fascination. Family holidays had taken her to many places, but never Scotland.

A year ago her parents would have considered Scotland too parochial, not exotic enough, and certainly not impressive enough to return to their respective social circles and boast about. 'How am I supposed to show my face around the girls after a holiday in Aberdeen when they've all just got back from Aruba?' Anna had questioned when Ryan had suggested Scotland for an Easter break three or four years ago. What had been strange, looking back, was that at the time he had completely agreed with her. How could he turn up to post-work drinks with stories about Scottish distilleries, when Japanese whisky was in vogue?

Arabella's landscape-watching was mostly silent, so Ryan busied himself with a copy of The Times and then The Telegraph. There was a major story in both around the diplomatic fallout between Britain and Pakistan after David Cameron had asserted that the latter was 'exporting terror.'

Now the Pakistani Prime Minister had declined an offer from Cameron to stay at his Buckinghamshire country retreat. Number 10 was denying this was a political snub, but rather a 'diary clash'.

Cameron. Cameron. It had to have been Cameron who had ended up winning in May. Now every time he picked up a paper, or turned on the news, he would see that name. A year ago, this would have been the result he had wanted. And if he was honest with himself, if he had bothered voting three months ago, he would have still have voted Conservative, but these days' politics seemed so irrelevant. He wasn't part of the apathetic politicians-are-all-alike-aren't-they collective. He knew there were major differences between the parties. Ending Labour's thirteen years of domination, stagnation, and eventual self-destruction in power was important. But was it as important as keeping his daughter safe? Was it as important as his friends and colleagues? Politics now seemed insignificant in comparison with the things that mattered.

The train came to a standstill at the platform and one of the Scottish lads confirmed this with a barely concealed belch. Arabella giggled. Ryan tried to look unimpressed.

They collected their luggage and made their way to the exits. People jostled in front of them, zigzagging in a disorderly disarray. 'Don't get lost,' Ryan instructed his daughter. 'Hold my hand.'

He put out his hand, but Arabella refused to take it.

'Dad, I'm not going to get lost.'

'It's a busy place. Stay close whilst I find a taxi rank.'

'Over there,' Arabella said, pointing to the line of black cabs near platform eleven.

'Well spotted,' Ryan said, impressed with his daughter's sharp eyes. He had been looking in completely the wrong direction.

They joined the queue. A few places in front of them were the lads from the train, now looking a bit worse for wear.

Ryan noticed more than once Arabella craning her neck to get a better look at them.

Once in the taxi, he gave the address of the hotel, and they were soon pulling out of the station and onto Waverley Bridge. They headed south. Like the station, the city was packed, the pavements a mess of tourists, locals, and buskers. It was the first day of August, a week before the Fringe festival kicked off but already the place was filling up. The taxi ride was short, their hotel was just on the outskirts of the south of the city.

The hotel they were staying at was a small, family-run affair, little more than a glorified B&B. Although Arabella had got used to staying in fancier places in her short eleven years, she was patient and unspoilt enough not to complain about the downgrade in accommodation. Ryan doubted many of her contemporaries at school would be so accepting.

Their rooms were opposite from each other, containing small, single beds, with bedside tables with racks of pamphlets for various tourist attractions around the city: Edinburgh Castle, the botanical gardens, guided tours of Holyroyd. Ryan flicked through a few of them whilst Arabella got ready for dinner.

The woman at reception had recommended them a pub a two-minute walk from the hotel, and after a long day on the train, both travellers decided that the place that required the least possible effort suited them best.

They were in the pub by six in the evening. It was mercifully quiet compared to the rest of the city, somewhat overlooked by the other tourists who rushed past on their way to more notable attractions.

'Can we go to The Elephant House?' Arabella asked as their main course arrived. Ryan had a pie and mash with a local ale whilst his daughter had ordered cod and chips and a coke. She had refused to order from the children's menu, stridently asserting that she was now old enough to order from 'the real menu'. Ryan was certain she wouldn't finish the enormous portion that she was currently trying to get through.

'What's The Elephant House?'

'It's where J.K. Rowling wrote *Harry Potter*.' She had recently devoured the entire series, locked in her room, each book seemingly more enormous than the last. Anna had been incredibly happy that she had shown such a voracious appetite for reading, and it showed in her school reports. English literature was by far her best subject at school.

'Sure. Where is it?'

Arabella, rather awkwardly, unfolded a map of the city on the table, and checked the index. 'The Elephant House, D6,' she said tracing her finger using the grid system. 'There it is.' Her index finger pointed to a spot a five minutes' walk from the station.

'You're good with maps, aren't you?' Ryan said smiling.

She beamed in return, happy that her achievement had been recognised. 'So can we go?'

'Only if you write a best seller while we're there.'

'Okay,' she nodded, as if this were a completely reasonable task for her to achieve.

'We can go tomorrow afternoon. We're getting up early to walk up Arthur's Seat, remember?'

'I remember.' She didn't seem as enthusiastic about the walk as she did about the café,

'Daddy has to meet a friend at some point. Would it be ok if she joined us in the afternoon?' Ryan asked.

'Don't say Daddy. Daddy is for babies. You are dad,' she said, somewhat frustrated.

'Is it okay if Dad meets someone tomorrow?'

'I guess that's fine,' she said, as she pushed her plate away, half the cod uneaten. 'I'm full.'

'I thought you wanted to order from the real menu?'

'But it's too much.'

'In that case, you won't want dessert.'

Her eyes swelled with anxiety. 'I'm not *that* full.'

'Hmm… well if you can't eat your main course, you wouldn't possibly be able to fit in dessert.' He picked up the dessert menu and flicked through it. 'Well, that means more for Dad. What shall I have? The chocolate fudge cake looks good. Or maybe the Knickerbocker Glory.'

'I want one of those!' Arabella pleaded. She may have been trying her best to grow up as fast as she could, but Ryan was pleased to know she was still a child in many ways.

The next day was brilliantly sunny and warm enough to walk in shorts and t-shirts. Ryan had bought them both new hiking boots before the holiday, but realised they weren't particularly necessary, as the well-worn path up to the summit wasn't too taxing. Ryan had kept with his fitness regime that he had started in December, and eight months of healthy eating and exercise had changed him dramatically. The night before, after getting out of the shower, with only a towel wrapped around his waist, he had looked in the full-length mirror in his bathroom and had been quietly impressed with what he had seen. He had lost a lot of weight, especially around the neck and the waist. His face, no longer supporting a double chin, looked five years younger. The muscles in his shoulders and upper arms were more prominent and for the first time in a decade the contours of his deltoids, biceps and triceps were liberated from the thick layer of fat. There was still a vestige of a beer gut, fat he doubted he would ever fully get rid of, but it wasn't something he was particularly concerned about; a bit of middle-aged slippage was to be expected, no matter how well you looked after yourself. If he had attempted this walk twelve months ago, he would have been bent over exhausted and covered in oily sweat. But now he could keep up with his daughter's boundless energy as she bounced a few metres ahead of him. Arabella's fitness was never in doubt. She was now a key player on her school's football team, and this interest in sport meant she could run for hours without getting tired.

She happily waved at the other hikers; families, young couples, elderly walkers plugging away with their hiking sticks that made them look like they were skiing uphill in slow motion. Whenever a dog ran past she would chase after it, animal and child dancing around, both ecstatic to play with each other. On more than one occasion Arabella asked if they could get a dog when they got back home. Ryan told her to ask her mum.

Ryan and Anna had joint custody of Arabella. She lived with her mum during the week in the house in Newnham and then Ryan looked after her at weekends in his rented flat in north Cambridge. He knew Kartik's parents lived in the same area, but didn't know where exactly. It was a pleasant, two-bedroom flat, that he was conscious not to furnish like a middle-aged bachelor going through a relationship crisis. He made sure Arabella's room was decorated to her liking, rather than a spare room filled with boxes that she got dumped in whenever she came to stay. He wanted her to feel at home, that she would be excited to see him, that she would want to stay as long as possible.

When they reached the top of the hill, they sat on the grass and looked out on the city. Ryan had made a packed lunch of sandwiches, fruit and chocolate that they shared whilst admiring the view. Bathed in the midday sun the city was an undeniably impressive sight, the castle standing to attention above the streets, like a gatekeeper on watch, ready to protect the throng of citizens below. To the north, the city seemed like it was swallowed by the brilliant blue expanse of the Firth of Forth.

'Who are you meeting tomorrow?' Arabella asked as she bit into a sandwich.

'Rachel. She's a friend of mine.'

'Is she your girlfriend?' Her gaze was on the cityscape.

Ryan laughed. 'No, she's not. I don't have a girlfriend. Besides, she's much too young. She's still at university.'

'Mum has a boyfriend.' It wasn't meant maliciously, just a statement of fact, by Ryan couldn't help but feel a bit upset that she would say it so bluntly.

'I know.'

'He's younger than her.'

'I know.' Anna had settled in with Alan, the naked man. He had never pressed charges. They didn't really talk about it and, wisely, the two men were kept away from each other as much as possible.

'So who is Rachel?' the ever inquisitive Arabella asked as she bit into an apple.

'Do you remember Cameron? The girl who had the accident on Jesus Green a few months ago?'

Arabella nodded. She had never met Cameron in person, but had subsequently heard about her.

'Rachel was her girlfriend.'

'They were lesbians?' Again, she was quite straightforward with her questioning.

'They were. And Rachel, as far as I know, still is.'

'I know about lesbians. We learnt about it at school. During sex education.'

'I'm glad you're up to speed.'

Ryan was impressed with how accepting this new generation was when it came to homosexuality. When he had been in school, there had been a guy who had been exceptionally camp and had been bullied endlessly for it, to the point where his house regularly got eggs thrown at it at night by the neighbourhood kids. Looking back, Ryan was horrified at having been part of this teasing, and he was quite glad that children of Arabella's generation were able to take different sexualities in their stride so easily. Ryan never did know what had happened to the kid he had used to bully, but there must have been some residue psychological pain.

'Why are you meeting Rachel here?'

'Because she lives here. She is back home for the summer holidays. She spends term time at Cambridge University.'

'Do you think I should go to Cambridge University? My teachers have mentioned it.'

'I would love it if you did,' Ryan admitted.

'Why?'

'Because it's one of the best universities in the world. And it will mean you're very smart.'

'Okay. I'll go there,' Arabella said with her unwavering frankness.

'You'll have to study very hard.'

'I study hard already. I know much more about photosynthesis than you do.'

Ryan laughed, remembering their study session together. 'It's a good start but it may take a bit more than just that.'

They finished their lunch, and Arabella sprang to her feet. 'Shall we head back now?'

Ryan agreed, and let his daughter lead the way, marching with purpose back towards the city.

CHAPTER THIRTY-FIVE

Arabella looked around, not able to hide a twinge of disappointment.

'What's wrong?' Ryan asked.

'It's not what I thought it'd be like.'

'What did you think it'd be like?'

'Not like this.'

'What did you expect? Hogwarts?'

'I thought it would be like Grimmauld Place.'

'I don't get that reference.'

'Yes, you do! It's in the *Order of the Phoenix*. Don't you remember from the films? We watched it together.'

'Oh, yeah. I remember now.' Ryan said, unable to remember much about the films he'd been forced to sit through. They all blended into one smudged memory of castles, wands, goblins, and wizards. He would have rather watched *The Great Escape* for the fiftieth time.

Although there was a large sign on the front of the café that announced it as 'the birthplace of Harry Potter,' the café hadn't adapted its interior to reflect its most famous regular's literary creation. There was no tacky Harry Potter décor or gift shop to buy wizard mugs or fake broomsticks. Instead, it had an almost creepy obsession with elephants; ornamental statues stood to attention on the windowsills; a cabinet by one wall contained at least a hundred figurines of different shapes and sizes; even some of the chairs had elephant faces sticking out the backs, expertly carved out of dark oak.

They ordered drinks from the counter and went through to the back of the café.

All the seats were taken in the tight confines of the café. They were about to head out again when a Japanese couple stood up from a small table by the window, gathered their things, and smiled politely indicating the now vacant seats. They moved into the newly empty seats and looked out the window. They had a brilliant view of the sheer rock face that Edinburgh Castle was built on.

'See that view? That's like something out of Harry Potter.' Ryan said encouragingly.

'Yeah, I suppose,' Arabella agreed.

'We'll have a look around the castle tomorrow. It's where they shoot a lot of the scenes in the Harry Potter films.' He didn't know if this was true or not, but it seemed plausible. Besides, he wanted to please his daughter. If he was wrong, Arabella didn't correct him. She had become distracted by two blonde girls sitting near them. They were roughly the same age as Arabella and were wearing red and yellow striped scarfs. He was almost certain these were the colours of one of the Wizard houses from Harry Potter, but the girls could have just been Bradford City fans.

The two girls had in front of them a board game, clearly inspired by the books. Arabella wasn't the only fan who had embarked on the Potter Pilgrimage. On the board were miniature wizards, trolls, ghosts, and other ridiculous things Ryan didn't recognise. Arabella looked on with a crushing hunger to join in.

'Looks fun, doesn't it?' Ryan said to his daughter.

Arabella nodded in agreement.

'Can I play?' Arabella asked.

'Well, it's rude to just interrupt someone else's game,' Ryan said.

Arabella looked up pleadingly, her eyes wide, almost desperate. It was a look that reminded him of a year ago, when she had pleaded with her mother to be able to join in a game of football in the park, much to Anna's disapproval. The idea of vicariously annoying Anna swayed it.

'Okay, let's go and ask.'

The two of them approached the girls' parents. Ryan felt slightly uncomfortable, suspecting what they would be thinking: here was a divorced man struggling to connect with a daughter whom he couldn't quite keep entertained himself for the duration of their time together. To be honest, it was only half true.

Ryan explained how Arabella was a big fan and how she would love to join in the game if possible. The parents, a very pleasant, well-mannered, Scottish couple a few years older than Ryan, were more than happy to accommodate Arabella. The twins, Amy and Susie, were just as welcoming as the parents, his daughter's easy-going, straightforward attitude instantly garnering a welcoming approval. Anna would have described the family, 'a good cultural fit', which somewhat took away from Ryan's goal to irritate his ex-wife from a distance.

He went back to the table by the window, and watched his daughter interact as he drank his skinny, decaf latte.

Ten minutes later his phone vibrated on the table, and a message popped up on the screen. 'Just arrived.' Rachel's message was nice and economic, and no sooner had he read it than he saw her walk into the room. She scanned the seats, and Ryan raised his hand to make himself known. She smiled and walked over.

'Hi,' he said.

'Hey,' she replied.

There was an awkward moment when they didn't know how exactly to greet each other. A handshake was too formal, but a hug a bit inappropriate, especially for Ryan, who was aware the twins' parents were looking at him meeting a girl half his age. He didn't want to give off the impression that he had taken his daughter along to a date, only to palm her off to another family so he could spend alone time with his mistress. In the end, they opted for a quick kiss on cheek.

'Can I get you a drink?' he asked.

'Sure. A cappuccino, please.

'You hold the fort,' he said indicating the table.

'That's funny, because it is near a real fort,' Rachel said pointing to the castle outside.

Ryan let out a weak laugh, not having intended to make a joke, and not entirely sure if it should have been considered one. 'I'm just going to see if my daughter wants anything,' he said pointing to Arabella, who was already engrossed in the game.

He ended up getting a round of hot chocolates for Susie and Amy, and coffees and cake for their parents, despite their overly polite protests that 'he really shouldn't have.' Despite their friendly remonstrations, he knew he had scored some serious brownie points. He'd made a career buttering up business leaders in some of the world's most renowned organisations. He'd be a chump if he wasn't able to impress a middle-class family in a tourist hotspot.

The lady behind the counter agreed to help Ryan carry his bulking order to the back of the café, and he sat down opposite Rachel, who was looking over at Arabella.

'How old is she?'

'Turned eleven in March.'

'That's sweet. Are they friends of hers?' She asked, nodding to the blonde twins.

'They weren't until about fifteen minutes ago. Now, I don't think they've got a choice.'

'That's nice.' Rachel smiled. She rubbed her hands together, and then stroked her knees. There was something on her mind, beyond the simple small talk, he could sense it.

Like everyone, she had changed since last year. She seemed both more relaxed, but also a little lost and worn down. After the funeral, she had been one of only two of Cameron's friends that he had stayed in touch with. This had been a surprise as she had been the one he had thought he had the least in common. What he had realised since was that this apparent lack of common ground had only been created because Rachel had been so engrossed with her then-girlfriend that she had barely acknowledged the existence of other people.

He himself had also been guilty of neglecting to see past the dotting, socially anxious, reclusive girl, who had hung onto every word of the girl that, for a few months last year, everything seemed to revolve around. Only in the months after Cameron's death did Ryan realise that they had all been using, perhaps exploiting, this incredible girl in their own way; they all wanted something from her, they all expected her to carry the weight of those expectations, to manage both her own life and their lives in one casual, sweeping movement; to echo brilliantly against the noise of the world, to help pull them all out of the mire.

Ryan had needed Cameron so he could impress people he had thought it important to impress. Rachel had needed a foundation of support to help her get through her first move away from home, and to ease her into the ridiculous academic demands of Cambridge. And Kartik? Kartik needed someone who could justify his almost nullified existence. Someone with talent and intelligence, whom he could stand alongside, one half of him hoping that some of her talent would rub off on him, and the other half praying that it never would, so whatever success may befall his friend, he could always be at her side, making facetious comments and pithy remarks.

'How's the summer been?' Ryan asked. They hadn't seen each other since May, when Rachel had returned to Edinburgh after completing her first year.

'Not bad. It's been a lot of work, catching up with last year, and prepping for next year. I still haven't really caught up with when my grades dropped at the start of the year.'

'Are your tutors still understanding?'

'Well… to an extent. But there is this relentlessness at Cambridge often regardless of personal matters. It's like you're drowning and they just stand there and watch.'

For some reason, Rachel had come to Ryan for support at some of her darkest times, a connection that was at the start bewildering to him, but that developed into a quasi-foster role, helping her keep on top of deadlines, manage her workload, and, most importantly, listening to her when she needed to talk about things away from academia.

'I can imagine. You've still got, what, another month or so before you go back?'

'Starting in October, yeah.'

'Well, it'll be good to have you back in Cambridge.'

'Are you still going to be there?' She was biting on her finger nails now. But it was a purposeful agitation. What did she really want to talk about?

'Yeah, why wouldn't I be?'

'Well, you were talking about moving back to London? Getting your old job back. You know, with everything that has been going on recently.' She meant the divorce, but she didn't say it in so many words.

'I think I'm going to settle in Cambridge for a while.'

'I didn't think small town living was for you?'

'It's growing on me.' Ryan conceded. 'Have you heard from Kartik recently?'

Her face snapped out of a half-baked daze and into reality. Was that what she was nervous about? Something to do with Kartik?

'I have. Do you remember that film he was working on?'

'*The Line*?'

'Yes. They just had a screening of it.'

'Did you see it?'

'Yeah. They showed it as part of a short film showcase at the Cambridge Picturehouse.'

'Freddy got them in, eh?'

'And you once told me nepotism was dead.'

'I doubt I was being truthful. How was the film?'

'It was good. Kind of strange and arty. I don't know if I'm the target audience. We engineering students take things quite literally. I think it was meant to be a metaphor about something.' She looked perplexingly down at her coffee. Her forehead creased, as if she were going to bring up whatever was on her mind, but then she paused and looked out of the window. Was it something to do with her and Kartik?

'Did Kartik mention anything?' Ryan asked. He hadn't seen him since the night on Jesus Green.

'About you?'

'Yeah.'

'He's not your biggest fan. You did punch him.'

'Keep it down,' Ryan hissed, nodding over to the parents currently looking after his child. They didn't look like the type that would throw a punch in anger, and would certainly look down on people that did. 'And that's not exactly fair.'

'Twice.'

'What?'

'You punched him twice.'

'Well yes, but I'm pretty sure he slept with my wife more than twice.'

'Ex-wife.'

'She wasn't at the time.' Why was he having to defend this? Why was Rachel being so protective? He was almost certainly sure he was morally in the right here. It had been Kartik who had acted dishonestly first, he'd just reacted. Was she being defensive of Kartik's actions because there was something between them? Her and Kartik? Together? Surely not. She had mentioned Freddy without a hint of unease or jealously. But still…

'But Kartik didn't know that when they…You know…' She trailed off.

'I don't think it matters,' Ryan said, trying not to take this very personal subject personally. 'He knew she was married, even if he didn't know who exactly she was married to. It still doesn't make it better.'

'No, it doesn't make it better. But it does make it a rather silly and ridiculous coincidence,' Rachel said. 'And besides, from what I've heard, he wasn't the only one.' She smiled. She meant it as a joke, but delivery and sensitivity clearly weren't her strong points when it came to humour.

'Nice.'

'Look, I'll talk to him. But I don't know how enthusiastic he'd be about meeting up or anything.'

'Thanks.'

Again, she looked away from him, this time towards the children. Arabella was animated and vivacious as she played the game. It looked like she was winning, a natural precocious talent, whatever she did.

They watched the game unfold for several minutes, the silence between them not entirely unpleasant. He had felt a little bit aggrieved that Rachel had been so blunt about his wife's affair. But she had an engineers' gift of mistiming and misreading social cues and nuances. It wasn't that she completely missed the target of societal decorum, but rather her comments would curl somewhere between her brain and her mouth, coming out skewed to what would usually be considered acceptable. It was a trait he would have found unforgivingly irritating a year ago. He didn't mind it (too) much these days.

'Can I ask you a question?' she asked, her voice not entirely steady.

'Sure.' He felt like they were getting to the crux of things now.

'You know I didn't mean to be blunt about your wife, right?'

'Is that what you wanted to ask?'

'No, I just want to make sure we're ok, that's all.'

'You're stalling.'

'Yep.'

'Why?'

'Because…'

'Because?'

'Because stalling is easier.'

'Really?'

'I think so.'

'I know there's something on your mind.'

'How perceptive.'

'You can talk to me about it.'

'Okay.'

'In your own time.'

Rachel took a deep breath. 'Well, I've kind of met someone.'

'Really?' He shifted in his seat.

'And I feel guilty.'

'Guilty?'

'Yeah.'

'Any reason?'

She fixed him with a how-could-you-be-so-stupid stare. It was a face that looked like a duplicate of Arabella's when she got frustrated with her father's inability to keep up. 'Really?'

'Look,' he said. 'It's fine to move on. You're going to have to at some point.'

'It feels like a betrayal. And I don't want to betray Cameron.'

The way she was talking made him certain of his earlier hunch about Kartik. He needed a way to tease the information out of her gently. 'Was it because this new person knew Cameron?'

Her eyes widened. 'How did you know?' Her raised voice made some heads turn.

'It was just a guess. And it's ok. I'm not judging you. When people are put together in traumatic situations, a bond develops. It's natural. It happens. It's your happiness that matters.'

'But I feel like everything that we have together is, I don't know, tarnished in some way. Like we're staining Cameron's memory.'

'Cameron was special. We all know that. She was one of a kind. And none of us are ever going to forget her. But we've got lives we need to get on with as well. And if you've found someone that makes you happy, then that is what matters. That is what counts for you now.'

'I know. But it doesn't make it easy. Especially considering it's the first time they've been with, you know, a woman.'

'Wait, what?' Ryan said, suddenly confused.

'You don't think it's their first time?'

'I'm pretty sure we both know that's not their first time.'

'Really?'

'We were just talking about it.'

'We were?'

'The infidelity?'

There was a long, pressing pause, that would have been funny if they both weren't so confused.

'Who exactly are we talking about here?' Ryan asked finally.

'Louise.'

'Louise?'

'Who are you talking about?'

'Louise!' Ryan let out a laugh so loud that a nervous

elderly couple at the next table visible jumped with alarm. 'You? And Louise? Together? Really? With Louise?' It was all so ridiculous that his brain had temporarily stopped functioning.

Rachel looked a little annoyed at the fact this had inspired such hilarity. 'Yes. Louise,' she said bluntly.

'I'm sorry,' Ryan said, wiping his eyes. He tried not to laugh again, but failed.

'Ryan!'

'Sorry, sorry. I know it's serious. But really? I never thought you and Louise would ever be a thing. How long has this been going on?'

'A couple of months. We became close after the funeral. I thought it was just as friends. Well, it was just as friends at first. Then things started getting a bit more serious. And then I left Cambridge for the summer and thought it'd be the end of it. But she came up to Edinburgh a few times on business. And we've met up. And things happened.'

'Wow. Okay. You and Louise. That's something.' Ryan realised he was shaking his head in disbelief.

'She's actually really cool. I know Kartik never really saw eye-to-eye with her. But she works hard, and has a great sense of humour, and is really lovely.'

'Sense of humour?' He tried not to raise his eyebrow, but failed.

'Yes!' Rachel said firmly. 'You just never got to know her like I do. We became friends around December time. I think we both felt we were somehow on the outside of this big group, and were forced together because other people wanted to spend time with each other. It sometimes felt like we only had walk-on parts in the Cameron and Kartik Show. They had all their little skits, and inside jokes, and a rhythm in the way they talked that I never thought I'd be able to catch up with. Whenever I contributed something it felt like it was out of place, or that I'd missed a beat and they were on to the next thing. It was like I had joined a dance troupe and everyone else had been rehearsing for years, and then I came along and messed up their routines. That's what it felt like anyway.'

'And it turned out Louise felt the same way. It wasn't that she didn't like Cameron and Kartik, but they had this way about them that rarely let others in who weren't like them. Because Louise was away so much with work, she felt they were quite haughty around her, like they looked down on her because she was pursuing a career in London and not drinking in a pub in Cambridge.

'When she told me about this, it completely changed how I saw her. Cameron had said Louise was cold and aloof, but she just felt like an outsider. Or an imposter. And it was exactly how I felt back then.'

'Like you were two extras in a movie that wasn't really about you? They were Butch and Sundance and you were the school teacher?'

'I'm not sure I follow.'

'*Butch Cassidy and the Sundance Kid*. It's one of the greatest movies of all time.'

'I've never seen it.'

'You've never seen *Butch Cassidy and the Sundance Kid*? Paul Newman and Robert Redford?'

Rachel shook her head. 'I'm sorry. I'm not very good with films. Cameron was. She and Kartik always did little skits from films and I never understood what was going on. It was another way me and Louise felt like clueless outsiders. Like, just because I haven't seen *Jaws* doesn't mean I can't join in your conversation.'

Ryan was just about to exclaim that he couldn't believe she had never seen *Jaws* but stopped himself. 'Trust me, you two weren't the only ones that felt like that. The last time I spoke to Freddy was just after the funeral and she felt the same way. And being older, I was in the same boat.'

'But you and Freddy seemed to join in so well. Like, you

just integrated yourself effortlessly and no one asked any questions.'

'It was all a façade, Rachel. I work in recruitment and Freddy worked as a producer. Part of our job description is the illusion of effortless schmoozing. It's never as straightforward as we make it appear. Anyway, you and Louise became friends…' Ryan continued, keen to move the spotlight away from himself again.

'Yeah. I don't know if you remember, but on the night of… the night that… on New Year's Eve,' she said eventually. 'We spent hours talking to each other that night. That's when I found out how she felt about the group, about how she didn't fit. And we just chatted. And it was nice. And then after that night, I really needed someone to reach out to, but I didn't know who I could talk to. Cameron was gone, Kartik reminded me too much of her, Andrew seemed a bit lost, I didn't know Freddy that well. And then there was you. And you were great to get back on track in terms of studying, but I couldn't talk to you about the truly personal stuff. I don't mean this in a nasty way, but I needed someone closer to my age. No offence.'

'None taken.'

'And so I called Louise. And we met up. And she supported me. And she listened to me. And I cried. And I bitched and moaned. And I did all these stupid things. And she just sat there patiently and listened. And we kept seeing each other. And she kept listening. And I listened to her. And then, one day, we moved from being just friends to being something more.'

'Wait, does Andrew know?' Ryan said.

'I think he's about to find out,' Rachel said, gritting her teeth awkwardly.

'I see,' Ryan said. Again he smirked. There was something unfailingly hilarious about the entire situation. It was like the tragedy and confusion of the past year had unravelled into a brilliantly timed punchline. 'If you think about it, it's still quite funny.'

'Thanks for taking this so seriously,' Rachel said sarcastically.

'I'm sorry,' Ryan said again, trying to sound calm and reassuring again.

Suddenly Rachel looked up. 'Who were you thinking of?'

'Huh?'

'Who did you think it was I was talking about?'

'In what way?'

'You seemed to think I was seeing someone else.'

'Ha, it's going to sound ridiculous now.'

'Go on…'

'Well, I thought it was Kartik.'

Now it was Rachel's turn to laugh. 'You've got to be kidding me.' She almost knocked over her coffee. 'You do realise that Kartik isn't a woman?'

'Hey, it still seemed more likely than Louise.'

'Trust me, I wouldn't date Kartik in a million years.'

And this time they both laughed together, Ryan genuinely happy for his friend.

Rachel became serious again. 'But, do you think I'm doing the right thing? It's not too soon?'

'There's no time limit to how these things work. You never know when you will meet someone, or when something in your life is going to profoundly change. You can't say 'I've got to wait X amount of time, before I am allowed to do Y'. You've got to do what you think is best for you, and for those around you. Do you like her?'

'Louise? Of course.'

'And does she like you?'

'I think so.'

'Then it doesn't matter. Look at me. You're not betraying Cameron or her memory. We all miss her. I miss her. I know you miss her. We will always remember her. But you've got to keep doing whatever you have to do to keep going.' Ryan scratched his head, unsure if he was any good at being reassuring. He looked over at his daughter again, and hoped he was.

A waitress came over and took away the empty cups, and wiped where Rachel's coffee had spilled. She smiled warmly at them as she did.

'Thanks, Ryan,' Rachel said when the waitress had left.

'I don't know if any of what I said makes any sense. But I hope it helps.'

'I think it's what I needed to hear.'

They sat and watched the girls play their board game for a while, the children lost in an innocent world, their lives protected from the violent shocks that come at us in waves as the years go by, changing us in ways that would have been unrecognisable if we were to see our present-day selves from the naive perspective of our childhoods. Two dice rattled in Arabella's hands before being released; they landed on a six and a four. This seemed to lead to a square of some significance, as the twins shook their heads in frustration. A card was drawn, a question was asked, and she was allowed to reroll.

Whatever the goal of the game was, Arabella seemed to be on the right path. Ryan hoped Rachel was as well.

CHAPTER THIRTY-SIX

The sun relentlessly beat down on the concrete of London's Southbank. If Edinburgh was busy with tourists in August, it was still dwarfed by the sheer magnitude of visitors that flocked to this side of the Thames. Sometimes it felt like entire villages and towns, from France, to Spain, Italy, Russia, China and Japan, had been uprooted, and dumped unceremoniously in winding queues to ride the London Eye, or to snap photos of the Houses of Parliament.

The recruitment consultant tried to feel energised by this hustle and bustle, but mosty felt frustrated each time he bumped into yet another stationary visitor gawping at the Thames. What was the fuss about? It was a bloody river. He was pretty sure they had rivers in Beijing, in Tokyo, in Paris. In fact, he had been to Paris a couple of times. He knew for a fact that there was a bloody river there. It was dark, and wet, and had boats on it, and really awful buskers playing music alongside it, just like the Thames did. So why did the French come to London and take photos of this river? Take photos of your own bloody river and stop getting in my way.

With herculean effort, he wormed his way through the crowd, his suit jacket removed because the sun and the heat of the crowd was making his back damp with sweat. He passed the Eye, went under Hungerford Bridge and past the noisy skate park on his right-hand side. He remembered his brief skating days when he had amazed himself by finally producing a half decent kick flip. Shortly after, he'd soon got bored and frustrated as he was unable to do any other tricks, and given up, never to ride a skateboard again.

There was a brief moment when he considered stopping to watch, and an even briefer period of thinking he would be able to pick up the hobby again, before he came to his senses and continued to his destination. He was in London now and he had to be purposeful in everything he did. That was what marked the true people of London from the amused crowds; a sense of striding tenacity and forward momentum in everything you did. To fit in you had to be a shark, swimming past the shoals of fish taking photos and buying cheap souvenirs.

Past the skate park were lines and lines of tables with second hand books. He decisively ignored these, and turned into the BFI Southbank centre. The corridors were dark and blissfully air-conditioned. He walked between the restaurant and bar and the front, and through a winding corridor where the ticket desks were. *Why were the ticket-counters at the back?* This confused him, but not enough to deviate him from his task in hand. Be a shark, be a goddamn shark.

He swam to his left to a bar surrounded by thin, dark, velvety ropes hanging from the ceiling. Again, he did not let these strange aesthetic choices divert his attention, and marched straight through them, and saw who he was looking for sitting in a corner on a dusty sofa, body hunched over a laptop, face illuminated by the screens placid glow. The figure hadn't noticed him as he traversed the hanging ropes, so he walked over until he was standing in a position that would be deemed acceptable for polite conversation. Still the figure did not look up, but instead hammered away at the keyboard, face contorted in deep concentration. He could tell straight away that this was a shark swimming with a purpose. He almost felt bad to interrupt, but he knew he had to complete his mission.

'Hello, Kartik,' he said.

Kartik stopped typing and looked up. Confusion quickly gave way to a wry smile. 'Hello,' was all he offered in way of response.

'How are you?'

'Not too bad. Yourself?'

'I'm good. Can I sit down?'

'Sure,' Kartik said, indicating the vacant chair opposite. There was a bizarre formality to the meeting. Was it because he was wearing a suit? He shouldn't have worn a suit.

He sat down and faced his old friend. Even though he was wearing cream shorts and a navy t-shirt, there was something quite workmanlike about his appearance. His hair was cut short at the sides and combed neatly on top, tidier than it had been at any time since the recruiter had known him. A close shave had removed the lazy stubble that had always given his face a look of lost vagueness, and his eyes were free of the puffy redness of a habitual stoner.

'You look good,' the recruiter said earnestly.

'Thanks. So do you,' replied Kartik out of politeness rather than earnestness.

'Thanks.' He laid his suit jacket on the empty seat next to him, then faced his old friend. 'So, Louise broke up with me.'

'So I heard,' Kartik replied. 'I'm sorry to hear it.'

CHAPTER THIRTY-SEVEN

Kartik didn't feel sorry as he sat opposite Andrew. He was glad his friend was finally out of the relationship that had burdened him for so long. His only worry was that Louise would do the same to Rachel.

'She's a lesbian now,' Andrew said. He seemed more confused than sad, as if he was working out how he hadn't realised earlier. Kartik, if he was being honest with himself, had wondered the same thing.

'Yeah.'

'With Rachel,' Andrew continued.

'Yeah.'

'Didn't see that one coming.'

'Me neither.'

There was a long pause, as they both digested this information that they both already knew. Then Kartik, unable to stop himself, started to laugh.

'It's not funny,' Andrew said.

'It's quite funny.'

'She was my girlfriend, Kartik.'

'And now she has her own girlfriend.'

'I don't see how that's funny.'

Kartik looked at his friend, trying to repress his smirk. He failed in this endeavour and then started to laugh again. This time, Andrew joined in and the air of strained formality started to evaporate.

'Are you okay?' Kartik asked after the laugher had subsided.

'Yeah, I think so. I don't know.' Andrew looked towards the little bar. 'Do you want a coffee?'

'In here?'

'Yeah. Why not?'

'I dunno. Why don't we go outside? It's a nice day. Sometimes I feel all I ever do is sit inside and drink coffee.'

'There are worse things to do with your life.'

'Come on, let's go down the Southbank. There are some nice pubs down the way where we can sit in the sun and get a pint.'

'And here I was thinking you would offer some grand alternative. But if it's not still around drinking coffee, it's sitting around drinking alcohol.'

'It's nothing if not a varied lifestyle that I lead.'

Andrew agreed, and Kartik packed up his laptop into a brown satchel that he slung over his shoulder, and they headed down a corridor to the exit. 'Hold on,' Kartik said when they came to a door that said, 'Staff Only'. He knocked and after a few seconds, Freddy opened it.

'Look who turned up,' Kartik said to Freddy, nodding towards Andrew.

'Andrew!' Freddy said with genuine delight. 'How are you?'

Andrew looked surprised by her sudden appearance, but equally pleased. 'I'm good. I didn't expect to see you here,' he said as they hugged.

'Kartik mentioned you may be coming over. It's good to see you again.' Behind her was a small office, two other staff members sitting at computers, looking on with a very vague interest.

'You're working here now?' Andrew asked, peering into the small office.

'Only on a temporary basis. Still based in Cambridge most of the time. But I'm helping out with the programming for the Film Festival here. Kartik's down visiting.'

'That's very cool,' Andrew said. 'Great place to work.'

'It's not too bad,' Freddy said smiling. 'What about yourself, where are you working now?'

'I've moved into recruitment. Next to Moorgate. Renting a place up in Stoke Newington.'

'Recruitment? Nice. Like someone we know,' Freddy said, looking over at Kartik, with a hint of disapproval. Kartik was still rejecting any attempt from Ryan to get in contact.

'We're going off for a quick pint,' Kartik said. 'To have a bit of a catch up. Is it possible to stash my laptop here?'

'No problem,' Freddy said, taking the bag from him.

'Fancy joining us?' Kartik asked.

'I can't. I'm not going to be finished until late,' Freddy said apologetically. 'We're putting the finishing touches on our Jean Luc Godard retrospect that we're doing.'

'Aboot Da Soof?' Andrew said, remembering a conversation from long ago.

'Close enough,' Freddy said. Her colleagues in the office smiled at the mispronunciation.

'I'll be back in a couple of hours,' Kartik said, kissing Freddy.

'Nice seeing you again,' she said to Andrew. 'We'll make sure we do it more regularly from now on.'

'Yeah, that'd be nice.'

Freddy went back into the office, and Kartik and Andrew headed outside onto the Southbank. They walked east, past the National Theatre and the television centre.

The conversation struggled to get off the ground at first.

There were pauses, there were starts, there were hesitations, and a good deal of admiring the scenery.

As well as intentionally freezing Ryan out of his life six months ago, Kartik had also inadvertently ostracised Andrew. After Andrew and Louise had moved down to London, Kartik had moved in with Freddy and he and Andrew had lost contact. But this lack of contact had done more than just superficial damage to their ability to hold conversation. There were hairline fractures in the foundations of their friendship now.

'I saw that film you made last year,' Andrew said as they passed the Oxo Tower. '*The Line*.'

'What did you think?'

'Yeah, it was good.'

'Yeah?'

'Yeah. I'm not really sure if I understood it though.'

'It was a little bit weird,' Kartik admitted.

'Did Freddy like it?'

'Yeah, I think so.'

'She's really into those arty-type films, isn't she?'

'She is really into those arty-type films.'

'I'm glad it's working out for you two.'

'Thanks.'

There was another silence as a jogger darted past them.

'We are going to start on another one soon,' Kartik said after the jogger passed. 'It's going to be a feature length film.'

'That's awesome.'

'And we've got a big enough budget that I'll even get paid this time.'

'You're shooting in Cambridge again?'

'No. London this time. Freddy and I are going to make the move down here in the next couple of weeks. She's hoping to get a permanent contract at the BFI.'

'You're moving to London? That's great.' It was hard to

tell if Andrew was genuinely pleased about this, or if he was just being polite. 'Wait, but what about Café Ristretto?'

'I'm quitting.'

'You're quitting?'

'I'm quitting.'

'You're quitting Café Ristretto?'

'In two weeks.'

'You're quitting Café Ristretto in two weeks?'

'That is correct.'

Andrew laughed. 'I never thought I'd live to see the day. I was worried you'd just end up there for the rest of your life.' He patted Kartik on the back. 'Good for you.'

They went under Blackfriars Bridge, and then came out with the Tate Modern looming up on the right hand side. In front of them was The Founders Arm, which had a seating area looking over the river. They got their drinks and then sat outside at a table looking over the Thames.

'So how are things with you?' Kartik asked as they sat down.

'You know. It's been okay. It's not been the greatest year. But things are looking better now. I think. I hope.'

'Are you still in touch with Louise?'

'A little bit. Not that much. It was too painful when we first broke up. But now it's a bit easier to talk to her.'

'Do you want to talk about it?'

'I don't know.'

'We don't have to.'

'I guess I should. They say that articulating your problems is the first step to solving them.'

'They do say that.' Kartik had never heard someone say that.

Andrew was watching a pigeon picking at a chip on the floor a few metres away. He took a deep breath. 'We hadn't been working for a long time. I think we all knew that. Something had changed. We thought it was because of Louise's job, and we decided that moving to London would solve everything. But it didn't. Things just got worse. Rent was higher than we thought. I got a job that was very demanding, Louise was working all the time and I barely saw her. And there's just something stressful about London. We both constantly felt exhausted. And I never felt like I had any free time. And that made things even worse, because we didn't spend any time together.'

'Then a couple of months ago she suddenly had all this business in Edinburgh. At first it was a one off. Then it was every other weekend. Then it was every weekend. Then one day she came back and told me everything, about how she wasn't happy with me, about how she wasn't happy in general, and how she had met someone else.'

The pigeon hobbled towards them, and Andrew kicked a foot out towards it. It flapped its wings in a panic and flew off to bother someone else. 'And then, to rub salt in the wound, she confessed that she had been seeing Rachel.'

'I don't know what to say,' Kartik confessed honestly.

'I'm not even mad. Not at Louise. Not at Rachel. I knew they had become close since the start of the year. But I didn't see what was happening.'

'And now I'm not entirely sure what to do. I've realised that for the past few years Louise has guided every decision in my life. I didn't do anything independently. I didn't do anything for myself. She controlled everything. But now I've lost that control, what the fuck am I meant to do? Everything's changed so much this year already, I just don't know what's next.' He played with his tie, loosening it to give him a better chance to breath. Then he took out a packet of cigarettes and offered one to Kartik, who declined. Andrew shrugged and lit his own.

'You're smoking now?' Kartik said, slightly surprised.

'Well, Louise would never let me. So I'm trying new

things.' He inhaled again, and struggled to disguise the fact that he wasn't really enjoying the experience.

'Good for you.'

Andrew nodded.

'Well, you're a recruiter now,' Kartik said, hoping it would sound positive.

'That I am.'

'Who are you working for?'

'Fusion Vision.'

'Fusion Vision?'

'Yeah.'

'Fusion Vision Recruitment?'

'Fusion Vision Recruitment.'

'You're working for Fusion Vision Recruitment?'

'I'm working for Fusion Vision Recruitment.'

'Really?'

'Yes.'

'Really?'

'Yeah. I spoke to Ryan when I moved down here.'

'Ryan suggested it to you?'

'He gave me a lot of advice. Even put in a good word with the London office.'

'How is it?'

'Better than I thought. Better than media sales anyway. It's a tough gig though. A lot of work. A lot of stress. I'm starting to understand why Ryan sometimes behaved like he did.'

'A greedy adulterer prone to outbursts of rage?' Kartik surprised himself by the venom of his own words.

'He's not that bad,' Andrew said.

'He's a prick.'

'Kartik…'

'He is. Don't try to defend him.'

'He's okay. Especially when you get to know him.'

'Trust me, I got to know him a little too well.'

'Yeah, but in unusual circumstances.'

'You know he was cheating on his wife?'

'You were also fucking his wife, so don't take the moral high ground.'

'I don't think there is any moral high ground here.'

'That's convenient. As soon as you're involved morality ceases to be the issue,' Andrew said firmly.

'That's the sort of thing Cameron would have said,' Kartik said. The past tense hurt them both.

'But it's true,' Andrew continued, his voice soft. 'You shouldn't pass the buck on these sorts of things. Take responsibility for your own actions.'

'Recruitment's really stuck a pole up your arse, hasn't it?'

'He's down in London on Friday.'

'Ryan?'

'Yeah, seeing some of his old colleagues.'

'They don't like him that much.'

'You're just saying that.'

'I overheard them talking when he set me up for some interview. They think he's a joke.'

'Whatever. You should get in contact.'

'He put you up to this, didn't he?'

'What are you talking about?' Andrew turned away and looked towards the people crossing the Millennium Bridge.

'That's the reason you're here. He's using you.'

'No, I came because I wanted to see you.'

'You're just another one of his pawns in his game.'

'There's no game here,' Andrew said, still looking at the figures as they criss-crossed each other on the bridge, some stopping to pose for photos, others just trying to get from A to B.

'For someone who works in an industry that plays it fast and loose with the truth, you really are a bad liar. You need to work on that poker face if you want to succeed.'

'I'm actually very good at my job,' Andrew said

indignantly, turning back to face Kartik, and stubbing his cigarette out in the ashtray.

'And yet you can't admit that you're here as a favour to your boss.'

'Regardless if he did or not – '

'Which means he did.'

'You should still meet up with him. He feels bad about what happened.'

'My face felt bad as well.'

'He had his reasons.'

'All I did was tell him the truth.'

'You slept with his wife.'

'I didn't know that at the time.'

Andrew sighed. 'We're going around in circles.'

Again silence took hold of them. A street performer was setting up a few meters away. He was draping himself in a long robe, putting on a harness with a fake arm and walking stick that attached to a base on the ground. When the robe was put on, along with an oversized Yoda mask, it would appear that the busker was levitating a few feet off the ground. Even though these types of buskers in London were more common than mice in the underground they still amazed small children enough to force the parents to cough up a few quid every time they passed one.

'It's amazing that people fall for that sort of thing,' Andrew said, pointing out the obvious illusion.

'They don't believe in it. Even a child can see past that. But people want to believe in something they know isn't true. Makes their drab lives a bit more interesting.'

'So cynical.'

The busker hoisted himself onto a concealed seat, and added the final touches to his costume, and was ready.

'It's not cynical. I'm glad they do it. It's better to have a bit of hope in the extraordinary, than to know for certain everything is boring.'

'It still sounds pretty pessimistic to me,' Andrew said.

The busker had only been in position for a few seconds when a small girl, no more than four or five, ran up in amazement to the floating Yoda. There was no way that she hadn't seen the busker constructing his illusion, but she still waved delightfully.

Andrew turned back to face Kartik. 'He knows something about Eden's Bonfire.'

'Huh?'

'Ryan. He discovered something with Philip.'

'What?' Kartik didn't want to seem too eager.

'I don't know. He didn't tell me. But he wanted me to tell you that he knew something.'

'A solution?'

'I don't know.'

'He mentioned it may be to do with the economy. Did he say anything to that effect?'

'Look, I don't know anything about it. I'm just the messenger.'

'So you are his little errand boy?'

'Okay, yes, he asked me if I would get in contact with you. But that doesn't mean I didn't want to see you as well.'

'Really?' Kartik asked sceptically.

'I don't see why it's so hard to believe. It's been good catching up. But think what you want. And do what you want. I just thought you would want to know that Cameron's work may have gone somewhere.'

The mention of her name didn't get any easier as time passed.

'I'll think about it,' Kartik said.

Andrew passed him a business card with Ryan's details.

'Right, well, I'm going to make a move,' Andrew said standing up. The turbulence of the past six months had created a steely maturity to Andrew's movements, mannerisms, and words. 'But genuinely, it was good seeing you again.'

'Yeah, you too,' Kartik said, also rising. They embraced in a not entirely easy hug, and said goodbye. Kartik watched as Andrew headed east down the Southbank, towards London Bridge. As he passed the hovering Yoda, he fished out a couple of coins from his pocket and tossed them into the performer's upturned hat.

CHAPTER THIRTY-EIGHT

'You know, Kartik, I am going to miss you when you leave.'

'Thanks, Gabor.'

'You were a good worker.'

'We both know that isn't true.'

'I am not making jokes. You helped me when things were tough. I would have not been able to keep this place going without you.'

'Thanks. It means a lot.'

Kartik was sat opposite the Hungarian in the cramped staff room of Café Ristretto. He had just delivered the news that he was quitting. In two weeks' time he would he serving his last coffee.

'I mean, you were not the perfect employee. There were times you got stoned and fell asleep in toilet during shifts.'

'Yeah,' Kartik smiled at the memory.

'And you were not very polite to customers. Only pretty girls if I remember.'

'Well, I'm a taken man now.'

'And your standard of coffee-making was not always good.'

'Right…'

'And you were very bad at keeping the store tidy.'

'Okay, Gabor, I got it. I had some imperfections.'

'Ha! You had many imperfections.'

'Well, I'll be out of your hair now.'

'Why were you in my hair?'

'Don't worry, it's just an idiom.'

'Hmm… but all that aside, you were very good with staff. Everyone liked you. We will be sad to see you go.'

'It was people like you that kept me sane these past two years.'

Gabor smiled. 'I have something I want to show you.' He reached up to one of the shelves and took down a thin, rectangular package. 'I was waiting for the next team meeting to tell everyone. But I show it to you now.' There was visible excitement on his face.

'What is it?' Kartik asked as his manager carefully unwrapped the mysterious parcel.

'It is what we all been waiting for.'

Gabor slid out a framed certificate and showed it to Kartik.

'Is that what I think it is?' Kartik said in a hushed, reverent tone.

'The Gold Star Store of Excellence Award!'

The words were printed in raised lettering on the certificate, with a large gold star on the bottom. Inside the star was a signature from the CEO of Café Ristretto, cementing the fact that their little corner of the world went above and beyond when it came to keeping the denizens of Cambridge well caffeinated.

'Congratulations, mate,' Kartik said extending his hand. Gabor shook it vigorously. 'All your hard work has finally paid off.'

'Not all my hard work. All *our* hard work. This belong to you as well. We earn this together. As a team.'

'Really?'

'Really.'

'Even though I fell asleep in a toilet?'

'Nobody's perfect.'

'Like Jack Lemmon in *Some Like It Hot*.'

'Yes. We all like it hot now,' Gabor said failing to grasp the reference. 'I am very excited to show to rest of team. It will display behind the counter, so everyone knows we are premier coffee house in city.'

He put the framed certificate back in the package and then back on the shelf.

'What do you do now?' Gabor asked.

'I'm moving to London.'

'To work on big films?'

'Well, not a big film. But it's enough to get by. I'm moving in with my girlfriend.'

'Ah, Freddy? I liked her. Nice girl. Strange name. In Hungary, Freddy is a boy's name. Like Freddy Mercury.'

'Yes, well it's an odd one. But, I can't really criticise someone for having a strange name.'

'Yes, you are right. I have always wondered about your name. It is not typical English name.'

'No,' Kartik said, trying to suppress a smile. 'It's Indian.'

'Why do you have Indian name?'

'It's a long story,' Kartik said. His two problems had resurfaced; his name and his future. He was happy that he finally had a decent response for the latter.

'Okay, well maybe I'll hear it sometime. I must be leaving now. The wife is texting me. You close up? Only the tills left to be counted.'

'No problem.'

Gabor gathered his things, said goodbye, and headed out of the staff room. Kartik watched him on the office CCTV monitor as he descended the stairs, went out the front door, and locked it behind him.

Kartik pulled out the cash register and started counting up the day's takings. It was usually a task he found boring and laborious, but knowing he only had two more weeks meant he completed the job with a strange sense of calm. Would he miss these mundane little jobs when he left?

It was as he was locking up the cash in the safe, and doing the final pieces of paperwork that he saw a figure on the CCTV monitor on the pavement, staring into the unlit café downstairs. Initially he suspected it was Gabor returning for a set of keys or wallet, but on closer inspection it was clear the body shape wasn't right. A passing customer wondering if they were still open? No, that wasn't it. They were hanging around too long, glaring into the dark, empty café, as if searching for something.

Kartik locked up the safe, left the staffroom and went downstairs. The figure stood by the glass doors, still peering into the darkness. When they saw Kartik, they pulled away slightly, an awkward, surprised movement. It was then they both knew who they were looking at.

Kartik went over and unlocked the doors.

'Hello, Kartik.'

'Ryan.'

'How are you?'

'We're closed.'

'I noticed.'

'How observant of you.'

'Can I come inside?'

Kartik shrugged and held open the door. Ryan walked in and sat at one of the tables opposite the counter. He was wearing a smart white shirt tucked into navy chinos. Kartik was still wearing his work uniform. He took off his apron and went behind the bar.

'Espresso?' Kartik asked.

'It's a bit late for coffee.'

'Are you sure? It's the best in Cambridge. We've been

awarded the Gold Star Store of Excellence. We've got a certificate and everything to prove it.'

'Impressive.'

'It is.'

'Maybe just a tea then?'

'Tea it is.'

He made two teas and set them on the counter. Ryan picked up his and took it back to his table. Kartik remained behind the counter.

'I'm guessing Andrew put you up to this,' Kartik said, sipping his drink.

'Andrew?'

'Yeah. I saw him the other day down in London. He said you wanted to get in contact.'

'Oh, yeah. He told me about that. He's become quite the recruitment consultant. Who would have thought it?'

'A prodigy of yours?'

'No, I just gave him a reference. Everything he's doing now is because of his own hard work.'

'Right.'

'But no, it wasn't Andrew who told me to come here. It was Freddy.'

'Freddy?'

'Yeah. I ran into her yesterday at the train station. She said you were closing up today. Wanted us to talk.'

'Freddy wanted us to talk?' Kartik said, feeling a bit exposed now.

'Yeah. Don't worry. I didn't say anything to her about, you know, everything. I didn't want you to get in trouble.'

'She knows everything.'

'About Anna?'

'About everything.'

'You told her?'

'Yeah. A few months ago. It was just easier that way. She's

not stupid. She would have found out eventually. And it was better to tell her everything all in one go.'

'How did she take it?'

'She said I acted stupidly.'

'Look, I was stupid as well.'

'Yeah, she said that too.'

'She's a smart girl.'

'She is,' Kartik agreed. He leant back against the back of the bar, not really sure what to do next. Part of him wanted to end the conversation there, insist he had to close up, and kick Ryan out. He still didn't like the man. However, part of him felt a softening, and a curiosity, for the person he had gone through so much with. 'So why did she want us to talk?'

'She said it would do you a lot of good. Do us both a lot of good. Give us a sense of closure or something.'

'Jesus, it's like she thinks we're getting a divorce or something.' Kartik realised what he had said too late. 'Oh, sorry. I didn't mean it like that.'

'Don't worry about it,' Ryan said, laughing it off.

'How are things?'

'It was difficult. But things are more settled now. But Arabella is doing well. She's back to being one of the best in her class. And she's on the football team. Quite the player. Like a young Lionel Messi.'

'As long as she's staying out of trouble. And how's Camilla? Sorry, Anna…' Kartik trailed off, not knowing if it was the best question to ask.

'Haha, yeah, Anna. She's well,' Ryan said. Whatever bitterness was once there had either been forgotten or he was very good at hiding it. 'She's with her new boyfriend now. You've met him before.'

Kartik looked puzzled for a second before he worked it out. 'The naked man?'

'Yes, the naked man. Or Alan Osbourne as he's known to his friends.'

'Well, I don't think he'd class us as friends, so I guess he's just the naked man.'

'That was a strange night,' Ryan said, almost nostalgically.

'Do you even remember it?'

'Well, parts of it. I remember a very well placed punch.'

'You've got quite a habit of doing that, don't you?'

'Trust me, Kartik, it was much more satisfying punching him than it was punching you.'

'Although I can image it wasn't entirely unsatisfying hitting me?'

Ryan didn't answer and instead stood up and looked at one of the pictures on the wall. An olive-skinned man was driving around the small streets of Rome on a Vespa, a pretty girl in a flowery dress on the back.

Had Kartik crossed a line? It was hard to know where they stood with each other. He decided to move the conversation on from that night on Jesus Green.

'Andrew mentioned something about Eden's Bonfire,' Kartik said.

Ryan looked uncomfortable for a second, body language that didn't come natural to his bulking frame. He turned away from the picture and faced Kartik again. 'Yeah, that's one of the reasons that I wanted to see you. To tell you in person. I talked to Philip a while ago about it.' He stopped, his shoulders seeming to shrink.

'And?'

'Maybe you should sit down for this.'

'I'm fine standing.'

'Unfortunately, the sceptics were right.'

'What do you mean?'

'It was a load of nonsense. It didn't mean anything. A massive hoax that somehow everyone got drawn into.'

'I don't understand,' Kartik said.

'It was a scam. A joke that got out of control. That team in MIT found out a week or so ago. It was set up by a couple of

South Korean twins, computer geniuses who wanted to mess with their friends. But then it started to get shared around and people started to take it seriously. And the twins kept going, writing, rewriting, and coming up with different puzzles, different clues. One was an autistic maths wiz who didn't know any better. He just liked making puzzles. And his brother was in it for, well, I've got no idea. Maybe he had finally found something he could connect to his brother with. It was all run on a series of different encrypted virtual machines that they changed around every few weeks. Highly advanced stuff. That's why no one was able to trace it back to their IP address.'

Ryan talked like a Catholic reciting his sins, his words flowing in an unstoppable torrent. 'They didn't make any money from it, they won't become famous for it, just notorious in a few academic circles. I suppose they weren't hurting anyone. And it's no different from making a crossword. A super complicated crossword. But it led people on. A lot of people are very pissed off. Philip was fuming. He's usually such a placid guy. But, when he found out, it was like he turned into a different person.'

Kartik didn't know how to react. He felt the air had been knocked out of him, that part of what he believed had been suddenly disproven, a flat-earth believer seeing the curvature of the earth for the first time. Why did he care so much? He'd never spent any time on the puzzle, never personally been invested, had barely even paid attention when the subject had been brought up.

'What does this mean for Cameron's work?' he asked.

Ryan shrugged. 'No idea. I guess it doesn't mean a thing now.'

'So she spent all that time on nothing? She spent the best part of a year chasing shadows?' Kartik felt anger rising. He tried to picture the twins, and tried to be angry at them, but they were too remote, too much of an abstraction. He thought about shooting the messenger, but realised that would get him nowhere either.

'I don't think she was wasting her time, Kartik. She spent her time doing something she enjoyed. She worked on something that she found satisfying. I don't think it matters if Eden's Bonfire had given us the answers to the world's finances, or exposed the identities of The Illuminati, or reveal the secrets of the universe. She wasn't defined by what the answer was.'

'But she was tricked. She spent her last few months unknowingly being scammed.'

'A lot of people fell for it,' Ryan said. 'Some of the smartest people in the world fell for it. And she enjoyed doing it.'

'But it tarnishes everything.' Kartik was almost trembling now. Her memory, her legacy, everything was gone. In death, she had somehow fallen victim to a gloriously destructive practical joke. No longer was she going to be remembered as a person, but instead as a punchline.

'It doesn't change anything about how she lived her life,' Ryan said.

'It changes everything.'

'No. The only thing that matters is how you remember her. What she meant to you. And what she meant to those that she was close to, Andrew, Rachel, Louise, you. The people whose lives she touched. Nothing is going to take away our memories of her.'

And it was then that something broke inside of Kartik, and he couldn't hold in the pain anymore. 'I just really fucking miss her, Ryan. Every single day. I can't stop thinking about her. I can't stop thinking about that night.' He was crying, but he didn't care.

Ryan walked over to the counter. 'I know. We all miss her. She was one of a kind.'

'You don't understand. You didn't know her like I did. I

can't get over it. I think about her all the time. Every. Single. Fucking. Day.'

'It's not a bad thing. *'Scars have the strange power to remind us that our past is real.'*'

Kartik looked up. 'She taught you that quote, didn't she?'

'You think I'd ever come up with something like that on my own?'

'You don't seem like the type.' Kartik tried to wipe away the tears but they kept coming.

'I'm not. Cameron said that to me after the night we caught Anna. I was a mess. I'd come here looking for you,' he motioned to show he meant Café Ristretto. 'But I found her instead. She talked to me about grief and salvation. I'm not sure if I understood it all, but it made me want to be a better person. That's how she helped people. She's still helping me.'

'It should have been me,' Kartik said. 'I should have done something stupid like walking out onto the ice. If I'd died, it wouldn't have mattered. Just one less idiot serving coffee. But Cameron? She could have changed the world.'

'Well, maybe it's our duty to change the world for her now.'

Kartik almost laughed at the idea, but the feeling of loss was still too raw. 'How exactly are we going to change the world?

'I don't know. Maybe not in an earth-shattering way. Maybe we're just destined to change our small little corners. Fix the messes that we got everyone involved in. I think we're making a start. Don't you?'

Kartik straightened himself up somewhat. 'You sound like you should have your own daytime TV program. Life Affirmation with Ryan Stanfield.'

'Would you tune in?'

Kartik took a tissue from the café counter and wiped his eyes again. 'I'm a bit busy these days. Moving house, the film, a girlfriend. I don't have much time for sitting around and watching TV.'

'How things have changed, eh? What happened to that guy that used to sit in the pub and spill pints on people because he had nothing better to do?'

'Oh, he hasn't gone. He's just been dormant for a little bit.'

Ryan slapped Kartik on the shoulder. 'Cameron would be proud of who you've become. She was always proud of you. I was always a little jealous of your friendship.'

'Really?'

'Yeah. It's rare to see two people so different, yet so well suited to each other.'

'Thanks,' Kartik said. He wiped his face again.

'You'll be alright, Kartik. I think you're finally on the right track.'

'And you?'

'I haven't punched anyone for months. So I guess things are better.'

'So what now?' Kartik asked.

'We just keep moving forward, I guess.'

'Keep moving forward,' Kartik repeated quietly.

'I suppose you'll be wanting to close up,' Ryan said when he finished his tea.

'Yeah, I suppose I should.'

Ryan headed to the door and Kartik followed.

'Good luck in London,' Ryan said stepping into the warm evening. 'I know it will treat you well.'

'I hope so,' Kartik agreed.

'And if it doesn't, I'm sure Freddy will look after you.'

'Thanks. She'll be happy that we've found some sort of closure.'

'Is that what this is?' Ryan asked with a wry smile.

'I don't know, Ryan. It just felt like the right thing to say.'

'Yeah.'

Ryan Stanfield waved goodbye and headed off down the

street. Kartik McNair watched him go and then finished up the last few tasks he needed to do before he could lock up. He looked around the dark café, trying to take in all the smallest details; the faces of the people in the pictures on the wall, the glimmer on the side of the coffee machine, the worn wood of the staircase. A sense of melancholic serenity took over him as he set the alarm and headed for the back exit.

Just keep moving forward. It wasn't the worse advice he'd been given.

EPILOGUE

Ryan stood on the school playing field, watching the children run back and forth, their formation surprisingly robust for twenty-two eleven-year-olds. The coach had clearly done a lot of preparation to keep them in an effective shape. This was in stark contrast to the boys' game that he had passed on the opposite pitch. There was a macho, hungry aggression to their play, every player running after and pouncing on every loose ball. The tactical arrangement was non-existent.

In contrast, the girls were disciplined and well organised, employing an intelligent zonal system, the defenders holding a strong back line, the midfielders creating the moves, and a two tall, quick forwards eager to make runs in behind the oppositions defence.

And right there, in the midfield was Arabella, the engine room that powered her team. She moved quickly whenever her team picked up possession, dropping her shoulder, off balancing her marker, always finding space. She played in the attacking midfield role, and whilst her runs didn't always result in her getting the ball (the holding midfielder seemed to prefer to lob a long ball in the hope of it dropping to one of the tall strikers rather than playing a smarter, more controlled ball along the ground to Arabella) she was always looking to trouble the defenders, to make space for her teammates on the pitch, to be useful with and without the ball.

The home side, Arabella's team, were trailing one-nil when Ryan arrived. He was one of a dozen parents standing on the touchlines. It was the first football game he had seen live since his father had taken him to Villa Park in the late seventies and early eighties. He could still remember the relentless chanting, the hurling abuse at opposing fans, the smell of fried food from the vans, the deafening roar when Villa scored, and most of all, the bitter cold of the midwinter games, breath rising from the terraces like black country smoke. He couldn't be further away from that atmosphere now; the crowd here were polite and respectfully, quietly encouraging when their own child had a chance, but remaining mostly silent for the rest of the time, only breaking for some soft chit-chat with one of the other parents.

Just before the halftime whistle, the holding midfielder - a slightly plump brunette with a number seven on the back of her shirt - frustrated with her lack of success with kicking thirty-yard-long balls to the strikers, held up the ball for a couple of seconds, shrugged off a tackle, looked for her team mates, and saw Arabella breaking into space just in front of the penalty area. The number seven rolled the ball along the ground into Arabella's path, who took a touch, turned on the ball and dribbled it with speed towards the goal.

She had just entered the penalty area when the challenge came. It was a bruising, crunching tackle, a defender almost twice her size upending Arabella with a two-footed challenge that completely missed the ball.

Ryan resisted the urge to roar in indignation, an instinct developed on those cold Villa Park terraces. Fortunately, he didn't have to make his displeasure known as the referee blew for a penalty. Arabella was rewarded for her hard work by being chosen to convert the kick. She lined up the ball, took four steps back, drew a quick breath and then raced forward, kicking the ball cleanly past the keeper and into the top left-hand corner of the net. The game was level.

Her celebration was brief, a few high fives with her teammates, before running back into her own half in anticipation for play to resume. What a refreshing display of focus and team work compared with the insufferable overdone posturing, taunting, and rejoicing that a Premier League player would indulge in after a goal.

The holding midfielder and Arabella continued to link up well after halftime, and as they approached the end of the game, the home side had scored two more, Arabella assisting with both. The game ended three-one and Arabella had been involved with all her team's goals.

It was within the last few minutes of the game that Ryan was joined by a familiar figure.

'I didn't expect to see you here,' Anna said.

'Thought I'd try and get as many games as possible, even if I'm not picking her up.'

'How is she playing?'

'Very well.' He filled his ex-wife in on her daughter's performance.

'That's great.'

'It is.'

'And how are you?'

'I'm good. Yourself?'

'Yeah, I'm ok.' Anna shrugged. 'I've got some news.'

Ryan suspected he knew what she was about to say, but let it play out anyway. 'Oh yeah?'

'Alan is moving in this weekend,' Anna said, looking at the girls on the pitch and not at Ryan. So it was all arranged. The naked man was moving in.

'That's good.' He thought he was being sincere.

Their daughter was shaking hands with the opposite

team. Once she had made sure to congratulate all eleven of the opposition she ran over to her parents.

'Did you see my goal?'

'Yes. You were amazing.' Ryan said. 'You should have been on the England team this summer. You would have won the tournament.' England had endured a torrid campaign in South Africa, crashing out in the second round to Germany in a humiliating 4-1 defeat. He didn't know how much he was exaggerating when he said Arabella would have improved their squad.

'Yes, well done, sweetie,' Anna said. 'Are you ready? Alan is waiting in the car.'

Arabella looked around, as if looking for an excuse to delay the moment. 'Do we have to go home now?'

'There are things that need to be done around the house, so we need to make a move, unfortunately.' Anna genuinely looked sorry for having to leave so soon. She started walking towards the carpark, taking Arabella's hand. Ryan walked on the other side of his daughter.

'What about you, Dad?'

'I'm not doing anything. But it's your mother's turn to take you home. I was just here to watch you play.'

'But I want to talk to you about the game.' Arabella was using her well-practised puppy-dog eyes.

Ryan looked towards Anna. 'How can you refuse that face?'

Anna chewed her lip, glancing briefly towards the car park where Alan was waiting, and then back at Ryan and Arabella. Ryan put his arm around his daughter's shoulders as they walked, joining them as a unit, mutinying against the proposal of an early bath.

'Do you have homework tonight?' Anna asked.

'I did my maths yesterday because I knew I was playing tonight. Then I have French translations but that's not due in till Friday.'

'How fantastically prepared, you are,' Ryan said. It was like she'd planned the entire thing.

Anna's resistance was starting to wane. 'Are you sure you have nothing else to do?' Arabella shook her head forcefully.

Her mother's resistance was no match for the adorability of Arabella's display, and eventually she gave in.

'Ok, go with your father for a little bit.' She smiled and looked at Ryan. 'Don't keep her out too late. It's a school night remember.'

'No problem.'

Arabella smiled and high-fived her dad.

'What do you say?' Ryan said, putting on his best parent voice.

'Thank you, mummy,' their daughter said, and then threw her arms around her mother, which took Anna by surprise. Anna was forced to take a step back to balance herself against the force of the grateful footballer. She put a hand on her daughter's head, and gently stroked it, a maternal act that Ryan was happy to see happen more frequently. He mouthed the words 'thank you,' to her. She almost looked like she was about to start to cry, when Arabella released her.

'Back by eight at the latest,' Anna reconfirmed, as they got to the car park. It was the same one they had had a blazing row less than a year ago after Arabella had got herself suspended. Ryan saluted her, and Arabella mimicked the action. 'See you later.'

Anna headed towards Alan's Audi Avant. Behind the wheel Ryan could just about make out the face he had punched the previous November. He wasn't entirely certain, but it looked as if the bridge of the nose was slightly crooked, which gave him a tiny sliver of satisfaction.

'So where are we going, dad?' Arabella asked as they got in his Range Rover. He had downsized in terms of property, but for some reason he couldn't quite bring himself to sell the Range Rover. There was something about the car that he still really liked. However, his driving had become a lot more patient in recent months. He even didn't mind sharing the road with cyclists. Well, most of the time.

'Well, there is a very good coffee shop in town. A friend of mine works there. A Hungarian chap called Gabor. He's just won a Gold Star Store of Excellence Award.'

'What does that mean?' Arabella asked, as she got in the passenger seat and did up her seatbelt.

'I've got no idea, but he's very excited about it.'

'Okay, I want to go there.'

'You're the boss,' Ryan said as he pulled out of the car park, his daughter smiling next to him.

Kartik picked up the paper in front of him and looked at the headline. Ed Miliband was edging closer to being picked as the new leader of the Labour Party, and the tabloids were having a field day. Already the nickname Red Ed had caught on, as well as the idea that he had stabbed his brother in the back to win the backing of the unions. In May, just after the general election, Neil Kinnock had endorsed him as leader, which, from the vicious right-wing press's perspective, was like being endorsed by a Stalin. It was as if his leadership credentials had been shattered before he had even been confirmed as the leader of the opposition.

'Kartik, come on,' Freddy said. 'We'll miss our train.'

'Coming.' He paid for the paper in the station and then headed to the ticket gate. He was pulling behind him a large wheeled suitcase. On his back was a backpack that was filled to bursting point. Together they represented everything he would be taking to London. Freddy was in the train stations main concourse, also flanked by a large suitcase.

'Have you got your ticket?' she asked.

'Right here,' he replied, showing her the cardboard ticket that he held in his hand.

'And it's the right one this time?'

'Yes, it's the right one.'

'Are you sure?'

He approached the ticket gate and inserted the card. There was pause when nothing happened. Kartik's heart skipped a beat and a horrible sense of déjà vu flooded through him. And then the ticket appeared at the other side of the machine, like a little tongue, the light went green, and the gate swung open. Mission accomplished.

On the other side he gave Freddy a smug look, who was sadly unimpressed that he had completed this rudimental task without any issues. They headed to Platform One..

Despite Freddy's insisting they were going to miss it, the train hadn't even arrived at the platform yet.

Kartik looked down at his watch. It was just past six on Wednesday. Arabella would have just finished her football game. He sent a quick text to Ryan and asked him how it went.

The train pulled up to the station and Kartik hoisted their bags into the luggage compartment, whilst Freddy got them seat. They sat opposite each other, a table in-between them.

'Do you remember the first train journey we took together?' Freddy asked.

'How could I forget?'

'You looked very dashing.'

'Dashing? Really?'

'There was something about the spent-the-night-on-someone's-sofa-look that fascinated me.'

'You know I had actually spent the night on someone's sofa?'

'Yes. You told me about that night.'

'It was an odd one.'

'I'm glad it happened. Otherwise we may never have met.'

'I couldn't stop thinking about you the next day,' Kartik admitted.

'I remember you when we said goodbye at the train station you tilted your head so that when I tried to kiss you on the cheeks I accidently hit your lips.'

'That wasn't me tilting my head,' Kartik protested. 'That was you!'

'It was not! That was all you!'

'Slanderous lies!'

'Well, whoever did it, I'm glad it happened,' Freddy said. 'Does that count as our first kiss?'

'I don't know. It was more a half kiss than a full kiss. It was like this…' Kartik leant over the table and Freddy did the same. Kartik went to kiss her on the cheek, but at the last moment Freddy turned ever so slightly and the side of their lips touched. They held themselves there for a moment. They looked ridiculous, but neither of them cared.

They pulled their faces a fraction apart. Kartik opened his eyes and looked deeply into Freddy's.

'Are you ready?' she whispered.

'Ready for what?'

'For our new life in London.'

There was a jolt as the train pulled away from the platform and slowly started to gather speed. They were on their way.

'Yeah. I think I am.'

How many coffees had he gone through now? He wasn't entirely sure, but he certainly didn't feel well. But that may have also been down to the fact that he hadn't slept for two days. This was too important. He had been making too much progress. They had all thought it was over, but he'd found a way back in.

The computer screen in front of him glowed, the

illuminating light hurting his tired, red eyes. He had missed work, he had avoided his family, all he had done was focus on the task at hand.

His hands danced over the keyboard, inputting the final calculations, calculations only made possible by Cameron's hard work. She had built the foundations, created the structure that he had built on. And even when it had seemed that the ground underneath those foundations had collapsed into a sinkhole of deceit, he had kept on. He had suspected there was something more to the revelation that the entire project was a hoax set up by an autistic South Korean and his brother.

In fact, true to the deceptive nature of the Eden's Bonfire, this lie had instead been part of the puzzle itself, the final clue that could be interpreted and used to find the solution. When everyone else had accepted this fraud, Philip Lawson had continued. Alone he had persevered, alone he had kept going, determined that there was something more.

Now his hand wavered over the enter button. The final calculation had been input, now he would see if all this work would be worth it.

He pressed and the screen changed. It was all there. It hadn't been a waste of time.

Philip leant back on his chair, exhausted, drained. He had done it. He was the first person in the world to see what he now saw on the screen.

Eden's Bonfire had been solved.

Printed in Great Britain
by Amazon